Richard Frederick Fuller

Chaplain Fuller

Being a Life Sketch of a New England Clergyman and Army Chaplain

Richard Frederick Fuller

Chaplain Fuller
Being a Life Sketch of a New England Clergyman and Army Chaplain

ISBN/EAN: 9783337055271

Printed in Europe, USA, Canada, Australia, Japan

Cover: Foto ©Raphael Reischuk / pixelio.de

More available books at **www.hansebooks.com**

CHAPLAIN FULLER:

BEING

A LIFE SKETCH

OF

A NEW ENGLAND CLERGYMAN AND ARMY CHAPLAIN

By RICHARD F. ₁FULLER.

"I must do something for my country."
"Dulce et decorum est pro patria mori."

BOSTON: ·
WALKER, WISE, AND COMPANY,
245 WASHINGTON STREET.
1863.

UNIVERSITY PRESS:
WELCH, BIGELOW, AND COMPANY,
CAMBRIDGE.

PREFACE.

" Poscimur :— si quid vacui sub umbra
Lusimus tecum, quod et hunc in annum
Vivat, et plures, — age, dic . . . .
    Barbite, carmen ! "

EREAVEMENT naturally leads us to recall the scenes of the life of the departed, to look over the memorials of his virtues and the souvenirs of his love. This employment has afforded a sad satisfaction, and the general interest manifested in the fate of Chaplain Fuller, as well as the historic scenes in which he participated, has led to the publication of his biography.

It is hoped that this labor of love may be of advantage to the family of the Chaplain, to whose benefit its pecuniary avails are devoted.

The pen of the Chaplain has been made to write the greater part of his biography. Especially in martial scenes does he make his own record.

As his character is unfolded in these pages, we think the pure and patriotic motive which led him to seal the devotion of his life with his blood, stands forth in bold and unmistakable prominence.

War scenes and incidents, historical personages and places, render the theme of this book of universal interest. The full and particular narrative of the combat of the Merrimac and Monitor, of which the Chaplain was an eyewitness, is one of his sketches of important events which have a value for historical reference.

And it is believed that not only the religious public, but the general reader, will be interested in the narrative which depicts a specimen of the New England clergy, a class remarkable for its position and influence among a free people.

Upon the Chaplain's childhood and youth we have dwelt with some particularity, not only because of their general importance as the key to the sequel of life, but also on account of the public interest in his sister Margaret, who was the loadstar of his early days.

CONTENTS.

PART I.

CHILDHOOD AND YOUTH.

PART II.

THE NEW ENGLAND CLERGYMAN.

PART III.

THE ARMY CHAPLAIN.

PART I.

CHILDHOOD AND YOUTH.

"How many are you, then," said I,
  "If they two are in heaven?"
Quick was the little maid's reply,
  "O Master, we are seven!"

"But they are dead; those two are dead!—
  Their spirits are in heaven!"
'T was throwing words away; for still
The little maid would have her will,
  And said, "Nay, we are seven!"
                                        WORDSWORTH.

CHAPTER I.

LINEAGE.

"Parvum Nilum videre."

HERE is a natural curiosity to trace a stream to its source — to follow it back to the hills from whose bosom it first springs to life. The more noble the flow of its current, the more beneficent its waters, in opening paths to inland navigation or furnishing food for man, so much the keener is curiosity to trace it to the crystal fountain of its origin. The undiscovered source of the Nile was for centuries the theme of speculation. Inquirers, after the ancient method, propounded this practical question to the oracles of reason, and drew from them the enigmatical responses of theory; never apparently thinking of the solution, which modern empiricism has reached, by actually threading back the stream, and thus working out the safe result of observation.

Human life, like the river, may attract little public notice in its playful early course, when prattling among the parent hills, or leaping in gay cascades on its downward way, to swell, eventually, into the graver, deeper current of manhood. But if, as its waters gather head, they furnish a spectacle of natural beauty in their flow or fall, or bestow public blessings in banks made green and fruitful, or bountiful fisheries, or bear upon their back the burdens of navigation, or attract attention by the glory of their exit into the sea, symbolizing the issue of life for time into the ocean of eternity, — then men turn their steps back to the early stream, and search out, in its source and surroundings, every presage of its destiny.

It is generally believed, that character, as a common rule, bears the impress of family origin. In the division of mankind into races, each race preserves in its history distinguishing traits, both physical and intellectual, so decidedly marked as to induce some ingenious naturalists to deny one common origin to all the human species. So in the subdivisions of race into families, we often observe the prominent characteristics repeated in successive generations. There is very much, it is true, to disturb this natural result. Marriage dilutes the family blood. Circumstances, which serve to evoke the fire of genius or talent, often allow it to slumber for subsequent generations. Especially is the success of parents wont to leave buried in the luxurious nurture or outward advantages of offspring those energies which the *res angustæ domi* first developed in their own childhood, early poverty nurtured, and a severe but kind adversity trained to wrestle in the arena of difficulty, till a surpassing strength was attained. From the influence of these disturbing causes, it is almost or quite impossible to calculate the share which family traits have in the problem of individual destiny. Yet a growing attention is paid, and, we think, reasonably, to this subject.

Genealogical trees are more assiduously cultivated. The ramifications of kindred are traced to the trunk; thence the root is sought out; and, still unsatisfied, the genealogist inquires for the seed, whence it germinated, what wind wafted it to the place where it fell into the foster bosom of the earth, and, if possible, from what tree did the seed come. Such inquiries may be sometimes too minute, or pushed beyond the clew of fact, into the worse than useless vagaries of mere speculation. Yet, to a reasonable extent, family history forms a legitimate introduction to a biography.

We are, happily, able to afford a glimpse at the ancestry of the subject of this narrative. His American forefather, Thomas Fuller, was lured to these shores by curiosity, in 1638. We have an authentic account of his tour and its results, in some verses, which, as they seem to possess few of the other characteristics of poetry, we trust are equally free from its propensity to fiction.* He declares that he was won over by the preaching of the famous Shepard, the echo of whose eloquence (saith our record) " after the lapse of two centuries has scarcely died away "; and that his converted heart was led to love liberty to worship God in the wilderness better than the flesh-pots of Egypt, left behind him in old England. An irreverent family tradition has mali-

---

* If the public deem us to speak too lightly of our honored ancestor, they can themselves try the poetical question by a reference to " Historical Notices of Thomas Fuller and his Descendants, with a Genealogy of the Fuller Family," contained in the New England Historical and Genealogical Register for October, 1859, and also to be found in the Appendix to the first volume of the edition of the Memoirs and Works of Margaret Fuller, published by Walker, Wise, & Co. Boston. 1863.

ciously dared to assert that the black eyes of a certain
Miss Richardson, who conditioned the boon of her
hand upon a New England residence, were the true
loadstars of American attraction with our worthy pro-
genitor. But, for ourselves, we at once and forever
repel the soft impeachment, not merely as reflecting
upon our ancestor's veracity and parole of honor (for
he was a lieutenant of militia) ; but because we are
sure no one could win enough the favor of the Muses
to coin rhymes, who would fail to acknowledge in his
verse so honorable a leading as the lustrous eyes of
a maiden in determining his line of destiny. The
supposition that, in the blind romance of first love, he
misconceived his true motive, is alike inadmissible in
the case of our American patriarch. No! that he
was a true Puritan, with a large place for the religious
element in his character as the controlling motive, is
abundantly proved, we contend, not only by his own
words and deeds, but also by the character and lives
of his descendants.

Third in the series from Thomas Fuller was Rev.
Timothy Fuller, who graduated from Harvard College in 1760, and was ordained in 1767, the first
settled minister of Princeton, Massachusetts, and, ultimately having moved to Merrimack, N. H., almost
exclusively applied himself to agriculture, and the
training of his five sons, all of whom became lawyers,
with no schooling, before their college days, except the
home teaching.* In Princeton, he was the proprietor

---

* These sons were Timothy Fuller (to be more particularly mentioned),
Abraham Williams Fuller, Henry Holton Fuller, William Williams Fuller,
and Elisha Fuller; of whom a brief account may be found in *Historical*

of the blue Wachusett, assigned to him as the parish farm, — a tract well able to "carry forests on its back," yet fitted to bear little else.

A descendant thus seeks to account for the parish grant to the parson being located upon this mountain,

> Bestowed by his society,
> To ear from thence his salary:
> For ministers, not then, as now,
> Used brains, without the sweating brow.
> Why his good people gave the mount,
> And kept the vale, we've no account.

Notices of Thomas Fuller and his Descendants, above referred to. They have all been gathered to their fathers. On the decease of Henry, in September, 1852, an eloquent tribute was paid to his memory by Hon. Charles G. Loring, in presenting to the Supreme Judicial Court the resolutions of the Bar on that occasion; to which there was a feeling response from Mr. Justice Fletcher. We should delight to dwell longer upon this nucleus of five legal brothers, were it not aside from our present purpose.

Besides the five sons, there were five daughters, who survived Rev. Timothy Fuller. From the time of his death, on the third day of July, 1805, till the death of his son Timothy, on the first day of October, 1835, a period of full thirty years, that family circle of brothers and sisters remained unbroken. Now all have passed away, except Mrs. Deborah Allen Belcher, of Farmington, Maine, who, though for many years a widow, still enjoys a green old age, honored and beloved by children and grandchildren.

Those ten children were much attached to each other, as well as to their parents, while living, and their memory when departed. Mr. Loring, in his address to the court on the death of Henry, before referred to, gives a touching picture of the ten children of Rev. Timothy Fuller, who, some quarter of a century after he had gone to his rest, and long after the family dwelling in Princeton had passed away, visited its site together. Nothing remained but its cellar, which time had partially filled, whose rounded excavation it had carpeted with greensward. Here the children gathered, and, seated in the charmed circle of what was once their home, sang again together the sweet hymns to which their tongues had been attuned in childhood, by their faithful parents, in the dearly loved home which had once rested upon that spot. They did not visit it again, in concert; and many of them sought it no more. Death, in a few years, broke that circle; and one after another they went, in quick succession, the way of all living.

But little produce, almost none
Could on the lofty hill be grown.
Yet, to conjecture, charity
Forbids that this the cause could be.
He was a pastor, — and, their sheep
Shepherds upon the mountains keep:
Or, that he might, like Moses, stand,
To look upon the promised land,
And, with uplifted thought, behold
The wonders of the heaven unfold;
While, still, upon his parish sheep
'T were easy half an eye to keep;
As they the fertile valley till,
Spread out beneath the lofty hill!

Rev. Timothy Fuller represented Princeton in the Convention of Massachusetts which voted to approve and accept the Federal Constitution. Being totally opposed to slavery, he voted against that instrument, on account of the insidious clause providing for the rendition of fugitives from service. This negative vote is claimed by his descendants for an hereditary honor; manifesting, as it does, that aversion to oppression which has characterized more than one of the family, and taking a first step in that antislavery path which descendants have followed on. In the light of recent history, may we not be led to believe that it would have been better for this nation had it, while in its cradle, strangled the little serpent of slavery, so cunningly insinuated into our Constitution, before it grew to the *monstrum horrendum, informe, ingens, cui lumen ademptum*, like the baleful dragon of the Apocalypse.

This antislavery origin was duplicated, in 1770, by the marriage of Rev. Timothy Fuller to Sarah Williams, daughter of Rev. Abraham Williams, of Sand-

wich, Massachusetts. He married Anna Buckminster,
a near relative of the distinguished clergyman, whom
Choate aptly styles " the glorious Buckminster," and
whose useful and brilliant career, brought to an untimely close, has been commemorated by his distinguished contemporary, Dr. Channing.* The honor
of this family connection was the occasion of bestow-
ing the name of Buckminster, as the middle bap-
tismal name of the subject of this memoir.

The eldest son of Rev. Timothy Fuller, bearing his
father's name, graduated from Harvard University in
1801, at the age of twenty-three, with the second
honors; having his only preparatory training in the
home school, when, *pari passu* with Latin and Greek,
he acquired those habits of industry and endurance,
which, even more than learning and talent, form the
sure capital of success in life. His high college rank
was the more creditable, that he was obliged to defray
his expenses by teaching school in the vacations, and
even during a part of the term, — an episode, which
not only encroached upon his time, but also tasked the
energies he would have been glad to apply solely to
the pursuits of a college student. He himself thought
he should have borne off the first honors, had he not
felt obliged to take an influential part in a college rebellion, which he regarded as justified and called for
by the students' grievances. He was admitted to the

---

* Buckminster, as a child, was a precocious and eager reader. It is related that he was, one day, intent on reading in a room by himself, leaning
against the mantel. He remained in this posture, entirely absorbed, for
several hours, till he fainted from exhaustion; and the family hearing him
fall, rushed in to find him on the floor in a swoon.

1 *

bar, after the usual term of preparatory study, and for many years had his office in Boston.

Timothy Fuller rapidly rose to distinction at the bar, being noted for close reasoning and high professiónal character. He joyfully devoted the first-fruits of professional success on the altar of family love, faithfully assisting his younger brothers in their struggles to obtain an education. He took Henry into partnership, — a favor he repaid years afterwards by conferring the same advantage upon Timothy's son, Richard. He was especially kind to those in humble circumstances, and readily espoused their cause in the forum for a small compensation, and often at the risk of receiving none.

He had a natural fluency and facility in extempore speaking, in which he was *semper paratus*, and more successful than in the labors of the pen. This afforded him ready entrance, and of itself almost drew him to political life. His moral and religious nature and characteristic benevolence led him to embrace the principles of republican 'democracy, whose mission he believed to be the general diffusion of knowledge, the elevation of the humble, the political equality of all races and conditions of men, and human brotherhood, as announced in the sublime epitome of the American Declaration of Independence. He was a member of the Massachusetts Senate from 1813 to 1816, a Representative in Congress from 1817 to 1825, Speaker of the Massachusetts House of Representatives in 1825, and a member of the Executive Council in 1828.

He is still remembered as chairman of the Committee on Naval Affairs in the House of Representatives of the United States, having the good fortune to perform the duties of that position in a manner acceptable to the naval service, as well as to the general advantage. His heart echoed the lament of the Seminole Indians, forcibly expatriated from their native hunting-grounds, and carried far away toward the setting sun. His long and elaborate speech in their behalf, which may be read in the records of the debates of the House upon that interesting topic, produced a marked impression, but could not stay that career of national wrong to the weaker races scandalously denominated " manifest destiny," the retributive penalty for which Providence seems now visiting upon us in the bloody scourge of civil war.

He also made a strong speech in opposition to the Missouri Compromise, maintaining that not an inch of territory should be left to the blighting influence of slavery. He thought that, while conflicting interests were a fair subject of compromise, principles of eternal justice never were. In yielding material interests by compromise, man is giving away what is his own; but in compromising the principles of justice, he is daring to give up something of those sacred claims of right which do not belong to man, and cannot be in any measure relinquished without robbing God. To say that we avoid a greater evil by sanctioning a smaller one, he regarded as a reflection upon the rule of human conduct laid down by the Almighty, requiring us to do right and leave the consequences to him. History has proved that all the compromises with slavery were really the onward marches of its encroaching waves, thus.gathering volume and momentum perfidiously to sweep over the barriers of "thus far and no farther," submitted to by the slave power as only a temporary expedient and means of fraud. He was also influential in the election of John Quincy Adams to the Presidency. A pamphlet, published by him, entitled "The Election for the Presidency considered," had a wide circulation.

Timothy Fuller was a religious man. While in college, he sedulously examined the evidences of Christianity, and reached, by patient research, a deliberate conviction of its truth, which could never afterwards be shaken. He at once joined himself to the Church, of which he remained a life-long member and a careful observer of its sacred ceremonies. He attended divine worship constantly with his family, and regularly ministered at the home altar in the "church, which was in his own house." Nor could he be induced, under any pretext, to perform secular business on the Sabbath. When he first went to Washington, he purchased a new Bible, known in the family as his "Washington Bible." He marked in it the twentieth verse of the forty-ninth Psalm, — "Man that is in honor, and understandeth not, is like the beasts that perish." Early in his professional career he cherished a project of becoming a preacher, but desired to first secure a maintenance, that he might discharge the duties of the sacred office with entire independence.

In 1809, he made a happy alliance in marriage with Margaret Crane, daughter of Major Peter Crane, of Canton, Massachusetts. The father served in the

Revolutionary war. He acted as chaplain, at one time, of his regiment in the army.

Margaret may be truthfully styled a " good match " for her husband, for her character was the complement of his, and each had prominent traits where those of the other were deficient. Thus, while he dealt in reason, and approached all subjects intellectually, her sphere was the fancy and imagination. His tastes were for the practical and useful ; hers for the ideal and beautiful. Each yielded to the wishes of the other. She leaned on him for views and opinions, discerning his judgment and implicitly trusting his results ; and he was careful to gratify her æsthetic tastes. Her ideality had taken especially the direction of flowers, and he provided for her an extensive garden, though, for sport, he insisted on his own bed of dandelions and marigolds, which, he laughingly insisted, far exceeded her exotics in real beauty and value. In temperament, too, they were admirably matched. He, always industrious and overworked, needed the elastic influence of her buoyant and exuberant spirits. With their diversity of traits, they had the oneness of aspiration and aim which is needed happily to cement the marriage union. Both were pious ; — he especially in the department of judgment and principle ; she, in that of religious emotion and affection. Both loved children and home ; — he, careful to provide, solicitous to develop and stimulate his children, and always anxiously reaching forward toward their future ; she, a sunbeam of solace and cheer, a tender mother to soothe each childish grief and to shed a radiance over the present hour. She did not

love the children more than he; but they appreciated
her love at once, while justice to his was deferred till
the retrospect of riper years. He was not, however,
by any means a stern parent. He gave each night
a touching proof of his fatherly tenderness, by visiting
the couch where the children had sunk to rest, and
pressing a kiss upon their unconscious lips.

Soon after his marriage, he purchased, for a resi-
dence, a large dwelling-house situated upon Cherry
Street, Cambridge Port. In this mansion, which the
children called "the Home House," were born Sarah
Margaret, Julia Adelaide, Eugene, William Henry,
Ellen Kilshaw, Arthur Buckminster, and Richard
Frederick. Julia Adelaide died in infancy; and all
have now passed from the stage of mortal life, except
William and Richard. On the year of the birth of
Margaret, her father set out a row of elm-trees in
front of the residence; which may still be seen, of
a large growth, stationed, like huge sentinels, before
the mansion. But, alas! they protect no longer the
family who first set them there, and resorted for a
while to their increasing shade.

Mr. Fuller first sought Cambridge as a residence,
in order to withdraw as much as possible from the
contagion of an epidemic, then raging in Boston; and
he never afterwards resided in the city.

CHAPTER II.

CHILDHOOD.

" The child is father of the man. "

ARTHUR BUCKMINSTER FULLER was born in Cambridge Port, Massachusetts, on the tenth day of August, 1822. Here he was nurtured, till the family removed, when he was about five years of age, to a mansion in Old Cambridge, which his father purchased of Chief Justice Dana. It was situated upon high land, near the Colleges, still called, from its original proprietor, " Dana Hill."

The family were much attached to the dwelling in Cambridge Port, styled the " Home House " ; though its attractions were chiefly intrinsic, consisting of the sunshine of family love and the charm of the birth-place. It boasted, however, a beautiful garden, se-cluded by a high, close fence, and decorated with trees, vines, and flowers. At its western extremity was a gate, always locked, behind which the sun set in glory ; stimulating by its mystery the children's fancy, to imagine, that, if opened, it would admit to a bright-er land.* The prospect from the mansion windows

* See Memoirs of Margaret Fuller Ossoli.

needed to be looked at through the medium of ardent love of home, to be attractive or tolerable. It consisted of salt marsh, unreclaimed as yet, or made land, occupied by dwelling-houses, interspersed with several laboratories of the useful arts. Arthur's mother used laughingly to relate, that, on the day of removal, he gazed wistfully his farewell look at the loved scene, sighing, " O, I shall not see the soap 'urks any more ! "

In Margaret Fuller's Unpublished Works,* we find the following reference to the Cambridge Port residence. She had just returned, at the time of writing, from a tour among the mountains. She says: " I feel satisfied, as I thought I should, with reading these bolder lines in the manuscript of Nature. Merely gentle and winning scenes are not enough for me. I wish my lot had been cast amid the sources of the streams, where the voice of the hidden torrent is heard by night, where the eagle soars, and the thunder resounds in long peals from side to side, where the grasp of a more powerful emotion has rent asunder the rocks, and the long purple shadows fall, like a broad wing upon the valley. All places, I know, like all persons, have beauty, which may be discovered by a thoughtful and observing mind; but only in some scenes, and with some persons, can I expand and feel myself at home. I realize this all the more for having passed all my childhood in such a place as Cambridge Port. There I had nothing, except the little flower-garden behind the house, and the elms before the door. I used to long and pine

* MS. Vol. II. p. 711.

for beautiful places, such as I read of. There was not one walk for me, except over the bridge. I liked that very much; pleasing myself with the river, the lovely undulating line on every side, and the light smokes which were seen in certain states of the weather."

Dana Hill was altogether a different spot. In the rapid growth of Boston and its suburbs, a few years have made dwellings to cluster on the site. But then its fair area was almost unoccupied save by the central mansion, whose casements, like the eyes of Argus, looked upon the green, flowery hills of Brookline and Brighton, and the glimmer of the intervening Charles River, dyed with the crimson glories of the sunset, or bright, in turn, with the bending azure of day and the silver lamps of night. From the house, a long avenue conducted to the road, lined with the blooming borders, where the mother's flowery retainers arrayed themselves, paying their tribute of beauty and fragrance, in return for assiduous protection and culture. In the lawn, on either hand, were fruit and ornamental trees; while, more in the background, like a reserve, was another garden of fruit and flowers.

Here Arthur's family resided for six prosperous years; while the younger children attended several private schools. One of these has a conspicuous place in memory, owing to the *régime* of its lady teacher. The birch was her sceptre; and, lest one should be weakened in its sway, she kept a bundle of them on hand. These she required the boys to procure for her; and woe to them, if they brought her other than

B

long, straight, and vigorous twigs! She indulged in
a feline diversion, when her quick eye could detect
a boy engaged in the proscribed occupation known
as "wool-gathering." Watching her occasion, and
creeping noiselessly behind, she dispelled the day-
dream with a smart stroke from her birch wand.
What an awakening was that! what a cruel return
from illusion to reality! It may be adduced, as an
instance of natural depravity, that the other urchins
sympathized with the teacher in this pursuit, and
eagerly watched her well-conceived project of surprise, wishing it success, though themselves liable to
be made the next victims; and when the rod made
its successful and sudden descent, the feat was greeted
with a suppressed applause, which the exclamation of
the culprit and the startled expression of his countenance by no means served to diminish.

On the elevation of John Quincy Adams to the
White House, Arthur's father expected a mission to
Europe, as a token of the appreciation of his influential labors on behalf of the successful candidate. But
the President did not "remember Joseph." In this
expectation, his daughter Margaret had been encouraged to look eagerly forward to visiting that Europe
in whose literature she had become so well versed.
Both were destined to disappointment. This check
may have contributed to induce the father to seek
a more retired sphere of life. But there were other
motives. He had been long gathering materials
for a history of his country, which he purposed as the
crowning labor of his life. He had, besides, a view
to the education of his children. Attributing his own

success in a great measure to the endurance and industry acquired by an early experience in the toils
of agriculture, he desired to subject his boys to the
same hardening process. Not a little influence, too,
may have been exerted upon him by the romantic
retrospect of the afternoon of life upon boyhood's
morning, in drawing his heart toward those New
Hampshire hills, whose blue walls enclosed its horizon;
feeling, —

"..... as in a pensive dream,
    When all his active powers are still,
    A distant dearness in the hill,
    A secret sweetness in the stream."

Induced by such motives, Arthur's father sold his
residence in Cambridge, and occupied the house of
his brother Abraham, on Brattle Street, in Cambridge,
for one year, while casting about him for a new location. While living here, an accident occurred to
Arthur and his younger brother, in celebrating the
glorious Fourth, after the manner of independent
boys. Arthur early manifested an enthusiasm for the
observance of this birthday of our liberty, with mimic
artillery and banner, which is thus pleasantly alluded
to by his sister Margaret: "'I'm independent!' as
Arthur shouted and waved his flag; when Eugene
cruelly stopped him, and made him come in to learn
his lesson." * His enthusiasm was more seriously interrupted on the occasion of the accident referred to.
The boys had several times discharged a little cannon,
running with shouts into the cloud of smoke, when
it was inadvertently aimed at the box of powder,

* Unpublished Works, Vol. II. p. 823.

which ignited with a fearful explosion, prostrating both children, and so burning them as to confine them for several days to their bed. .

The new family residence was in Groton, Massachusetts, a prosperous town of Middlesex County, distant some thirty miles from Boston, and at that time principally devoted to agriculture.* The house and grounds had been fitted up with much care and expense by Samuel Dana, a Judge of the Court of Common Pleas. The white mansion, situated upon a gradual eminence, looked complacently upon the blue Wachusett, Monadnock, and Peterborough Hills. It was quite attractive to childish eyes, its ample front bathed in the sunlight, seeming, on approach, to expand into a smile of welcome. Alas! we little anticipated, as we crossed its threshold, the bitter cup of family sorrows we were to drink there! Yet that discipline was not without a beneficent compensation for those who submissively acknowledged that God "in faithfulness afflicted them."

Here opened a new field of activity for all the family. The father applied himself to superintending the husbandry of fifty acres, and making alterations and additions to the buildings. Nor did he wholly decline the professional avocations which still sought him out in his retirement, and led him again occasionally into the forum. He also gave some hours to his projected history, and applied himself especially to the training of his children. In the last-named department he was careful to form the children to

---

* Caleb Butler, Esq. has composed and published a careful history of Groton, containing many interesting facts.

habits of early rising, promptness in action, industry, and concentration upon the matter in hand. Regularly were they summoned in the morning; and there was no more "folding of the hands in sleep." They were obliged to respond at once with their feet striking the floor. It happened that the butcher usually drove into the yard at the same time; and the rumbling of his chariot, as it broke upon the dream-land, and seemed to suggest the father's call, serving as its unwelcome prelude, made the useful vender of meats unpopular with the boys. *

The observance of the Lord's day he regarded as of the first importance, and strictly enjoined it upon his children as he did also a reverential regard for the public Fasts and Thanksgivings, instituted by our pious Pilgrim fathers. The church edifice stamped its picture on the children's memory. Arthur thus alludes to it in his remarks at the public dinner on the Bicentennial Anniversary of Groton: " I remember the ancient church, then unchanged by the hand of modern improvement. I can see to-day those old-fashioned pews, so high that only by a peep through the rounds which ornamented their tops could I discern the faces of youthful comrades; and there seems yet to echo in my ear the hearty slam with which the pew seats, raised during the prayer, descended in a rude chorus of accompaniment at the signal of the minister's ' Amen!' — a not unwelcome word, I fear, to undevout children of that day or this." Quite as impressive to the youthful mind was the high pulpit, ascended by a winding stair, on whose dizzy elevation the preacher was just visible, emerging

from the damask cushion *toto vertice supra.* What
lent a great interest to the minister in the childish
view, was his apparently critical position of immi-
nent peril from the huge hemispheral sounding-board
suspended by a frail tenure above his head. There
was nothing to indicate to the child's speculation that
this massive superstructure was hollow, and therefore
adeqfiately secured by the apex fixed to the ceiling.*
Noteworthy also was the psalmody, especially the
agonized moment when the strangely assorted instruments strove to take the pitch. The individuality of·
the surly bass-viol and the intensely strung fiddle was
never lost in their assembled harmony. Alas! the
glory of those orchestras has forever passed away!

In family government, Timothy Fuller did not
wholly dispense with the rod, though we recall but
one instance when Arthur was made the subject of it.
That occasion is well remembered, because, from participation in the punishment, it made a marked impression both upon the back and mind. Arthur and
Richard (by two years his younger brother) had been
quarrelling, in that unmalicious, but bearish brotherly
style paternally denominated "squabbling." Smarting with reciprocal wrongs, they resorted to the legal
father as the fountain of family justice, each prefer-
ring his complaint. They did not fail to obtain what
Molière's Scapin so little relished,—justice: but, though
no reproach could be cast upon the unsullied ermine
of the family judge, yet the result of the cause discouraged them from afterward submitting their griev-

* A witty clergyman compared these old-fashioned pulpits to a hogshead,
with the minister speaking out of the bunghole.

ances to the same tribunal. Hardly were the pleadings in, when the proceedings began to assume an ominous aspect. The father proposed to adjourn to his chamber, as affording a better opportunity to sift the matter. Among the family effects was a certain black riding-stick, with which the children, in their equestrian efforts, were wont to invigorate the energies of the tardy family steed, known as " old Charley." The father accompanied his proposition to adjourn to the chamber by the assumption of this stick, which may have resembled the black rod of Parliament. This significant act justified the apprehension that the case would have an unpleasant issue for one or the other litigant, and, before the die was cast determining which, the rod cast an unpleasant shadow upon both. The boys felt some disposition to withdraw, for a settlement *in pais*. But *galeatum sero duelli pœnitet*. In other words, the *locus pœnitentiæ* was reserved for a later stage of the proceedings.

Arrived at the chamber, the parental judge directed Arthur, as the eldest, to open the case. In vain Richard attempted to break in, with an indignant protest against the allegations and arguments. The court calmly but firmly enjoined silence upon him till Arthur had first fully enjoyed his constitutional right to be heard. When his breath or narrative had given out, the signal was made for Richard's wordy onset. Arthur, in his turn, was thwarted in eager attempts to interrupt the younger advocate. When both sides had been duly heard, the court, with no dilatory *curia advisare vult*, proceeded forthwith to deliver a somewhat elaborate judgment, reviewing the variances as

well as coincidences in the statements of each side,
and drawing from the latter the inference that both
were to blame; concluding with the sentence that
the boys should take off their jackets, in order that
the black rod might be more closely applied to their
backs. As the father assured them that the infliction
would pain him much more than them, they indulged
the hope of a light chastisement; in which, as in
speaking, Arthur, from priority of age, had the first
lot. This expectation proved illusory; for, though
the whipping was calm and deliberate, it was eminently thorough; nor did he " spare the child for his
crying."

Another illustration of home government was furnished soon after the removal to Groton. It was
early summer, the skies blue and bright, the breezes
grateful, and the birds melodious. How dull and
dingy the school-room in comparison! Out-of-door
laborers seemed to enjoy a comparative holiday to
Arthur, who had thus far only applied himself to
work when so inclined, for variety, and had no conception of the *labor improbus* which *omnia vincit*. He
also persuaded Richard to be of the same mind; and
they both besieged father and mother with entreaties
to allow them to work instead of study. The father
held out long against them, assuring them that they
would soon find labor very irksome, and wish to return
to study again. But no! they were sure they should
enjoy labor in the free air better than the pent-up
toil of the school, in the beautiful season which lured
all creatures forth. He advised them to try the experiment, before a final choice, offering to let them

work for a few days on trial, and to continue it or return to school, according as they should find most agreeable. But they were so sure they should like work, that they preferred to sever the school tie, and make choice of it at once. The father, having warned them that, if they made this election, it would not be revocable, thought it would be a good lesson for them to have their own way.

Great was their delight in getting rid of school; and for the first half-day they exulted in their choice. But presently blisters and fatigue came, and they began to waver. They held out for a time, ashamed to admit their folly, but gradually gave way; and then they pleaded for leave to go back to school. This the father firmly declined. The boys fretted and murmured, but failed to move the father. As a last resort, they fled from the work one day, and ran to entreat their mother, throwing themselves upon the floor, and bewailing their sad fate. The mother was much moved, and soon joined her entreaties with theirs to bring over the father, who had followed the boys, and stood a calm spectator of the scene. He replied, that to yield would have a very bad influence upon the boys; that they had chosen to rush into the difficulty, despite of counsel and warning, and ought now to bear the consequences of such conduct, as they would have to on the stage of life, for which they were training; that they had entered into a fair and deliberate engagement, and ought not to wish nor to be permitted to violate it. The adamantine statue of Themis would have swerved as soon as he; and so back the boys·

2

had to go to their inglorious toil. That lesson was not forgotten.

Yet the father did not bear too hardly upon the boys, nor require them to work too many hours. He carefully watched their powers of endurance, and imposed no task upon them which might trench upon the elasticity of childhood. He furnished them suitable opportunities for sport and recreation, in which he cordially sympathized. Spartan endurance he desired them to acquire, for he possessed and prized it himself. He was in advance of his day in cold-water bathing, which he regularly practised, in a cold room, even in winter. He slept with the window open all winter; a practice which at first dismayed his wife, but which she learned herself to value. In winter, he occasionally ran barefoot a considerable distance in the snow, to which feat she never was reconciled.

Plodding manual toil never suited Arthur's mercurial temperament. He sympathized with Daniel Webster, whose scythe never hung to suit him, except when it hung in an apple-tree. He relieved his tasks, however, by an active and playful imagination, recounting fables to his companion Richard, and constructing air-castles for his amusement.

He would represent a rich man rolling in a coach with gilded trappings, to bear him to congenial scenes of wealth and luxury, but leaving the aggravated Richard ignobly plying his hatchet at the tedious brush block. Or else he would personify and weave into his narrative the grotesque traits of every person who crossed our path having any singularity. After a while he brought together these caricatures

into an assemblage called "The Universal Band";
whose adventures beguiled many an hour of work.
After the boys had retired, too, at night, Arthur
continued these humorous narratives, with such an
exhilarating effect upon him and his audience of
one, that their peals of laughter disturbed the family,
and the parents came and enjoined silence. One
of Arthur's imaginary personages was an eccentric
man, who never could be converted to the electrical
theory, and would wear a brass hat for his protection in thunder-storms; nor could repeated lightning
strokes beat into his cranium a different conviction;
he always attributing his wonderful preservation to
his brazen covering. Another was a tall individual,
with an ardent thirst for overhearing conversations,
and a faculty of projecting his ears for this purpose
several yards from his head, till they had drank in
the desired information. Another was a person of
very timorous temper, constantly interrupting the most
festive discourse with his unseasonable croak of alarm.
We forbear to spin Arthur's yarns over again, lest
they should not impress the public risibles as they
did our own, in the blithesome days of early boyhood, before the shadow of death fell upon our household. Suffice it to say, that, though we have read
Dickens with hearty merriment, he never drew from
us that almost self-annihilating laughter with which we
were seized in Arthur's recitals.

We ought not to omit, in this connection, our first
military experience in a company of martial boys,
organized and drilled on our common, by William A.
Richardson, then attending school at Groton, after-

ward Arthur's classmate in college, and now our honored Judge of Probate and Insolvency for the County of Middlesex.

Arthur's father instilled into him lessons of nature, for which he had a passion, and the Groton scenery opened fair pages. He walked forth with his children in the sparkling crystal mornings, holding their hands in his, and sympathizing in the exuberance of their buoyant spirits. At such a time, when asked if he found his rural retirement suited to his taste, he declared that he only regretted he had not taken the step earlier. He added to the pleasures of the walk by genial conversation, encouraging the children to enter upon themes sometimes beyond their years. He spoke of the short-sighted pursuits in which men were ordinarily absorbed, unworthy of the capacities and aims of immortal beings. He touched upon human greatness, declaring that the pen wielded a greater power, and secured a higher and nobler as well as more lasting fame than the sword, — instancing this by Walter Scott, whose name, he said, would have an increasing lustre when Napoleon's star had grown dim. He seized occasions to commend industry and economy in the little things of life which make up the mickle, and to point out the folly and peril of pecuniary speculation.

The changing scenes of nature, with whose everyday face out-of-door occupations and sports made Arthur familiar, impressed his mind indelibly and gave a habit to his thought. His very active fancy could not be bound down to the slow round of manual labor, and was perpetually star-gazing, or sky-gazing, or giving a voice to the wind and waterfall. Hence it happened, in his after life, that, habitually in public speaking, he appealed to the current events of the natural world as a commentary to his thought; and if any change passed over nature's face, even while he was speaking, he made use of it as aptly as if he had expected it, or its very mission were to serve him for illustration. The overcasting cloud, the returning triumph of sunshine, the rainbow, the showers, the snows, the wind, the sun, moon, and stars, day and night, spring, summer, autumn, winter, — these were his alphabet or vocabulary, learned by heart in his childhood's intimacy with nature. In his remarks at the Groton Bicentennial Dinner, before alluded to, he thus refers to the scenes of nature : "The pleasant walks by day in your beautiful groves and fields, our sports on the river's bank, the moonlight pastimes beneath the ancient elms near my honored father's dwelling, the regard of my young heart for those once living on earth, and now no less truly living in heaven, can never be forgotten."

Before the house was a semicircle of two or three acres, at the bottom of which ranged some pines, where the redbreast robins regularly sang their tuneful loves, and in the same nests, year after year, laid their blue eggs. As their melodies told of their home joys, their parental anxieties and triumphs, when their little ones were hatched, nurtured, and at last committed to the air on full-fledged wings, he reminded the children that we could learn to be considerate of them, by reflecting upon their own domestic attachments. He indulged the children in keeping pets. To each was a

chicken given from the spring brood. Of course this
chicken must survive the ides of Thanksgiving, and
must hatch one or more broods of new exempts next
season. In this way, like Jacob's speckled cattle, the
poultry-yard soon passed to the children, and we remember the father repossessing himself at least twice
by purchase.

Arthur had also a tame blue dove he called *Divie*,
which was a constant companion in the house and
field, her master's finger being her favorite perch.
This lovely bird, in the familiarities of several months,
endeared itself to the hearts of all the household, and
cruelly were they lacerated when it fell a prey to the
spirit of evil in the form of a cat. Arthur was so
much affected by the loss that he would never have
another dove.

In this varied development, under the happy auspices of a loving father, was Arthur's childhood faithfully improved. But the even tenor of his life in
Groton was destined soon to be interrupted by a fearful shock of fate, which was to precipitate upon his
tender years the cares of manhood, scarcely permitting
the orphan to weep for his dearly loved sire, in the
pressure of new and grave duties.

His father had a naturally delicate constitution ;
although, fortified by strict temperance, a spare and
regular diet, cold-water bathing, and habitual exercise
in the open air, he had been enabled to endure the
fatigues of public life and the exhausting labors of a
lawyer in full practice. As a little child he was puny
and sickly, and though he rallied so as to acquire an
average strength, his health always demanded careful

attention. As he returned to farm labors, he seemed to fancy himself a boy again, and able to engage in its pursuits as actively as ever. His spirit was as eager and vigorous and resolute, but the frame of fifty had neither the elasticity nor endurance of the age of fifteen. Neither he nor his family appeared to realize this. His energy prompted him to inspirit the men he employed by his own example, and they sought for the triumph of the physical over the intellectual by outdoing him and putting his strength to the test. We remember him, in the violent heat of summer, loading grain, with the perspiration flowing over his brow, while the hired man was endeavoring to pitch on the load faster than it could be arranged on the cart. After such efforts he was compelled to lie down on his bed from exhaustion, yet no one thought of evil consequences.

Among other farm improvements, he paid particular attention to draining low lands, and bringing to fertility the mines of agricultural wealth borne thither and deposited by the water. Vegetable matter while saturated decays slowly, but when the water is let off and the warm sunbeams admitted, decomposition is rapid. Arthur's father, in the summer and early autumn of 1835, had caused some low lands to be thus drained and opened to the action of the sun. It was afterwards thought (with how much justice we do not undertake to decide) that malaria was exhaled from this drained land, and led to the severe family sickness of that season. Certain it is, that Margaret at this time was brought near the gates of death with typhus fever. Soon after her recovery, her father was seized with Asiatic cholera, and the same autumn the two boys, Arthur and Richard, were ill with fever. The fatal sickness, however, of the father, at least, may have had other causes. Perhaps his constitution, naturally so delicate, had worn out. Not long before his death, while as yet having no symptoms of sickness, he expressed to Arthur a presentiment that his departure from earth was near at hand. He spoke of it seriously, but with cheerfulness. Perhaps he may have been admonished by a declension of strength incident to the wearing out of the body, as it draws towards the close of its term. Or the proximity of the spiritual world may have touched some delicate chords in his nature, and made itself apprehended by a new and spiritual experience.

On the morning of the thirtieth day of September, 1835, Arthur's father had appeared in usual health; and for dinner had partaken of rice and milk, his favorite repast. In the afternoon of the day, while in the house, he was seized with sudden illness, vomiting and sinking helpless to the floor. He was immediately taken up, borne to his chamber, and laid upon his bed. As soon as he was carried there, he declared calmly that he felt his sickness would be mortal; and was able to say little else, such was the agony of his sickness. The family physician, who was speedily summoned, pronounced the malady to be Asiatic cholera, although there was at that time no other known case of this fell scourge in New England, and though, from habits of strict temperance, and simple, abstemious diet, he was an improbable subject for the disease. Yet the symptoms were indubitable; and the doctor's opinion was afterwards confirmed by a post-mortem examination conducted by several physicians.

The conflict between the defensive forces of nature and the assault of disease was short but terrible. For twenty hours, alternate spasms and chills, attended with a cold perspiration beading the marble brow, evidenced the progressive parallels with which the besieging foe advanced to storm the citadel of life. But no groan, no murmur of complaint did the sufferer permit to escape him. At last there was a lull, preparatory to the final onset, which was to break upon his life and liberate the tried spirit, to know no more pain, no more sorrow, no more death. He now, in a faint whisper, being too much reduced to speak aloud, expressed his desire to bid farewell to his family; and, as they gathered about his bedside, he smiled faintly, but with undimmed love, upon the dear weeping circle. The parting kiss he strove to return with his cold lips, while his eye irradiated undying love, and the light of the familiar smile flickered transiently upon his pallid features. The seal of that kiss could never be forgotten or effaced. It attested a love stronger than death; and it pathetically reiterated the lessons of fatherly admonition, counsel, and affection which those lips could no longer utter. The speechless symbol was more expressive than fluent language. It served as the solemn authenticating seal set to the children's life commission by the dying father, and mutely expressed what he could no longer speak. His undying affection in the dying hour crowned the uniform kindness and tenderness of his life. *Finis coronat opus.* And the perfect re-

2 * c

pose of his trust in God in that time of utmost need ennobled him in his children's view, and threw a glory over his virtues.

Soon after this farewell scene, he was released from his sufferings. It was evening when he breathed his last. The children slept, and were first awakened to know themselves orphans by the solemn tones of the minister's prayer, proceeding from the chamber of death. Sad indeed it is, when the young child first says to himself, "I have no father!" The mother's love lacks the father's power to protect, provide, and open the path of life. Yet in this case the gloom of the occasion was soothed by the repose of the father's face, as he lay low in death. All trace of suffering had passed away, and the features had not been emaciated in the short season of sickness. The expression of his countenance was pleasant and almost smiling, seeming bound by the lightest spell of slumber; and, except that the eyes were closed, looking as the children had seen him when engaged with his papers, humming to himself some gentle strain.

His age at his death was fifty-seven years. He was temporarily interred in Cambridge; and, finally, in the family lot at Mount Auburn.

CHAPTER III.

YOUTH.

"The individual man, — how does he, on his birthdays, reflect upon the period of life already gone! behold, as it were in vision, the solemn pageant of scenes long passed away : look on paintings, hung in Memory's gallery, of deeds performed in bygone years, and over which the veil is generally drawn as too sacred for common and uncaring eyes. .... How does he rejoice in the thought of early struggles as requisite for the development of his character, and early hardships suited to task and strengthen his powers of endurance." — *Bi-Centennial Address, delivered at Groton, Massachusetts, Oct. 31st, 1855, by REV. ARTHUR B. FULLER.*

Y the death of the father, the main pillar of the family edifice was stricken away. Not merely was affection lacerated by the loss, and the aching void of afflicted love felt in the place which the honored parent had filled, but there was also a sense of helplessness as well as loneliness ; and forebodings of the future mingled their shadows with the gloom of bereavement. This was not exclusively from lack of property inheritance, but still more from an entire inexperience in business, and a strong distaste for it, in those on whom the management of affairs now devolved. The mother was as naturally inapt for finances as one of her flowers, cherished by her as she herself had been by her husband's fostering care. She was characterized by quick perception, devoted affection, and constant delight in all the forms of beauty ; but she had never

learned to calculate ; and she felt wholly helpless as the
managing head of the family.   Her daughter Margaret
was her main reliance.   But that daughter, though
learned in the lore of many tongues, and gifted
with force, courage, and energy, had one weak point,
and that was *business*.   She dreaded computation.
Mammon she felt never looked auspiciously on her
destiny.   She was not a votary at his shrine ; and the
offended *numen* did not shine upon her fortunes.

Of the rest of the family, Eugene, her younger
brother, was engaged in the study of the legal profession.   He had as yet acquired little knowledge of
business, and could not relieve his mother and sister
from the weight of care.   William, still younger, was
at a distance, engaged in mercantile pursuits.   Arthur
was but thirteen years of age.

The property left by the father was mostly real
estate, and, though unembarrassed with debt, was but
little productive.   Lands he acquired he generally
retained.   The Cambridge Port house had never been
sold, though it rented for but a trifling sum.   He left
two farms ; but farms are proverbially unprofitable,
except to owners applying their own hands to the
task of culture.   It may be well this should be so ;
at any rate, so it is in New England.   One of these
farms, situated in Easton, Massachusetts, came upon
his hands under peculiar circumstances.   He had been
professionally employed to draw the deed of convey-
ance.   The purchaser, making no mention of the
grantor being married, it might not have been deemed
the duty of one employed merely as a draughtsman
to insert the release of dower.   This was omitted ;

the husband died, and the widow came forward to claim her thirds. Acting from the dictates of a delicate sense of honor, the lawyer himself assumed the purchase; and thus came to be the owner, till his death, of a distant farm, from which he never received an annual return of two *per centum* of the cost. He visited it yearly, accompanied by some of his children. It abounded in stones, which had been built into walls of many feet in thickness, that might have served to defend a city. On it stood an old red house, boarded in the ancient permanent style with white oak. Here the widow enjoyed her "thirds"; living in a sort of contest of longevity between her own tenement of clay and the oak-boarded red house. She succumbed at last; but she outlived her cotenant.

There was also a little land, of trifling value, in Salem, Massachusetts, a few bank shares, and the mortgage for the purchase-money of the estate on Dana Hill, Cambridge; property appraised at something over twenty thousand dollars, yet, as will readily be perceived, affording a slight income, and small means for the family maintenance and the education of several children. It required a very different style of life from what the family had been habituated to while the father managed affairs, and his professional earnings were equivalent to a handsome annuity.

Arthur's mother now relied upon Margaret for judgment and counsel. The devoted daughter, with a noble spirit of self-sacrifice, gave up her plans of foreign culture, just ripe for fulfilment, her literary ambition and pleasures, in obedience to the call of the

nearest duty. She said she felt she should not otherwise be at peace in her mind. But it was a great
disappointment to her; and she was further depressed
by a sense of incapacity for her new post. Yet she
determined to make up by courage and energy for her
deficiencies in business faculty. And she succeeded,
though at the cost of some shadowed and melancholy,
yet unrepining hours.

To perform her task, she felt that the boys should
be duly impressed with their condition and the necessity laid upon them in life, and that the family affairs
should be fully explained and unfolded to them. The
family had frequent gatherings, like the Indian at
his council-fires, to discuss future prospects, and terribly gloomy and portentous did they seem to the
young hearts. Fear and helplessness sat at the coun-
cil-board.

Arthur was thus seriously affected, and his every
power called out. We cannot doubt that the lessons
he now learned were of life-long value to him; and,
especially, that what he had to undergo roused his
energies, and trained him to the resolute habit of
grappling with difficulties and overcoming obstacles
which characterized his manhood.

During the season succeeding the father's death, the
farm was carried on by the boys, assisted by an inexpe-
rienced hired man, whose ignorance was only equalled
by his pretension. Arthur, in the improvised curtain
narratives which have been alluded to, denominated
him "The Haughty," making a caricature of his rash
and clumsy method of farm-work, and visiting upon
him an ideal retribution for his presumption. In the

course of the season the man became constantly more offensive, and Arthur planned a *coup d'état* to get rid of him. He selected a stout cornstalk-but for himself, and another for Richard, and, during the husking operations, headed an onset upon "The Haughty." The immediate object was not gained, for the defendant was a full-grown and athletic man. The cornstalks proved too frail a weapon, and were soon broken in the vigorous assault, which the party attacked finally repelled, and even carried the war into Africa. The matter was thence adjourned to the civil tribunal, where Margaret acted as judge. Here "The Haughty" was loud in his charges, while Arthur justified the assault as provoked by many grievances, and instigated by the spirit of our heroic revolutionary fathers. Margaret regarded it as a balanced case, and would not censure the boys. Not long after the man's term expired, and no new engagement was made with him. This cornstalk engagement we deem the more memorable, because we believe it was Arthur's first martial encounter, and his second was the battle of Fredericksburg. We never knew him on any other occasion to have any conflict with man or boy. As a child he was spirited, and always believed in the right of self-defence ; nor would he have tamely submitted to insult or injury. But his demeanor was not such as to invite aggression, and he was always too kindly and considerate to provoke strife.

The following season the family were so fortunate as to secure the services of a faithful and efficient man,* who managed the farm affairs as well as if his

---

* Since a prosperous farmer upon acres of his own, in Groton.

own, and obtained unprecedented crops. This year, with such efficient aid, it was felt that Arthur could be spared from the farm, and that the time should be diligently employed by him in his college preparation. He accordingly attended school at the academy in Leicester, Massachusetts, of which his father had once been a teacher. He made considerable progress here in his studies, and, what is more important, he received serious religious impressions at prayer-meetings. As early as this, or even earlier, he set his heart upon becoming a minister of the Gospel; and from this purpose he never wavered; nor did we ever hear him, in the whole course of his ministerial career, in the sunny side and the shady side of the clergyman's life, in trials or successes or disappointments, express one regret that his choice had fallen upon a calling which he ever regarded as most useful and noble.

During the next season the whole farm-work devolved upon Arthur, at the age of fifteen years, aided by his younger brother. The plan and the execution of farm culture, the buying and selling, were left to them. And the farm was thus successfully carried on, with an occasional day-laborer, and steady help during the toils of the hay-field. Arthur overcame his natural repugnance to labor, and prosecuted farm pursuits with the same energy and enthusiasm which he afterwards manifested in other fields. Occasionally extreme heat or fatigue from incessant toil disposed the younger brother to give way, but Arthur would hear no such word as retreat. He never worked harder than in these fields of home, nor did any retrospect afford him more satisfaction than the remembrance of his farm labors. An idea of the extent of the work may be gathered from the statement, that the boys tilled some five or six acres of corn and potatoes; and about twenty tons of hay were harvested. The stock consisted of three good cows and a pair of oxen, besides hogs.

The dairy was cared for by the diligent mother, who achieved laborious triumphs in the making of butter and cheese, which fully sufficed for the family use. Although her house labors were more than equal to her slender strength and health, and her years bordering on fifty, yet she would not permit her numerous coterie of garden flowers to suffer, nor would she incur the expense of the ·assistance of a gardener, nor divert the boys from the necessary and crowded avocations of the field. Her flowers she fostered herself, in every hour she could snatch from household pursuits, toiling in the heat of the sun, and obliged by her near-sightedness to stoop to close proximity. Yet her ideal darlings sprang up, bloomed and faded, neither choked by weeds nor faint through want of irrigation.

As has been already stated, the family employed occasional help in the farming. Such men as worked for them no doubt have always their counterpart in society. But a few of these characters, who have long passed from life's stage, must be sketched here, because they were painted on the easel of boyish fancy, and their idiosyncrasies furnished sportive themes for Arthur's epics, while they enjoyed the honor of being enrolled in his "Universal Band." One of them, familiarly called "John," was an inveterate follower of Bacchus, in his cheaper and grosser cups. His only merit was good-nature. We have not been able to obliterate from memory his always placid but bloated countenance. His excesses had fearfully recoiled upon him. With other boon companions, he lived ·with a neighbor in the working season. This neighbor himself adhered firmly to principles of total abstinence — from water! He boasted that he had not been thirsty enough for twenty years to drink it. And nature had conformed to his tastes, by giving him a jug figure, surmounted with a bald head like a stopper. Certain friends of his, congenial spirits, of which charmed circle John formed a link, lived with him in the summer season, doing just days' works enough to pay for a little meat and a great deal of drink; and, when they got " out of spirits," taking up their winter-quarters in the poorhouse. Such specimens of depravity tended to give the boys a horror of those habits which had wrought their degradation ; and the mother did not decline to employ them occasionally, in special exigencies, as their conversation and deportment were not objectionable when their friend Alcohol had deserted them in their need, and they were trying to obtain the golden lure to draw him back. Her pity for them exceeded her censure, as it did in the case of all the degraded and unfortunate. This they well knew, and were sometimes emboldened to enter the garden, which bordered on their own demesne, when she was engaged with her flowers, under pretext of admiring her favorites, but really with an eye to the fruits which abounded there. We well remember one occasion, when John had entered the garden and climbed into a choice cherry-tree. There we spied him among the green leaves, his red and bacchic countenance like a huge cherry engaged in devouring the little cherries, as the rod of Aaron swallowed those of the magicians. We boys contrived to hint to him that for certain reasons these familiarities with the fruit were not entirely agreeable to us, and John was magnanimous enough to leave the banquet, alleging his preference for the indigenous fruit of the same species whose distilled virtues, he boasted, garnished the generous cellar of his host.

When we employed John and his compeers, some oversight was necessary to keep them to their tasks. They delighted to beguile their toil with narrative of fact and fiction which they represented as having once occurred in the vicinity; and they sought often to pause and lean upon their hoe, or other implement, the better to point out the *locus in quo*, or lend to their descriptions the animation of gesture. But Arthur was not to be circumvented in this way. Like an efficient speaker or moderator, he continually brought them back to the matter immediately under discussion, namely, the row they were hoeing, or whatever work was in hand.

One of our day-laborers brought with him a large mastiff, of whose pugnacious exploits he bragged till Arthur grew weary of the theme, and asserted that he could vanquish the dog himself. The man, with wounded vanity, declared he would like to set the dog on and try it. Arthur would not recede from what he had said, and the result was the dog was set on, and rushed, with bristled hair and tail erect and bare fangs, to the encounter. For about five minutes Arthur plied his boots with rapidity and vigor against the dog's chest and chaps, occasionally bringing the canine jaws together with the tongue unpleasantly sandwiched between them, till the dog ingloriously lowered his caudal flag, and, despite the invective of his master, turned back from the proceeding with a bugle-note far different from the trumpet-bark which sounded the charge.

Interspersed with farm toil was the relief of rainy days and our rare public holidays. One of the latter was the old Election-day, on the last Wednesday of May; at which date it was the rule among farmers, to have the planting completed. This was a sad day for the birds, whose exulting spring melodies were wont to be cruelly interrupted, and their nestlings bereaved by the sports of the hunter. The law now has not only transferred the election day to another season, but shields with its broad ægis the little birds' nests, protecting their domestic joys from the ruthless sportsman. Arthur and Richard, we believe, only once assumed a musket, in the Election-day hunting; and we do not know that Arthur, on any other occasion, discharged fire-arms till the battle of Fredericksburg. Their father kept a brace of pistols in the house; but he always cautioned the children against them: and his warning had the more effect from the powder explosion by which, as we have narrated, Arthur and Richard were injured in Cambridge, and from an incident which occurred on one occasion, when he exhibited the pistols and the manner of firing them to gratify the curiosity of the family at the fireside. We have a lively recollection of that occasion. " Now, children," said he, " I know perfectly well that these pistols are not loaded ; yet, in showing you the opera- tion of the lock, I shall not point the pistol at the head of some one, as a boy might do, for bravado. For instance, I shall not point it at your sister Mar- garet." With this remark, he directed the weapon to the wall, near the floor, and drew the trigger. Great was our consternation when the pistol exploded, and discharged a bullet through the wall into the cel- lar. This unlooked-for result was explained after- ward, when it was ascertained that some one had been practising with the pistols, and inadvertently left them loaded.

On the Election-day referred to, Arthur and Rich- ard sallied forth to the hunt, musket on shoulder. The first bobolink they levelled at was considerably agitated, broke off his jubilant strain, and took his flight, the boys claiming that they had drawn blood. Several other birds, after the discharge of their pieces, paid to their sportsmanship the compliment of retir- ing to a distance. But, after a while, the bobolinks seemed to get an inkling of the true nature of the case, and to shake their sides and wings, convulsed with songs of derisive merriment. After several hours, the boys returned home, without a single feather as a trophy ; and they did not try the gunner's sport again. They were more successful in angling, on the banks of Nashua River, or floating in boats upon the mirror-depths of Martin's Pond.

After haying was finished, the farmers usually in- dulged themselves in a day's pastime, spent in a fishing

excursion. The men employed to help in haying,
the season Arthur and Richard carried on the ·farm,
made a great point of this day of sport; and the boys
accompanied them on the occasion. They procured
some spirituous liquors; and, after themselves imbib-
ing, strove hard, by ridicule and persuasion, to induce
the boys to partake. Arthur was firm in his resistance, but Richard was prevailed upon, in spite of
Arthur's entreaty, and warning that he should let his
mother know of the affair. On retiring that night,
the mother visited Richard's bedside, and administered
to him a solemn reproof, which he never forgot.
This was Arthur's first step in the temperance cause,
in which he afterwards faithfully labored.

In the Groton experience, Arthur's education was
by no means neglected. The mother and sister regarded the grand purpose of preparing him for the
arena of life as far transcending the convenience and
expediency of the hour; and nothing would have
tempted them to sacrifice his welfare to the family
needs. It was very justly believed, conformably to
the father's views and plans, that the hardships of
farm labor might form a very valuable part of educational training; while the complemental part of mental
discipline Margaret heroically assumed. Her rule
was to study, in the summer, the out-door literature,
traced in the expressive characters of nature, with its
" books in the running brooks, sermons in stones, and
good in everything": while in the winter she applied herself to human lore. This was her *régime*,
also, with the boys. As soon as the farm harvests
were garnered, the seed-time of in-door teaching com-

menced; and for several hours a day she presided
over the family school. This was a very great sacrifice to her. Her own mind was amply stored,
and she longed now to create, in emulation of those
masters who had won the laurels of literature. To
teach children, scarcely in their teens, was as much
below her bent as for Apollo to tend the flocks of
Admetus. Nor could she, like him, beguile the occupation with the lyre. Her father's death, the aban-
donment of her plan of European travel, and the new
weight of uncongenial family cares had depressed
her, and her harp hung for a time tuneless upon the
willows.

As a teacher few have excelled her. Not merely
did she faithfully train to good habits of mental application; not merely did she store the mind with the
treasures of learning; but she constantly sought to
kindle and stimulate noble aspiration. When in their
studies they came upon the feats of Roman, Greek, or
modern patriotic devotion, she would expatiate upon
them with glowing eloquence. Little did they expect,
when they·thus learned and admired the devotion of
Curtius or Scævola, or the modern Swiss who broke
the assailing phalanx by gathering with the embrace
of his extended arms a sheaf of pointed spears into
his own bosom, that their own times would add new
narratives to the legends of glory; that the Italian
War and the American Rebellion would furnish many
instances of devoted heroism, unsurpassed by the
bright pages of history; and that in these scenes the
aspiring teacher, Margaret, and the ardent pupil,
Arthur, would participate.

No doubt her personal influence on Arthur was
more important than what she could impart to him
in those early years. A noble spirit is catching ; and
Arthur was quite capable of being lighted with her
enthusiasm. She herself remarked this, expressing the opinion that in his mind he resembled her
more than the other children. The formative influence she hoped to have on the boys and upon her
sister Ellen, who composed the trio of her family
school, she regarded as much more important than
the rudiments of learning, which she would have
willingly committed to another teacher, and which it
much tasked her patience to communicate. Her own
great quickness and astonishing rapidity in the acquisition of knowledge led her to expect the same
in her pupils ; and tardiness on their part was very
trying to her. The little awkward ways which sometimes fasten on children annoyed her inexpressibly.
Among these may be mentioned a habit the boys
fell into of incessant movement of the hands, as if
catching at succor in the recitations, when they were
drowning in the deep places of Virgil. 'It seemed
absolutely impossible for them to think of the hand
and keep it still, while agonized with classic difficulties and trembling in dread of the doom of a bad
recitation. Sometimes their bright answers in geography or history made her laugh outright. She
preferred to laugh rather than weep, which was her
only alternative. Some of these bright responses she
recorded at the end of the geography *in perpetuam
memoriam.* We have in mind a passage, which may
still be seen by any one who can obtain access to that

text-book, — "Richard, being asked where Turkey in Asia was, replied that it was in Europe!"

In a subsequent letter to Arthur, while he was absent, completing his college preparation, Margaret thus refers to her family school : —

"You express gratitude for what I have taught you. It is in your power to repay me a hundred-fold by making every exertion now to improve. I did not teach you as I would; yet I think the confinement, and the care I then took of you children, at a time when my mind was so excited by many painful feelings, have had a very bad effect upon my health. I do not say this to pain you, or to make you more grateful to me ; for, had I been aware at the time what I was doing, I might not have sacrificed myself so; but I say it, that you may feel it your duty to fill my place, and do what I may never be permitted to do. Three precious years at the best period of my life I gave all my best hours to you children ; let me not, then, see you idle away time, which I have always valued so much ; let me not find you unworthy of the love I felt for you. Those three years would have enabled me to make great attainments, which now I never may. Do you make them in my stead, that I may not remember that time with sadness. I hope you are fully aware of the great importance of your time this year. Your conduct now will decide your fate. You are now fifteen ; and if, at the end of the year, we have not reason to be satifised that you have a decided taste for study, and ambition to make a figure in one of the professions, you will be consigned to some other walk in life.

For you are aware that there is no money to be wasted on any of us; though if I live and thrive, and you deserve my sympathy, you shall not want means and teaching to follow out any honorable path. With your sister Ellen's improvement and desire to do right, and perseverance in overcoming obstacles, I am well satisfied. . . . . . May God bless you, and make this coming year a prelude to many honorable years !

" Next time I write, I will not fill my whole sheet with advice. Advice too often does little good ; but I will not believe I shall speak in vain to my dear Arthur."

Early in the year 1839 a purchaser was obtained for the Groton place ; and the family willingly bade adieu to the scene of their first great calamity, and many consequent hardships and trials. The step was the more advisable, because Arthur and Richard had arrived at years which called for a more exclusive application to study than the cares of the farm admitted of.

Margaret, in a letter to her brother, thus dwells upon the Groton trials : —

" You were too young to feel how trying are the disorders of a house which has lost its head ; the miserable perplexities of our affairs ; and what your mother suffered from her loneliness and sense of unfitness for her new and heavy burden of care. It will be many years yet before you can appreciate the conflicts of my mind, as I doubted whether to give up all which my heart desired, to enter a path for which I had no skill and no call, except that *some one* must

tread it, and none else was ready. The Peterborough
hills and the Wachusett are associated in my mind
with many hours of anguish, as great, I think, as I am
capable of feeling. I used to look at them, towering
to the sky, conscious that I, too, from my birth had
longed to rise ; but I felt crushed to earth. Yet
again, a noble spirit said *that* could never be. The
good knight may come forth scarred and maimed
from the unequal contest, shorn of his strength and
unsightly to the careless eye ; but the same fire burns
within, and deeper than ever. He may be conquered,
but *never subdued.*

"Yet if these beautiful hills and wide, rich fields
saw this sad lore well learned, they also witnessed
some precious lessons given, too, — of faith, of fortitude, of self-command, and of less selfish love. There,
too, in solitude, heart and mind acquired more power
of concentration, and discerned the beauty of a stricter
method. There the heart was awakened to sympathize
with the ignorant, to pity the vulgar, and to hope for
the seemingly worthless ; for a need was felt to attain
the only reality, — the divine soul of this visible creation, — which cannot err and will not sleep, which cannot permit evil to be permanent, or the aim of beauty
to be eventually frustrated, in the smallest particular.
. . . . . Ought I not to add, that my younger brothers,
too, laid there the foundations of more robust, enterprising, and at the same time self-denying character ? "

After some months' study at a private school, taught
by Mrs. Sarah Ripley, in Waltham, Massachusetts,
Arthur entered Harvard University. He passed the

four years of college life happily and profitably, and graduated with an honorable part in 1843. Among his classmates were Rev. Dr. Hill, now President of the University, Judge Richardson, before mentioned, Rev. Frederick N. Knapp, of Washington, now engaged in the labors of the Sanitary Commission, and others who have become well known. During the first year he maintained a position at or near the head of the class, but his health giving way, he was obliged to relax his efforts.

While in college the concerns of religion were not forgotten in the pleasures of the Castalian spring. His serious impressions ripened into church-membership, and he united with the church of the University. In attendance upon the round of college duties he was regular. In associating with his fellows he guarded against exciting the ill-will of that portion who did not propose to themselves a serious aim in college pursuits, yet he was careful not to suffer his time to be frittered away. He lays down, for one about to enter college, the following rules to regulate his conduct, before he has learned the character of his companions: " I advise you on no account to miss a single prayer or recitation; but do not boast of it, or those who have missed a great many will dislike you. Be sociable and agreeable when any one calls on you; but do not yourself call much on others."

During his college course, to eke out his finances, he taught a district school in Westford and in Duxbury, Massachusetts. His love for children rendered teaching for him a pleasant and successful task. He engaged in the work animated by the same enthusiasm which characterized him in every pursuit of his life. Imagination, hope, and a buoyant temper cast a roseate coloring over all. In a letter from Westford, he declares that the children in his school are "very intelligent and pretty, every one." He did not fail to please, in his turn, those who were so agreeable to him, and to obtain access also to the regard of the parents through the sure way of the children's hearts.

He was no less successful in Duxbury, where, we are happy to learn, his labors have not been forgotten. From Duxbury he writes, "I have thirty-nine scholars, *all* good ones, *all* love me. I am so fortunate, also, as to please the parents, and, in fact, was never happier in my life. I have a great deal to do, however, besides the regular school labors, in teaching evening schools, visiting the parents, and studying myself in order to instruct them well." And again he writes: "I have been invited to several balls and parties. The former I never go to, and the latter always." Shortly before he closed his school, a meeting of the district was holden, which passed the following preamble and resolutions.

"Whereas, Mr. A. B. Fuller, our accomplished and much-esteemed instructor, is about to close his school in this place, and we feel desirous of expressing our warm approbation of his course while with us, and our sincere gratitude for his earnest and faithful labors; therefore,

"*Resolved*, That the thanks of this meeting be tendered to Mr. Fuller, for his able and successful exertions in imparting that knowledge to our children which the world can never take away.

"*Resolved*, That we approve of the methods which Mr. Fuller has taken to instruct the pupils consigned to his charge; that we believe his influence has been of the most beneficial tendency, in preserving uncorrupted the characters and hearts of our children; that both his precept and example, while with us, have tended to inculcate and sustain a sound, elevated morality."

From reminiscences of our district-school teacher, kindly furnished us by one of his former pupils, we make the following extract.

"We boys were sometimes invited to spend the evening at his rooms, and then we enjoyed ourselves heartily. He entertained us with stories, anecdotes of history and philosophy, and a sight at the ' Master's ' literary treasures, such as seals, colored wax, transparent wafers, and other knick-knacks, which seemed to our admiring eyes like Oriental treasures. The literary entertainment was followed up by a feast of nuts, apples, and oranges, very congenial to our boyish appetites. These favors made us look up to and love the teacher, endearing to us, too, the master's room in the old red cottage on the hill; and many a well-recited lesson, I ween, has been the result of those happily spent evenings.

"He introduced evening schools into our district, made interesting by spelling-matches, debates, and lessons he gave us in reading. At one of these evening schools we were much annoyed by a crowd of vandal boys, with adult forms, but undeveloped brains, from a neighboring district, who boasted that they had put down the evening spelling-school in their own district, and were bound to stop ours. They assailed us with various hideous noises at the windows, and even with pebbles. Our master of a sudden donned his hat, and with but two strides, as it seemed to us, sallied from the school-house and pounced upon the ringleader, a lad as tall and nearly as heavy as himself, seizing him by the collar, to the boy's surprise and the confusion of his comrades, and shaking him nearly out of his boots. He then required his comrades, who to the number of six or eight were gathered round their chapfallen leader, to give him all their names, and thoroughly dismayed the whole set, who never troubled us more."

Arthur's school-teaching drew from his sister Margaret, who was never lavish of commendation, the following terms of approbation, in a letter to him: "I am satisfied that your success, and the tact and energy, by which you have attained it, are extraordinary. I think of you with great pleasure, and am only anxious about your health."

In a letter, some months previous, she imparts to Arthur her views of the methods of teaching: a subject which she had carefully considered, in connection with her practical experience; as many gifted minds have done, especially in classic times; and as all cultivated minds should do, having no right to shut up in themselves the treasures of learning and thought.

"About your school," she says, "I do not think I can give you much advice which would be of value, unless I could know your position more in detail. The most important rule is, in all our relations with our fellow-creatures, never to forget that, if they are imperfect persons, they are still immortal souls, and treat them as you would wish to be treated, in the light of that thought.

" As to the application of means, — ' abstain from punishment as much as possible, and use encouragement as far as you can, *without flattery.*' But be even more careful as to strict truth in this regard towards children than to persons of your own age. For to the child the parent or teacher is the representative of justice ; and as the school of life is severe, an education which in any degree excites vanity is the very worst preparation for that general and crowded school.

" I doubt not you will teach grammar well; as I saw you aimed at principles in your practice. In geography, try to make pictures of the scenes, that they may be present to their imaginations, and the nobler faculties be brought into action as well as memory.

" In history, try to study and paint the characters of great men : they best interpret the leadings of events amid the nations.

" I am pleased with your way of speaking of both people and pupils. Your view seems from the right point; yet beware of over-great pleasure in being popular or even beloved."

CHAPTER IV.

BELVIDERE, OR THE MISSIONARY.

"These are the gardens of the desert, these
The unshorn fields, boundless and beautiful,
And fresh as the young earth ere man had sinned, —
The prairies."
BRYANT.

"In the morning sow thy seed."

"He that watereth shall be watered also himself."

ON graduating, in 1843, Arthur Fuller commenced that career of enthusiastic and tireless public activity, which was never intermitted except by the tribute of sleep he grudgingly paid to the night, and the occasional protests of overtasked nature in the transient form of illness, till he rested forever from his labors on the battle-field of Fredericksburg. The ink of his college diploma was scarcely dry, when he started for the prairies of the West, on a mission of teaching and preaching. He embarked not only his whole soul, but his whole fortune in this enterprise; investing the several hundred dollars still remaining of his patrimony in the purchase of an academy in Belvidere, Illinois. He attached himself to this institution, as he did to the pastorate of several churches afterward, at the nadir of fortune's wheel, sure that it could go no lower, and hoping to give an upward impulse.

3 *

The academy at Belvidere had been discontinued,
and was now re-opened. It was an expired light, in
a locality where its lamp, well trimmed and burning,
might radiate afar, without a rival, over a new, broad,
and interesting field, as a much-needed beacon of
knowledge and influence. We always thought the
principal who now started the Belvidere academy
into new life was admirably calculated for the Western field, by reason of the animated, almost fever-
ish impetus of activity, which would not let him rest,
and which was in harmony with the rush and onward
sweep of Western life. Here, too, his delight in nature could be amply gratified, as he rode over the
level or rolling prairie, with its beautiful flowers
nodding among the verdure, its occasional park, and
its broad horizon, regaled by the melodious song-
ster, the long-drawn strain of the turtle-dove, the
clouds of pigeons, like the arrows of Persia, darkening
the sun, and made romantic, too, and even dangerous,
by the prowling packs of rapacious wolves. Such were
the Illinois prairies in 1843. Belvidere, the shire
town of Boone County, already numbered nearly a
thousand inhabitants, and every day swelled its census.
The town is located on the eastern head-waters of the
Rock River, in a region of unsurpassed natural beauty.

Margaret, in 1843, thus depicts scenes of Rock
River: "It is only five years since the poor Indians
have been dispossessed of this region of sumptuous
loveliness, such as can hardly be paralleled in this
world. No wonder they poured out their blood freely
before they would go. On one of the river islands
may still be found the ' *cachés* ' for secreting pro-

visions, the wooden troughs in which they pounded
their corn, and the marks of their tomahawks upon
felled trees. When the present owner first came, he
found the body of an Indian woman, in a canoe, elevated on high poles, with all her ornaments on. This
island is a spot where Nature seems to have exhausted
her invention in crowding it with all kinds of growths,
from the noblest trees down to the most delicate plants.
It divides the river, which there sweeps along in a
clear and glittering current, betwixt noble parks,
richest green lawns, pictured rocks, crowned with old
hemlocks, or smooth bluffs, three hundred feet high,
the most beautiful of all. Two of these, the ' Eagle's
Nest ' and the ' Deer's Walk,' still the habitual resort of the grand and beautiful creatures from which
they are named, were the scene of some of the happiest hours of my life. I had no idea, from verbal
description, of the beauty of these bluffs ; nor can I
hope to give any to others. They tower so magnifi-
cently, bathed in sunlight : they touch the heavens
with so sharp and fair a line ! This is one of the finest
parts of the river ; but it seems beautiful enough to
fill any heart and eye all along its course ; and nowhere
broken or injured by the hand of man." *

On the twenty-sixth of September, 1843, Arthur
started upon his Western mission, with a quick ear and
eye for observation, and a thirst for information, which
made the world an instructive book, from whose pages
he who had gone forth to teach should himself be
taught. Early in his journey, a scene in the railroad
car furnished the first lesson. Arthur has himself recorded it.

* Margaret Fuller's Unpublished Works, Vol. II. p. 677.

"A little boy of twelve years of age, poor and ragged, came into the car. There was a slight shrinking from him manifested by some of the well-dressed passengers. He took his seat quietly near me; and a sea-captain, who entered at the same time, told me his touching story. I learned that he was a poor orphan, and, three days before, had been wrecked. A vessel which had seen the accident sent forth its boat, to save from a watery grave any who might be rescued. They spied the little boy, floating amid the waste of waters, and approached him; but he, with a generosity, alas! too rare, cried out: 'Never mind me! save the captain: he has a wife and six children.' Poor fellow! he knew that the captain had those who loved him and would need his support. The captain, in telling me the story, was much affected, and said, with a sympathy characteristic of the mariner, 'The boy has only the clothes you see, sir; or he would not be so ragged. I care not so much for myself, though I too lost all; but the poor lad will have a hard time of it.' Several persons, on hearing this story, gave small sums to the poor orphan; and advised him to make a statement to other passengers, who would doubtless give something. 'I am not a beggar,' was his only answer; 'I don't wish to beg their money.' At this moment, a fine, benevolent-looking individual arose in a seat near me, and unostentatiously offered to plead for him who would not prefer his own claim. Most successful was the warm-hearted appeal which he made to the passengers; and ten dollars were collected.

"The plain, practical, common-sense way in which

this person manifested his sympathy for a fellow-being won my regard, and I entered into conversation with him. 'I 've been a sailor myself,' he said. 'The generous fellows ought not to want, when misfortune, not vice, has rendered them destitute. I know this brave captain would share his last dollar with any one in distress.'

"He sat down in the vacant seat next me; and more and more was I pleased to find that his religion was no mere theory, no barren speculation, but an active principle. I asked his name. 'Jonathan Walker,' was the reply; and the branded hand full well attested the fact. Yes! upon this man, so benevolent, with a heart so tender, had the friends of slavery wreaked their shameful vengeance!"

Borne on with the great tide of travel, he soon finds other objects to touch his heart. On board the steamer, he visits the steerage, and here his pity is stirred by a poor mother with her ragged babe. In his diary, he says: "She pressed her infant, sick, cold, and hungry to her bosom, and gave it the best of her scanty shawl; while her haggard look of despair told what she endured. God help the poor, and keep them from temptation! Do they live in this sad, wretched, starving way, and we look on, and pity them not? How can I complain, because I have little, when they have naught? Some of these poor creatures are sleeping now; and can forget their cares, and can dream of food and happiness. Happy sleep! Thrice happy the sleep of death, if they rest in Jesus; for then they will go to their Father! They go now to New York. How many temptations will assail them there! and what have they to sustain them in the trying hour? Starving and naked, will they not sacrifice the little they have learned of goodness and morality to keep the soul within the body? Can we wonder, when we behold the wreck of womanhood, or the besotted being who seeks to drown care in the maddening bowl? Is it strange to find that receptacle of vice and infamy, the 'Tombs,' crowded with inmates? And yet many can look on with indifference or brutal contempt; some can *laugh* at their squalid misery!"

Arrived at Belvidere, the teacher's labors began in earnest. Some sixty scholars gathered at the opening of his school, of various ages, numbering among them two or three young ministers of the Christian Connection, who suspended preaching for the benefits of his instruction. He soon found plenty of good work to do, with an increasing number of pupils, but almost no money. There was everything else in the West except currency. That, even in the coin of Lycurgus, was minus. Parents were glad to have their children taught at the academy, if the principal would take his pay in grain, wood, or even land. He was compelled to this course, and had to turn his commodities into money as he could, sending them to another market. All this he underwent, acting in the double capacity of teacher and merchant, with the hardihood of a pioneer. But this was by no means the sum of his employments, for he also did the work of an evangelist.

He gives the following sketch of the field of his labors.

"The Western man who would be useful must be

no mere theorist; he must employ every physical, moral, and mental power, or he will never succeed. An earnest laborer alone can claim or secure respect here; none other can move the heart or influence for good. My own situation is one to be sought by a person who sincerely desires to benefit his fellow-men; by one who is willing to devote his every energy to the cause of humanity. To such a one, a wide sphere of usefulness is offered, — none wider. Here he will find men thirsting for light and knowledge, and ready to learn 'what is truth.' He will indeed see much of ignorance, the inseparable though deplorable attendant upon all new settlements; but he will find the people are longing for instruction, and sighing for those privileges which their Eastern brethren enjoy. An earnest, philanthropic man should seek such a situation; but it is one to be feared by him who loves wealth or ease. Let him shun it, for here is no happiness for him. I daily feel how much more self-devotion I need, how much more of a spirit of prayer and consecration to the work.

"I knew long since the sacrifice I was making, and chose to relinquish ease and worldly promise in the hope of doing something for humanity. I love my work better and better. The more I contemplate the fields, white already for the harvest, the more I bless God that I am permitted to be one of the few humble reapers. I am resolved to struggle on, to bear up in a Christian spirit, and look to God for assistance and strength, knowing I 'shall reap if I faint not.' Besides, I am rewarded when I see so good a work going on. I have found here the sphere I have long sought,

and am happy, yes *happy*, amid all the toil and privation, — privation which you can never know till you
visit us.

"Our Christian brethren have well broken the
ground, and cheerfully unite with us, heart and hand,
in every good word and work. I have found among
them true zeal and love, and have joined and often
speak at their social conference meetings. Yesterday
I communed with them, and never felt more like meeting the disciples at the table of our common Master.
On Saturday last we had a fellowship meeting, as it is
termed; and truly it was a precious season. The
writer spoke twice, and it would have been no easy
task to remain silent. I have also, by request, attended and spoken at a Baptist social meeting, and
was pleased with all I saw and heard."

In a home letter he gives the following sketch of his
religious labors: "I go every Sabbath about eleven
miles, take charge of a Sabbath-school at ten, preach
at eleven, have an intermission of half an hour at half
past twelve, preach again a long sermon, take tea at
once, and ride over the chill, bleak prairie, directly
home, which I do not reach till late in the evening.
On week days, besides the hours of teaching, I lecture
and aid in debating-societies, and so forth, so that I
can scarcely find time to write even these poor letters."

He has given us an amusing account of a performance in the debating-society of Belvidere. It was
the discussion of the temperance question in the form
of an indictment, returned against one Alcohol, charging him, in various counts, with murder in the first

degree, arson, robbery, larceny, subornation to perjury, street-walking, vagabondism, and all the other crimes. The principal of the academy acted as prosecuting officer. A lawyer was judge, twelve honest men were impanelled for a jury, and Alcohol retained in his defence a wily advocate. The case for the government was strong. Abundant evidence was adduced to prove that Alcohol had been an accessary before the fact, and therefore, in the eye of the law, principal, in all the crimes charged ; nay, that he had been the prime instigator of the same. The government rested their case ; and now came the ingenious defence. A gentleman, on whose nose and other features Alcohol had placed the proprietary mark which is wont to distinguish his retainers, came forward to be sworn for the defence. The government's attorney prayed the judgment of the court on the admissibility of the witness, objecting that he was evidently under the influence of the defendant, and not disinterested, and in fact that he furnished another instance of the very crime of subornation charged in the indictment. The defendant's counsel, with all the indignation of offended virtue, protested against the imputation of the government. The court decided not to take cognizance of the objection made to the witness so as to pass upon it judicially, but to allow the jury to consider it in connection with the weight of testimony.

The witness was sworn ; and a keen deponent he proved to be. He testified, as an expert, that Alcohol did not have the effect upon his associates of stirring up the passions and depleting the pocket: thus encountering with a general negative the specific posi-

E

tive proof of the government. He was made the mark of a raking fire of cross-examination, which he very adroitly parried.

"Do you pretend Alcohol has benefited you?"

"I do."

"What has he done for you?"

"Made me happy."

"But did not your pleasure soon turn into bitterness and pain?"

"Ah! that was because my friend Alcohol left me. The moment I got him back again, I was happy once more."

On this evidence the defendant's counsel founded a panegyric of Alcohol; trying, by a sportive vein, to induce the jury to think lightly of the charges "trumped up," as he said, against his client. But the government's attorney effaced the impression of this plea by a pathetic picture of ruined families, weeping wives, and destitute children, society at large corrupted, and the individual temple of God in humanity desecrated and turned over to the habitation of demons. The judge charged fairly, laying down the law with precision. The jury brought in a verdict of guilty; on which a judgment was rendered against Alcohol, as a nefarious criminal; and he was branded, in that community, as an outlaw.

In his vacation, our missionary scorns the scholar's *otium cum dignitate*, and starts upon a missionary tour, which he thus describes: "I left Belvidere in an open wagon, upon my way to Geneva. I arrived, about eleven in the evening, after a fatiguing journey, and quite exhausted from the effects of the heat, from which

the interminable and shadeless prairies afforded no protection. The next day being the Sabbath, I preached
both morning and afternoon, and enjoyed much pleasant converse with our friends in regard to the state
and condition of the religious society. The following
Monday, Brother Conant and myself rode to Ottawa;
and thence, taking a boat, we proceeded, amid most
lovely scenery, to St. Louis. The high, frowning
bluffs, the majestic rocks, and ever and anon the smiling prairie, afforded a scene of never-ending pleasure."
Thence he went to Quincy, where he preached, and
from there, " We next proceeded to Warsaw, where
three days were passed. Brother Conant and myself
each preached upon a week-day evening. The people,
however, were too much engrossed with Mormon
troubles to make us deem it advisable to remain over
the Sabbath...... From Warsaw we went to Nauvoo,
and passed ten days at the Nauvoo Mansion, kept by
Mrs. Smith, the wife of Joseph Smith, the founder of
Mormonism. I certainly never heard such an amount
of the novel and absurd as was uttered during those
ten days. Still, while I believe the leaders to be vicious
deceivers, I found many sincere and worthy people in
the place; and nowhere have I received more polite
attention. I saw and conversed with a large number
of their elders and chief men, and became more and
more amazed that any could believe their absurdities.
The erection of the temple at Nauvoo continues without cessation; and unwearied are their efforts to complete the structure. How much is it to be regretted,
that so much zeal and effort cannot be expended in a
better cause ! Many give nearly their all; and those

having naught else give the labor of their hands for
the erection of this temple of delusion ; while, among
us, those who hold a rational and liberal faith ofttimes
refuse a pittance for the extension of truth, or give
but grudgingly a mite from their abundance."

Having reached home, he says : " I look upon this
journey with satisfaction and pleasure, as not having
been wholly in vain. . . . . . We have distributed those
silent but persuasive preachers, our tracts, at many
places where the boat stopped but for a few minutes ;
and have sown the good seed broadcast, in the hope
that much of it will take root in good and honest
hearts."

On another occasion, he speaks more particularly of
his tract distribution : " Often a tract was left when
the boat touched for but a few minutes to take in a
fresh supply of wood, where only a solitary log-cabin
could be seen for many a weary mile. The inmates
would hail these few pages with delight, as promising
to beguile their lonely hours, or as furnishing food for
thought upon the day of rest. Sometimes not a book
could be found in the cabin, and a tract thus given
would supply the only ' reading material ' to a poor
but intelligent family. I wished very much that I had
a few good books to place where they would have
been so faithfully used. . . . . . Long before I reached
home, the stock of tracts we had taken was exhausted,
and several opportunities to benefit others were un-
avoidably lost.

" We sometimes hear persons declare, how much
they wish they could preach. To such I would say,
Your wish can be gratified. Take with you some

tracts, and freely give to those who will, through curiosity, as freely receive. Do this, not officiously, but from a desire to do good, and fear not but that it will be accomplished. Often a light is thus shed beneath the humble roof of the Western pioneer which diffuses joy where before was gloom. All, both men and women, may thus become missionaries, and eternity only can reveal how effectual is such preaching. . . . . . But against one mistake we wish to guard. We desire no mere trash. A worthless book is worthless the world over, and here would be doubly pernicious. A good book, however old, is a good book still, and will be profitably and gratefully read."

It may be well, in this connection, to cite what he says of the importance of the Western field; for the state of things to which his words were applicable twenty years ago still exists, and will long continue, though farther removed toward the setting sun. "We cannot disguise the fact, if we would, that the West, now rapidly becoming peopled with an untrammelled, bold class of men, will at no distant period have the predominating influence in the councils of our nation. If we refuse to impart to them, by our missionaries and publications, that light which cheers our own hearts, if we hold back our hands, which contain the antidote to the impoisoned draught of infidelity, then shall we be responsible for the anarchy which shall ultimately prevail. No one need fear that Western communities are not capable of appreciating the efforts of learned and intelligent missionaries, or of reading with interest and profit the various newspapers, books, and tracts. I can bear willing testimony to the intelligence of those whom it was my privilege to address in different portions of the West."

On another vacation missionary excursion, he raises the banner of Christ in a log-cabin. He thus refers to this occasion: " Here, in this humble log-cabin, were gathered men anxious to hear of Christ, and learn the way of salvation. I preached, and seldom have been more moved than when gazing upon the eager countenances of my auditors. At the East, we call a sermon one hour or more in length wearisome ; but here, where few religious opportunities are enjoyed, a shorter discourse would leave the audience unsatisfied. I have, too, found it better to throw aside all notes when speaking ; the tastes, habits, and perhaps prejudices, of the people demand it.

" After the sermon, according to custom, I invited a free expression of feeling and of interest in the cause of Christ. Elder Walworth spoke with much earnestness, and the Methodist class-leader testified to the value of such meetings, and the worth of the souL That log-cabin, and the feelings there expressed, will be long remembered."

The young missionary by no means restricted his labors to his denomination. He commenced his career with ardent longing for Christian union, and a love for all the branches of the True Vine, which ever animated him, till the last beat of his heart. Rev. Mr. Conant writes of him : " Mr. Fuller is invited to address the Sunday schools, to participate in the social meetings, to lecture, and even to preach to the Orthodox societies. He lately received a request from some of the Presbyterian Society of Crystal

Lake to preach to them. I mention these things as incidents illustrative of what I have said of the confidence and respect which he has secured. He attends to all these calls, as far as time and strength and his other duties will permit, — preaching, lecturing, and talking to the people."

To the Methodists he always felt nearly related. In a letter from Belvidere he says: "A few Sabbaths since, after teaching a Sabbath school, which I had collected in a settlement about nine miles from this place, and preaching twice, I attended a Methodist meeting about half a mile distant. We sat quietly some time, waiting the arrival of their clergyman. Time passed swiftly, yet he came not; and I was strongly solicited by the class-leader and his brethren to officiate in the place of him they had expected. At first the request was declined, on account of a feeling of fatigue, but upon being renewed it was complied with, from a fear that a further refusal might be misinterpreted. I preached, and am sure that at least my own heart was benefited."

The academy, meanwhile, had nearly doubled the roll of its members, and was enjoying a high prosperity. But the zeal of the young preacher and teacher was burning out too rapidly the fuel of life. The flesh began to show itself too weak for the willing spirit. This he hints at in the following letter, which, while it furnishes a slight sketch of his labors, breathes something of that heart's desire for Israel which inspired his efforts.

"You wish," he says, "to know of my labors; and I will briefly inform you. Teaching in the acad-

emy, and having the whole oversight of its three departments, and attending to all the business inseparable
from an institution like mine, sufficiently occupy my
week-day hours. Upon each Saturday I start for some
destitute settlement, and lecture during the evening,
and preach thrice upon the Sabbath. In one place I
have a large Sabbath school, which I visit once in
three weeks. The scholars are from families of various denominations, and have no books nor any teacher
save myself. In the evening I usually ride home, in
order not to be late at school the next morning. My
health is wretched ; and may drive me from this wide
and promising field. Still there is too much to be
done for me to feel that I have a moral right to remain unemployed ; the harvest is too plenteous, and
the laborers too few.

" It is not until recently that I have felt it my duty
to preach thus regularly ; but the people in this region
are now fairly awakened, and would ' know of the doctrine.' It matters not how the storms rage over these
cold, barren, and bleak prairies, crowded audiences
listen eagerly. O, why will our clergy leave this noble
West unaided by their counsels ? Why will not more
of our strong men do battle here in the cause of truth
and Christianity ? Our missionaries are obliged to
ford rivers, face the rude winds, and preach in log-
cabins or barns, wherever their voices may be heard ;
yet we feel that the cause of truth is onward, and
many are coming to a saving knowledge of religion.
. . . . . I have generally preached in destitute settlements, where otherwise the living voice would seldom tell, upon the Sabbath, of life's responsibilities
and duties.

"Such is my present employment. I deeply feel a desire to obtain a more thorough theological education ; and, should I leave Belvidere in the spring, it will be with that intent, and on account of ill-health. My public speaking is wholly extemporaneous, and my week-day labors preclude the possibility of its being otherwise."

But he now felt compelled to leave this fruitful Western field ; not merely by the warnings of his overtasked health, but by his desire to lay a more solid foundation for usefulness in a profession whose enlarged sphere of action, and constant demand for new treasures from the storehouse of thought, his experience led him daily more highly to appreciate. Yet he yearns toward the field he must leave, and longs to have a fit successor. "In order that he may truly succeed," he says, "let him be an earnest, prayerful man, a *laborer* in the vineyard ; not one who comes simply to contemplate beautiful scenery, or to benefit his health, though both may be done. He should be so filled with the importance of his mission, that he could speak from the overflowing heart, without being always fettered by written sermons ; willing, too, to preach during the week occasionally, where he found inquiring spirits ; and above all one who scorns not the humble log school-house, so that he may benefit immortal souls."

The labors of our young missionary were valued highly by his coworkers in the blessed cause. One of the elders of the Christian Connection writes thus: "Brother Roberts accompanied me to Belvidere, and. we called on Elder John Walworth, who resides in

4

the place. Here seven ministers providentially sat
down together, — Elders Walworth, Roberts, Stick-
ney, Thomas, and Barr, of the Christian Connection;
and Brothers Conant ·and Fuller, Unitarian. How
delightful the interview! It was good and pleasant;
for all were of one heart, united by bonds stronger
than death. Belvidere is a beautiful place, and an
interesting point. It is a county seat, settled by an
intelligent, enterprising class of inhabitants. Brother
Walworth travels extensively, and his labors are abundant through the wide circle of his travels. But his
field was too large, and the coming of other ministers
has afforded timely aid. We have a first-rate academy
at Belvidere."

Again Elder Oliver Barr writes: "Belvidere is a
place of much interest. There is a flourishing academy here, under the supervision of Professor Fuller, a
young man of splendid talents, fine accomplishments,
and eminently qualified as a teacher. Professor Fuller
is a clergyman of the Unitarian order, but a humble,
ardent Christian, and zealously devoted to the advance-
ment of spiritual Christianity, — strongly sympathizing
with the Christians, and wishing to see our interests
and efforts identical in the West."

Rev. Augustus H. Conant writes: "Brother A. B.
Fuller, Principal of the Belvidere Academy, is exert-
ing a quiet, but *deep* and *strong* and *constantly* widening
influence."

Elder John Walworth thus expresses his regret at
the departure of the missionary teacher: "We regret
that we are compelled to relinquish our claims upon
the successful labors of Brother A. B. Fuller, Princi-

pal of the Academy, on account of his ill-health. The
confinement and arduous labors of the school-room
were fast undermining a constitution which was not
naturally strong, nor fitted to endure such constant
application. He has found it necessary, in order to
regain his health, and if possible his constitution, to
return to the East, in hopes that comparative relief
from *so much* labor and care will in some measure, if
not entirely, restore his health. Mr. Fuller felt desirous to sell the Academy to friendly persons; which
he did, by sacrificing considerably in order to continue it in the hands of our friends. . . . . . He has.
acquitted himself honorably as the principal in this
institution, as an accomplished and competent teacher.
He leaves the school deeply regretted by the students
and their parents and friends, who will long affection-
ately remember his unwearied exertions to benefit his
pupils. He leaves many friends here who ardently
wish him health and prosperity, and who hope, should
his life be spared to enter another field of labor, that
extended usefulness and success may continue to attend him.'

We have in the welcome extended to the zealous
labors of our young missionary by other denominations
a pleasing proof of the cardinal oneness of Christian
faith. And is there anything more satisfactory than
to see the standard-bearers of Christ, his representatives upon the earth, complying with his touching
prayer, — " that they may be one " ? They will be
one in heaven ; and can they refuse to be one on
earth ? It was at the prompting of this union spirit
that " Brother Fuller " (such is the record of Elder

Barr) "offered himself as an associated member with us, to aid in the great work in which we are engaged. We received him as a Unitarian minister, yet a brother beloved, faithful, devoted, zealous, and commended him as a member of this conference. If this be 'a paradox,' be it so. I would to heaven there were more of that catholic, fraternizing spirit among Christians generally! Subsequently to this, Brother Fuller's impaired health required him to leave his flourishing school in Belvidere."

Thus we have given a brief statement of a Western experience of two years; and we think those two fleeting years form as bright pages as any in this biography. We believe God accepted the devotion of the young, zealous heart, like the grateful offering of Abel's sacrifice. And the reaper received wages.

CHAPTER V.

DIVINITY SCHOOL.

"The proper study of mankind is man."

N his return from the West, in 1845, Arthur Fuller entered the Cambridge Divinity School one year in advance ; having already, amidst his active duties, gone through with the first year's studies of that institution. Thus, in what Choate describes as "fitful, fragmentary leisure," he had laid up half the allowance of a student in theology, while performing the double function of teacher and preacher. More than the other half he had learned from the book of nature and man. He had stored his mind with grand images from the vast level or billowy roll of the prairie ; he had entered heart and soul into the onward rush of Western life, and had thus obtained a momentum of activity, an energy of enterprise, which continued to impel him through life. He had acquired a copious, flexible, extempore utterance, a power of suiting his thought to the audience, an aptitude in moulding to his purpose the lessons of passing events. A Western audience, in those days, was held by no conventionality, and would go out at any point of the speaker's address, when his attraction ceased. He must interest, or have no hearers, and when he ceased to interest he had immediate notice of it by a vanishing audience. Thus the student gained an admirable discipline in the school of human nature, and learned to "catch men."

In the classic shades of Cambridge our student now devoted himself to study, contemplation, reasoning, and prayer. Those momentous themes of humanity, redemption, immortality, and heaven, the eternal interests of . the soul, which have exercised the most earnest intellects through all the ages of man, he zealously dwelt upon, grappling with doctrinal questions, settling his own convictions, and studying modes of reasoning by which to impress his convictions on others. Yet he was so far a practical man, that he could take no cloister-like pleasure in reading and reflection, and was incessantly seeking the most available application of truth to life, the associated life of the race of man.

Vacation was the signal for him to engage in some new expedition as a preacher. The first was usefully spent in Montague, Massachusetts. Five persons, during his ministration, joined the church in this place, which had not for three years before had a single addition. He also lectured on temperance to a crowded house. His second winter vacation he spent in preaching at Windsor, Vermont. He writes home from here, describing his labors apart from his regular Sabbath preaching: "I have established a Bible-class, which includes young and old, and meets on Tuesday evenings; also a Sabbath school which I superintend myself; and I preach on Thursday evenings. My time is all taken up. Last Sunday evening fifty persons assembled to see me at my residence." Again he writes : " I know that I am a miserable correspondent this winter ; but I am hurried, hurried, hurried. The society is deeply interested now in the concerns of religion, and I have to visit a great deal and write two sermons .every week in addition. I prefer to write discourses, as being at present best for me. My audiences have largely increased, and I believe I am doing some good."

He seemed to hear the sighing of the prisoner in the State penitentiary established at Windsor, and could not be content without visiting that institution. He writes in reference to it as follows : —

" The humane efforts of those who have charge of the convicts have done much to alleviate the suffering inevitably attendant upon long confinement, and great exertion is made to provide for the best interests of those whose crimes have brought them into this gloomy place. It caused me, however, some surprise as well as gratification to hear, as I approached the door, the voices of many strong men united in singing ; and I never felt more thankful to God for the power of music to soften and purify the heart, than when looking upon that band of prisoners whose whole attention seemed absorbed by their song. It was my purpose to deliver a temperance lecture, since intoxication in this State, as well as throughout the civilized world, is the prolific source of crime. The convicts, I found, were practising temperance melodies. It was touching to hear the strains of that household song, ' Long ago,' echoed amid those gloomy walls ; and as I gazed upon

countenances where sin and painful thought had written somewhat variant lines, I could not but believe
many were thinking of bygone and innocent days,
when brighter hopes illumined their pathway, when
guilt had stained neither hand nor heart. Nor was
this 'long ago' with a large portion of that number,
who were yet young, scarce having reached the age
of twenty-five. When the chaplain told me how few
had ever been under religious influences in childhood,
and that most of them had been neglected boys, educated only in vice, my heart refused harshly to con-
demn them, nor could I feel anything but profound
pity. How many, now honored and respected by the
world, would have been equally stained, had they been
nurtured only amid scenes of infamy.

"I incidentally endeavored, in the course of my lecture, to convince the auditory, that the object of government in punishing crime is to protect society;
yes, often to protect men from themselves; and that,
if they were pardoned to-morrow, or had never been
detected, punishment, from its nature, would still be
inevitable, because conscience would harass with its
bitter reproaches, and *they* would have known their
undiscovered guilt and *God* also.

"Upon Monday, I accompanied the chaplain once
more to the prison, and through the favor of its officers
was allowed to converse freely with any of the convicts. I cannot tell you how much satisfaction this
gave me; they seemed generally so ready to acknowledge their wrong-doing, to be penitent, and desirous of
reform. Alas! many of them may break those resolves, or the world's harsh treatment and cold scorn

may drive them once again to mad crime; yet for some I believe and hope better things. It was gratifying to find men who at least were not cased in self-righteousness and vanity, which as a coat of mail shields from any warnings. The wages of sin had been received by them, and the coinage was burning and fearful; *that* these men knew. Hardened wretches there were, it is true; men who seemed to have no mercy for themselves, and no care for others; yet, thank God, I am not their judge.

"I saw Clifford, who murdered his wife and innocent children, and through life must be imprisoned. He sat in his cell *alone*, — always alone, save with the bitter musings of his depraved spirit. Scarce thirty-eight, and looking still younger; he rocked to and fro, glaring at me with scowling brow, and fierce, mad eye, while my few words through his grated window drew no response. Poor, degraded wreck of humanity, — how sullen and vindictive! No word has passed his lips for months, but brooding over the past, he remains, refusing all sympathy, all counsel. Yet who can tell but the voice of those who would gladly save him from himself may yet arouse some smothered spark of feeling in that scorched and seared heart? Clifford has attempted suicide, but failed, miserably failed. When a keeper essayed to remove him from one cell to another, the ferocious convict endeavored to throw him over the balustrade, and thus kill one who had treated him only with kindness.

"I shall never forget how that wretched man looked upon me; nor did I fail to mark how fearful is the power which man possesses of thus stifling nearly

4 *   F

every good thought or germ of tenderness implanted in his bosom. How low, how terribly low he, 'made but a little lower than the angels,' may fall!

" There are now fifty-seven prisoners; only three of whom are confined for murder, and one even of these for murder in the second degree, having committed the act while intoxicated. There is but one negro among the whole number, an abandoned, desperate fellow; his crime, murder. Years ago he escaped from slavery, and who of us can tell how much that burning wrong may have goaded and maddened, how its degradation, more bitter than death, more cruel than the grave, may have cankered the heart, till it was revengeful and beastly. If this be so, where, *where* rests the awful responsibility? Now that corrupt African is a dangerous being, and recks little for the blood of those who would control his passionate outbreaks.

" And yet another, a young man, drew my attention. He was the son of a respectable clergyman, was scarce twenty-one, and for eight long years must render unrequited and silent toil. O how deeply affecting to gaze upon his handsome, intelligent face, and to hear him talk of those whose affections he had crushed and hopes blighted! 'I shall be almost thirty when released,' he said, as he turned his dark eyes upon me, who attempted to teach him how much of life would still remain to him; that he might yet be happy, if here he resolved to do well and wisely for coming time. Idleness and bad company had wrought the dark thread in the cord of life for this young man. Temptation had thus made him her victim; and *now*

where were those companions? How many of them
ever thought of his misery, or laughed less loudly
from the thought of his sad fate? But there are those
who do care for him; those who often love most tenderly the erring and world-forsaken, — his mother,
and his family. He spoke of the letters his mother
wrote him, and which were angel visitants to his sad
cell.

" There is a strong desire manifested by some of the
convicts to learn to sing, and one of their number has
been a teacher of music. But they have no singing-
books nor means of procuring them. A very few temperance melodies, which those already knowing common
tunes can sing, are all which have enabled them to have
any singing. Of course methodical instruction is now
out of the question. Yet what greater solace or benefit
to the poor prisoner than music? Perhaps nothing could
avail to soften his heart more ; and shall such means be
denied? One of the reasons of that joyous welcome,
' Come, ye blessed of my Father,' which it is the Christian's hope to receive, is that the prisoner has been
visited. If any cannot visit personally, send those
books which shall seek out the erring, nor loathe their
cells. Idleness and bad company brought many a
wretched one to these dark walls ; let them be taught
an accomplishment which shall be a companion in solitude. Afford them innocent and useful recreation,
and you have done much to guard from temptation.
Let the plaintive song of penitence echo within these
walls, and hearts may be touched where otherwise
no chord could vibrate. Those convicts have been
promised by me six, or, if possible to get them, twelve

copies either of the 'Carmina Sacra' or 'Boston Academy's Collection' of music. Let no person think my promise unadvised; for whether these books can be got of others or not, no self-denial would be equal to that of allowing such an opportunity for good to pass unimproved."

At the close of vacation, our student returned to Cambridge, and at the end of the term regularly graduated from the Divinity School.

He now felt fully prepared for the great work of the Christian ministry. The spiritual unction, the facile speech and animated delivery, had secured for their auxiliary in the Christian warfare a sound learning, derived from books "rich with the spoils of time," together with intellectual method and discipline. Would that the physical man had been meet to sustain the spiritual flame! But in this respect a disproportion between the mind and body at once struck the observer. His figure, of a medium height, all alive with the restless nervous temperament, showed a chest too narrow to be in equilibrium with the largely developed brain.* The mind constantly advanced beyond its unequal yoke-fellow, the body, and the latter frequently gave out in the course.

* His head measured twenty-three and a half inches. It may interest some readers to learn that his head was once examined by Mr. Fowler, the well-known phrenologist, whose chart indicates ideality, benevolence, and the reasoning faculties as his leading traits, with a full development of moral and religious character. Let this go for what it is worth. Our own observation has led us to think the contents of a head more important than its capacity.

PART II.

THE NEW ENGLAND CLERGYMAN.

"Work of his hand
He nor commends nor grieves.
Speaks for itself the fact ;
As unrepentant Nature leaves
Her every act."

EMERSON.

CHAPTER I.

MANCHESTER.

"Though meek and patient as a sheathèd sword,
  Though pride's least lurking thought appear a wrong
To human kind ; though peace be on his tongue,
Gentleness in his heart ; can earth afford
Such genuine state, pre-eminence so free,
As when, arrayed in Christ's authority,
He from the pulpit lifts his awful hand,
Conjures, implores, and labors all he can
For resubjecting to divine command
The stubborn spirit of rebellious man ?"

WORDSWORTH.

N graduating from the Divinity School, Arthur Fuller preached a few Sabbaths at Albany, New York. Here, he writes, " I have been attending a course of antislavery lectures by Frederick Douglass, the fugitive slave, and have become greatly interested." The field of religious labor in Albany seemed too arduous for his then state of health. He says: " I will tell you what is the strong desire of my heart, — a good large parish in the country. I wish a *religious* society; for I believe my motives in entering the ministry are, in all sincerity and humility, to save souls. This is no idle talk with me, as you will believe. And this doing good, in a contented, quiet, conscientious way, is *my ambition.*" On returning to Massachusetts he was engaged to take the place of Rev. Edward T. Taylor, the Bethel preacher in Boston, usually styled " Father Taylor," who was to be absent about three months. It was no easy task to hold the attention of the rough salts who made up a good part of the audience, and who were habituated to the dramatic preaching and truly ' wonderful though eccentric eloquence of Father Taylor.* But here Western experience stood our preacher in good stead. He made the billows roll in his discourse, and levied contributions from Neptune's every mood, to arrest the ear, and depict in nautical guise the Divine truth.

On the return of Father Taylor, our young minister preached for three months at West Newton, Massachusetts, when he received and accepted a call from Manchester, New Hampshire. Here he was soon after duly ordained. The condition of the church and society when he assumed the charge is thus depicted in an editorial article in the Manchester Mirror: —

" The Unitarian Society in this place, like a youth of early promise, on which consumption had laid its wasting hand, seemed to be fast sinking into a premature grave. Its dissolution was so strongly anticipated by some of its scanty members, that a few of those who had helped by their money and influence to sustain it for years left it, from reluctance to witness its dying struggles, and connected themselves with other societies. Still there were a few who, crowned with

---

* An instance of Father Taylor's style occurs to memory, which will illustrate his figurative speech. In a very dry time he had been requested to pray for rain, and complied in the following terms: " O Lord, the thirsty earth sends up its prayer to thee in clouds of dust!"

that rich jewel, Hope, continued to strive on against the calumny of foes and worse desertion of friends.

"In this their darkest hour, Providence sent to them a pale student, whose physical frame, tender as the summer plant, seemed ill-adapted to feed a robust brain, and little fitted to endure the toil requisite to the performance of the arduous and often perplexing duties of pastor to a society which had hardly a name to live. The gentleman had been sent to supply the pulpit for only one Sabbath, yet with but little intermission he has supplied it ever since. We need not say the person above alluded to is their present efficient and eloquent pastor, Arthur B. Fuller." The congregation, when he commenced his labors, says the same authority, "embraced about fifty persons." The church was at a low ebb, "attenuated to but the square of two."

Soon a change passed over this scene, which is thus described by a writer in the Christian Inquirer: "In his (Rev. A. B. Fuller's) charge at Manchester, New Hampshire, I was permitted to see a congregation vitalized by his fervor and permeated by his Methodistic spirit. I had known the church when it was feeble, lifeless, and doubting. Under him, it changed as by a miracle, as no one thought of withstanding his influence: old and young were brought into an earnest sympathy with their pastor, as beautiful as it is rare. Other denominations gathered closely around him, whom they call Orthodox and Evangelical. The pews were full as often as he was able to occupy the pulpit. Prayer-meetings, which he loved more than any of us, were a perfect success."

The pastor's earnestness and eloquence had a deep foundation. He believed himself in a perishing world, whose only hope is in the Lord Jesus Christ. He recognized the need of regeneration. These great doctrines are well suited to kindle the ardor and nerve the energy of one who loves God and man, and who feels himself called to preach the everlasting Gospel. But it was not merely the necessity of religion : it was the delight which the preacher felt in the law of his God, the deep joy of heavenly communion, the fountain of immortal satisfaction, which he partook of in the contemplation of God's attributes of love, majesty, and power, which gave for him divine charms to temple worship and the meetings for social prayer. Nor was religion with him an insulated sentiment or emotion, without a leavening influence on the associate traits of character. The whole man was pervaded by it. It gave and received influence from the intellect and the practical life. His preaching partook of this character, seeking to thread all the mazes of life with the pervasive irrigation of religion ; to make religion practical, and the practical religious ; to render the intellect religious, and religion intellectual ; to secure the joint, harmonious action of mind and heart ; to cherish aspiration, not as a detached emotion, but as the normal, combined operation of all the faculties in every channel of activity.

"We had the pleasure," says an editorial in the Manchester Mirror, speaking of the Rev. A. B. Fuller, "of listening to a discourse by this pastor, in which was developed one of the great secrets of his success among the people, which consists not more in his chaste and flowery language and winning style, than in his presentation of the great practicability and adaptation of Christianity to all the purposes of life. In his discourse, he entered familiarly into all the social and business relations of man with his fellows; showing the imperative duty of honest dealing in buying and selling, as well as in our social relations to be guided by the Christian sentiment of love and goodwill one towards another, our obligation to have our religion manifested by works each day of the week as well as on the Sabbath, and not to clasp in our Bibles or lock up in our churches our religious obligations and duties. Religion has something to do with the whole man; and those who profess Christianity, and would adorn their profession, should follow its teachings, and carry into practice its requirements, at all times and all places and under all circumstances."

He was very conscious of the importance of pastoral visiting to success in the ministry, and assiduous in paying visits, encouraging his people also to call on him. Yet, to prevent this part of his duty from encroaching seriously upon his labors in the study, he arranged a system of proceeding. He writes: " I have adopted regular rules for the employment of my time, and find it advantageous. I give notice of it to my people, that they may observe my hours."

The influence of the prayers of the new pastor, and of his exposition of truth, through the Divine blessing, became more and more manifest, not merely in an increasing audience, but, what was better, in an awakened religious interest, and souls gathered in as the precious seals of his ministry. The Divine grace, falling first as the noiseless but refreshing dew, then in occasional reviving drops, descended at length in a blessed shower.

" Yesterday," he writes, " was the happiest day of my ministerial life. My society has heretofore prospered outwardly and to a certain extent in religious things; but there has been at no one time any united movement such as is often termed a revival, and in which many souls at once seem full of concern, and others obtain a bright and blessed life. But for the few past weeks there has been that earnest state of feeling, and yesterday some seven persons presented themselves before the altar to unite with Christ's visible Church, and consecrate their lives to his service. It was a morning of deep feeling. The whole congregation were moved, and all those to whom I spoke at noon seemed much affected, most even to tears. This is but the beginning of a true revival of pure religion and self-consecration, as I hope and believe. I rejoice in it. In my mind there is no prejudice against a well-conducted and carefully guarded movement of this kind, in which excess does not necessarily mingle. Give me even excitement rather than apathy. Those who united yesterday were influential business men and most devoted women. I could tell you sweet things about nearly all of them. To-morrow evening, we hold a meeting of the church, to be followed by a meeting of inquirers, in which we shall set our church all to work, and answer the questions of those who long to know what they shall do to be saved. Rejoice with me, dear brother, that such a season of refreshing and revival is now vouchsafed to my church and society."

In the pastor's success it must not be supposed that he encountered no difficulties, no discouragements. He always had his full share of conflict with obstacles ; but, armed with the shield of faith, the helmet of salvation, and the sword of the Spirit, he did not yield, nor withhold the counsel of God.

At one time the most wealthy and influential man in the society, the pillar and mainstay, was exasperated by an earnest sermon against the great wrong of slavery, and dwelling upon the black crimes the slave power had perpetrated by the aid of a supple North. The gentleman called on the pastor, and told him that sermon had determined him to quit the society, and connect himself with that of another denomination. The pastor received this announcement in a very different manner from what had been anticipated. He assured his parishioner that he approved of his resolution. "I have preached to you," said he, "a considerable period of time, and with little apparent effect. Probably my mode of presenting truth is not adapted to your case. I hope a style of preaching which dwells more habitually upon the sterner themes of Divine truth may affect your heart."

The parishioner, finding he should not punish the minister by going to another church, declared he would not go to any. The pastor expressed sorrow, but would not yield an iota of the independence of the pulpit, in preaching the whole counsel of God. There the matter dropped, and there for some months it rested. The pastor, meanwhile, was always courteous when he met the lost parishioner. At length as he was passing one day the bank with which the gentleman was connected, he was surprised to notice his ex-friend beckoning to him to enter. What was to come off he could not imagine, but he expected nothing agreeable. On entering he was requested to be seated by the former parishioner, who was writing at a desk. He patiently complied, and presently his parishioner, approaching, placed in his hand a check for twenty-five dollars, saying, " Mr. Fuller, I respect you for your independence, and I give you that as a token of my appreciation." The pastor was much affected, and felt inwardly to thank God, not so much on his own account, as for the change which had been wrought in his parishioner.

The harmony between them was never afterward interrupted. The parishioner would listen quietly as a lamb to the occasional philippics which the pulpit did not neglect to thunder against " the sum of all villanies." The parishioner died not long after, bequeathing a handsome legacy to the society, and his pastor delivered an affecting eulogy upon the departed. Was it not better for the clergyman thus to do and dare, trusting in the Lord ? Was it not far better for the parishioner ? Was he not taught to trust the sincerity and fidelity of the pastor, who he saw would not yield his Master's cause to the pressure of golden influence ?

Our pastor encountered also a similar temporary reverse with a most happy ultimate result, in his pulpit presentation of the cause of temperance, — a subject which he not only advocated zealously to secular assemblies, but pressed home upon his people with his characteristic earnestness.

He had prepared a temperance address, which he delivered in a neighboring town on a special occasion ; and, impressed .with the religious importance of his theme, he threw it into the sermon form, and delivered it from his pulpit. It happened that a wealthy man in his society was engaged in the sale of spirituous liquors. He took umbrage at the sermon, declared it was personal, and written expressly for him, and he would go to meeting no more. So he retired, like Achilles to his tent. ' But it was no easy matter to persuade his children to the like course ; for they were attached to their pastor, who always loved children, and drew them closely to him in the Sabbath school, and had a smile and pleasant word for them wherever he met them, calling his lambs by name, occasionally too devoting a half-day 'service and sermon especially to them. Nor was the wife willing to forego her religious privileges for the grievance of her lord. So the rest of the family still attended church, and the head of the household was thus often reminded that there was such an institution, and, strange to say, it was still in progress, notwithstanding his dereliction.

Meanwhile the pastor was equally civil to the father when he met him, and equally cordial toward the rest of the family. At length the wife asked him if he could not send some message to her husband, who was by no means happy, yet, with the fancy rankling in his mind that the offensive sermon was written especially for him, could not be reconciled. The pastor said that he had nothing to take back about the sermon ; but if it would be any relief to her husband, she could tell him that it was originally written as a temperance

lecture to be delivered in another locality, and with
no thought of him. Now again the relieved parishioner appeared in his place at church. He did not,
however, expect the pastor to refrain from temperance
sermons. Nor did he now wish it, for he himself
gave up the traffic in spirituous liquors, and put his
hand to the temperance cause.

Not long afterward, on a dark night, two men found
their way with a lantern to the pastor's residence, to
engage him to give a lecture on temperance in a
neighboring town. One of them was the reconciled
parishioner! What an unlooked-for issue was this
to the difficulty! What a sunshine succeeding the
shadow which had briefly rested on the faithful preacher's heart! For, though persevering in fidelity to
his appointed duty as watchman on Zion's walls, he
could not be indifferent to the hearts which he must
alienate in proclaiming the Divine displeasure with
iniquity.

In Manchester, as everywhere in his ministerial
labors, our pastor loved that garden of the Lord
where the buds of childhood and the opening bloom
of youth are fostered, a favorite resort of the Divine
Gardener, where he finds a sweet perfume, — the
Sabbath school. In a sermon relative to the share of
duty which falls to the congregation, in the joint work
of pastor and people, he says: " This city contains
hundreds, perhaps a thousand children, who are members of no Sabbath school, and who seldom or never
enter a church. If you think this a high estimate, go
to those who have searched, and you will be astonished
at your previous incredulity. Now shall we do noth-

ing to gather these souls, fast contracting the taint of vice and corruption, into the place of religious instruction? Great God! is it nothing to us that these little ones, for whom Christ died, and whom he has pronounced our own brethren, are treading the highway to death, trained only in iniquity and crime?"

He says, on another occasion, in enforcing parental duty: " Begin, dear parents, early to teach your children religion. I am persuaded that many, very many, are converted in childhood, and so in very youth ripened for heaven. Yes; there are parents in my audience who know, either of the living or departed, that this is gloriously true! The seeds of sin, too, sown in the heart of childhood, or found already there, will spring up to yield a fatal harvest, unless by prayer and effort parents early begin to educate their children for heaven. Else must the parents be called to comfortless mourning for their offspring, and bitter memories be garnered in conscience, even for eternity."

We find our pastor, too, at Manchester laboring as one of the committee of the public schools, and lectur-ing on moral and educational topics to promiscuous assemblies. He advocated there and in neighboring towns the passage of the Maine Law. He delivered courses of lectures, giving sketches of prominent Scripture personages; also upon the respective duties of parents and children, and the sphere of woman. He spoke to teachers' institutes and literary associations. In a published address he delivered before the Academy in Bedford, New Hampshire, he indicates the religious importance of education in the following terms.

"It is our sincere opinion, that intellectual culture is immortal in its tendency and nature, and by
strengthening man's mental faculties, increases his
capacities for bliss and the acquisition of spiritual
knowledge hereafter. The mind, the thought, can
never die ; they live on, immortal as God from whom
they came. I could not advocate so earnestly the
acquisition of knowledge, if limited to this brief life.
I plead for it, because philosophy and just reasoning
teach us that such acquisition is of eternal value, and
fits for a higher sphere of spiritual enjoyment hereafter.

"I have been grieved sometimes to hear Christian
men and women speak slightingly and disparagingly
of human learning. Ah, Christian ! where were that
Bible you value, save for that human learning which
translated it into a language familiar to your ear ?
Where were it, had not some poor wise man discovered the art of printing ? Where would have been
the Protestant Reformation, had not Luther known
other languages than his own, and translated from the
"crooked Greek" the Book of books, for the use of
the common people ? Christian ! look again at your
Bible, ere *you* deprecate human learning, or array
yourself against the friends of education ; for

> 'Piety hath found friends
> In the friends of science, and true prayer
> Hath flowed from lips wet with Castalian dews.'

"All honor to our Puritan forefathers ! They were
not indeed perfect; but their faults were those of their
age, while their virtues were not of their age, but, by
the grace of God, their own. Long may the church
and school-house stand, as they wisely placed them,

side by side, each as a safeguard against the mistakes of the other. To the educated clergy of New England and their zeal for knowledge, to their early establishment of schools and universities, is due much of our prosperity, our greatness."

Having thus slightly sketched the pastor's labors, we glance now at the home where his heart rested and his mind composed. For more than a year his mother was housekeeper at the parsonage. In a letter, he thus refers to her: "She is quite well now, yet has not much strength, nor will she ever have again. Her years press heavily upon her; yet in her feelings she can never grow old." In another letter, nearly of the same date, he says: "This is mother's birthday. She speaks of you with that love which so tender a mother uniformly feels for her children. To-day she is sixty-one. Her years with us must now be few. May we do all in our power to make those few happy."

In the same letter he thus refers to his sister Margaret: "She is a most affectionate and gifted sister. We have in our family all the elements requisite for great happiness." Alas! that happiness was destined to a tragical interruption!

> " Life is a sea. How fair its face,
> How smooth its dimpled waters pace,
> Its canopy how pure!
> Yet hidden storms and tempests sleep
> Beneath the surface of the deep,
> Nor leave an hour secure."

The kindred tie linking the hearts of this family together was strong and affectionate. Especially Margaret was regarded with loving pride by the dear brothers and sister for whom she had sacrificed so

much, and by the widowed parent·who had leaned on
her in place of the staff death had stricken from her
hands. One way the mother had of expressing her
affection in life, and her love stronger than death, was
in the culture of her daughter's favorite flowers, fostered in the garden, and ultimately cherished to breathe
the balmy incense of affectionate ·memory over the
cenotaph, commemorating the daughter when her spirit
and body alike could no more be found in earth.

She thus in a letter exhorts her son : " I wish you
to pay especial attention to Margaret's favorites, sweet
pease, mignonette, and mourning bride. Many bouquets have I made of them for her."

Margaret, on her part, fully reciprocated her mother's affection. She writes to Arthur, anticipating her
return home again from foreign lands : " I hope to
find you in your home, and make you a good visit
there. Your invitation is sweet in its tone, and rouses
a vision of summer woods and New England Sabbath
morning bells. It seems to me, from your letter and
mother's, that she is at last in her true sphere. Watch
over her carefully, and do not let her do too much.
Her spirit is only too willing, but the flesh is weak,
and her life is precious to us all."

But the time had now come for death to make
another breach in the family, prostrating Margaret, its
noble column, and this by an assault singularly unexpected and severe.

She had been absent on the Continent for three
years. During this time she had been united in marriage with a noble Roman, captain of the Civic Guard,
and a brave combatant in the Italian struggle begin-

ning in 1848, which martyred so many patriotic lives for the time in vain. The union was a happy one, and is thus described by Mrs. William W. Story in a letter to Mrs. James Russell Lowell: "You ask about Margaret's marriage. I think she has chosen the better part in marrying. Her husband is noble by nature as well as by birth, and seems more the lover now than even before marriage." This union had been blessed by the birth of a beautiful boy.

The trio were on their return voyage in the summer of 1850, and the mother, brothers, and sister were hourly expecting to greet again that loved and gifted member of their family circle with the added treasures of affection she brought with her. But "O the heavy change!" The paper which should have announced the vessel's arrival contained instead an awful telegram, with the stunning tidings of the vessel's wreck, and the graves those loved voyagers had found in the tempestuous sea!

The family, when this ill news flew fast to them, lightning-winged, were waiting to repair to New York, where the vessel was expected to arrive. They now went thither, — but how sad a journey! — for the vessel had foundered on Fire Island, an exterior barrier of New York harbor. When they reached the scene of the terrible drama, the angry sea, not yet calmed, was still rolling its mountain billows over the stranded wreck, its poor ruined victim swept over by its waves at scarcely a stone's throw from the firm shore where the grief-bowed mother, the afflicted brothers and sister in vain strained their eyes into the foamy deep to catch any vestige of the noble and loved form of Margaret. The body of the babe alone the ruthless ocean relinquished, after life was exhausted, to be borne away for burial in a sweet spot watered by tears and garlanded by living flowers.

The mother endured this sorrow through "the dear might of Him who walked the wave," and who will not lay upon us a trial greater than we are able to bear. But she contracted from it (such was her physician's opinion) that malady which, nine years after, terminated her mortal career. Arthur bore the affliction with fortitude. He writes some months afterwards : " There are sad memories which at times oppress me, and the sense of the loss we have met only grows deeper as time passes. But I know it is not right to be absorbed by these griefs ; neither right towards those living in this world, nor those living in the other ; and I seek only to remember what Margaret has been, is still, and *shall be* to us."

In the autumn of this year our pastor took a step which had been deferred by the family bereavement, but which a regard for his afflicted mother's health, no longer adequate to a housekeeper's duties, rendered it prudent to delay no longer. He was happily united in marriage with Elizabeth G. Davenport, of Mendon, Massachusetts. We will describe her in his own words, contained in a family letter : " I find one who bears with me my burdens, and who is already greatly beloved by my people. Gentle, yet uniformly self-possessed, she deserves and always secures respect. It is a great relief, too, to be able to share all my thoughts and feelings with one who sympathizes warmly with me. I have great cause to be thankful to God."

It is sometimes imagined that the expansion of the heart over a wide field comprising multiplied objects must diminish its love for that home where it originated, and whence it has enlarged in concentric circles, like the smooth surface of a lake into which some listless hand has dropped a pebble. We believe this to be a false surmise. Love partakes of the infinite capacity of its Divine Original, who glories in it as his name, and it " grows by what it feeds on," strengthened in its first generous affections by its enlarging range. So it certainly was with Arthur Fuller. His filial and brotherly love could be supplanted by no new ties, nor by his unlimited philanthropy. Pleasing proofs of this we can adduce from his family letters ; a few of which we will cite, not only for this purpose, but also for the sentiment they contain, and the light they throw upon his character.

The following letter is addressed to Richard and his companion, on the birth of their oldest son.

" I rejoice with you in your new blessing. Married life is comparatively sad, if no children are given to increase attachment to one another and to life. You will find great satisfaction in training this young immortal in all good things, physical, mental, and spiritual. I have named the three in their proper order of development and attention ; for education is *educing*, developing, not grafting on, or producing. His physical well-being, the laying of a good foundation of bodily health, will deserve your especial attention. Too many parents foster the mind's growth at the body's expense, and allow the wick of life, in giving too much light, to waste the candle. You will not be so unwise.

"It is looking a good way forward, to think much now of the little boy's mental culture. Yet that should begin early. Try to give balance rather than precocity.

"You will both of you, as parents, have additional reason to care for the regulation of *your own* lives and hearts. Man is an imitative being, and especially assimilates, in his mental growth, the lessons, however minute, which parental example inculcates. Your *deeds*, not your words, will be the copy which his youthful hand will inscribe with indelible lines upon his heart.

"Spiritual training, distinctively so termed, I name last, as last in order. True, this forms part of physical and yet more of mental education, and should blend with them all. If he have a sound body, he will be free from the vexations of ill-temper which ill-health produces; if a sound mind, then he will readily see the relations between right and wrong, and discriminate as to truth and falsehood. Do not seek to form his *opinions*, but his *character*. Religion is character, not opinion. The sound heart will never allow the head to err as to *saving* doctrine. Do not seek, therefore, to give an undue bias on either side, but look well to the fountain, for 'out of the *heart* are the issues of life.'"

We will cite also a letter occasioned by the event which makes the opposite to birth; closing, as that opens, the mortal drama.

"DEAR EUGENE AND ELIZA: —

"A few days since the sad intelligence of your mutual and heavy sorrow reached me. I do not call it your loss; for how can it be so to have a treasure transferred to heaven, which may lead you more and more to fix your hearts where is stored your precious jewel. I once viewed death and earthly separations differently from my present thought; but the more deeply I drink life's cup, by so much the more do I long to taste that of immortality, even if death's bitter draught must first be drained.

"Doubtless our Father, in his love for *his* children, considered what you would suffer; yet sent the death-angel in mercy to teach the sad lesson of mortality.

"I had learned already to love this little niece whom I have never seen, but whom I *shall see* at no distant day.

"I could not refrain from saying these few words to you. I feel that our laments of earthly separation are but the preludes to the glad songs of heaven, where these loved infant voices will greet us again, never more to be hushed in death."

The fountain of pleasantry which had played up so spontaneously in Arthur's childhood, imbittered by the tears of his early orphanage, and chilled afterward by many a hard life lesson, sobered, too, by assiduous labors and pressing cares, lost its early exuberance. Yet it occasionally works free of mingling tears, and sheds again its refreshing on his way. We find a few instances of this in his letters, which, though passing from grave to gay, we think may be cited as not out of keeping with the tessellated course of life.

In a January letter from Manchester, when the skies of fortune also wore a wintry aspect for railroad stocks, he writes: —

5 *

" This really cold day convinces us that winter has not been omitted from the list of the seasons. I suppose in your warm office you are not, like us, exasperated by the biting salutations of Jack Frost, who dares to breathe his cold aspersions upon the most reverend heads in New Hampshire, and makes the exposed front feel as well as look like a marble brow.

" I shall be in Boston next week on Wednesday, and meanwhile should be glad if you would exercise your financial abilities in the sale of a little stock and the purchase of other for me. The Providence shares have never seemed, in any but a satirical sense, a providential thing for me. To keep those two shares would be a tempting of Providence, and I doubt not be the cause of a further fall in my pride consequent upon a further fall in the stocks.

" At any rate I want to sell to a young man like you ; though I fear it may be needful to seek some one still younger, who has confidence, and does not rail at all railroads. With the proceeds please make insurance doubly sure, by purchasing two shares additional to the two of that ilk which I already possess."

Again Januarius exhilarates him to the following letter, all charges in which the recipient would have it clearly understood he distinctly repels.

" I wish you would write that you have searched, and that my great-coat is or is not in Boston. I wrote to you some time since a letter upon no other subject, save that I closed with a hope that your health was good. You replied, or rather wrote a note, giving ample assurances in regard to your health, but *not one word* as to the coat. I put the subject in the postscript of another letter, knowing that the postscript is the most important and noticeable part. Not a word in reply yet. Now I suppose that the great-coat *is* convenient to you, and that possession is nine tenths of the law, — but not of the *gospel*, remember! I shall get out a writ of ejectment, if I hear of your parading that coat on Washington Street. It *does* look well, I know, but then — "

He alludes to the general subject of playful spirits in another epistle written upon his birthday.

" I duly received your letter calling on me for a 'jocular reply.' Gayety has not for years been the prevailing mood of my mind, and is much less so now. My frame is rather that of calmness and serenity. Life has been a serious, thoughtful business, and has shown me too much suffering in the world, too much need of inward conflict, to admit of much mirth. Yet I am seldom if ever sad, and after seeing you, or some friend of more care-free hours, I am gay again. Yet the fountain of mirth does not overflow, unless some angel visitant troubles the waters.

" This is my birthday. I have risen early, and am writing to you. You will not expect mirth to be in my heart on this morning of reflection. Yet I think myself very happy, much happier than as a child. Then I had much to endure, without the inward support to enable me to bear the petty ills that assail that period of life. Now I am in feeble health, but that does not sadden me. I am pastor of a good and appreciating society, and above all have a glimmering of those bright joys to come, which even now would be

more than a reward, were I wholly self-consecrated.
Ah! were I not conscious of faults and of departures
from the one true path, by coming short of the full
discharge of duty, then I should be perfectly happy!
Were I to live my childhood over again, I would do
everything to gain a sound, strong constitution; for
lack of strength has hindered my best efforts from
full success. I would gain, too, accomplishments which
might beguile sick hours, and would be taught methodical habits. Father's death, and the consequent griefs
and anxieties, probably prevented all this. Yet how
soon at the longest shall I go to that home where
neither physical strength nor aught but holiness will
be needful! I think much of mother and of you all
to-day, and with ever-increased love."

The year 1853 opened with a notable providence
in the life of our Manchester minister. On New
Year's day he writes: "I am now in manhood's
prime, — thirty years of age. The sands of my life
must be more than half run out. I feel a solemnity
not easy to express." A few days after this he visited
his brother in Massachusetts, and on his return, over
the Boston and Maine Railroad, a remarkable accident
occurred, which he describes in one of the newspapers
in the following terms: —

"You desire me, Mr. Editor, to write out the particulars of the distressing railroad casualty. The train
left Boston at quarter past twelve at noon. There
were about forty in the car where I was seated. A
portion of the passengers were in a sportive mood. I
recollect particularly some young men jesting upon
the phrase of their passenger tickets, 'Good for this

trip only,' and speculating for how many other trips the same ticket had been and would hereafter be used. And yet to some that trip doubtless has proved the last. We were on an express train, and only stopped at Wilmington, Ballardvale, and South Andover; at each of which places more passengers got in, thus increasing the number in our car to about sixty. At South Andover General Pierce and his lady, accompanied by their interesting little boy of thirteen, entered the car, and took seats in the front, near where I sat. We had gone about a mile and a half further, and were at our full speed, — I was looking out of the window, — when we felt a severe shock, and the car was dragged for a few seconds, the axle of the front wheel being broken.

" In another second the coupling of our car parted, and it was whirled violently round, so as to reverse the ends, and we were swung over a rocky ledge into a place many feet below the railroad grade. I retained my consciousness perfectly, and had no expectation of escaping death. I shall never forget the breathless horror which came over us during our fall. There was not a shriek nor an exclamation till the car, after having turned over twice on the rocks, was arrested with a violent concussion, parted in the middle, and then broke into many thousand fragments. I received personally a few bruises and flesh cuts of no particular moment, and found myself amid a mass of shattered glass and splintered wood and groaning men and women, with no limbs broken, and with a heart to praise God for his sparing mercy. The car was a fragmentary ruin, and there was no need to make the exit

from door or window. The next moment a man, covered with blood himself, — a noble fellow, — cried,
'We are alive ; let us help others !' I passed from
one frightful part of the scene to another, which
seemed like a dreadful vision. Men came up on every
side dripping with blood, and few escaped without
some cuts or bruises. Before all were rescued, the
top, covered with oil-cloth, took fire from the stove,
adding to the general horror and suffering.

"Among the many terrible incidents, two especially
impressed me. On the bank sat a mother, clasping her
little boy some three or four years of age. He had
been snatched from the ruin which had strown the
rock with splintered fragments, and her own person
was considerably burned ; but she was shedding tears
of gratitude over her rescued child, and rejoicing in
his safety, unmindful of her own pain. A few steps
from her I saw the most appalling scene of all. There
was another mother whose agony beggars description. She could shed no tears, but, overwhelmed
with grief, uttered affecting words which I can never
forget. It was Mrs. Pierce, the lady of the President
elect ; and near her, in that ruin of shivered wood and
iron, lay a more terrible ruin, her only son, one minute
before so beautiful, so full of life and hope ! The
blow by which he was killed instantly struck his fore-
head.

"Soon we were able to convey the wounded and
the dead to the nearest house. After the head of the
little boy had been tenderly cared for by the physicians, and all possible done to restore the look of life,
he was carried by us to the house which he had left

so recently. I shall never forget the look of extreme pain that child's face wore ; and yet there was something resigned and tender impressed even by the awful hand of death. The form which had left that house but little more than an hour before, full of life and happiness, was now borne back to those who had parted from him, — the heart hushed and still, — the form motionless, and the limbs fast growing rigid under the icy touch of death."

The day following the disaster, he thus writes to his brother respecting it.

" I write to you from the land of the living. I am a good deal jarred and bruised. I did not feel it at all at first ; others suffered so much more, especially General Pierce and lady, who were so terribly bereaved. I shall never forget that scene of horror. It is before my mind every moment, and will not away. Nothing but the mercy of God saved any of us from utter destruction. It is wonderful that any live to tell that fearful story. I expected to die, and looked death in the face with calmness. I was astonished to find myself alive amid that awful ruin. I was blessed in being of some service to those bereaved parents, most heavily stricken in the midst of their greatness, and also in aiding the wounded and suffering. How thankful should I be ! What a life of holiness I ought to lead ! Surely no pride should require the repetition of that dread lesson, that in the midst of life we are in death.

" How little did I think when I left you at the railroad station, that the interview we there terminated bid fair to be our last ! All our meetings ought to be so profitable and true, that, if the last, the survivor might feel no regret, and the dying have a sweet and calm conscience. Such may ours ever be !

" I always felt that I should not live beyond thirty ; yet when the axle of that car broke, I was laying plans for the future, when in a moment the thought flashed on my mind, ' For me there is no earthly future. In a moment I must meet my God.' I am very thankful, especially on account of dear mother and my wife, and those who love me, who would have felt the shock of another violent death in the family."

The plans which he says he was revolving in his mind when the railroad catastrophe occurred, very likely related to changing the place of his pastoral labors. He had some months before received a call from the New North Church in Boston, which he felt bound to refuse, by reason of the great unwillingness of his people to part with him. The call was, however, pressingly renewed, and after much hesitation he concluded to accept it. He thus states his reasons in his family correspondence.

" It costs me a pang to leave here, and I go to a very arduous post ; but I feel it to be the call of duty. I make no pecuniary gain by the exchange, and must work harder than ever before. Yet I hope not only to accomplish much good in the great heart of our denomination by my efforts, but also to have more time for study and to elaborate my sermons than I can have here. My own mind needs further develop-ment. Here I have almost no exchanges, have access to no large library, and have to write two sermons nearly every week, besides a vast deal of parish visiting. A change of location will aid me in these respects, as I have a good stock of sermons now written, and shall be near Cambridge library and have plenty of exchanges. I shall, too, be near you and other members of the family."

We have been favored with a letter from Hon. Daniel Clark, United States Senator from New Hampshire, respecting the pastorate in Manchester, the place of the senator's home residence ; with extracts from which we close this chapter.

" Your lamented brother was held by me among my most esteemed friends. I took much interest in him ; and with my family he seemed almost ' as one of us.'

" My little boys would leave at once their sports, and always run to see Mr. Fuller. And Mrs. Clark always regarded him with an interest stronger, I think, than she ever felt for any pastor save Dr. Peabody, late of Portsmouth, her native town.

" Your sainted mother, too, was very dear to us. She was an angel on earth, — kind, affectionate, pure, sympathizing, and devoted. My little ones always called her ' Auntie Fuller.'

" The ministry of your brother at Manchester was a very successful one. Not only with his own society was he very popular, but with all others.

" He was so sincere, so zealous, and so devoted, that he entirely disarmed sectarianism, and won his way to the hearts of all. He came to us when feeble. He built us up ; but when he left our strength was gone.

" When he died for his country, he had been absent from us many years ; yet I may truthfully say, from the time he left us to the day of his death he was con-

H

stantly rising in the estimation of our people. He never 'wore out,' as many do.

" With the schools he made himself familiar ; and all who were in them at that time were very fond of him.

" But I may not enlarge. When he fell, I supposed he had not resigned; but I have since learned that he had, — life and commission together.

" He was earnest and devoted. He said to me, when talking of a place as hospital chaplain: ' If I cannot get a place where I can save my health, I will go back to my regiment, and die with them ; for I will sooner do it than quit the service of my country.'

" Noble martyr to a noble cause ! Surely his country should not permit his family to mourn, uncared for."

CHAPTER II.

BOSTON.

"Thy converse drew us with delight,
    The men of rathe and riper years;
    The feeble soul, a haunt of fears,
Forgot his weakness in thy sight.

"On thee the loyal-hearted hung,
    The proud was half disarmed of pride,
    Nor cared the serpent at thy side
To flicker with his double tongue."

                                    TENNYSON.

UR pastor was installed in his new charge on the first day of June, 1853. His parish was in Boston, at the North End, — a location once the centre of fashionable residence. His dwelling was numbered 31, on Sheafe Street, near Copp's Hill. The latter is a swell of land opposite Charlestown. The British planted a battery there, at the battle of Bunker Hill. It is an ancient place of burial, and contains the graves of many well-known Boston citizens; of whom Cotton Mather may be named as one.

His religious society was at a low ebb when he entered upon its ministry; owing, in part, to a cause which might be counteracted, but not overcome. The native population was constantly receding from that section of the city, and giving place in part to mercantile and manufacturing occupation, but mainly to resi-

dents of a foreign birth and different religious persuasion. This cause was constantly operating with a
greatly increased momentum. Building up the religious society, therefore, was like the stone of Sisy-
phus, raised only by the constant application of superior strength, and relapsing again the moment effort
was intermitted. Members of the church and congregation were constantly caught away by the tide of
population, and borne to southerly parts of the city;
while those from whom recruits could be hoped to supply the broken ranks were, under the influence of the
same law of change, departing also.

It is not impossible to explain these changes in the
focal centres of city residence, when they are once
in motion, for the very force of the current, taking
away those who were congenial and attractive, and
substituting heterogeneous occupants, easily accounts
for the continuance of a change in the character of
population once begun. But what gave it the first impulse, how long it will continue in the channel it runs
in at any given time, in what quarter it will set next,
— these are questions as hard to solve as the causes
and courses of ocean and atmospheric currents. As,
in many regions, geology indicates a former inhabi-
tancy far different from the present, so the local history
of but a few generations in Boston designates spots,
formerly the centres of wealth and influence which
have since shifted to localities once little likely to be
the magnets of such attraction. An instance of this
may be found in the neighborhood of Fort Hill, a spot
adapted by nature for pleasant residence, and not a
great many years ago the court-end of Boston. But

the inscrutable law of change led its inhabitants to give place to the crowded occupation of the poor and humble. And now this population, in its turn, seems to be receding before the onward march of the granite blocks of commerce.

Such was the field to which our pastor was now transferred; induced, as he declares, by the unanimity and earnestness of the call tendered to him once and again, and even by "the very depression and urgent need" of the new pastorate; and such was the adverse current against which he labored successfully, but with impossible permanence.

The power of the pulpit was by no means his only instrument. His insight led him to recognize the Sabbath school as the necessary means, not only of attracting the lambs to the fold, but the sheep also, by the strong though scarce appreciated influence which the rising generation exercise by the ties of love upon their adult kindred. He knew, too, the power of conference prayer in drawing down from the Source of every good and perfect gift the dews of Divine grace and the refreshings of the Holy Spirit. Meetings of this character were regularly held in his vestry. He says respecting them: * "I believe such meetings have been productive of much good, and would here warmly commend them as an instrumentality which you cannot too faithfully use or too carefully cherish. Let us return to the *ancient* usage of this society, and, as did

---

* A Historical Discourse, delivered in the New North Church, October 1, 1854. By ARTHUR B. FULLER. Boston: Crosby and Nichols. In this Discourse the interesting annals of the New North Church, from the time it was founded in 1714, are briefly reviewed.

its founders, meet often together for prayer and religious converse ; and may God grant that attendance
upon these meetings may soon become as general as
attendance upon the sanctuary, and that they may be
well sustained by those who are ready to testify to
God's goodness, and seek to win souls to Christ; that
there may be many ready to address God in prayer,
and to sing his praise. So shall he ' revive his work '
among us."

He also reanimated a benevolent society in his parish, which continued in active and beneficent existence
during his pastorate. And with its aid he founded a
parish library.

To fully understand the instrumentality which he
put in operation for his labors in the Lord, we must
not forget his faithful parochial visits. His love for
the children, and their love for him, welcomed.him to
the open portals of his people's dwellings. Wherever he went, we shall find the young attending upon
his steps, — in the pastoral charge, and even upon the
tented field. On his way from church they clustered
around him, and he needed the arms of a Briareus to
take them all in, or to lend a hand to each of the little
ones who sought this token of fellowship and guidance
betwixt the man and the child. Nor was he a re-
specter of persons or conditions in his intercourse. He
felt his Master's words, " Of such is the kingdom of
heaven," and delighted to regard the unfolded capacity, the unstained innocence of children ; while hope
painted to him the bright possibility of their future,
and love made him seek to draw them thus early to
the only sure shelter from the storms of time and eter-

nity, the ark of safety, Christ Jesus. The destitute children, too, who had been gathered into his Sabbath school from the highways and hedges, won the honor of the pastor's hand on the way from church.

He had two good angels to help him in the home work of the pastor, — his mother and his wife. Both were earnest laborers with him in the Sabbath school; both were unexceptionably beloved by the people. " His domestic life in Boston," writes one of his parishioners, " seemed very delightful to him, and was especially pleasant to his people. The death of his wife was felt by his whole society almost as a personal loss, so greatly had she endeared herself to all who knew her. His mother, who afterward cared for his household, was so wise and good, that I never saw or heard of any who did not revere her and prize her sympathy and counsel." Alas! how little time has elapsed since we saw this trio in the Sheafe Street parsonage ; and yet centuries could not more effectually have placed them in the unseen, irrevocable past than has been done by the course of a few fleeting years. A picture of them recurs to memory, as they sang together a Methodist melody entitled " We are passing away," the wife leading at the piano, and • the mother and son standing near. They were very fond of that expressive hymn, which accompanied each verse by the chorus, " We are passing away," sung in a sad, dying strain, but immediately changing to a closing note of triumph, " Let us hail the glad day ! " Those blended voices have, at intervals but briefly removed, vanished from earth, and, we doubt not, they have in the raptures of heavenly song hailed,

once again united, the glad day of eternity, to know
no setting, to know no shadow upon its ever orient
sun !

To promote the interests of the Sabbath school,
which were at a low ebb, he organized an association
of teachers, which "interested them in their work,
and tended to their mutual acquaintance and improvement by regular gatherings for study and conversation."* He also sought to encourage the children by
picnics and by anniversary observances. Some of the
Christmas and New-Year exercises of his Sabbath
school filled the church with a pleased and attentive
audience.

He took a warm interest in the consecration of children. He did not regard it as a rite of mystic effi-
cacy, nor as indicative of a union formed with Christ,
which faith only can accomplish. But he valued it
as giving the children up to God, as Abraham devoted Isaac ; as symbolizing somewhat, like the Jew-
ish rite of circumcision, the covenant blessings trans-
mitted through parents ; but especially as a solemn
recognition of the supreme Fatherhood of God, and
his sovereign claim upon the children, accompanied by
. the undertaking of the parents to bring them up in the
nurture and admonition of the Lord. He believed,
too, that the unconscious subject, though deriving
from it no mysterious influence, would in after life be
led to regard it as a solemn pledge of the affection and
consecration of his parents, and their desire and prayer
to win for him Heaven's choicest influence. Thus natural affection would give an impulse to religious aspi-

* Letter of a parishioner.

ration, and mingle the loved parent's voice, when perhaps hushed in the grave, with the whisperings of the Holy Spirit.

Many a pleasant occasion did the pastor enjoy of the consecration of children, as well as of older persons. In his pleasant Sabbath-school picnics, they were brought and came forward garlanded for this beautiful ceremony.

He enforced the necessity of conversion, and held it up as the aim of Sabbath-school instruction. In a convention, he says: " The specific object of the teacher should be the conversion of the scholar. The human heart is a great battle-field. While religion is a most natural thing, it is supernatural. There is much in the heart that tends heavenward, but there is much that is grovelling. A conflict is continually going on, and it is the teacher's province to turn the scale. There is a time when the heart is changed. The conversion is often sudden and startling, like the tornado, and oftentimes almost imperceptible and gentle as the result of a mother's prayers, like the zephyr that follows the storm, causing the leaves to kiss each other, and the flowers to gently nod before the soft and noiseless wind. Children need to be told, like other people, to come to Christ. The natural heart of the child knows no more of God than it does of mathematics. Nicodemus was probably a kind man, with many excellent virtues; yet the Saviour said he must be born again. Except a *man* be born again, — these were the words, — and they applied to all men. He did not believe in calling the infant a sinner, nor in original sin; but there were tendencies in the child to depravity, to sin, and he

6

needed conversion. It was a dangerous doctrine to say that children did not need a change of heart."

It was not, therefore, to keep, but to acquire, religious character, that he labored with children, that they might obtain Christ in the soul, who alone can preserve the innocence, simplicity, and guilelessness which characterize childhood; and, by transmuting its lovely, spontaneous impulse into *principle*, appropriated as the intelligent volition of a religious mind, furnish the young heart with a safeguard for virtue and a means to counteract and destroy the tares with which the busy adversary has left no heart unsown. This was the belief which nerved the pastor's energies, to labor in season and out of season, to pray and not to faint, to seek to wreathe the lovely buds of childhood, which always attracted him in every condition of life, into the Saviour's garlanded crown.

He earnestly pleaded the cause of the Sabbath school from the pulpit. In a sermon devoted to the subject, he says: " Well do I recollect an occasion when I exchanged with a brother of the Wesleyan Methodist connection, and, by his request, remained at the Sabbath school, which took place immediately after the morning services. When I had dismissed the congregation, I was astonished to find all but some fifteen or twenty, who were mostly casual attendants, remain to take places in the Sabbath school. The ages of the members of that school ranged from the child of five to a mother in Israel whose form was bowed by the burden of eighty years. The whole congregation were engaged in the work. The old gave character to the school, the young life and vivacity. In some classes, each in turn became the teacher. The congregation was poor in temporal wealth, not a rich man in it. Many wondered how it lived, for there are no conference funds among the Wesleyans. But I did not wonder, after seeing the Sabbath school.

"In my judgment, the plan they pursued is the true one. Our Bible-classes ought to be thronged, and many younger classes gathered. The whole congregation should in some way, either as teachers or pupils, be members of the Sabbath school. It would be worth while even to dispense with the afternoon service, if this result could be secured."

The pastor's varied labors were fruitful of good. An interesting instance of his mode of dealing with the young hearts of his charge, who sought to follow the drawings of the crucified Saviour, and leave all to come to him, occurs to memory; and we relate it, as illustrative of his treatment of a delicate subject. A young man unbosomed himself to him, relating his religious experience and his desire to unite himself with his newly found Saviour by a public profession. But his parents opposed it, and he was under age. The pastor counselled him, that it was no doubt his duty to leave father and mother for Christ's sake, if that should be necessary; but he should first try rather to win them to the Saviour, and bring them with him. The convert was their only, dearly-loved son, and they were without religion. They probably regarded him as under the influence of a transient impression, and the pastor hoped, if they found he had a permanent desire to unite with the church, they would finally yield to the wishes in spiritual things of one they had ever indulged in the temporal. He therefore advised him to defer his public profession for some months, and see if the parents would not be persuaded to come round to his wishes.

Such, indeed, was the result; and better still! When the parents found their darling child had really permanently set his heart on uniting with Christ, they resolved to gratify him, and announced to him that they no longer opposed his wishes. Nor was this all. They had viewed religion in others as bigotry or excitement or unsoundness; but what was this which, without any induction on their part, had obtained a hold upon their son? It had not made him less observant of their wishes, but more dutiful. It had blended with his amiable natural traits, and transfigured them with a new glow and radiance. Might there not, then, be a reality in religion? Thus they also were led to inquire the way of life, and ultimately followed their son in giving their hearts to the Saviour, and professing Christ before men.

A prominent theological trait in our pastor's character was a love for Christian union. Heads might differ on the most difficult problems submitted to the intellect; inadequacies of language might further widen this variance, and often give it an apparent reality when it in fact existed only in a diversity of meaning attached to words; but Christian hearts at least might agree and combine, and surely ought to do so, instead of turning the spiritual weapons given them to vanquish the world to the unhallowed purpose of internecine strife. Christian union, he believed, gauged truly Christian love, and indicated the completeness

of the transformation of the natural heart to the likeness of Him who breathed up among his last petitions
the touching prayer that his disciples might bo one,
even as he and the Father were one.

He liked not denominational shackles, and he induced his people in Boston to adopt a form of organization ; the first article of which reads as follows : —

" ART. 1. The church connected with the New
North Religious Society shall assume no sectarian
name, desiring simply to be known as a branch of
the Church of Jesus Christ."

Afterward, when engaged in the duties of army
chaplain, he was more than ever drawn in heart to
desire the oneness of the followers of Christ; and
he declared, if ever settled over another parish, it
should be independent.

His preaching was principally practical, seeking to
bring home the Gospel to the soul, and to induct it
through all the channels of spiritual and secular life.
So far as was requisite to this, he preached upon doctrines boldly and distinctly, yet dealing kindly with
those who differed from him. He sought to distinguish the good ingredient in each extreme, while himself pursuing the golden mean, as if he made his motto,
Medio tutissimus ibis. He thought lightly of the badges
of sect. He thus writes, in reference to a clergyman
who had left the Unitarian body: " Let each man
find his true place in the army of Christ, where his
sympathies and convictions lead him ; and, in whatever regiment he fights, if he is a soldier of Jesus, he
has my God-speed."

He would by no means consent that the dominion

of religion should be abridged, or the sceptre of the Almighty Sovereign excluded from any sphere of public or private life. Especially did he regard politics as the right domain of religion. Where the government is intrusted to one ruler, his religious training in regard to his high public responsibilities is admitted to be an essential safeguard of his justice and virtue and permanence of authority. And where the sceptre is intrusted to the people, the same rule must apply with a force by no means diminished. He insisted upon the discharge of his sacred trust in this respect in his new position.

In a published discourse, entitled "Our Dangers as a Republic, and Duties as Citizens," the pastor defines his views of political ethics. "I envy no man," he says, "in whose bosom is no glow of patriotism. . . . . . It is an unholy and dangerous divorce, a sundering of things joined by God, which separates religion from patriotism, Christian principle from political action. Our fathers ventured not into the struggle till they had bent reverently within consecrated walls. I cannot too strongly enjoin the necessity of personal religion. He who enters the arena of politics without it, goes to the battle unarmed.

"Every American citizen should be the uncompromising advocate of liberty throughout the land. Let us soon and ever justly be able to say of our beloved country, as Curran proudly says of him who takes refuge in Britain, 'No matter in what language his doom may have been pronounced, no matter what complexion an Indian or African sun may have burned upon him, no matter in what disastrous battle his liber-

ties may have been cloven down, no matter with what
solemnities he may have been devoted on the altar of
slavery, — the first moment he touches the sacred soil of
Britain, the altar and the god sink together into the
dust, his soul walks abroad in his own majesty, his body
swells beyond the measure of his chains, that burst
from around him, and he stands forth redeemed, re-
generated, and disenthralled by the irresistible genius
of universal emancipation.' " *

The pastor did not doff the robe of office to make
stump-speeches, and in the pulpit he was no party
advocate. He had some warm friends in the congregation who were entirely opposed to him in political
life, who yet declared they honored his independence,
and liked to hear him speak his mind; and when he
was nominated for political station, some opponents
voted for him, as a tribute to the man. In this connection it may be pertinent to state, that in 1857 he
was nominated, by the Republicans of Suffolk District
Number Two, for the Massachusetts Senate ; but, with
the other candidates of his party in that district, he
failed of an election.

The pastor was a careful student of public events,
and failed not to point out their moral in his discourses.
When the sad news of Daniel Webster's death was
announced, he expatiated upon it from the pulpit.

---

* While boasting Britain secretly leans towards the side of slavery in the
American rebellion, this celebrated quotation cannot be too familiarly cited,
in order to call a blush to the cheeks of the Empress of the sea. In
America, too, it should never be reckoned trite, till it becomes true of our
own liberated soil. Till then, we may say of it, as a clergyman replied
to one finding fault with his repeating a sermon, " I ought to preach it till
you practise it."

"On this calm Sabbath morn," said the preacher, "he who had lived amid the conflicts of the forum and debate in national assemblies, the thunders of whose eloquence had been hurled against those who opposed what he deemed the country's welfare, — *he* rests from his labors; he on this quiet morning lies cold and passionless as the lifeless marble! Forgetful of all political differences, a nation is shedding, and will continue to let fall, tears of regret for this sad event. Every noble heart to-day will throb with sympathy and solemn sadness.

"One after another the brightest jewels have been plucked from our nation's crown by the ruthless hand of death. Last of all, he has now fallen whose heart, whose mind, in its wondrous grandeur, was American in its every pulsation, its every thought. Differ from him as some of us have honestly done, all that is forgotten at his grave; and we mourn together. Never more shall we meet the gaze of his cavernous eyes, in whose depths we seem to look upon his mighty intellect. Never more shall Faneuil Hall be filled with that deep, sonorous voice, whose every tone was full of meaning. Never more shall a listening senate hang breathless on his word. No more shall his utterances flash like lightning across the continent, while the Austrian despot trembles at his pleas for Hungarian freedom.

"Daniel Webster is dead; and even in the house of God we sit in solemn sadness at the thought, and say, Alas! our country! Yet, my friends; it cannot be that such a mind, such a spirit, should die! God is not so prodigal of mind and spirit as to strike out such from the circle of being. They must be immortal as He from whom they came. It is only the body which lies cold and lifeless; the soul can never die. Thank God that in his last moments he uttered imperishable words of faith in immortality, and faith in the Bible, and that among his last words were those of prayer. O ye who revere his memory, let that lesson of faith sink into your hearts! The great, the mighty, must die ; but they shall live again ! It is not ours to judge of their faults, but rather to learn from whatever was good in their example ; while we are reminded that the body dies, but the soul lives forever, and yet forever!"

In the cause of temperance the pastor labored on, both in the pulpit and out of it. In 1858 he was chosen by the State Temperance Convention a member of the Executive Committee, and in the same year was elected a director of the Washingtonian Home, better known as the Home for the Fallen.

He loved these enterprises, not merely for the main object, but for the incidental result of bringing men of different callings and religious persuasions into friendly nearness. In an address to the Sons of Temperance, he asks, "Has the order accomplished nothing, if it unites men of different denominational names on this platform of philanthropy ?"

In the Home for the Fallen, too, he took a warm interest, on account of its benefits conferred on the class to whom it was devoted, and the genial influence which co-operation in benevolence has upon the philanthropist. "He liked the institution," he said, at one of its public meetings, "because it was not sectarian,

6 *   I

because of its broad principle, and because it was not adapted to any nationality, but to those of all nations and climes."

After the Maine Law had become a Massachusetts statute, he appeared before the Mayor and Aldermen of Boston to advocate a petition for its enforcement, which had been subscribed by clergymen of all denominations, and, among other signers, by eighteen hundred and sixty women. He alluded to the rendition of Burns, the fugitive slave, which the city government had aided in, alleging that they must sustain the law, though contrary to their own convictions. He urged them to prove the sincerity of that allegation, by a like scrupulous loyalty in enforcing the Maine Law. The city authorities took no action. But such efforts are never lost, and ultimately result in good, even after they have been forgotten.

We find the pastor in Boston, as elsewhere, faithfully laboring as a member of the public-school committee. Nor did he forget the cause of popular education in the pulpit. When a sacrilegious hand was stretched forth to withdraw the Bible from the public schools, it led him, as well as others of the clergy, to an earnest protest from the sacred desk. " No question," he said, in the language reported in the public press, " had ever arisen of so vast importance in our midst; and the discipline, the usefulness, the perpetuity of that system which our fathers established, were hanging in the balance. We needed to keep the Bible in the schools to prevent our land from becoming a land like France or Spain, or other countries where the Bible was set at naught. Knowledge without morality was power, but it was power for evil; and whence could we draw higher morality than from the Bible, to guide and strengthen knowledge?"

We find him, too, speaking before the New England Female Medical College, in terms approving of that enterprise. On the important subject of woman's rights he often expressed himself. We cite as a specimen his ideal of womanhood, delineated in a published discourse, occasioned by the death of Mrs. Louisa Sophia Swan.

"This ideal simply demands for woman the right to do all she can do well; considers that her true sphere for which organization and capacity adapt her; recognizes her neither as man's handmaid and servant, nor idol and superior, but his helper and equal. With this class, woman's rights and woman's duties are synonymous. Home, it believes, from her very constitution, the law of God, written in lines of sinew and vein and bone and the very texture of her being, home will ever be her chief sphere of action; but whenever a Joan of Arc leads her countrymen to victory and to freedom; whenever a Florence Nightingale makes of the hospital of the Crimea a scene of angel ministry to the wounded; whenever a Grace Darling saves life by daring almost more than manly; or a Mrs. Patten guides her dying husband's ship safely into port, herself its commander; or a Mrs. Stowe writes the tale of suffering beneath the foul oppression of slavery; or, in the strife for Italian liberty, a woman in immortal Rome does immortal deeds of beneficence, watching over the helpless Roman soldiery when they were dying in the hospitals, and dying, as did some Americans of old, for human rights and dear liberty ; * — then to all these, and such as these, those who accept the ideal of JESUS, utter the plaudit, ' Well done,' and declare that these women have not forgotten their sex, have not departed from its duties, but have nobly fulfilled them all, and are truly womanly women.

" My friends, for one, I rejoice that a greater than Solomon taught us by his word, yet more by his example, what should be the rank and sphere of woman ; that she should not be man's vassal, and say, as Milton represents Eve to say, —

> ' What thou bid'st,
> Unargued I obey; so God ordains;
> God is thy law! thou mine; to know no more
> Is woman's happiest knowledge and her praise.'

And yet more, I rejoice that he rejected the sad, awful view which regards woman as the mere toy of man's idler hours ; to be loved only when young and fair, and then neglected ; to be flattered, but not truly reverenced, and at last to find in him the careless husband, the forgetful reveller. Ah, thank God,

> ' The days are no more,
> When she watched for her lord till the revel was o'er,
> And stilled her sad sorrow, and blushed when he came,
> As she pressed her cold lips on his forehead of flame.
> Alas for the loved one! too spotless and fair
> The joys of his banquet to chasten and share;
> Her eye lost its light that his goblet might shine,
> And the rose on her cheek was dissolved in his wine.' "

When the great refreshing from the Lord, in 1857, swept over the community with wondrous power, it

---

* Referring to his sister Margaret.

found our pastor a servant girded for the work.
While he deprecated a superficial, illusory excitement,
and especially artificial contrivances to forward that
which the Spirit of God can alone accomplish, he
earnestly approved and rejoiced to labor for a deep
spiritual work of grace. That great revival attested
the presence and commission of the Messiah as much
as, if not more than, his miracles in the flesh. One of
its most melting and beautiful effects was manifested in
bringing together pastors of all denominations. One
meeting in every week was especially for them, as
brother prophets to bow together at the throne of
grace, and with thanksgiving supplicate the continued
prosperity of the Divine work. Pastors spoke in mis-
cellaneous assemblies, where sect was forgotten in the
presence of the great Head of every true church.
Christians were astonished to learn here that members
of other denominations were moved by the Holy Spirit
to the same heavenly affections and desires as their
own. "If that be Unitarianism," said one of another
sect, after listening to our pastor on such an occasion,
"I would be a Unitarian." He sought to have thanksgiving mingle with the supplications of the prayer-
meeting. He wished it remembered "that praise is
an important element of prayer. We did not want
always to be in sackcloth and ashes, but to remember
the Father's loving arms spread out to embrace his
children. There was infinite love behind the clouds
of earth. Let us think of that. In our Pentecostal
season, let us rejoice in the love of God, the cheering
symbol of which shines in the unclouded heavens
to-day!"

One of the grateful incidents in our pastor's toil
was the warm friends he acquired. Few were more
fortunate than he in making "friends indeed"; those
who do not waver nor slacken in their regard, and
who, once gained, are lasting. One of them perhaps
furnishes the key to this good fortune in characteristics
of our pastor, which he thus describes: "He was
always so genial and hearty, so glad to meet his friends.
There was never anything cold or indifferent about
him, no doubtful reserve to make you question your
welcome. So, when I heard him preach, besides the
satisfaction of hearing a faithful word feelingly spoken,
I had a pleasure in the voice of a warm-hearted, earnest friend, who was sure, after the service, to give
me a cordial greeting, more refreshing and comforting
to me than the best sermon." His friendships were
not confined to his own parish nor his own denomination. As a happy instance of this, we may refer to
the kindly relation which subsisted between him and
the Rev. Rollin H. Neale, D. D., of the Baptist denomination; and we are glad to insert here a communication we have been favored with from that eminent
Christian pastor.

"I cheerfully comply with your request to furnish
some personal reminiscences of your brother. It so
happened that I was present at his installation in Boston. Wishing to hear the addresses of the gentlemen
who were announced to speak on that occasion, especially the sermon of Rev. Dr. Peabody, now of Cambridge, I had the pleasure of seeing him as he first
entered upon his ministry in this city. Our personal
acquaintance, however, did not begin until some time

afterwards. I frequently heard reports of his earnestness as a preacher. Members of other denominations, intending of course to pay him a compliment, said that he was strictly evangelical, and preached the Gospel. He became known as an advocate of temperance, a friend of the poor and the outcast, and, indeed, was prominent (though with no spirit of bitterness) in favor of every moral reform.

"My personal acquaintance with him began in a way that proved to be of much interest to myself, and which I regarded as quite a favoring Providence. I had been appointed to preach the Dudleian Lecture, which that year was to be on the subject of Romanism. I had thought of various ways of treating it, all of which were unsatisfactory. I had taken up and rejected one theme after another, until I was quite in a fever of anxiety as the time for fulfilling the appointment drew nigh. I reluctantly accepted an invitation to an evening party. Your brother was present. In the course of conversation, I said in pleasantry: ' Mr. Fuller, I see by the newspaper advertisements that you are delivering a series of lectures against the Orthodox; I hope you will not be hard upon us.' ' O no,' said he, ' I am only telling how much good there is in you. I see a great deal of truth in all churches, and in all doctrines, — the doctrine of the atonement, the doctrine of regeneration, and of the Trinity. And I only try to bring out what is good and true, and leave the false and the corrupt to take care of itself.' He went on in the same strain for I know not how long. I looked at him, very respectfully of course, but became somewhat absent-

minded. 'Is not this,' I thought, 'the true way to
deal with Romanism?' And before the interview was
ended, I had got my theme and the plan pretty much
worked out: 'The Elements of Truth in the Romish
Church.' I explained to him afterwards how much
relief this incidental conversation had given me, and
how much aid I had thus received in preparing for a
dreaded occasion. From this time our friendship became intimate and unreserved. He was perfectly open
and frank in the expression of his sentiments, never
seeking to conciliate favor by compromise or conceal-
ment of his own views; but he was not inclined to
controversy or to a negative faith. The things which
most impressed him, both in morals and religion, and
which, therefore, were most prominent in his conversation, were such as would, with men and Christians
generally, find a ready assent. Hence, without seeking for popularity, he was universally beloved. I
never heard any one speak to his disparagement.
This is the more remarkable, as his preaching and public addresses were never of the milk-and-water stamp.
He was so obviously sincere, so honest, and withal had
such a fund of good-nature, that it was impossible, even
for those whose conduct came under his severest
denunciations, to speak or think ill of him. When I
heard of his appointment as an army chaplain, my first
thought was, 'That is the right man for the right
place. He will love the soldiers, and they will love
him.' And so it has proved. No church was ever
more attached to a pastor, no affectionate children
more closely bound to a loving father, than the members of the Sixteenth Regiment were to him. He was

with them in their frequent and tedious marches, with them in the night-watches, with them in the hour of sickness and sorrow, and with them on the field of battle and of death. His published letters from the army are exceedingly characteristic. Breathing the spirit of unaffected piety, there is no moroseness. You see him everywhere, and at all times, active, cheerful, and full of life and hope.

" I met him in Boston a short time before his death. He had been sick, but was anxious to hasten back to the field of duty. I wanted him to speak at a public meeting, but remarked about his unministerial-looking costume. ' O,' said he, ' I have to rough it, and dress accordingly.' He spoke at several of the religious anniversaries with more than his usual enthusiasm and patriotic ardor.

" When I heard of his death, my heart sank within me. I thought of his wife and children, of the soldiers whom he loved so well, of you, my dear sir, his brother, and of my own personal bereavement. But of these private griefs I will not speak. I am glad that you are preparing a biography. The best memorial of him, however, is that which he has written himself, and which will long live in the hearts, and I trust in the improved characters, of those who knew him."

We have thus briefly glanced at six laborious years of our pastor in connection with the New North Church in Boston. All earthly relations, longer or shorter, must cease ; and his Boston pastorate was now brought to a close. He found his strength unequal to cope longer with the adverse current, expending upon it a

toil which could not there obtain any lasting success,
and he sent in his resignation, having resolved to
accept a call extended to him by a society in Watertown, Massachusetts. His society in Boston parted
from him with regret, and some three years afterward,
having settled no other pastor, sold their house of
worship.

The public press appropriately noticed his resignation. One paper says: " His sympathies have ever
been with the people, and his labors, unremitting and
constant, have ever been for the people, and conse-
quently the PEOPLE have loved him." Another remarks: " He has overtasked his strength, and needs a
respite from hard work. He will be a loss to Boston,
and particularly to that section of it wherein he has
devotedly labored. The time is near at hand when
the Protestant churches at the North End must seek
some other spot, if they would perpetuate their existence."

Another paper reports him as saying, in his farewell
discourse, that " he had preached life more than doctrine. He had preached against sin, especially against
slavery; and he thanked God that he had done so.
He spoke strongly and unequivocally when our noble
Senator fell beneath a dastardly blow. He spoke with
severity against the repeal of the Missouri compromise
and against every aggression of the slave power. He
had spoken freely against individual and national sins,
but never as a partisan. He had denounced intem-
perance and the supineness of the city authorities.
But, most of all, he had preached repentance, regeneration, holiness, charity, and active benevolence.

" He regretted that their evening meetings had not generally been successful. He was persuaded that his parishioners entertained love for him. His own for them was deep and fervent, and would only cease with life.

" He glanced at the progress of the church since his connection with it. Their debts had been consolidated and lessened, and no longer embarrassed them, and he left them with money in their treasury. Their house had been remodelled. Their church-membership had increased fivefold, and their Sabbath school three-fold."

The very day on which this farewell discourse was pronounced, the pastor's mother entered on her ever-lasting rest. He knew not the event was so near, though he refers perhaps to her critical sickness, when he alludes in the sermon to the many seasons of sorrow he has attended, and adds, " Voice after voice, dear to my ear, has died away, and others will soon be hushed in death." He had lost his wife three years before, and perhaps from being deprived of the home which had been so dear to him, and afforded him such genial refreshment in his toil, he felt the less able to continue his pastoral labors, in a scene, too, which always reminded him of what he had lost.

In the next chapter we propose to take a more interior and familiar view of his Boston life ; and, meantime, we close this with the following tribute from a valued parishioner.

" It was his custom," he says, " at one time, during a prevalent revival in Boston, to hold daily afternoon and evening prayer-meetings, in which all were invited to participate, without regard to doctrinal views. On an occasion, when the various denominations blended with peculiar harmony and cordiality, one of the congregation struck up ' The morning light is breaking'; and it was never sung with a greater zest or livelier feeling of common brotherhood. His congregation was at one time so large that the aisles of the church were temporarily furnished with extra seats.

" The sad intelligence of his death, on that mournful Sabbath, caused more than one heart to throb painfully as they realized that a friend had gone, that a noble soul had, in the impulsiveness of a heroic nature, and at what he considered the imperative demand of duty, which appeared to be his guiding star through life and his watchword in death, passed from the Church militant to the Church triumphant."

CHAPTER III.

EPISODES.

"Tears of the widower, when he sees
A late lost form that sleep reveals,
And moves his doubtful arms and feels
Her place is empty."

"Dearest sister! thou hast left us!
Here thy loss we deeply feel."

"He passed; a soul of nobler tone:
My spirit loved and loves him yet."

"My mother! when I learned that thou wast dead,
Say, wast thou conscious of the tears I shed?"

MONG the extra-parochial labors of our pastor was the issuing a new edition of the works of his sister Margaret. She left a large quantity of manuscript, which the pressure of her occupations and the frailty of her health had not permitted her to put into book form. This task was now achieved by her brother, partly as supplemental to books already published, and also in a new volume entitled *Life Without and Life Within*. The first book he issued in this way was *Woman in the Nineteenth Century*. He writes in reference to it: "I have done my best and hardest work on this book. The labor of compiling and superintending such a publication and correcting the proof is greater than I could have conceived possible. It is done, and I thank

God for giving me strength to do it. I pray that it may contribute to do justice to her merits. That is all the reward I can expect, and that reward would be so noble, so holy ! "

The profits from the sale of her memoirs and works were applied to paying her honorary debts, which she had contracted with friends, on a fair understanding of her present and probable future inability to repay, and which her family ultimately had the satisfaction to cancel from the posthumous fruits of her character displayed in her memoirs and her writings edited by her brother Arthur. He had the satisfaction at last to announce : " Margaret's debts are all paid, every dollar ! That sacred trust to us is now fulfilled."

In his private correspondence, he frequently alludes to these books. " I think," he says, referring to the first named, "it has something adapted to every capacity. The story of " Aglauron and Laurie" must interest the most careless reader, and the letters will arrest the attention of the most hurried, while the *Woman in the Nineteenth Century* meets the wants of the profound thinker."

Again he writes in relation to his editorial toil : " This has been a labor of love, which I have joyed in, and have esteemed a privilege, and not a burden. If I only live to send forth Margaret's works from the press, as they should appear, I shall not have lived wholly in vain." He says in another letter : " One of the things for which I have labored most in these latter years, and wish to complete before going hence to be seen no more on earth, is the erection of suitable memorials to Margaret's memory. These are not to be the cold and passionless marble only, but volumes of her warm and earnest thoughts, so high and so noble ! "

The reverential affection which he gratefully cherished for this sister led him also earnestly to co-operate with his mother in adorning the family resting-place in the Mount Auburn Cemetery in Cambridge. This had been a favorite resort of Margaret; here she loved to walk and meditate. And here the mother had purchased a spot, comprising several lots, for her cenotaph and monument, the commemoration also of her gallant husband, and the last resting-place of her little Angelo. To this spot, too, the bones of the never-forgotten father were removed, and suitably commemorated. And here bloomed the fair and cherished favorites of the mother, whose flowery tongues told the tale of affliction, faith, and love, while they breathed up the aromatic tribute of devoted memory. The lot is situated upon Pyrola Path, not far from the tower.

Alas ! death soon gathered into this green garner other forms, cut off in the bloom of life. In 1856 he was fatally busy with the pastor's household and kindred. He opened the year by removing a young wife and mother from the bosom of Richard's family ; and before the year's close, two who had mourned for her were laid in the same resting-place, — the pastor's wife and sister.

It was the fourth day of March when his wife was suddenly snatched from the family circle, leaving an infant but a few weeks old. In reference to this event, he writes: " It is God who alone can speak to me words of comfort ; and through the Holy Spirit he does so. Much as I mourn, I am sustained." Nor was he wanting, too, in the balm of human consolation poured into the wound by near friends, and by a people who tenderly sympathized with him. His parish not only took upon themselves the funeral obsequies, beautifully performed in the church and burial-place, but they passed a kindly vote of condolence, with some weeks' leave of absence.

In September of that year, his sister, Mrs. Ellen Channing, died in a decline. The flame of her spirit burned with increased brilliancy in the hectic of her cheek and in the eye's seraphic radiance, just before it was caught up, to burn with the lights above.

> Hers were the bright brow and the ringlet hair,
> The mind, that ever dwelt i' the pure ideal;
> Herself a fairer figure of the real
> Than those the plastic fancy moulds of air.

The sorrows of the pastor led him to seek occasionally a change of scene. But he never wished to intermit his labors in the Lord; and we still find him advocating the loved cause of his Master. He made two visits to Judge Nahum Ward, at Marietta, Ohio. From this place he writes: "I am pleasantly situated here. I have everything needful for my comfort, and enjoy the beautiful scenery. Marietta is the most ancient place in Ohio. It was settled in 1788, by inhabitants of New England, and retains all its early characteristics. It is indeed more of a New England than Western place. Mr. Ward is a grandson of General Artemas Ward of the American Revolution, and is a noble, generous-hearted man, preserving also great energy and a fine religious character. As proof of his generosity and Christian zeal, he has built a church here, the handsomest, if not most costly, in the State, and all at his own expense ; and now he will pay the minister's salary, and that generously, certainly for a time. I find him a very intelligent companion, abounding in reminiscences of his journeyings and adventures in his early days. Lafayette visited him when in this country, and presented him with a cane, on which he had often leaned when in the Austrian dungeon at Olumtz. Mr. Ward has travelled widely in Europe, and seen there many celebrated men."

Our pastor was the first preacher in this newly-erected church, and had the satisfaction to found the Sabbath school there, which remembered him after his death.

He frequently gave the public an account of his journeys, through the medium of newspaper correspondence. He thus speaks of Trenton Falls : " That deep ravine worn through the solid rock, that river of amber water, assuming every shape of grandeur and beauty, now scatters pearls in torrents, and now reposes in a deep basin, whose dark depths reflect the arbor-vitæ trees, and fair flowers fringing its banks and stooping down to kiss the sparkling waters. Who could behold all this without a thought of that river of life, whose waters are clear as crystal, which wanders through scenes yet more resplendent with glory, and whose banks are adorned by the tree of life, of which the arbor-vitæ is an emblem, and flowers that never fade ? "

He gives an account of a lady preacher who officiated, on the Sabbath, at Trenton village. " A rude

7   J

platform," he says, "had been erected; but it looked
finely, decorated with oak-wreaths and adorned with
flowers. The meeting was toward evening, when the
glare of the sunlight is over, and only the shimmer of
light among the leaves is noted. The preacher, taste-
fully dressed in white, was evidently a modest, unpretending woman. We had some fear lest her words
should mar, rather than aid the effect of the occasion,
but were happily disappointed. Her quiet manner,
clear articulation, and purity, even holiness of look and
word, were in unison with the scene and the hour.
Her text was from Psalms, 'Your heart shall live
forever.' She aimed to exhibit the undying nature
of human affection, and to prove therefrom both the
immortality of the soul and also the immortality of
those pure friendships, domestic ties, and holy relations
which, on earth, make almost heaven in our homes
and hearts. The sermon did not exhibit much origi-
nality or power of thought; yet its purity of tone,
earnestness of appeal, and fervent sincerity commended
it both to the heart and judgment of the hearers, while
her modest bearing disarmed any prejudice against
her as a woman seeking to be a public teacher. Her
intonation and articulation were almost faultless."

From Trenton he proceeds to Niagara, of which he
writes : —

"This magnificent scene grows upon the mind
and heart every hour. One may be soon satisfied at
other places; but here the old feeling and request
comes up, 'Master, it is good for us to be here!' Let
us build tabernacles, and abide till the death hour;
yea! be buried on these banks, and let this mighty

organ-pipe chant our requiem, while the rainbows which span the falls by day, and no less on each moon-light night, speak auguries of hope and heavenly glory to the departed soul.

" But who can describe Niagara? What voice, save its own mighty one, can speak its charms ; what pen but that of inspiration could write adequately of its glories? I think, in a reverent mind the all-absorbing feeling is, that *God is here ;* this is his temple ; he is speaking ; and when the Lord is in his holy temple, and speaks to man, *let all the earth keep silence before him !*"

He sought recreation, too, on the White Hills, in New Hampshire. " Here I am," he writes, " pay-ing a visit to the ' Old Man of the Mountain.' This locality is grand and beautiful beyond my conception. ' Echo Lake '. deserves its name, repeating some twenty times the cannon's loud report, and returning the notes of the bugle as if a band of music were in full play. To-morrow I go to the Flume, where my friend, Mr. Smith, was struck dead. The scene will be mournful, yet attractive too. How much beauty there often is, even in sadness ; as these mountains sometimes look most beautiful when veiled in clouds, from which the rainy tear-drops are falling."

The mountain beauties roused his devotional heart to make a Bethel of the place, and raise his voice in exposition of the grand language of Nature. " We had a sermon," says a correspondent of the press, writing from the mountains, " from the Rev. Mr. Fuller, of Boston, which I scarcely ever heard sur-passed. In speaking of the mountains, he traced the hand of God in every waterfall and every rock ; everything which he had seen had talked to him of his Maker."

In his journeyings, the pastor often turned aside from the habitations of the living to meditate in "the village of the dead." His repeated bereavements led him to think much of death, but never with gloom. He regarded it as the portal of glory for those who sleep in Christ, on whose solemn threshold he loved to muse. His faith was entire. He said he could say of his trust, "I *know* that my Redeemer liveth." He did not wear the mourning weed for his friends; and he always wished the light of faith to relieve the shadow of natural grief in the funeral obsequies of the Christian. To him cemeteries were eloquent with life-lessons taught in the memorials of death. He was thus led to trace thoughtfully the time-worn inscription, and he published many accounts of cemeteries. Among these may be mentioned descriptions of the burial-places of Quincy, Waltham, and Newton. He has given an account, too, of the solemn prairie cemetery, seeming in the vast emerald reach of the horizon like burial at sea.

The little graves had for him a voice of peculiar pathos, yet of glad faith and hope. On this theme he says: "How beautiful, though sad, is death in childhood! Beautiful, for it is only death in semblance, and in reality the beginning of a painless, joyous life! Beautiful, because with the death of that infant form, all tendency of disease whether in soul or body, all fear of becoming a sinner, all temptation, all grief, have to that soul died. I never feel surer of immortality, than when looking upon such a casket, from

which the angel we call Death has removed the jewel.
There *must* be a land where that bud shall unfold,
those undeveloped capacities be expanded, those un-
tried powers put forth, and the end of such a creation
answered. This life were a sad, a vexing problem —
yes, and a wretched boon to man — were not another
and a better life attainable beyond it. The future
must be the interpreter of the present, its compensation too."

During the period of which we are now treating, our
pastor was twice elected a chaplain in the legislature
of Massachusetts, — in 1854, of the House of Representatives, and in 1858, of the Senate. It happens
that one of his prayers in the legislative body was
transcribed, and we insert it here as a specimen of the
brief and comprehensive supplication, which he thought
best adapted to such an occasion.

"O wise and beneficent Being, who dwellest in
light ineffable, unseen by physical sense, but visible to
the eye of faith! we approach thee now with filial
confidence and trust!

"Earnestly do we covet the best gifts, — that faith
which can remove mountains of obstacles from our
pathway, that charity which suffereth long and is kind,
that love which worships God by serving and helping
our brother man, that hope which is an anchor to the
soul amid all life's storms!

"O Lord! help us really to live, — not merely to
exist and to while away our passing hours, but to live
in deeds more than years, live in high thoughts, pure
emotions, lofty desires! O Heavenly Father! how
many of those who think they live are really dead, —

dead in trespasses and sins, dead in all but the animal nature ; whilst many whom the world calls dead yet truly live, yet speak to us, think for us, and influence us, by their deathless thoughts, immortal deeds and memories ! Help us to live much, even in few years ; and if, when we perish as to the body, the silvered locks and furrowed brow be not ours, yet may our time have been long, because useful, our death not premature, because we had early accomplished life's great end !

"And Thine shall be the praise forever. Amen!"

We have been favored with a note from Colonel Robert I. Burbank, a gentleman favorably known in the legislature and forum. Having been a contemporary member of the House, he thus speaks of Chaplain Fuller.

" I take very great pleasure in stating, that during the whole session his punctuality, his urbane and genial manners, his patriotism, his fervency in prayer, and his Christian spirit and devotion, were the theme of universal admiration.

" I remember well to have noted, and frequently at the close of the session to have heard it said, that so appropriate had been his language, that from no words of his could be inferred his political or denominational sentiments.

" He was exceedingly beloved by us all. His zeal in the fitting discharge of his duties then was only the offspring of those noble qualities of heart and soul which impelled him, near the close of his useful career, to deeds of prowess, which have immortalized his memory."

The summer journeyings of our pastor were the

occasion of pleasant family letters, which blended the musings of a pious heart with expressions of family love. From life's meridian, he thus writes: "This is my birthday, and brings with it many meditations as to the past and presaging thoughts of the future. Yes, to-day I am thirty-five; and have lived half the term allotted to man! I ask myself whether half life's work is done, and if so, cannot but feel how little will be the entire sum. Yet these years have teemed with incident, much that is tragic, more that is sweet and pleasant. The tide is bearing me on to the grave; nay, not so! rather, I trust, toward heaven's shoreless ocean, where my little bark, so long tossed on life's heaving sea, may float forever on those joyous waters, where the breath of the Spirit shall swell its sails, and waft it from one scene of beatitude to another."

In 1859, when his mother's ill health had assumed a character so serious as to denote an issue not far removed, he thus writes to her, on the 15th of February, her birthday: —

" I will not let this day go by without a word expressive of my constant love and daily memory of you. This, too, is the birthday of my little boy; and I blend together in my thoughts the two dearest objects of affection, — my children and my mother.

" And now, my dear mother, I have only this word of greeting to utter, — may God bless you and make this year full of happiness to you; and if it prove your last, or witness your birth into another sphere, may it yet be fraught with richest, choicest, most precious blessings, and be the happiest which your life, so varied in its sorrow and joy, has ever known."

In a letter to Eugene he thus refers to his mother's sickness, which confined her for several of the last months of her life to a sick-chamber: "I have just returned from Wayland, where I go every two or three days to visit our beloved mother. We found her still quite ill, but more comfortable, always thinking of you and her other dear ones, expecting death, whenever it may come, as a solemn but sweet reality, and as the herald to a brighter region."

In another letter to the same brother, he refers again to his mother: "Nothing could be more serene and radiant than her sick-chamber. The little children all seek it, as the one joyous, sunny spot in the whole house, where they are ever sure of wisdom and love, blended together in every word."

Thus did she draw near eternity. But Eugene reached it several weeks in advance, through the ocean portals, being lost overboard in his homeward voyage from New Orleans. In the mother's state of health it was thought best not to communicate an event to her which might add a mortal pang to her last hours and speed her malady. Finding no allusion made to Eugene, she asked Richard if he had gone before her, a remark which he evaded without answering. She saw in a moment the purpose to withhold from her sad and exciting tidings, and meekly suppressing the anxious questioning of a mother's heart, she never alluded to the subject again.

She continued cheerful, fully supported by her beloved Lord, and drawing near with bright and joyous anticipations the heavenly world which, with her Saviour, held so many of her heart's treasures. We remember turning to hide a starting tear on an occasion when she spoke of her interest in the growing corn, hoping a plenteous harvest, without one sigh at the thought of the other harvest-home where she would then be gathered.

She entered sweetly on her glorious rest, on Sabbath morning, July 31st, 1859, the same day that terminated the Boston pastorate of her son Arthur.

In her sickness she watched with interest the growing attachment of her son for Miss Emma L. Reeves, a sister of Richard's wife. She expressed a wish that the marriage might not be deferred on account of her departure for the better land, and it took place accordingly in September of the same year.*

---

*. We take the liberty to insert a few unpretending verses from the pen of the bride, in reference to her husband's children.

> " Maidens wove white buds and leaflets,
>   Sweet and pure as they,
> Feverfew and mignonette,
>   In a fair bouquet.

> " But a loving hand brought dearer,
>   Fairer flowers than they,
> And he placed them in my bosom,
>   Not to fade away.

> " One a bud, but just revealing
>   Rich and roseate shades,
> With a sweetness aromatic·
>   As the Indian glades.

> " And beside it is my Lily's
>   Alabaster cup,
> Raising pure and perfumed petals
>   Gently, heavenward, up.

> " Ye are welcome to my bosom,
>   Choice, immortal flowers!
> Heavenly Gardener! help me train them
>   For thy fadeless bowers! "

7 *

The husband, in a private letter from the army, thus refers to his second marriage : "In my mother's sick-chamber appeared a ministering angel. Her love for my mother, and devoted, tender care for long, weary months, her love of flowers and children, her poetical tastes, and, above all, her consistent piety, and the evident leading of Providence, caused me to form another attachment as true and tender as the first."

He now entered upon house-keeping in Watertown, which he continued till he was appointed army chaplain, a period of his life to which we shall now give exclusive attention.

PART III.

THE ARMY CHAPLAIN.

"Who is the happy Warrior? Who is he
That every man in arms should wish to be?
—It is the generous spirit, who, when brought
Among the tasks of real life,
 . . . . .

Controls them and subdues, transmutes, bereaves
Of their bad influence, and the good receives:
 . . . . .

Who comprehends his trust, and to the same
Keeps faithful with a singleness of aim ;
 . . . . .

And, through the heat of conflict, keeps the law
In calmness made, and sees what he foresaw ;
 . . . . .

Whom neither shape of danger can dismay,
Nor thought of tender happiness betray ;
Who, not content that former worth stand fast,
Looks forward, persevering to the last,
From well to better daily self-surpast ;
 . . . . .

Finds comfort in himself and in his cause ;
And, while the mortal mist is gathering, draws
His breath in confidence of Heaven's applause :
This is the happy warrior ; this is he
Whom every man in arms should wish to be."

          WORDSWORTH.

C'HAPTER I.

THE GREAT REBELLION.

"And after that he must be loosed a little season."
APOCALYPSE.

"Whence and what art thou, execrable Shape,
That dar'st, though grim and terrible, advance
Thy miscreated front?
            .   .   .   .   .   .
Art thou that traitor Angel, art thou he
Who first broke peace in heaven, and faith till then
Unbroken, and in proud rebellious arms
Drew after him the third part of Heaven's sons,
Conjured against the Highest?   .   .   .
      .   .   .   . Back to thy punishment !"
PARADISE LOST.

HE attention of our New England pastor now became closely fixed upon national affairs, which daily wore a more threatening aspect. He watched the issue with the anxious regard of a patriot, a Christian, and a minister of the Gospel. With the children of the Puritan, these three terms are convertible. American patriotism is not solely the love for the Republic, which burned in the breast of the devoted Roman, or instigated the Greek to almost superhuman valor. The Puritan had sundered the natural, and sacrificed the mere instinctive love of country, to seek beyond the vast ocean a new country, where he would be at liberty to worship God according to the dictates of his own conscience.

This he sought, and this has bound his heart to his new home. His love of liberty and of country is, therefore, always a love of the open Bible, with freedom of unfettered development in all directions of the manhood which speaks in every original feature the likeness of its Divine Maker. Therefore patriotism in America, more than anywhere else in history, is an intensely religious sentiment; and they are found to love their country most who love God most, — to render the best military service on the battle-fields of patriotism, who are the best soldiers of the cross. Nor do they doff one uniform when they don the other. They see in the loved stars and stripes of the Union the standard of the cross; and they follow their Master to war against rebellion, as did the Israelites the pillar of cloud and fire, as did the army of Constantine the crucifix which glowed in the sky.

The guardian, therefore, of the religious interests of the Puritan race watches carefully, too, the vestal flame of patriotism. An important part of his theology is the history of his country; and as a watchman on Zion's walls, it is his duty to signalize every approaching foe to freedom. The politician does not study public affairs more intently than the pastor; and, as he takes the lead in religion, he holds the same place in patriotism. Thus our Gospel ministers, in the almost theocracy of American liberty, are like the Elijahs, Ezekiels, and Isaiahs, who guarded the integrity of the nation as a part of their spiritual charge.

In the country, too, of the "Church without a Bishop," there has been no apportionment of religious ethics, assigning one share to the laity and another to

the clergy. What is right for the one is for the other.
And what the Christian clergyman may not do is
alike unlawful for the Christian layman. Hence, not
only have the clergy of America sent their petitions to
Congress against the expansion of the national area
furnishing new fields for slavery propagandism; but
when the guns of Fort Sumter proclaimed the out-
breaking of rebellion, they rushed to their country's
standard, some in the pastoral robe, some sword in
hand, captains or privates in the Church militant; no
more hesitating for clerical punctilio, than they would
to serve as *posse comitatus* of the angel Michael for the
imprisonment of the Dragon.

The religious nature of American patriotism has given
it a characteristic very puzzling to those who understand
only the instinct of patriotism. The Bible has enlarged
the Puritan's heart to the utmost borders of the world.
Religion has transformed it from the contracted geo-
graphical sentiment to a cosmopolitan patriotism, whose
country is the world, whose countrymen are all mankind. It cannot be restricted to the earthly precinct
hallowed by the accident of birth, although it loves it
because of its Gospel liberty, and as affording a step-
ping-stone to a better country, that is a heavenly.
Therefore its declaration of rights does not say, *we* are
free and equal; but *all men* are born free and equal,
endowed with certain inalienable rights, among which
are life, liberty, and the pursuit of happiness. It will
not, therefore, be accessary to fetters imposed by another; nor can it be satisfied while there are any groaning under oppression, by whose bonds it is galled, as
bound with them. True, while it insists upon washing

its own hands in innocency, it will seek to deliver those oppressed from other's wrongs, by prayer to God and by the power of public opinion, rather than by carnal weapons. Yet it cannot be indifferent nor inactive, in its legitimate moral sphere, while the sighs of a downtrodden brother-man are wafted to it by the farthest wind.

The religious character of the sentiment makes it repudiate with holy horror the maxim, " Our country right or wrong," if the latter phrase be taken to mean more than a mistaken policy, and imply further the perpetration of national crime. The Puritan's children love their country as a province of God's domain; and while they will, with a cordial willingness beyond others, render to the subordinate government all which is not due to higher claims, they will never take its part in rebellion against the Supreme Ruler.

These remarks explain the participation of our clergy in the work of suppressing rebellion, and furnish the key to the course of Chaplain Fuller, to be unfolded in our narrative. They are not, probably, at all needed by our countrymen and times. Yet the voice of a published volume is liable to extend to other countries and other times, to whom our holy cause ought to be fairly presented.

For the same reason, we deem it necessary to make a very brief statement of the causes which have led to a rebellion against the best government mankind has enjoyed, and which has been the repository of the world's hopes of freedom, — a rebellion with no precedent upon earth, and but one in heaven.

Briefly, then, let it be noted, that, as in the days

of Job, where the children of God resorted, the Adversary also came with them; so, in American colonization, with the Puritan purpose was embodied an antagonistic element. Not merely did the lovers of God seek a sanctuary of freedom in the new world, but devotees of pride, indolence, and Mammon, and needy adventurers, hungry for spoil, came also. In Mexico they sacrilegiously bore the crucifix in a crusade of plunder and oppression; while in South America a desperado, who had been foiled in petty villany at home, so magnified the scale of his robbery as to take his place among those giant Scapins, who make up the catalogue of earth's conquerors.

In the Southern colonies of North America, too, the same element obtained a place, implanting the tares of oppression in the area of liberty, and misotheism in the see of religion.

These elements did not for a time develop their antagonism; but as they were shaken together in the course of history, a ferment was inevitable, and finally an irrepressible conflict, till the sure triumph of God's eternal day should forever dissipate the night. Wickedness always evinces its lineage from the Father of Lies, by dissembling, while its end can thus be accomplished. Hence, in American history, while the word *slave* was carefully excluded from the Constitution, as thrusting a lie in the face of the instrument, it obtained an anonymous place in the fugitive clause, hiding in liberty, till it should grow strong, and confident to raise its crest. *Latet anguis in herbis.*

In the growth of the country, slavery finds leisure for political plotting while the attention of liberty is

K

absorbed in thrift and industry. It concentrates, too, its attention and energies upon the one purpose of self-preservation and aggrandizement, while sectional interests are unwarily permitted to weaken the majority it seeks to control. In its own domain it hateth the light because its deeds are evil, and violently excludes public instruction, while, by grasping the landed property, it impoverishes and at the same time degrades those whose lot is not cast with itself. Thus the slave oligarchy rules, in its own States, a poor, ignorant white population of twenty times its number, and by means of this is able to control the policy of the rest of the nation. Its eye is on the citadel of liberty, to which it advances by secret parallels, and these parallels have the plausible name of Compromises.

The Cerberus of slavery looks with a green-eyed watchfulness. from its own wasted domain, to the far exceeding increase of the children of liberty ; and it is constantly contriving devices to offset this augmentation which threatens to.so outnumber slave representation as to be no longer manageable. Slavery, like the locusts, can only flourish by spreading from land it has ravaged to newly acquired territory. This leads to the acquisition of Louisiana, Texas, the war with Mexico waged for more domain ; and by compromise the slave oligarchy partitions the fairest regions for its blighting spread. Yet wickedness cannot grow so fast as virtue and industry and invention, nor the darkness of slavery increase like the light of liberty under the presiding sun of Christian righteousness. Slavery is alarmed for her supremacy, and as she fails to keep step with Freedom in advancing over the new fields, she contrives fraud and crime. She raises her crest, thrusts forth her hissing tongue, and would strike her fangs into the fair bosom of Liberty. Kansas is the first theatre of unblushing crime attempted by the slave oligarchy, now become desperate. A supple tool of its own occupies the Presidential chair of the nation, and all the means of government are at its command. Bribery, corruption, terror, violence, are alternately levelled at the ark of Liberty, — the ballot-box.*

But the crime is too outrageous for the Christian light of the nineteenth century to look upon. The "north star is at last discovered." The people withdraw their absorbed attention from worldly increase, and fix it in astonishment upon the slave power, wearing now a disguise so thin as to reveal its horrid deformity. The nation is about to speak, and in its ominous murmur, which already begins to surge like the first low breath of an overwhelming tempest, the quick ear of the slave power discerns the presage of doom, and rouses to the climax of crime, "having great wrath, because he knoweth that he hath but a short time."

The slave oligarchy had now installed in the White House a President whose public career has given his character no alternative but treason or beetle-blindness; which horn of the dilemma shall be awarded him we leave to the sentence of History. Conspiracy was in his Cabinet, transferring the munitions of war

* It cannot be necessary to refer the reader to the masterly *exposé* of the crimes of the slave power contained in the speeches of the Massachusetts Senator, entitled, "The Crime against Kansas," and "The Barbarism of Slavery," and indeed all the utterances of that eloquence, whose burden has still been, *Delenda est servitudo!*

to the rendezvous of treason, with the army reduced
to a shadow, and the navy despatched to distant seas.
The nation spoke at the ballot-box, and commissioned Freedom to the presidential office. The com-
mencement of Abraham Lincoln's administration found
the rebellion armed and equipped from the national
storehouses, and the government disarmed and de-
pleted by the preceding administration.

The guns of Fort Sumter signalled the onset of
barbarism and oppression upon the fairest domain that
genuine religion, public education, brotherhood, and
liberty had ever acquired. In no heart did it awaken
a more patriotic response than in that of the subject
of our present narrative. We indeed arrogate for him
no superiority nor singularity in this respect, for, thank
God! the heart and voice of twenty million freemen
in this exigency was as that of one man.

Enthusiastic Union meetings were holden in every
city and village of the Free States. The national stars
and stripes streamed from the church, school-house,
mart, factory, and private dwelling; so that bunting
speedily rose to a fabulous price, and could not be had
at that. Every profession and calling vied with each
other in patriotic expressions. Committees of citizens
waited upon the few presses or individuals who manifested any symptoms of disloyalty, and compelled them
literally to display their colors, and define satisfactorily
their position. It was felt that the nation's critical
hour had come, and called for prompt and united
measures.

Patriotic and military enthusiasm pervaded all classes.
Boys organized themselves into armed bands, and would

gladly have shared the campaigns of their sires. Among these may be mentioned a military organization of young soldiers in Boston, called " The Fuller Rifles," in compliment to the chaplain.

Among the public meetings everywhere holden, we have the account of one in Watertown, in which " the Rev. Arthur B. Fuller protested against 'any further compromise with slavery. Thus far, and no farther.' He was in favor of the Constitution of these United States. He was in favor of a settlement; but, in the language of Hon. Charles Sumner, 'Nothing is ever settled, that is not settled right.' Let us stand right ourselves, and then we can demand right from others. He urged the Republicans to stand by the election of Lincoln and Hamlin. Protect and sustain them. He was opposed to compromise, — even to the admission of New Mexico, — because it would be in violation of our platform, and at variance with the opinions of such honored statesmen as Webster and Clay, and because it interdicted the spirit of the Gospel."

After the Sabbath labors of his own pulpit, he went to the camp, where the soldiers were gathering, and preached to them in the temple not made with hands. Here his extempore facility and pliancy of address to the needs of the occasion proved very effective, and rendered his preaching especially valued by the soldier. He was soon chosen chaplain of the Sixteenth Regiment of Massachusetts Volunteers, and, on the first day of August, 1861, was duly commissioned by Governor Andrew.

We have a newspaper report of a sermon he preached at Camp Cameron, Massachusetts, which may give some idea of his manner of address in his new position.

"The text selected was the sevententh and eighteenth verses of the thirty-second chapter of Numbers : ' But we ourselves will go ready armed before the children of Israel, until we have brought them into their place : and our little ones shall dwell in the fenced cities, because of the inhabitants of the land. We will not return into our houses until the children of Israel have inherited every man his inheritance.' The sermon was specially designed to assure those who were about to go to the war that the cause they were going to serve was a holy one, and had the approbation of the Lord in the same way as that alluded to in the words of the text. There was something, the speaker said, extremely similar in the circumstances of our inheritance here in the North, on this side of the Potomac, and that of the Jews. They said, ' We will not inherit with them on yonder side of Jordan ; because our inheritance is fallen to us on this side Jordan eastward.' This, our inheritance, it was proper we should protect and defend from its enemies, who loved not America ; that we should subdue the land to recognition of just government, and afterward return, and be guiltless before the Lord, in the which should be a possession. If we did not do so, then the words of Moses to the children of Reuben and Gad would be applicable to us ; we would sin against the Lord ; and we might be sure our sin would find us out. The families of all such as would go out to battle in this religious war — for it was a religious one — would be well protected and cared for. Without a successful subjugation of the enemy of the inheritance we had to bequeath to our children, that inheritance would be valueless; and hence our duty to go forth, fearlessly and valiantly, for the rights of those we loved. This was the motive which every man had at heart; and going to battle in the name of the Lord they would carry it out."

On receiving the commission of chaplain, he resigned his pastorate in Watertown. In his letter of resignation he says: "The moral and religious welfare of our patriotic soldiery cannot be neglected save to the demoralization and permanent spiritual injury of those who are perilling their all in our country's cause. The regiment represents Middlesex County on the tented field, the county in which I was born, and which my honored father represented in our national Congress; and one company is from Watertown, where for nearly two years I have been a settled minister, — circumstances which give this call of duty a peculiar claim upon my mind and heart. I am willing to peril life for the welfare of our brave soldiery, and in our country's cause. If God requires that sacrifice of me, it shall be offered on the altar of freedom, and in defence of all that is good in American institutions."

Before leaving for the scene of war, he was gratified by a presentation visit from his friends, of which the following account was given in the public press.

"A very pleasant gathering of the friends of the chaplain of the Sixteenth Regiment, Rev. Arthur B. Fuller, took place at his residence in Watertown on Wednesday evening. Yesterday morning a committee, of whom Dr. Samuel Richardson was chairman, presented to Mr. Fuller the handsome sum of two hundred and fifty dollars, stating that, but for the stringency of the times affecting all classes, a much larger sum could have been easily raised. Among the donors are *members of every denomination* in Watertown, Rev. Mr. Flood, the Catholic priest, being among the number.

" The following brief but appropriate address was made by the chairman of the committee, Dr. Richardson : —

" ' Respected and dear Friend : As you are about to leave us for a new field of action, your friends of various denominations in this community desire to present you with some testimonial of their affection and high esteem for you as a minister, a citizen, and a man. I am requested to present you this purse, with their sincere prayers for your safety and welfare. May you soon return to your beloved family and friends, and may we once more have the privilege of grasping your hand in welcome and gladness at the close of this war, as we now with sadness press it in parting with you to take part and do your duty in its stirring scenes as a patriot and a Christian.'

" A beautiful and well-stored writing-desk and several other substantial packages were also presented Mr. Fuller by his friends in Boston and vicinity."

Among the closing scenes at Watertown, we remember a prayer-meeting in the Methodist Episcopal Church. In the desk sat the pastor, Rev. Henry E. Hempstead, afterward Chaplain Hempstead, and Chaplain Fuller. The topic of prayer and remark was our country's crisis. An army officer present spoke of the dangers he was about to encounter, and of death upon the battle-field. The two clergymen poured forth earnest patriotic prayers. Much evident solicitude for the soldier was manifest in the assembly, seeming to lament in advance his expected life-sacrifice in his country's cause, as did the Trojans in bidding farewell to Hector when he went forth against Achilles. Danger for the clergymen was not thought of; yet, in the issue, the army officer resigned, and returned home; the chaplains continued in their country's service, and both laid down life upon the altar of patriotic devotion within a few days of each other, at Fredericksburg. The one fell from a hostile bullet; the other sacrificed his life in taking care of the sick and wounded, and the incidental exposure. So little do we know of the future!

8

CHAPTER II.

FORTRESS MONROE.

"I confess to having enough of the war spirit to feel a pride in Bunker Hill and other scenes of our Revolutionary struggle. War is a terrible evil; but tyranny is a greater; and, to expel the latter poison from the body politic, war is needful. After all, what is life but one great battle-field, on which a most momentous war against temptation and the tyranny of our passions and appetites is waged by each human soul? And what spirit has made its way to any true nobility of character, any real self-government, without passing through a field of moral battle, which has been to it a Bunker Hill, a Marathon, or a Platæa? And the debased soul, alas! has known its Waterloo, from whose deadly conflict it came not off victorious!"—*Family letter of* REV. A. B. FULLER, *written June* 17, 1852.

"Though lodged within no vigorous frame,
His soul her daily tasks renewed,
Blithe as the lark on sun-gilt wings
High poised.'

N the 17th of August, 1861, Chaplain Fuller left Boston with the Sixteenth Massachusetts Regiment for their Southern destination. He writes * that on their departure "there was less elation, less display, than usual, perhaps, but more of stern determination and clear realization of the object to be achieved and the hardships to be endured than has been felt before."

Respecting his regiment he says:—

* We shall cite in the following pages, without particular reference, the Chaplain's private letters, and his correspondence published in the Boston Journal, Boston Traveller, New York Tribune, Christian Inquirer, and other papers.

" The character of the men composing it is generally such as promises fresh honors to a county which contains Lexington and Bunker Hill, Concord and Cambridge, Watertown and other places historic in our earliest struggle for freedom. The officers are skilled military men, selected for capacity, and not because of political influence.

" You have doubtless learned by telegraph of the safe arrival of our regiment in this city, but a few particulars of our journey and position here may not be unacceptable. Our route witnessed one continued ovation, city and country vying in patriotic demonstrations and exhibitions of good-will toward those who were on their way to the scene of peril, but we believe also of honor and of ultimate national triumph. On many a hillside, in the evening, bonfires blazed, and at every way-station enthusiastic cheers rent the air, and many little gifts and leave-takings of those who to us were entire strangers evidenced that in this great cause the people are one in heart and opinion.

" At Fall River an escort of a juvenile company of Zouaves and of many citizens awaited us, but Colonel Wyman wisely avoided fatiguing the men by marching through the streets of that city. Indeed, throughout our journey the same judicious plan has been pursued by our officers. We only touched at New York; we did not land from the steamers, and no unnecessary steps have yet been taken, and no unnecessary display made. We were compelled to journey on the Sabbath, owing to the present exigency, which imperatively demands all our available force near the capital. This fact caused us to find in nearly every town in New Jersey, as we passed through, the people in their best attire, and ready to welcome us. It would have pleased our friends at home to have seen the general good order of the men, and to find that they were not unmindful of the fact that, though 'we were marching on,' yet it was the Sabbath day, and 'hymns of lofty cheer' and true religious patriotism were alone in order.

"Our greeting in Philadelphia, although at midnight, exceeded our leave-taking in Boston. A fine collation is always given by the most substantial citizens of this place to each regiment as it passes through the 'city of brotherly love,' no matter what the hour, or from which of our loyal States. Our fine brass band — and there is none better connected with any regiment — 'discoursed most eloquent music,' fitted to the day and the occasion.

"We *marched through Baltimore* yesterday, the *nineteenth* of August, thinking of another *nineteenth*, that of April, when another Massachusetts regiment marched through also. We were not enthusiastically received as a general rule, for Baltimore is as to its leading influence disloyal to the Union, and hates to-day that 'Star-Spangled Banner,' which still floats from Fort McHenry, and loves not that whole country for which Washington fought. Why not, then, be consistent, and take down their proud monument to the 'Father of his Country'? Here, of all places, might patriotism be expected, and sad enough is it to find it otherwise. A large part of the population yet remains true to the old flag, and manifests itself loyal in a noble manner."

For a few weeks the regiment was stationed at Baltimore, which at that time had not been wholly relieved from the poison of the oligarchs. The government were still vainly endeavoring to temper the needful austerity of war with the ill-assorted moderation of peace, mistaken by the foe for timidity, weakness, and indecision. The Chaplain thus expresses the results of his observation: —

"You can hardly imagine how much the evidences of a

more stern dealing with traitors and a more vigorous prose-
cution of the war inspire the soldiers with fresh hope and
confidence. Fremont's proclamation meets with almost un-
qualified approval, *especially from Union slaveholders.* It is
a move in the right direction, and would be imitated to advantage in this State, and in all our semi-loyal States.

" The presentment of treasonable newspapers by grand
juries, and the suppression of others by the government, is
especially to be commended. It is these which hound the
rebels on to their treasonable deeds, and they should be forced
to be 'dumb dogs, which dare not longer bark.' But why
are such tolerated in Baltimore? No less than three such,
the South, the Republican, and the Exchange, are published
there, and are most defiant of the government. They daily
incite to insurrection, and the consequence is that our officers
and soldiers are daily insulted there, and it is done with perfect impunity. One of the soldiers of our regiment was fired
upon in broad daylight by a woman, before we left that city,
while he was pursuing a deserter, and in the discharge of
his duty. I have seen secession flags flying, and had them
flaunted before my face while walking quietly, unarmed, in
the streets. I have heard cheers, long and loud, for Jeff
Davis, and groans for the Union. This is always done by
women and children, it is true, for that is the cowardly,
sneaking nature of rebellion, avoiding risk of summary vengeance from our manly soldiers. But ought these things
to be allowed? and may not another massacre like that of
the 19th of April ensue if these things are not nipped in
the bud, and if a traitorous press remain unsilenced?

" Our officers and soldiers did not always bear contumely
in silence, though they could not strike down their tormentors
when such were women and children. Sometimes they answered such scoffs with fitting words. 'Are you a Massachusetts soldier?' said a woman, elegantly dressed, and doubt-

less deemed a *lady* in Baltimore. 'I am, madam,' was the courteous answer of the officer thus addressed.* 'Well, thank God, my husband is in the Southern army, ready to kill such hirelings as you.' 'Do you not miss him, madam?' said the officer. 'O yes, I miss him a good deal.' 'Very well, madam, we are going South in a few days, and will try to find him and *bring him back* here with his companions.' You ought to have seen how angry she was! 'You are from that miserable Boston, I suppose,' she said, 'where there is nothing but mob law, and they burned down the Ursuline Convent, — the Puritan bigots!' 'Some such thing did happen in Charlestown many years ago, when I was a boy,' said the officer, 'at least I have heard so, and am very sorry for it. But can you tell me what street that is?' 'Pratt Street,' was the unsuspecting reply. ' *What happened there, madam, on the* 19*th of April, this very year?*' He got no answer from the angry secessionist, but the loud shout which went up from the Union bystanders, who generally are of the humbler orders, atoned for her silence. People that live in glass houses had better not throw stones. The same officer, riding in a chaise with a gentleman who showed secession proclivities, but was courteous in their demonstration, was told by the gentleman that the horse which was drawing them was called 'Jeff Davis,' in honor of that distinguished rebel, and asked if he 'did not object to driving such a horse.' 'O no, sir,' was the instant reply; 'to drive Jeff Davis is the very purpose of our coming South.' Our secession gentleman imitated his sister traitor in preserving a discreet silence."

The religious object of the Chaplain's commission no martial preparations could make him forget. He had come as a religious teacher, ready to practise what he preached, and he was impelled by his sense of the

* The officer was Chaplain Fuller.

especial importance of religion in the terrible experiences of war. He writes : —

"Our encampment is hardly settled enough yet for definite arrangements to have been fully carried out. After this week, however, the arrangements are as follows: Sunday school at nine, A. M.; attendance to be wholly voluntary. Preaching every Sabbath at five o'clock, P. M., the old hour at Camp Cameron, and the best hour of the day for the purpose. Prayer and conference meeting (when practicable) every day at about six and seven, P. M.; attendance of course voluntary. These services will be fully attended. Even now, every night there are quiet circles for prayer and praise.

"Besides these services, there are Bibles and religious volumes to be distributed to the men, and books for singing God's praise. We find the 'Army Melodies' useful among us, and were not the writer one of the editors of the volume, he would say much of the necessity and usefulness of supplying religious and patriotic music and words to every regiment and every naval vessel, in place of the ribald songs so sadly common in the army and on shipboard. No more refining or religious instrumentality than music can be used."

That threadbare subject, the *weather*, acquires an original interest from new circumstances.

"This topic, so common when people meet who have not much to say, assumes real importance when 'the children of Israel dwell in tents,' and when the weather exercises so much influence over the health and spirits of the men. We have been generally favored with genial skies, but the rainy weather has now set in, and the last three days have been uncomfortable in the extreme. Particularly inconvenient is it with reference to religious exercises. These are necessarily suspended every rainy day, and yet on no day do the

men so much need the cheering and reviving influences of
social conference and prayer, and particularly of *singing* God's
praise. We have a choir organized, who sing from the 'Army
Melodies,' and most of the tents are vocal every evening with
its patriotic and religious songs."

As there was no new outbreak in Baltimore, and
its agitated elements gradually subsided, the Chaplain
found occasion to contemplate some of the interesting
features of that locality. Among these was his favorite resort, the last resting-place.

"Close by us is the famous Greenmount Cemetery, the
Mount Auburn of Baltimore. This ground, too, was recently
desecrated by the traitors of Baltimore. Immediately after
the 19th of April last, the chapel of the cemetery was seized
by order of General Trimble, and used as a storehouse for
rebel guns and powder. Now Massachusetts soldiers walk
quietly through its shady paths, and think, not of death, but
of the immortality of blessedness which awaits every loyal
soldier who dies a martyr for liberty, and for the Christian
principles involved in this struggle.

"And well may a Massachusetts soldier love to walk solemnly in these paths; for in yonder enclosure lie the remains
of the gallant Major Ringgold, who died at Palo Alto. His
only monument is a stockade of Mexican guns and bayonets
captured in that conflict. Colonel Watson, who died at Mon-
terey, sleeps, as to the mortal part, peacefully near. But not
before these soldierly memorials do we linger longest. In
yonder mausoleum laid for days our Massachusetts dead of
the 19th of April, 1861. The soldier whose last words were,
' God bless the Stars and Stripes!' slept here until Governor
Andrew's noble missive was carried into effect, and their
bodies, cared for 'tenderly,' were restored to the Old Bay
State, which will ever cherish their memories."

He thus writes of Druid Hill Park: —

"These beautiful grounds are frequently occupied by the Federal forces, though at present no regiment is within their limits. The citizens of Baltimore have recently purchased this site, and have made a liberal expenditure to beautify its precincts. No finer drive exists than its roads afford, and no better ground can be found for an encampment, though the government is chary about using it, in courteous deference to the wishes of the citizens. On our way thither we passed by many beautiful residences, mostly occupied by secessionists, for they comprise the wealthy men here. On one residence, however, the 'Star-Spangled Banner' still proudly waved, and there it has waved in the breeze every day since the 19th of April of this year. All through the reign of terror, as the Union men designate the ten days succeeding that infamous massacre of our soldiers, that flag floated in the air, surrounded by secession emblems."

He thus speaks of Fort McHenry: —

"It occupies a splendid location to command the city and suppress rebellion within its limits. The large shell mortars and heavy columbiads and other weapons of destruction are kept constantly ready for service in case of an insurrection against the government, and the destruction of Baltimore would in such a case be inevitable. Monumental Square, where secessionists mostly reside, the 'club-house,' where treason is said to be hatched, Pratt Street and its bridge and market, — these would in such an emergency soon be scenes of terrible carnage and vengeance on the enemies of our government. And the star-spangled banner would wave over smoke and flame from that very fort where its appearance in the gray, misty morning called forth from the author, imprisoned in a British ship, an immortal song of patriotic fervor,

8 *   L

the tribute and prophecy of the permanence of the old flag of our country."

Death, too, whose painful volume, crowded with repeated lessons, was now to be the Chaplain's daily text-book, thus opens the first chapter and teaches him to moralize : —

"In the afternoon I attended the funeral of an excellent man, J. D. Prentiss, formerly of Medfield, Massachusetts, a graduate of Harvard, and for many years President of Baltimore College. He was a firm Union man, and I had enjoyed the hospitalities of his home for several days of the past week. He attended our religious services only the Sabbath before, and in all ways had testified his love for old Massachusetts and her soldiers and their holy cause. He had spoken to me of the peril to life in the army, and now he lay in that beautiful home a mangled corpse, killed by a railroad accident. He had so many friends in Massachusetts, and has been so devoted a friend to our soldiers, that his memory claims this mention. His fate is an illustration of the truth that death is everywhere, not only on the battle-field, but in our very streets ; and many of those who pity us and fear for our fate may themselves earliest be called home, and by a bloody death. It matters not, if we are prepared. He always dies well who has lived well, die when, or where, or how he may."

On the 1st of September orders came for the regiment

"to report at Fortress Monroe, and without an instant's hesitation rations were dealt out, tents struck, baggage hurried into wagons, and we were soon on board the Louisiana. Our march through Baltimore to the boat was very different from our entrance into that city. Secessiondom was discouraged by the Hatteras Inlet news, and stayed at home; but the Union men and women and children of Baltimore were out in full force and in high spirits. It made one fancy himself at home in good old Boston to hear such loud cheers for the Union. Ladies presented choice bouquets to the officers and soldiers as they passed, and a patriotic enthusiasm was manifested, which, if followed by patriotic deeds, will yet redeem the fair fame of Baltimore."

On his brief voyage he writes : —

"I am surrounded by naval and military men who were in that glorious conflict. Trophies of the splendid triumph are freely exhibited, consisting of swords, flags, surgical instruments, &c. Our boys of the 'Sixteenth' are cheering pretty loudly on deck, and in one part of the steamer the brass band are discoursing their liveliest strains. You would think our soldiers on board had all turned Methodists to judge by the shoutings; the companies from Lowell, especially the 'Butler Rifles,' largely Catholics, were heartily joining in the chorus of 'Glory Hallelujah, we are marching on.'" *

The regiment were destined to stay several months in the fortress, and here the Chaplain was enabled to prosecute his labors with vigor. The following is a sketch of the religious work.

"I have among my auditors, every Sabbath, a large number of Roman Catholics, and also members of every Protestant sect. It requires no forbearance on my part to preach on those great themes only, and in that spirit only in which all the disciples of our common Master can take an interest, and feel that their conscientious opinions are respected.

---

* Nothing could be more expressive of the enthusiastic determination of the North to maintain its inherited free institutions, than the sudden and universal popularity of this anonymous song.

Shame on any citizen, in these times, who has not a mind too patriotic for partisan strife ! shame on any nominal Christian who has not a heart too large for sectarian controversy ! I believe *to-day* is not the day for any discussion, but how best we can save our country and save souls ; that among citizens there are only two classes, — patriots and traitors ; among believers, only two classes also, — those who love God and Christ and man, and those who love them not. This love of the Father and his Son and our brother man, — *this* is the 'threefold cord which cannot be broken '; for it is vital *religion*, — the bond which connects the soul of man to his God, and with all that is goodly or may be made such.

"Every Sabbath, I now preach in the morning at the Hygeia Hospital, just outside the fortress, where I have been appointed as chaplain *pro tem.;* and in the afternoon, in the encampment of my own regiment, whose service I never make subordinate to any other.duty. The attendance by the regiment is nearly, if not quite universal, and a more quiet, decorous congregation I would not ask. The men are mustered into their respective companies, and, led by'their officers, march to the parade-ground, where they form a hollow square. In the centre a rude platform is erected, on which the chaplain stands. The officers and soldiers are generally furnished, by the liberality of the Unitarian Association, with the Army Melodies, from which they sing. These simple and cheerful strains are better adapted to the soldier than any more formal tunes. They evidently enjoy them ; and from every tent, at night, you will hear the soldiers singing 'Homeward Bound,' 'Joyfully,' 'Freedom's Era,' 'The Star-Spangled Banner,' 'We are Marching On,' etc. Nothing is more refining and elevating, nothing more *religious* in its tendency, than good music, when accompanying patriotic or devout words; at least, this has been my experience among the soldiers here and at the hospital, and in other regiments with whom it has been my fortune to come in contact.

"But the instrumentality which at present seems most potent for good, is the social conference and prayer meeting. This is held in front of my tent every evening, and is as orderly, and *more* numerously attended than any vestry-meeting in New England.

"We conduct it rather differently from any other with which I am acquainted. The first half-hour is devoted to hearing from the chaplain an account of what is going on in the great world from which we are comparatively isolated. Few soldiers can afford to take any daily papers, or buy those which occasionally are brought to our camp. It seems to me a part of my duty to inform them of any items which come to my knowledge, whether of a national or literary nature. Above all, any news from dear old Massachusetts, and best-beloved Middlesex County, where our homes are, is welcome indeed. Then we spend about ten minutes in conversation as to topics upon which the chaplain can give counsel, — how the soldier can safely transmit money to wife or mother, how break himself of a habit of profanity, or any one of a hundred questions he desires to ask. Perhaps he wants to tell, himself, some news from the quiet town from whence he and his company come. After these few minutes' talk are over, there is a decorous silence, broken at last by the voice of prayer; and then an hour is spent in prayer and conference, and in frequent singing of familiar hymns from the Melodies. Both officers and soldiers participate in these meetings, several of the captains and lieutenants being members of churches."

The discomfort at first experienced from lack of a place of worship was soon obviated. The Chaplain writes : —

"Our friends in Boston have just sent to me a beautiful chapel-tent for religious services. It is to be dedicated next

Sunday, and the various regimental and naval chaplains in this vicinity are to take part in the services. The soldiers are preparing wreaths of the holly, with its ruby berries, and live-oak, with its brilliant leaf and delicate acorns. Bouquets of tea-roses, and other flowers still blooming here in the open air, will also grace the tent on this occasion. I have felt that, being set apart for sacred uses, it should be consecrated by a regular dedication service. I assure you that no congregation ever felt more grateful than my army congregation, that they have now a place of shelter from rain or heat or cold, or the unwholesome evening air. We shall not usually need it for day-services while the weather is as pleasant as now; but it will grow colder; the chilly sea-winds will soon sweep over this exposed Point Comfort, and our evening prayer-meetings were already impracticable till this tent came."

This chapel-tent, which the Chaplain, in a home letter, calls "his pride and his joy," was the first Lord's tabernacle pitched among the army tents during the war of the Rebellion, and it was suitably consecrated with exercises which the Chaplain thus describes : —

"Yesterday was a noteworthy day with the Sixteenth Massachusetts Regiment, for on it we dedicated our beautiful tabernacle tent. This tent was presented to us by various patriotic and benevolent citizens of Boston, who desire that religious services may not necessarily be suspended during the sultry heat of summer, or during the fall of the rain, so copious in Virginia, and that our evening prayer and temperance meetings may not necessarily be held in the open air. The subscriptions were secured by a most excellent lady, and she receives the grateful acknowledgments of our entire regiment. The day of dedication was also Forefathers' Day (Dec. 22), which was very appropriate for a Massachusetts regiment, having their tabernacle in the wilderness, as did their fathers. The presence of Hon. Charles R. Train, Representative in Congress from that district of our State from which the entire regiment comes, was most opportune. As his stay could only be for a few hours, and the dedication of an army tent is a patriotic as well as religious occasion, our chaplain cordially invited him to make one of the addresses, which he did in a most eloquent and acceptable manner, and in a spirit every way appropriate to the solemn service.

" Both army and navy chaplains participated in the exercises. The chaplains were representatives of nearly every sect, including Roman Catholic, but there was entire harmony, and a sweet blending of devout sentiment and Christian, patriotic utterance. Chaplains from North and South East and West, were there, and from sea and shore, yet no discordant note was uttered. The tabernacle tent was trimmed with holly and live-oak wreaths and crosses, made by the soldiers with a taste which would have surprised our female friends. The ladies of the Hygeia Hospital, who were present, contributed a beautiful cross of mingled evergreen and flowers. Our regimental band played the ' Star-Spangled Banner' admirably, and the regimental choir sang the hymns written for the occasion in a manner which elicited, as it deserved, much praise. Rev. Mr. Fuller's dedication discourse was founded on the text in Isaiah iv. 6, — ' And there shall be a tabernacle, for a shadow in the daytime from the heat, and for a place of refuge and for a covert from storm and rain.' " *

* The hymns for the dedication are in a vein suited to the occasion. The first is from the pen of Dr. O. Evarts, Surgeon of the Twentieth Indiana Regiment.

" From home and kindred far away,
    Upon this soil we bend the knee,
And, from the midst of war's array,
    Thy children still, — we look to Thee !

The house of worship having been obtained, an
army church was organized.

"An Army Christian Association has been formed in the
Sixteenth Massachusetts Regiment, at Camp Hamilton, near
the fortress, which promises most beneficent results. It supplies the place of our parish and church organizations at
home, and gives the chaplain of the regiment some reliable
coadjutors in his religious duties. The members of churches
scattered throughout a regiment find some nucleus about
which they can rally, and thus become identified as Christian
disciples. Soldiers also longing to break from the thraldom
of sin, and feeling as never before the need of being Christians, find here a home and sympathy and loving watch-care.
I look upon it as the most important movement of a moral
and religious nature yet inaugurated in the regiment. It
receives not only professing Christians into its fold, but
all who desire to be guided by Christian principles; nor is

> "No love of self, no lust of power,
>   Nor greed of gold, hath brought us here;
> But, in thine own good time and hour,
>   We come to see thy light appear.
>
> "Let ' use,' not ' fame,' inspire our arms,
>   And our first love be love for Thee!
> That Freedom, with her heavenly charms,
>   May make us, also, truly free!
>
> "And when, O Father, over all!
>   Nor in this tent, — nor in this field, —
> In life's great battle we shall fall,
>   O bear us off upon thy shield!"

The following was also written for the occasion: —

> "To Christians in New England homes,
>   Where sons of pilgrims love to dwell,
> Once more the ancient summons comes,
>   ' Up to your tents, O Israel!'
>
> "We come, but trust not princes, Lord,
>   Nor arm of flesh, nor human skill;

it restricted in membership to any sect or to Protestants, but welcomes all who desire to be guided by duty and acknowledge fealty to the law of God. It may lead to a church organization ultimately; but if so, its basis must be equally simple and truly liberal. This is no place for the building up of any sect or combination of sects, but for the upbuilding of the kingdom of the Redeemer in the hearts of all who desire to be soldiers of Jesus Christ while soldiers in the American army."

Nor was this church inactive. The Chaplain writes:—

"On Tuesday evening we have a meeting for prayer and counsel. It is conducted just like our church and class meetings at home, only, thank God! we know no name but the all-prevailing one of Jesus, the divine and ever-blessed Redeemer. It is under the special care of a most excellent soldier, J. A. Smith, who is a local Methodist preacher, and untiring in his religious efforts here.

> With faith we lean upon thy word,
> The counsels of thy holy will!
>
> " For thy pavilion, Lord of hosts!
> We pitch the chief tent of the field;
> Thy leadership the army boasts,
> And trusts thee more than sword or shield!
>
> " Here, in thy temple, still thou art,
> Where voices in devotion rise,
> Hymned with the melody of heart,
> To own and bless the sacrifice!
>
> " Throughout the camp may earnest heed
> To truth, here uttered, be bestowed!
> For none so much as soldiers need
> To lean upon the arm of God!
>
> " ' How amiable, Lord of hosts,
> Thy tabernacle!' shall exclaim
> The soul that in salvation boasts,
> Adoring here God's holy name! "

"The chaplain finds in these brethren noble coadjutors, and desires they should have full and ample credit for their aid. They ask no such praise, yet they most thoroughly deserve it. But for their hearty and earnest co-operation little could have been accomplished for the spiritual welfare of the soldiery. This Tuesday evening meeting is especially valuable to strengthen the hearts of Christians and prevent their becoming weary in well-doing, or being tempted to desert the ranks of the army of the living God, and enlisting in the service of sin, whose bitter, hard-earned wages are spiritual death. Away from home and home influence, that man is arrogant indeed who believes he stands so firm that he is in no danger of falling if he neglect to seek loving, fraternal watch-care, and Christian sympathy."

The tabernacle worship was not without musical aid. The Chaplain says : —

"A choir has been formed in the regiment, composed of officers and soldiers, for conducting the musical services of the sanctuary on the Sabbath, and at our other meetings. It is duly organized by the choice of chorister and organist and the assignment of the regular parts of music. I say *organist*, for we have at present a very sweet-toned melodeon, which formerly belonged to a secessionist young lady at the Hampton Female Seminary, and has been kindly loaned us for a few weeks by the military authorities."

The Chaplain congratulates the Old Dominion upon the introduction of the New England system of free schools.

"The American army, especially the Massachusetts soldiery, are fast transplanting Northern ideas and New England institutions to the sacred soil of Virginia. They will flourish well here, we doubt not, unless overshadowed by the Upas-tree of slavery, beneath whose poisonous shadow every good and Christian plant sickens, and ultimately must die, except the axe be laid at the root of that tree, and it 'be hewn down and cast into the fire.' This week we commenced a school in the chapel-tent of the Sixteenth Massachusetts Regiment, under the superintendence of the chaplain of the regiment, assisted by five competent teachers selected by him from among the non-commissioned officers and private soldiers. As its tuition is absolutely free to all who attend it, it may certainly be denominated a free school, and, so far as the writer knows, is the first entirely free school in Virginia, with the exception of those established for the contrabands here. God grant that this New England plant may take root and thrive !

" We have scholars in all the primary branches, — in writing, — in fine, just the same branches are taught as in the common district schools of New England."

The Chaplain also organized a Soldiers' Teachers' Association, whose objects are thus set forth : —

" The teachers who have in charge the regimental school feel the need of unity of plan and counsel, and to compare and agree upon methods of instruction together. They, therefore, are to hold meetings every Friday evening for these purposes, at the tent or 'log-cabin' of the chaplain. It is my intention, in some future letter, to give the names of those non-commissioned officers and private soldiers, who so nobly devote themselves to instructing their fellow-soldiers, with no reward but the pleasure of doing good. Lest it should be thought strange that so many could be found in a Massachusetts regiment who need primary-school instruction, it ought to be mentioned that all, or nearly all, the scholars are of foreign parentage, and have not had early advantages, through no fault of their own.

" They are earnest for knowledge, and though a holiday was

given yesterday, because of the illness of the chaplain, and no school is regularly held on Saturday, the men declined the holiday, and the school was continued both yesterday and on Saturday, by the assistant teachers, at the urgent request of the men. There has not yet been a single instance of insubordination or disrespectful word or look on the part of these earnest scholars, who, though uncultured, desire strongly improvement, and are deeply grateful for the opportunity afforded them. God bless them and their noble soldier-teachers!"

The true New-Englander, though duty may call him to don the martial garb and repair to the tented field, yet does not leave his religion behind him, and cherishes still the emblems of its continued presence and power. The hallowed chime of the home Sabbath bells cannot indeed be heard, but the sacred day is re-membered; The Chaplain thus alludes to its observ-ance : —

" Yesterday was even more than usually a hard-working day with me. The idea of rest for the clergy on the Sabbath is certainly obsolete. I held two services with my own regi-ment in their chapel-tent, and then, by request of the First Delaware Regiment, preached in their encampment to a kind and attentive audience. It seemed a little singular to me to be invited to preach to a congregation all of them from a slaveholding State, and many of them slaveholders, and none of them Unitarians. It certainly is not because my views of State policy or Christian truth are unknown here, though I am no partisan or sectarian anywhere. The chap-lain of this regiment, an Old-School Presbyterian, is now absent; and I understand it was at his suggestion the invita-tion was given me. I enjoyed much the occasion. On my way thither, I was requested to visit a dying soldier in the hospital of the Ninety-ninth New York Regiment (Naval Brigade). It was a sad, sad sight, — that young man dying far away from home! Yet the kind attentions of every soldier present, and their sympathy with the sufferer, must have soothed him, and also his parents, could they know of it, when tidings reach them that their son's last battle is fought."

The Pilgrim days of Fast and Thanksgiving were also duly honored. Of the former the Chaplain writes : —

" This was solemnly observed in our regiment. Indeed, the day seemed more like Sabbath than almost any since we left home. At ten o'clock in the morning a discourse was preached to the attentive congregation of soldiery by the chaplain of the regiment. His text was Isaiah lviii. 5, 6, and he dealt frankly with sins individual and national, pointing out the only remedy in *forsaking* as well as repenting of them. God will judge our nation till we do righteousness and ' break every yoke and let the oppressed go free.' This is the part he requires at our hands. But we must be patient and bide his time, assured that it will come."

Thanksgiving, too, was gratefully observed, though a shadow rested on the feast. The Chaplain writes : —

" A few weeks since, I recollect hearing a person of somewhat despondent turn of mind remarking that 'governors must have hard work writing their proclamations for Thanksgiving this year,' as our country had met with little else than reverses, and these must cause suffering in every loyal State, while Massachusetts particularly had been called to mourn many of her most loyal and brave officers and soldiers, either perishing on the battle-field or pining in rebel prisons. Then came Governor Andrew's proclamation, answering bravely all this sceptical and ungrateful feeling, which existed in more hearts than one. · I think it the best Thanksgiving proclamation I ever read, — so noble, so heroic, so pre-eminently *Christian.* And yet that proclamation was written while we were still smarting beneath defeat, and Massachusetts herself bleeding at every pore as a result of the repulse at Ball's Bluff. But now the scene has changed. The winter of our discontent has become glorious summer again, and the most short-sighted of mortals can recognize the loving hand of God stretched forth to save this Israel. Truly we see now causes for devout, joyous, yet solemn thanksgiving. And we Massachusetts soldiers are to observe our State Thanksgiving also. Yesterday the chaplain read at divine service the Governor's proclamation, and announced that he should hold services next Thursday morning, and preach a sermon appropriate to the occasion, in accordance with regular Massachusetts usage.

"And yet our friends must not blame us if our Thanksgiving has its cloud as well as sunshine, and we cannot be merry as in bygone days. Perhaps this will be more in unison with the purpose of the day than has been the former method of its observance by many of us. *We are away from home,* and we shall feel the fact more on that day than any other of the whole year. The sweet voices which have been the music of our dwellings will not fill our tents and our hearts with melody; the smiles of loving wives and children, which have been our sunshine, will not gleam on our pathway. Yes, we shall have sad as well as joyful hours here next Thursday, and beneath the rose of happiness will be the wounding thorn of pain. And will they not miss us at home, too? O, how many vacant chairs in the domestic circles! It is not because we do not love our homes and the dear inmates, that we are absent, but because we *do* love them so strongly as to be willing to peril life in their defence.

And then, too, we shall think of our many brave soldier-brothers who have offered life upon their country's altar, and of Massachusetts homes, O so many! where the places recently vacated will never be filled again by the noble men who once occupied them. Ah, well! our harp of Thanksgiving will have its chords of solemn and sad as well as of joyous strain, and our day of rejoicing may know not only the sunshine of smiles, but a few rain-drops of tears in private, which we hope are not unmanly. Yet God bids us be glad, and truly has he given us rich and abundant cause for gratitude. We may soon meet again those friends who are in our earthly homes; and those brave brothers who have died so gloriously for their country, we, if faithful, shall surely meet *them* in the home which is heavenly, and on that day whose thanksgiving shall be eternal."

In his religious labors the Chaplain fully appreciated the aid of the Bible and Tract. To the American Bible Society he writes: —

" The liberal provision made by your society for the supply of religious reading to the regiment of which I am in charge as chaplain entitles you to some account of the distribution of these ' leaves for the healing of the nations'; and certainly most of the leaves of your books do grow on ' the Tree of Life,' judging by those which I have received from your depository. I am not of the same denomination with yourself, as you are aware, being a clergyman of the Unitarian household of faith; but I most cheerfully bid ' God speed' to your society in its holy work.

" Is it not one blessed result of this present strife for freedom and righteousness, that different religious sects can thus co-operate together in the warfare against sin, as divisions in the army of the living God, just as different regiments in the army of our country, can strive side by side against treason and rebellion?

"Our Catholic soldiers receive and read the Bible most cheerfully, as a general rule. I do not seek to proselyte them, thinking it would be wrong in the position I occupy, but I do endeavor to aid them in the religious inquiries which naturally arise in their minds, and in that work 'the word of God is quick and powerful.'

"I thank God, too, that your society does not blink the great question of the inalienable rights of man. God bless all who 'remember those who are in bonds as bound with them,' and may He 'who maketh the wrath of the heathen to praise him,' bring out of this fearful but holy strife that noble era when 'the sun shall not rise on a master or set on a slave.'"

Again he says : —

"Whatever new inventions there may be of warlike weapons and implements offensive and defensive, the Old Bay State believes that the shield of faith and helmet of salvation and breastplate of righteousness can never be supplanted, and that *no* man is thoroughly furnished for our country's defence without these and the Spirit's sword.

"Company K of my regiment were presented each man with a Bible by the Methodist Church in Watertown, Massachusetts, before leaving home, and though many were Catholics, yet no man refused the gift. The Massachusetts Bible Society have donated about five hundred Bibles and Testaments in addition, all of which bear the imprint of the American Bible Society. They have all been called for, and, with those given as parting gifts by wives and mothers, there can be but few in this regiment not now supplied, and I know *many*, very many, would on a march part with every other book, or even much clothing, sooner than leave behind their Bible. If the knapsack be too full to hold it, why then the owner would wear it in his bosom to shield in the day of battle the heart its divine truths had first purified.

"In two of our companies, probably the majority are professing Christians, and are here as actively engaged, as the rules of camp life will permit, in organizing Sabbath schools among the contrabands and poor whites in this region."

Nor was that cause forgotten which not only results from, but clears the way for, true religion, and which the Chaplain had loved from childhood, — temperance. We have the following account of it.

"We celebrated the close of the year 1861 by forming in the Sixteenth Massachusetts Regiment a Division of the Sons of Temperance. At an early hour the new chapel-tent of the regiment was filled to overflowing with soldiers eager to listen to an exposition of the principles of the organization, and to unite in the movement, if it commended itself to their judgment. Over one hundred officers and soldiers were proposed for initiation. Authority had been received by the chaplain from the Grand Division of Massachusetts to organize this Division, which is to embrace not only soldiers of this regiment, but Massachusetts men connected with other regiments at or near Camp Hamilton, or with the naval vessels lying off the fortress. The *per capita* tax on divisions connected with the army has been kindly remitted by the Grand Division. Great need is felt of regalia for officers and members of these divisions.* The Grand Division have permitted their operations as army divisions without this paraphernalia, but none more than soldiers, accustomed to uniforms, would so much appreciate and value regalia, and yet, away from home and with scanty means, it would be impossible for them to procure them. The temperance movement among soldiers deserves the encouragement, not only of professed temperance men, but of all who have at heart the moral welfare or wholesome discipline of the

* These were soon afterwards generously furnished by the home organizations.

9   M

army. The organization in this regiment is not intended
to supersede the old-fashioned total-abstinence society which
has been already organized, and is efficiently working, but
to aid its movements. Public meetings for addresses, &c.,
will continue to be held, and in the division the members
will be encouraged to literary efforts, and the exercises
will be diversified with recitations, essays, declamations,
and discussions which would be impracticable in a general
meeting, but will be of great intellectual and moral value
to the soldiers. We need some wholesome recreation and
intellectual and moral stimulus in the army, deprived as
we are of those enjoyed at home."

The Chaplain had some trials connected with his
army work, one of which had to do with this very subject of temperance. He was a staff officer, and his
comrades, as also other officers he met, regarded the cup
as a pledge of good-will, and the rejection of the social
glass as an indication of coldness or dislike. Besides,
such of them as were without religion were especially
pleased to see a chaplain disregard those rules of self-
denial which might have been at home a necessity of
the profession. A complimentary dinner, given to the
Colonel, was the occasion of a trial of the Chaplain's
temperance principles. As the pledges were drunk,
each officer in turn, and all in chorus, in vain urged
the Chaplain not to refuse the social proof of good-
will. At length, however, when the affair was becoming unpleasant to all parties, the Colonel rapped
on the table, and requested three cheers for the Chaplain, "a man whom we all honor the more, because,
in public and private, uniformly consistent with his
principles."

He had an earlier trial, of a different sort, in connection with the officers' mess. As an army chaplain
has almost no secular duties assigned to him by the
army regulations, advantage is sometimes taken of his
obliging temper. Of one clergyman an officer remarked, " his preaching is not of much account, but
he is so convenient to do errands ! " Of Chaplain
Fuller, it was expected that he should provide the
officers' mess. This he found would take up so much
of his time that he could not discharge those religious
duties which had led him on his army mission. He
therefore wrote a letter to the Colonel declining, for
these reasons, the care of the mess, citing the words
of the Apostles (Acts vi. 2), "It is not reason that
we should leave the word of God and serve tables."
This affair caused a coldness for a while on the part of
the Colonel, which was, however, dissipated upon longer
acquaintance, and gave place to mutual appreciation.
One of the last regulations the Colonel established,
before his death in the Peninsular campaign, was a
prohibition of profanity in the regiment.

Among the coincidences between the chaplaincy at
the fortress and the pastorate, we must not forget the
army *Parsonage !* The Chaplain thus describes it : —

" I hope it is with no feeling of undue pride that I announce myself as a householder and house-owner here in the
Old Dominion. Candor requires me to state, however, that
said house consists of rude, unhewn logs, with a chimney,
built of old bricks, in one end thereof, and a roof of boards,
with only the cracks between shingled. It boasts, however, a
window, made of a sash from a secessionist's house at Hampton, the broken panes being supplied with glass somewhat

too large, but kept in place with tacks. The American flag serves as a curtain to this window, the rebel relic and the patriotic bunting not having quarrelled yet. Several of the panes in the secession window are in the same condition as the former owner's brain, — a little *cracked;* still it serves well enough its purpose. My tent adjoins, and in that is my kitchen, with its camp cooking-stove ; while the 'shanty' room, with the 'fly' of the tent over it as a roof, makes a good reception-room, or will do so if the weather is ever pleasant again. Its walls are covered with pictures from Harper's Weekly and Leslie's Illustrated, which please my soldier visitors, and occupy their attention, if obliged to wait a short time before seeing me. This mongrel tent-shanty and log-cabin would certainly be scorned as a home or laughed at in New England, but it is by no means despicable here. A description of it may convey some idea to your readers of how we soldiers manage to live in Virginia, away from home comforts and luxuries. With the exception of the price of a few boards, my habitation has at least the merit of being an inexpensive building, having cost nothing but the labor of building, kindly contributed by the soldiers of my army-congregation. They call it the 'Parsonage,' and so I adopt that name. It is in close and convenient proximity to the chapel-tent."

Again he writes home : — .

" David * is beautifying about my house, setting out stately cypress and blooming plum and apple trees, besides currant-bushes and flowers. A large number of soldiers have volun-

---

* David Orr, whom the Chaplain, writing from his fortress island, calls his good man Friday, was one of those God sent from every condition in life to minister to and strengthen the pastor and chaplain in his pilgrimage. They were like angels to him, except that they were not few nor far between. Of David Orr he says, " He labors for me a great deal, and will accept no compensation." At another time, he writes, " The comfort of my life, David Orr, my good soldier-friend, accompanies me."

teered,. and are making paths covered with beach-sand of pure white. Stars and circles cut in the sod of emerald green show their ingenuity, and my log-cabin promises to be very lovely. A tea-rose is put before each window as a sort of screen or curtain, and they grow so luxuriantly here as to promise the best possible results in an artistic point of view."

He adds : —

"I always have two bouquets of tea-roses and other deli-cate flowers for my room and for the table, and occasionally a ripe fig fresh from the tree."

In a home letter he further refers to the Parson-age : —

"It does seem cheerless when returning at eventide to find, not my home and my wife, but only my tent and servant-boy. O those returns to what should be home! It is then that the sense of loneliness creeps over the heart, and, for a moment, love seems to triumph over patriotism, and we sigh for home. But, look about you! My humble tent has been boarded, and is to be papered. An underground brick furnace of curious construction removes cold and dampness. A table lighted with candles gladdens the heart, for on it are letters from my wife and dear memorials of darling children and of many loved ones at home, while all about the tent are kindly faces of soldiers who love me, and some of whom would, I verily believe, die for me. Ah! I have *a* home, if a humble one, and it is a dear one, too, if *another* in New England be dearer!"

His attachment to the soldiers was quite as strong as theirs to him. He writes : "Money would not induce me to go back and leave my regiment. My heart is in my work here. I am doing good, and that pays for all."

And soon the Christian reaper began to receive wages. He writes: "There is much religious interest in my regiment. I should not be surprised if it resulted in a true revival of religion."

The expanded circle of sympathy and love could not supplant the home affection. Nor could his adult "boys" (as he always styled his fellow-soldiers) make him forget the little ones who always drew his heart. He writes from his island tent: —

"Believe me, I cannot forget one flower of affection strewn along my pathway, nor a word spoken in season, of counsel or love. Little F.'s letter is one of those flowers, and from little G.'s shell, which I hold to my ear as she desired, I hear a mystic song of sweetness. Thanks for the flower and shell, flung by loving little hands on this margin of the sounding sea."

The Chaplain's labors were by no means confined to his regimental parish. While he was careful to do this, his first and nearest duty, he was anxious. not to leave the more remote undone. In this exterior province he was especially interested in the contrabands. He thus refers to a

"class whom we meet within the fortress, on the exchange, in the encampment, everywhere, for their name is legion. These are the 'contrabands,' the fugitive slaves of rebel masters. Now we may trust they are free from oppression, and that from their limbs the chains, and from their minds and spirits the shackles, have fallen forever. To-day these are not slaves, they are men ; and it must not be forgotten that General Butler first argued for their reception and protection from pursuit, and giving to them honorable employment and treatment, such as is due to all human beings.

" I can well believe, however, that the question what to do with them embarrasses the government. Here are two thousand and two hundred men, women, and children thrown on its guardianship. They impress me as a remarkably intelligent class of Africans ; probably only the smartest and most intelligent have the energy to escape from bondage, or the shrewdness to accomplish it. I have seen much of them, and taken great pains to ascertain their condition.

" I have attended several of their religious meetings. My friend, Chaplain Lockwood, now takes the guidance of them, ·by authority from General Wool. They are a little more demonstrative than I am accustomed to or suits my taste, but, for men and women so ignorant, less objectionable on this score than could be expected ; and often these former slaves possess a rude and simple eloquence which is most affecting. On Sabbath last, together with Brother Lockwood, we performed the marriage service for some ten or twelve couples, at the African meeting-house, who desired this sacred service to sanction their domestic union, and which service their former masters had either forbidden or declared unnecessary for slaves.

" Many of these ignorant and heretofore deeply injured people are now desirous of learning to read. It would touch any kindly heart to see how eagerly the poor creatures crave knowledge, which they feel to be essential to any progress for them as individuals or as men. By the laws of Virginia, to teach a slave or a free colored person to read is a crime, but one I would love to commit every day of my life.

" The other day I attended a funeral of one of their number. The African loves form, and here there was much of it, but nothing absurd, as I had been led to fear. They chanted many of their plantation religious songs. O, they were so mournful, so despairing (who wonders at that ?) in their view of this life; but they changed to wild pæans when they spoke of an immortal state. The number present was very large, and they were very much moved; for the negro is, beyond all others, an affectionate race, and death touches each sympathetic chord in his feeling heart. But with all the demonstration of woe which was made, not one note, not one word or deed, of those poor, ignorant, neglected, oppressed people was discordant to good taste or feeling."

In another connection he says : —

"I have talked with many of them, and am confirmed daily in my faith that no genuine man, white or black, was ever satisfied with slavery, and that the normal condition of every race and individual is *freedom*. Their situation here is now much improved, and benevolence is doing much for their welfare, while the authorities are not negligent of their comfort.

"However sad this war may have made many of us, it certainly has brought, and must yet bring, much blessing to the oppressed and enslaved African. These three thousand at and near the fortress, who by the war have been made FREE, — they indeed may and should fill the air with songs of solemn thanksgiving. And they do rejoice, but not with noisy hilarity. They come together rather with prayer for the diffusion yet more widely of the boon of freedom. Yesterday, though a holiday and a day of unutterable gladness to this long-suffering people, I saw not one colored person intoxicated, nor heard of one in that condition."

Again, referring to the contrabands, he writes : —

"Every day brings fresh arrivals of these fugitives from bondage. As the enemy withdraws, a portion of his property is destroyed by fire, and thus takes to itself wings of smoke and flame and flies away, and other 'property,' household chattels, takes to itself legs, and runs off to the fortress as fast as possible. Ungrateful beings, to desert masters and mistresses who have been so kind, and to leave a state of servitude which South-Side clergymen declare to be almost Elysium! What ignorant fools, to prefer freedom to slavery!

"And here let me contradict a report, that the contrabands in this region are unwilling to work, and have many of them run back to their masters. Both statements involved in this report are untrue. The contrabands are, as a general thing, willing to labor, though complaining much that the government does not pay them wages, as they had been led to expect. But I speak from personal observation, when I say they are anxious for any employment reasonably remunerative. My tent-door has been besieged with applications from boys and men desiring to be servants. I was over-persuaded, at last, to take a contraband youth into my service for a few days, who proved diligent, faithful, and industrious beyond my expectations. I had engaged another servant for the place, who yesterday arrived; but I have seen enough of this poor African lad to know that some of his race, at least, are skilful, truthful, and energetic. On board the United States flag-ship Minnesota, there is a boat's crew of contrabands. I was assured by one of the officers the other day, when visiting the frigate, that this crew excelled in fidelity, and was the only one which needed not an officer to accompany them when they went ashore, as not a man of them would get drunk or desert.

"As to their returning to rebeldom, it would not have been a matter of surprise if some few of a race proverbially affectionate had returned to their former homes and masters (no doubt some of them kind ones), and, above all, to their kindred left behind when they fled; but, after thorough inquiry, I cannot hear of one such instance, and am assured, by those who are in a position to know, that not one such case has occurred. I have been thus particular in this refu-

9*

tation, because here the colored race are being tested as to their desire for freedom and adaptedness to it. The question is one which must and will soon interest the whole nation, and a decision cannot long be postponed."

He gives an instance of service rendered by the contrabands : —

"The Sixteenth were paid off a day or two since, but I question whether that agreeable incident gave them as much pleasure as an exploit by Company F of this regiment, under Captain C. R. Johnson, of Lexington. This energetic company were on picket-guard a few nights since, when some slaves (ever our friends and the friends of the Union, when that is understood to mean freedom) gave notice that two rebel spies were about Fox Hill, near our pickets. A patrol was sent promptly out, consisting of only four men, under the command of Sergeant Morris, the two slaves acting as guides. The patrol force proceeded under this guidance to the house of a Mr. Topping, who has heretofore made loud pretensions of Union and loyal sentiments, has taken with the utmost cheerfulness the oath of allegiance, and had a pass and protection from the federal military authorities, yet nevertheless has been a traitorous spy, and actually in the service of the rebel army as their sutler.

"He has been in the habit of procuring gold here, and exchanging it for Confederate bonds for a high premium. He has also procured other supplies, especially *information*, of which the rebels have always stood, and still do stand, in great need, though not of the sort Mr. Topping has given them. On arriving at the house, Mrs. Topping assured Sergeant Morris that her husband was not at home, which fashionable announcement our soldiers declined believing. She protested ' on her honor as a Southern lady' that he was not in the house, but absent in the rebel service, and she ' had

not seen him for three months,' but Sergeant Morris dis-
trusted the lady's eyesight and word, rather than that of the
whilom slaves who acted as guides.

"After search, the sutler was found attempting to go 'on
tick,' in spite of our boys' declaration of 'no trust,' which a
sutler ought to understand. In other words, he was found
by our distrustful soldiers snugly ensconced between two
bed-ticks, whence he was rather roughly dragged forth by
Sergeant Morris. Subsequent search revealed his pocket-
book, containing several confederate bonds, several rebel
passes, and his 'protection,' now outlawed."

And here follows a picture of a woman of the despised race : —

"Do any of your readers remember my writing, a while
since, about a noble and gifted colored woman in this neighborhood, Mrs. Peak, and her sweet little daughter, called by
the soldiers 'little Daisy'? Mrs. Peak, her husband and
child, would scarcely be known as colored persons, being
almost white, and the child having blue eyes and long, flowing brown hair.

"Mrs. Peak has nearly all her life been a teacher. She
was an accomplished scholar, and possessed a singularly gifted
mind, and all her talents she devoted, unselfishly, to the elevation of her own race. She might have easily separated herself from them; she was free-born, and though her husband
had been a slave, he had years since purchased his freedom,
-and, by his industry and her exertions, had earned a goodly
property, so that, before the fire at Hampton, he owned two
houses and several thousand dollars. All was lost by that
rebel incendiary conflagration. But she refused to separate
herself from the race with whom she acknowledged kindred
blood, which, though slight in her *veins*, was never forgotten
in her *heart*. She established a school here for the ' contra-

bands,' the first of its kind; she devoted herself to gratuitous teaching, and doing this in a cold room, the best her means could procure, soon became sick; consumptive symptoms were aggravated, and she was confined to her bed. Even there and then she taught the poor colored children. But her end was near.

"At midnight, Sunday, the cry, 'Twelve o'clock and all 's well!' came over the waters from every naval vessel in our harbor. It was 'all well' with Mrs. Peak then, for at that moment she breathed her last sigh, felt her last throb of pain, and 'passed on' from midnight's gloom of earth to the high noon of radiant Heaven. I saw and prayed with her on the last day of life. That day was as calm, as holy and happy, as any of her earthly days could ever have been. She loved to sing, and sung then, 'Homeward Bound,' and 'There is rest for the weary,' tunes which our soldiers sing from the Army Melodies, and the contrabands are not slow in learning and applying in their own hours of sorrow. Mrs. Peak was a remarkable woman, irrespective of her race, and deserves to be ever remembered. Like Moses of old, she refused to be separated from her despised and enslaved people, or to be exempt from their trials; and chose rather to suffer afflic-tion with them than to enjoy worldly pleasure."

Chaplain Fuller was glad to mingle his services with those of the noble philanthropists, who, by caring for the sick and wounded soldier, have won fadeless lau-rels, if not of earthly honor, at least of that heavenly fame, which

> "lives and spreads aloft in those pure eyes,
> And perfect witness of all-judging Jove,
> As he pronounces lastly on each deed."

He says of the Hygeia Hospital: —

"This is admirably conducted under the skilful superintendence of Dr. Cuyler, surgeon in the regular army, and long a resident at the fortress. Here, too, are refined ladies as nurses of the sick, under the appointment secured by Miss Dix, who has been indefatigable in her care of all the army hospitals. Several of the sick soldiers of the Sixteenth Regiment were quartered here, and it seemed good to see a woman's kindly face again, and have her gentle ministry in our weary and painful hours. Here, too, I find many wounded soldiers of the Great Bethel fight, — some Germans, some Americans, and all so patient, so willing to lose life or limb for their native or adopted country, and only mourning that they did not achieve a victory. It is a privilege to visit and pray with such noble men. God bless the wounded soldiers of our patriotic army, and send them always as good care as they get from the physicians and nurses of this hospital at Old Point Comfort. Once this was *the* hotel of Virginia. Here President Buchanan loved to come, not forgetting to bring his ' old rye ' as a companion. In the very room I occupy, and whence I write, Senator Mason, only last year, in the summer, was an occupant. These walls have looked on many a nest of rebels, and listened to many a plot of treason.

" In the beautiful hall, with its splendid mirrors, once the ball-room of the Hygeia Hotel, we held our religious services yesterday. Your correspondent preached from the text, Isaiah xxxiii. 24: 'And the inhabitants shall not say I am sick ; the people that dwell therein shall be forgiven their iniquity.' My effort was to point to the heavenly land and its hopes, as a solace for the trials of this, and to show the sick and wounded soldiery, that if their physical wounds are gained in their country's cause, and are patiently endured ; if, too, they are ' soldiers of the living God,' as well as loyal American soldiers, all such shall ultimately be victors, — ' conquerors though they 're slain,' — and shall dwell forever in that land no one of whose inhabitants need to say, ' I am sick.' "

Again, upon the same topic, he writes : —

" Yesterday was a good day for us, and seemed more than
usual like a Sunday at home. It is not our custom to have
preaching in the morning, as camp duties interfere with it
early, and by ten o'clock A. M. it becomes insufferably hot.
Your correspondent was, therefore, again enabled to hold
services at the Hygeia Hospital, with the sick and wounded
soldiers there. It was a great gratification to find Miss Dix
present, from Washington, who came to the fortress personally to investigate the sanitary condition of our soldiery
in the hospitals and camps. In the afternoon Dr. McCay,
Miss Dix, and the writer visited each of the hospitals, as far
as practicable, and the fine seminary building near Hampton,
which will doubtless be used as a hospital in winter, and
afford most comfortable quarters for the sick. O how
the countenances of the wounded or ill gleamed with gladness as they saw once more a woman's friendly face, and
heard her kindly voice. The soldiers of the Sixteenth, sick
or well, were delighted as she inquired into their wants and
condition. God bless all who seek to comfort and soothe the
suffering among our brave men, and those, too, who tell them
how to avoid illness and make hardship seem light."

After these labors of the day he preached in the
evening to the contrabands.

He also writes to his family from the fortress, that

" the new seminary hospital has just been opened a quarter of
a mile from here. It has six hundred and eighty patients, and
I am the only army chaplain to visit and comfort the poor
fellows. I go almost daily to pray with the sick and dying,
and bury the dead. It is very trying; but I am sustained in
looking on ghastly wounds and pallid faces, and hearing dying
groans. Ah! how serious life looks to me now! I shall
never be very gay again, I think, though always cheerful.

Usefulness, goodness, not happiness, seem to me now the
great objects of existence, and, to make each other nobler
and better, our chief duty."

In connection with the hospitals, he also says : —

" This hospital is admirably conducted at the fortress, so
far as attendance upon the sick is concerned, by the kind and
noble ladies who have charge of that department. Soldiers,
when sick, go there dreading the confinement and treatment,
but soon they learn alike to love and honor the saintly ma-
tron, Mrs. Dulley, and her worthy associates. I do not use
too strong a term when I say *saintly*, for what else is it for
a cultivated and intellectual woman thus to leave home, and
devote herself to the sick and wounded soldiers, receiving but
a poor pittance as wages for the most exacting toil ? I am a
constant visitor of the hospital here, and speak advisedly
when I use these strong words of commendation."

Of Mrs. Dulley he says, in a letter to his wife :
" Next to my mother and sister and Lizzie and you, I
honor her most of the women I have known in real
life." In a published letter he says, that she

" is loved by every soldier who has ever come under her care.
They regard her as a mother, and she could not be more tender, more kindly in her care of her own brave sons, than she
is of these wounded and dying soldiers. I know if this tribute ever meets her eye she will deprecate its praise ; but after
months of viewing her laborious self-sacrifice in a public hospital, and hearing from so many soldiers yet more fervent
words of praise and blessing, I cannot refrain from this testimonial. If ever we have a saints' calendar in our church,
the name of this devoted woman, who so long has toiled
amid sickness and danger and death, must not be forgotten."

Of a death in the hospital of his regiment he writes : —

"A few days since, there died within its limits a young man named James Kavanagh; and a most solemn sight was presented, as his company came to take their last look at their comrade. He was dressed in his soldier's uniform, though his battles are all over. He looked calm and joyous in death, and as if the flag of his country, which draped his coffin, called to his face one glad, loving, triumphant smile. For that flag, and what it symbolizes, he died, as truly as if he had perished on the battle-field, and not of typhoid fever in the hospital. It was touching to see on a table near, unopened letters, directed to him, whose loving words he will never read. Poor James! And yet we cannot pity him, but honor rather the memory of one whose sweet privilege it was to die for his country."

He thus refers to another death : —

"An orderly sergeant of Company H, after calling the roll of his company, went to the hospital, and almost instantly expired. He seemed sleeping in his chair, but on examination he, too, had passed on to answer the solemn roll-call which is ever being responded to by that innumerable company who are constantly hearing the summons of the 'great Captain of our salvation.' Death on the battle-field, — that is sad, though glorious, but death in tent or hospital, with no mother or wife to close the dying eyes, though equally the result of a patriotic performance of duty, that death seems sadder; and a funeral, with no relative to follow the bier, with only the soldierly train, and martial though plaintive music, ah! *that* seems saddest of all. Die when I may, let me be buried at home, and let my dust mingle with that of 'kindred and loved ones.'"

Again he writes home of the Seminary Hospital : —

"We average three funerals a day. Though none of my regiment are in this hospital, and I have no official duty in

connection with it, yet it is without a chaplain, and I cannot
know of such a spot without seeking to do all in my power
for these dear brother-soldiers, suffering, dying, far from
home! O how small seem the trials and hardships which
the majority endure, compared with the sufferings of these
men! I am weary of any plaint from the favored of earth
when I compare their homes and their luxuries with the lot
of the wounded and sick soldiers. The other day I prayed
with and addressed the wounded Vermonters, one hundred in
number, in the seventh ward of the Hygeia Hospital. They
were sweetly patient and bravely cheerful, though many have
lost a limb, and many more will never leave those beds on
which they lie until borne forth to burial in a stranger's and a
soldier's grave, with only a pine head-board, on which their
names are pencilled, to mark their resting-place."

Victory was a potent physician. The Chaplain
says : —

"I visited the hospitals yesterday, and found the wounded
and sick soldiers there so improved that I wondered for
a while what patent elixir they had taken to make them all
feel so much better and make light account of wounds received in their country's service, or of disease which had
laid its hands upon them in her camps, but soon found that
the charmed medicine was a specific and panacea for all
their complaints, and is labelled VICTORY. Ask them what
had wrought the change, and they would tell you that Mill
Spring, Fort Henry, and Roanoke had been their physicians,
till the lame could almost leap for joy, and the most weary
and disease-stricken take up their beds and march forth to
share in further conquests. The released prisoners from
Richmond, whose wounds were too severe to permit them
to go to their homes when landed here, were not among the
least joyous."

In these hospitals the wounded and sick rebel prisoners were nursed as tenderly as Union soldiers, and it was sometimes charged that the former were the most tenderly cared for, in the anxiety of Unionists to heap coals of fire upon the enemy's head, while they evinced also that in their holy war hate was not enlisted and love had not been left at home. The Chaplain often spoke touchingly of sick and wounded rebels, who at first repelled his ministrations, but were generally won over by his kind address. Such was the case of a young officer from South Carolina, who had lost both his legs. As the cots of Union and Rebel soldiers were placed promiscuously, the Chaplain sometimes knew not which he addressed. He was struck with the lustrous dark eyes of the young man, who bore the marks of tender nurture, and to comfort him referred to the reward of the good soldier. "But do you know who I am," said the prostrate youth. "I suppose a Union soldier." "No," the other rejoined, "I belong to a South Carolina company." "Ah!" said the Chaplain, "I grieve for that. Your cause is at best mistaken. But we take no advantage of your position to reproach you. If you have thought you were in the right, may God forgive you!" The scene ended by the youth asking the Chaplain to stoop over and kiss him, while he threw his arms about his neck.

In a published letter on this topic the Chaplain says:

"In the hospital, no surgeon, no chaplain, recognizes any distinction between Unionists and Rebels. Shame were it if we did! Let our national enemies forget humanity if they will, we cannot, we will not, except first we forget the precepts of that blessed Book which, while it sternly declares the necessity of war and bloodshed in sin's remission and the world's progress, yet also demands, as the highest of duties, visiting the sick and imprisoned, feeding our hungry enemy, and the forgiveness of every repentant man. May the North, which has answered so nobly when war's dread clarion sounded, listen also and heed and bless those who on suffering beds are dying for their country, or on them expiating their offence, till we whisper, Father, forgive and bless them all!"

The labors of the Chaplain in the hospital furnish a marked parallel with those of his sister Margaret in Italy, which are thus recounted in a letter of the American Consul, Mr. Lewis Cass, Jr., which has not before been published.

"In the engagements between the Roman and French troops, the wounded of the former were brought into the city and disposed throughout the different hospitals, which were under the superintendence of several ladies of high rank, who had formed themselves into associations, the better to insure care and attention to these unfortunate men. Margaret Fuller took an active part in this noble work, and the greater portion of her time during the entire siege was passed in attendance upon the inmates of the Hospital of the Trinity of the Pilgrims, which was placed under her direction.

" The weather was intensely hot, and her health was feeble and delicate; the dead and dying were around her in every form of pain and horror, yet she never shrank from the duty she had assumed. Her heart and soul were in the cause for which these men had fought, and all was done that woman could do to comfort them in their sufferings. As she moved among the dying, extended upon opposite beds, I have seen their eyes meet in commendation of her unwearied kindness, and the friends of those who there passed away may derive consolation from the assurance that nothing was wanting to soothe their last moments. And I have heard many of those who recovered speak with all the passionate fervor of the Italian nature of her whose sympathy and compassion throughout their long illness fulfilled all the offices of love and affection. Mazzini, the chief of the Triumvirate, often expressed to me his admiration of her high character, and the Princess Belgiojoso, to whom was assigned the charge of the Papal Palace on the Quirinal, which was converted on this occasion into a hospital, was enthusiastic in her praise. And in a letter which I received not long ago from this lady, who is gaining the bread of an exile by teaching languages in Constantinople, she alludes with much feeling to the support afforded by Margaret Fuller to the republican party in Italy. Here, in Rome, she is still spoken of in terms of regard and endearment, and the announcement of her death was received with a degree of sorrow not often bestowed upon a foreigner, and especially one of a different faith."

CHAPTER III.

FORTRESS INCIDENTS : INCLUDING THE CONTEST BETWEEN
THE MERRIMAC AND MONITOR.

" If there be movements in the patriot's soul,
  From source still deeper and of higher worth,
  'T is thine the quickening impulse to control,
  And in due season send the mandate forth;
Thy call a prostrate nation can restore,
When but a single mind resolves to crouch no more."
                    WORDSWORTH, *Ode to Enterprise.*

" And the Philistine said to David, Come to me, and I will give thy flesh unto the
fowls of the air, and to the beasts of the field."

AR'S stern front occasionally had a feature
of pleasantness, and even its desolations
were adorned with a flower. Of the ruins
he writes : —

" I have always felt a desire to journey abroad and behold
the ruins of the Old World. How often we are told that we
have no ruins to make the landscape picturesque, no ' deserted village ' to inspire a Goldsmith's poetic strain. But
this is true no longer of America; alas! sadly untrue will it
be before this desolating war, which rebellion has instituted,
is ended."

From these ruins a practical advantage was also
derived.

" A foray, authorized by the proper officials, has just been made by us upon the ruins of burned Hampton. From them have been brought to our camp boards, stoves, and whatever was needful to preserve our men from suffering, and many a relic of these picturesque ruins and remembrancer of rebel outrage and recklessness will reach in due time our Massachusetts homes. Cruel and wanton was the destruction by Magruder's men of this once thriving and beautiful village; but the deed was done, and those scarred timbers are silent, and many homeless wanderers are eloquent witnesses of the atrocious character of this rebellion.

"Some of the half-melted or burned articles taken from these ruins look singularly like antiques from Herculaneum or Pompeii. I have a portion of the metal of the noted bell which was given to the ancient Episcopal Church at Hampton, long before the separation of our country from Great Britain. Besides this relic, some odd half-melted coins, and books (one more than a century old), I have been permitted to retain as relics."

"Beauty for ashes!" exclaims the chaplain: "such is the prophetic promise of Isaiah, when, 'the spirit of the Lord God being upon him,' he announced the joyous era which was to succeed the then present desolation of Judæa and Jerusalem. I could not but be forcibly reminded of this awhile since, as I trod amid the ruins of Hampton. This once thriving city was burned by the torches of the rebels, and ancient churches, modern school-houses, and once goodly and beautiful dwellings, are now blackened ruins or an indiscriminate mass of ashes beneath the foot of the gazer. As I looked about on these scarred and tottering walls, or the dark and fragmentary mass which strewed the ground, all seemed desolation, and the once fair city is fast becoming a howling wilderness, — a change wrought by traitorous hands. The scene was indescribably mournful. But even there I saw God's promise fulfilled. A beautiful rose, which the fire had not utterly killed, had been made more luxuriant by the ashes heaped around its roots, and was blooming more profusely than it ever could have done before. Yes, — 'beauty for ashes.' The dear God, who loves not desolation and human ruin, — who crowns the most frowning cliff with some coronal of love, — he had made this flower bloom amid that fearful scene of ruin and human wrath, as a token of Divine benignity. Let us accept the omen, and believe that God, from the desolation and ruin of this war, will yet cause the flower of Liberty to bloom and flourish with redoubled splendor. He who shielded that tender shrub amid the tempest of flame, and caused it to rear anew its head, and perfume the air with its fragrance, — nurtured to more radiant beauty by that very storm of human wrath and the ashes of its destructive flames, — he shall shield the tree of Liberty which our fathers planted on these Western shores, even amid these times, when the flames of civil war are carrying desolation in their pathway; and so, when the war is over, and as a result of the war, gazing nations shall find that tree blooming with more than its pristine beauty, above the ashes of our battle-fields, and sending even a holier perfume upward, as incense of gratitude to Heaven."

The buried ruins of humanity, too, Nature's fair hand forgot not to decorate. The Chaplain says of the fortress cemetery: —

"We turned at last from our toilsome but interesting ride on the sandy shore into a path which led through the woods. How changed the scene! At the entrance was the picket-guard, looking picturesque in their house of boughs, or beneath the pines, with their rifles stacked near and ready for use at a moment's warning. That ride through the Virginia forest we shall long remember. The live-oak abounded, with its brilliant green leaf. It was twined and wreathed

with many a vine, lending it grace and charm in return
for the support its strength afforded. There, too, stood the
holly-tree, with its splendor of clustered berries, making it
seem decked with rubies from the crown to the very skirt
of its green robe of leaves. Riding on, we soon came to a
paling, and there, within, were many graves of soldiers who
have died near or in the fortress, in past years, or in this
eventful one, so soon to be numbered with the past. The
cemetery is in a little pine grove, and the lofty trees seemed
sighing a sad yet noble requiem over the graves of the
soldiers. Ah, well! by the side of most of these graves
wife or mother never stood, to chant the solemn requiem,
or let fall the tear of sorrow! Let the winds of heaven
sing the strain through the pine-trees above, and let the
clouds drop tears pure as the sweet heavens over these
graves which kindred may never see! It looked almost
strange to observe in that soldiers' cemetery one or two
graves of women, and one wherein the passionless forms of
two twin children slept. These, doubtless, belonged to the
families of soldiers, who followed them to the fortress, and
here found — a grave.

"The cemetery has a rustic entrance, a portion of which
is formed into that emblem dear to every Christian, though
once an emblem of obloquy, — the cross. A part of the
fence has fallen, however, and, despite the picturesqueness
of the spot, the graveyard looked neglected and somewhat
desolate, as is almost unavoidable here and now. Very beautiful are the sighing trees ; and typical of ' glory, honor, and
immortality' are the chaplets of live-oak and holly which
stand near the bed of those silent sleepers ; but very cold
and desolate look those graves beneath, made in the sand,
whose whiteness speaks of the winding-sheet and the pallor
of death. Just without this enclosure is another cemetery, in
which we noticed that the graves were mostly of marines and

sailors of the navy, whose bodies have been borne here for interment; those who once tenanted them departing life in the harbor or near the shore. We spoke no word in that army and navy cemetery; and yet not wholly voiceless was that solitude, deeper, more solemn, and yet more sweet than the eternal dirge which the pine grove and the resounding sea near it are chanting. Our hearts heard a voice telling us not chiefly of death, but if we and those silent sleepers were true soldiers of the cross, or if those departed sailors had Jesus for their pilot over life's solemn sea, that voice spoke for them and us a nobler strain, and it was — IMMOR-TALITY. . . . . .

"I have seen many a marble monument and visited many a beautiful cemetery, and yet confess that seldom have I been more touched than by the simple memorial erected in this one consecrated spot, a religious oasis in war's desert, to the memory of some humble private soldier."

Life in the fortress the Chaplain declares is not monotonous.

"There is always some war-tidings, true or false, to stir a ripple on the sea of existence, and the varied drills, dress-parades, mountings of guard, &c., furnish sufficient variety of occupation. Occasionally the booming of cannon from Sewall's Point, or from the rebel encampment almost opposite our own, give our soldiers hope that the enemy will pay us a visit, when their reception would be warm indeed, and of such a nature that many of those who made it would never return to their own homes.

"God avert unnecessary bloodshed, yet if attacked I have no hesitation in praying for victory, however dear the cost to us or our foes. Above all, may *our cause* triumph, and it is of less moment how many of us die, if Liberty and Our Country yet live. How beautiful is the scene now before

10

us! The Chesapeake, with its gleaming waters, its waves
at play as though they did not run between hostile shores,
both of which they kiss and lave as if anxious for peace
and to wash out the stains of this fratricidal war.   Yesterday evening, when the moon was shining most brightly, I
watched the gleaming fires on the hostile shore.   How
friendly they looked! how hospitable!   Yet, had I or any
Massachusetts man shown ourselves within range, how soon
would other fires have flashed forth with deadly meaning,
and all because the Old Bay State loves that Union which
Virginia once was united with her in forming and upholding,
but now has deserted and is in arms to overthrow."

And there were other than æsthetic advantages derived from the Chesapeake.   For it

"swarms with fish, among which the sea-trout is especially
delicious.   Then, too, all along the shore are large beds of
Virginia oysters, and great quantities of crabs and other
marine delicacies, which the contraband population bring in
for us abundantly for a few pennies."

And there was other game, though exempt from the
hunter.

" Walking down to the sea-shore yesterday morning, I was
reminded, as often lately, of the great abundance of wild-fowl
in the vicinity.   Firing is not allowed near the fortress, except
for military reasons, and shot-guns are not easily procured by
those who would go at a proper distance from the lines.   The
wild ducks appeared fully aware of their immunity from danger, and would float saucily up almost to the very feet of the
sentinels pacing the shore with loaded rifles, and, looking
pertly up, swim lazily away.   Other game abounds on these
long heaths and in the forest, but is equally out of danger.
Indeed, wild-fowl and other game seem to seek this region,

like the contrabands, for safety, to the great aggravation of hunters of beasts, birds, and men. My sympathies are with the *hunted*, not hunters, in each case, and I am glad for the immunity which the wild-fowl and the forest bird and the timid hare and the oppressed black man here enjoy."

Winter, for a while, seems loath to banish the symbols of milder seasons. The Chaplain says : —

" It seems so strange to read of an accident to children skating on the ice in Massachusetts, and to hear from friends of grand sleighing already enjoyed in some portions of the good old Bay State. Here the waters still sparkle and gleam, unfettered by the despotic sway of Winter, who is so apt to make his approach felt ere he be fairly seated on his glittering, icy throne. I still bathe almost every day, when the tide is at its height, on the strand. And near my tent, in Mr. Segar's orchard, an apple-tree is capriciously covered with untimely but beautiful blossoms. A soldier has just passed with a rose in his hand, gathered in the open air."

Yet, Winter's forbearance was not of long duration. The Chaplain writes : — .

" Our first snow-storm came last evening. As in the war, so in the season, the ' sunny South ' seemed gaining the first victories, and the cold North had been repulsed from Virginia. The Queen of the South, Summer, was reigning in Virginia, in place of the King of the North, Winter, to whom at this season dominion of right belongs. But now all is changed. Yesterday morning I gathered a beautiful bouquet of tea-roses, Southern flowers, blooming in the open air. But last night the chilly wind blew, then came sleet, hail, and at last snow, and lo! Winter had come ; the frozen North had subdued the sunny South, asserted his lawful right to reign at this season, even in the Old Dominion.

"I confess my first sympathies had been with the Southern Queen, Summer. True, she had no right to stay longer, and claim supremacy in December; true, her kisses were deceitful, and her hot, sultry breath had caused the death of many a brave soldier by its malarious influence; but still she was crowned with flowers and had so many enchanting, if arrogant and capricious ways, that after all we loved her. But she is vanquished now; her wreathed wand was shivered last night when it ventured to try its strength against the sceptre of Winter, who, tardily, but sternly, at last asserts his right to reign. And beneficent, if austere, is his sway; for fever yields at once and flees in the train of the fugitive Summer; the stains of Virginia's soil, polluted by treason, are covered over with a pure white, a cold and snowy mantle. Yes, Winter has at last conquered Summer, even here on Southern soil, just as the loyal North will ultimately conquer the rebellious South in this strife for Union and Liberty.

"Well; Winter, King of the North, thou shalt be welcome, though thy aspect be cold and forbidding, and we will be loyal subjects of thy sway! Farewell, Queen of the South, thy reign is evidently over; we will not mourn thy departure, for with thee we hope fever and a host of other diseases and ills may depart also."

Another page of nature, the character of man, furnished for the Chaplain features of instruction and interest. He thus groups some of the points of interest on Old Point Comfort: —

"Leaving my tent at Camp Hamilton, on horseback, in company with a few friends, we were much impressed with the variety presented by a short ride in the vicinity. Passing through the German regiment (Max Weber's New York Twentieth), I was struck with the neat aspect of the vast number of little shanties, with which the soldiers of that thrifty and industrious nation have supplied the place of the showy but cold tents with which they have been provided. Their camp really looks like a smart Western village, and yet every cabin has been built of refuse lumber brought from the ruins of Hampton. Internally these shanties are the pictures of neatness, and their ingenious arrangements make you realize how akin the Germans are in many notable respects to our own New-Englanders. My friends alighted from horseback, and entered these humble substitutes for houses, and were much gratified. Almost every shanty had a few pictures on the wall, or at least a wreath of evergreen, as a mark of taste and love of the beautiful.

" Passing through this camp, we next entered that of the Naval Brigade. It hails from no State, but claims to represent the Union, its officers being commissioned directly by the President, and it is intended for land or sea service as the exigency may require.

" As we pass along, we leave at our left the Chesapeake Female Seminary, with its noble dome. The building is owned by the State of Virginia, and is now used chiefly as a hospital and for quarters for officers and some of their families.

• " Still farther, the fortress rises on our left, with its frowning walls and its many cannon peering curiously out of the portholes at the passers-by, and ready to give any disloyal visitants a reception more warm than pleasant. As we claim to be thoroughly loyal, they have no voice for us, though their mouths are wide open. On our right lie a large number of gunboats, transport steamers, schooners, the storeship Brandywine, and, more beautiful than any others, the flagship Minnesota and the Roanoke."

Of a high military character at Newport News he writes : —

"It was my privilege to visit this place a few days since and see that tried and veteran soldier, General Phelps, who achieved honorable distinction in the Mexican war. I found him unpretending, affable, and every inch a soldier. He is a skilled artillerist, and as the 'News' is strongly intrenched, the foe would meet a pretty bloody reception should they come. The entrenchments are provided with the formidable Sawyer's and other rifled cannon, which would deal out death by wholesale to assailants. The remnant of the regiment of Ellsworth's Zouaves went there yesterday morning. They are hard boys, and may fight bravely, but I am more and more convinced that the best moral men, yes, and the best Christians, are also generally the best and most reliable and the bravest soldiers."

And in the humbler walks he finds those to commend.

"In our Holliston company (Company B) is a man by the name of Fiske, a former resident of Georgia, which place he quitted abruptly a few weeks since, not, however, until he had become acquainted with the beauties of the only law which our Southern neighbors seem to respect, — lynch law. He was tarred and feathered, and treated with much indignity, and robbed of all his hard earnings. Fiske had never been an abolitionist, nor an opponent of slavery, though not holding it exactly a divine institution. His only crime was being a native of Massachusetts and not in favor of rebellion. He was a peaceful man, but on arriving here, at once enlisted in our regiment, and only wishes to go 'way down South to Dixie's land,' with plenty of good Massachusetts soldiers in his company. He is calm now, but *terribly in earnest* in this strife, and with no personal revenge in his heart; yet hates slavery, — the fount of all our woes, — and desires to see an end put to treason and rebellion in the Southern States."

And thus he speaks over a soldier's grave : —

" Stuart was an excellent young man, and died willingly, trustfully, feeling that he was giving life for his country. His were not the *éclat* and glory of death on the battle-field; yet his life was no less an offering on the altar of liberty. His humble pine coffin was followed to the grave by his captain and his company, and by the colonel of the regiment. The solemn burial rites fitting for a soldier were performed by the chaplain of the regiment, and then three volleys of musketry were fired over the insatiate grave in which we had placed the remains of him who, so few days since, was earnest in his patriotic zeal. On the following Sabbath, a discourse suggested by his death, yet more by his life, so far as we knew it, was preached by the chaplain to an attentive regiment. Massachusetts — yes, and America, too — will write on her heart of hearts the names of all who, in this perilous hour, die in her cause. Names the most humble shall henceforth become glorious."

He finds one, too, reminding of " The boy stood on the burning deck." He says : —

" Just as I was leaving Boston a lad of fifteen appeared, with proper vouchers, and entreated to go as a servant in the regiment. His father had been major in the regular army, but neither father nor mother nor other known relative of his now lived, and he had no way of earning honestly his bread. He is a Boston boy, of American parentage, and from one of our Suffolk schools. I took him, finding his card indorsed by good citizens, though not specially needing his services. On arriving at this encampment I was called to the city by business, and, leaving him standing in front of the head-quarters, told him to stay there till I returned, which would be before long.

" Business detained me, however, and knowing the boy

would have every kindness, I was not anxious about him.
Returning next day at 10 A. M. I found that during the
rainy night he had stood at his post, refusing to leave it,
because his orders were to the contrary. He had not gone
in to supper, nor did he leave, though without an overcoat,
when the rain-storm came on, till, falling asleep, he was
carried in by one of the servants. That is a boy who
'obeys orders,' and will make a good soldier. I had never
dreamed of being obeyed so literally, but confess I was
pleased with the implicit obedience of this little soldier's
orphan."

The fortress furnished melancholy spectacles.

" At the fortress wharf here, on that same Friday, we saw
fifty-seven patriotic and brave men who were wounded and
captured by the enemy at the battle of Bull Run. O what
a scene it was, — those poor mangled, wounded, *half-starved*
sufferers ! There was a young man who had lost a limb ;
and another whose whole existence must be a living agony,
a dying by inches ; yet only after long years may he be so
privileged as to 'sleep well, life's fitful fever over.' May
their grateful country not wait till the grave closes over
those maimed and sickly forms, ere she does them what
slender justice she can. And may the kindness of home,
and the sunshine of loved faces, and the music of friendly
voices restore to health some of these who must soon have
died, surrounded as they were in their gloomy prison-house
by the foes of human liberty, who scowled their hatred of
its defenders, and uttered only harsh words to these brave
men who had poured forth their blood as a libation on Freedom's altar."

Sights more cheering sometimes are met on the
shore.

"The sun, which was veiled in clouds on Saturday, shone again on the Sabbath.

"Well it might, for it seldom has looked upon a gladder scene than its setting rays gilded with a smile of holy joy. At that hour the steamer, which had been up to Norfolk with a flag of truce, returned, laden with a precious freight, even our released prisoners from Richmond and many another house of Southern bondage. As I went on board, I saw Colonel Lee, Colonel Cogswell, Colonel Wood, Major Revere, Captain Keller, and over three hundred other brave officers and soldiers, who were mostly captured in the courageous and sanguinary, but ineffectual, fight at Ball's Bluff. It was a different scene from what I expected, less noisy and more solemn, fewer 'hurrahs' and more exclamations of 'Bless God!' 'Bless God!' Ay, 'Bless God,' indeed; for Secretary Stanton spoke a truth we need ever remember, when he declared that to Jehovah's name, and not chiefly to any man's, belongeth the highest glory. Without underrating the valor of our brave soldiers, the wise strategy of commanders or statesmen, but heaping chaplets on their honored brows, we would at the same time remember that 'His right hand hath gotten us the victory.'"

The Chaplain thus describes another scene : —

"It affords a pleasant change from camp scenes to go a while each day to the fortress, and especially to the marketplace, which lies just without its walls and near the various steamboat landings. There you see every variety of men. Here are a group of naval officers, with their round caps and broad gold bands and brilliant uniforms. They are talking over a theme always pleasant, — the Hatteras Inlet victory, which was emphatically a naval triumph, although the brave German soldiers and our own gallant Butler did their full part in its achievement. The venerable man to whom they

10 *   o

most attentively listen when he speaks is the brave Commodore Stringham, who, to the regret of many, is to be transferred from this command.

"Near them is a band of soldiers eagerly asking whether they are not to have lot or part in some hazardous expedition for their country's service and strike a blow which shall sink Manasses and Bethel beneath the sea of oblivion. Patience, brave men, you will not long remain ungratified in your desire, and when the blow is struck, may it be so strongly dealt, so surely aimed, that under it rebellion shall reel and stagger to her final overthrow. You notice that the soldiers are of different States, but chiefly from New York and Massachusetts, who have stood shoulder to shoulder during all this warfare; of different nationalities, too, Germans, Irish, Americans, but united wholly in heart and mind, and all calling America their fatherland, for whom they will seek all service to do, and in her cause, if must be, die.

"But there comes a file of men who do not look so eager and expectant, albeit not half so ill as I had pictured such men to look. These are captured Secessionists, who have just been brought here to try the invigorating air of Old Point Comfort. That row is just from Baltimore, and is composed of most distinguished and gentlemanly, but bitter enemies of their country. For them I have no sympathy; they deserve none. They have sinned against the best and most lenient government upon which sun ever shone, and have sinned knowingly, and because of personal ambition.

"That other file of prisoners, and we have one or two such every day, is more deserving of pity; it is composed of ignorant men, misled by leaders like the first class of rebels who just passed us."

The Chaplain had an interview with some released rebels, which he thus describes : —

"While I stood on the deck of the Roncoos, as our flag-of-truce boat is named, there came upon deck a young man, dressed in full uniform as a naval officer, who touched his hat courteously to me, and called me by name. I did not recognize him, but, stepping aside to speak with him, was introduced to a captain and lieutenant, also in full naval rig, with swords by their sides. After customary words of introduction, my new friend said: 'Well, it seems good to get on the water again.' 'Ah,' I said, 'you have not been with your ship lately.' 'No,' was the reply, 'I had other duties.' 'Well, sir,' I remarked, 'it is to you naval gentlemen that the country is now looking to strike terror to the hearts of the Secessionists and crush out rebellion.' 'Sir,' they replied, in a loud chorus, 'we have *resigned.*' 'Indeed,' was my response, 'I am sorry you should be out of health at a time when so many important naval expeditions are on foot.' 'That is n't our reason.' I turned the conversation a little, somewhat enlightened, but still not willing to believe that these gentlemen, wearing Uncle Sam's uniform, were yet ready to fight against, but not for, a government whose cash they have long drawn as salary. 'Are you from Boston, gentlemen?' 'Just arrived from there.' 'How do things look in the good old city?' 'We went about but very little.' 'What part of the city did you stop in?' '*We have been residing for the last few months in Fort Warren, in Boston Harbor,*' was their answer. We all laughed. Then and during the rest of our conversation we better understood one another. My new-found acquaintance it appeared had seen me in Boston a few years ago, and remembered me, though I had forgotten him."

In the Fortress, the Chaplain was under a new *régime*, the law martial; a change not so noticeable to those who were a law to themselves, but of necessary severity with delinquents. He writes : —

"My heart is sad amid these beautiful Virginia scenes; and war's dread array has as yet presented to me no sight so sorrowful as our regimental guard-tent exhibits; for within those canvas walls are two men sentenced to be shot.

"Do you ask the crime of these men, whom the court-martial has thus sentenced to a summary execution? I answer, a very heinous one in military eyes, and rightly so regarded, yet not necessarily involving moral obliquity, — it is sleeping on their post as sentinels at night. This endangers the whole army, and the sacred cause for which we are contending; and unless extenuating circumstances appear, death is the awful yet righteous penalty. Still we cannot refrain from deeply sympathizing with those whose offence implies no malice, only that negligence and lack of watchfulness often equally pernicious and fatal to ourselves and others. But whatever my judgment says, my heart pleads for these men, — pleads for them before the tribunal of God, and will induce me to plead for them before the tribunal of men; and I cannot but hope and pray for that one sweet word which all we sinful mortals need, — PARDON!" *

The capture of two arch-traitors caused joy at the fortress. The Chaplain says : —

"It is they, and such as they, who have brought upon this State and our whole country sorrow and the sufferings of civil war. A friend near me suggests that he, for one, is glad that the Virginia 'architect of ruin' is no longer a free Mason; and those who know Slidell assert that he is even more inclined to all political evil and crime than his Virginia confederate in treason. It seems strange to us Massachusetts soldiers, far away from home, defending our institutions and liberties, to hear of citizens of Boston furnishing these plotters of disunion and avowed enemies of our government with

* The sentence of these men was commuted.

every luxury. We endure hardships and privations cheerfully; we desire no unnecessary severity towards these men who are largely the cause of our hardships, but we believe our government and State and citizens have done enough, and all that is honorable to themselves, when they treat *as well* and make as comfortable these rebel prisoners as they treat and make their loyal soldiery.

" By the way, if Mr. Mason now visits Massachusetts, and more especially Fort Warren, will he go 'as an ambassador,' as he once promised Mr. Winthrop?"

Of their release he says : —

" I find but one opinion in this division of the loyal army in reference to the surrender of Mason and Slidell. It is of reluctant but entire acquiescence. Their fangs are drawn ; let the serpents go. They are harmless, save to their friends in rebeldom or Great Britain."

Of the preparation of the expedition which captured Beaufort he says : —

" On returning to the fortress, I found the harbor and vicinity one forest of masts. Interspersed among these were the smoke-pipes of a countless throng of steamers. The decks of both ships and steamers were alive with armed men, — soldiers and marines. At night the scene was one of the most beautiful that human eye can ever see. Innumerable lights gleamed from every deck, and were reflected from the waters, glancing and sparkling as the light waves played ; strains of patriotic music arose from the bands or from human voices, and were wafted in sweet cadence to the shores. O, with what pride and joy, with what an infinitude of hope, and yet a blending of anxiety, did every patriot look on that floating city beneath our fortress walls ! How often have we expected it to sail during those radiant,

serene days and still October nights, when all seemed so
auspicious, and every morning we looked, thinking, half
hoping, that, in the silence of the night just gone, those white
sails would have been spread like the wings of sea-birds, and
those vessels have glided away, followed by the laboring
steamers as companions, on their mission of peace to loyal
men, of death to traitors. But those anticipations were long
disappointed, until at last, in the gray mists of morning, that
marine city did melt away like a night vision, and we saw it
sweep out of the harbor with the mists, and followed it with
our prayers and our blessings. A few hours sufficed to hoist
every anchor and set every sail; and when we looked anew
at those placid waters, the fleet which had ridden safely upon
them was gone, — *where* could only be conjectured, and con-
jectures, let me assure you, were numberless,.save among the
very few who believed they knew."

He thus alludes to the dreadful tempest which succeeded the departure of the expedition: —

"Scarce a day had passed after the fleet had left our
waters, when the sky, which had been so cloudless and azure,
became overcast, and the still waters were lashed to fury by
a fierce wind. All night it blew; it prostrated many of the
humble tents in our canvas city, and kept cold and comfortless the inmates of them all; but I think few thought much
of personal discomfort in comparison with the great interests
we felt were imperilled by the unwelcome storm. But that
night of wind and tumult was as nothing when considered in
relation to the driving, furious tempest of Friday and Saturday last. It did seem as though the powers of light and
darkness were striving for the victory, and the latter were
likely to get the better in the contest, or as if the very elements of nature were assaulting one another, and earth, sea,
and air were mingling in an indiscriminate strife, the result

of which to us poor half-drowned denizens of the tented field
was a very doubtful one. All Friday night the winds howled
over sea and main, and torrents of rain fell, or rather beat
upon sea and shore, and when morning came the white-crested
waves were rushing upon the beach like plumed squadrons to
the battle. Throughout the whole day the storm continued,
till our anxieties for the fleet, freighted with a nation's des-
tinies, reached a climax. Still we had one resource, — we
could do nothing in our human powerlessness to aid, but we
could look to Him who rules winds and waves, and know that
He who doeth all things well could and would care for that
fleet, and give it both protection and a prosperous event to its
undertaking, if in his wisdom that were best for the welfare
of our country and humanity. And never have I heard more
fervent prayers than those which have arisen from the soldiers at our humble prayer-meetings, as they invoked Heav-
en's blessing on the great expedition."

Every hour and scene were liable to martial interruption, and the frowning fortress was obliged, like
the Eastern sage, to sleep with the eyes open. Of
such an interruption, while religious services were in
progress, the Chaplain writes: —

"We worship, as did our Pilgrim Fathers, with arms in
our hands, ready to pray or fight, as God and duty may
require, and believing one not inconsistent with the other
in a holy cause, such as is our country's. A portion of our
regiment immediately proceeded to the scene of action, determined, if the enemy would desecrate the Sabbath by an
attack, we would consecrate 'Forefather's Day' with a victory. But the enemy were repulsed ere our companies
reached the field, and I met the ambulances bringing back
four wounded men of the German Twentieth New York
Regiment, our neighbors. Eight or ten of the rebels were

killed, but the foe saved themselves from further loss by retreating at the tenth volley. The enemy's force consisted of one regiment of infantry and one company of cavalry. Many colored men were in the enemy's ranks, the rebels having no tender scruples about arming the slaves. The number of the rebel wounded is not known. None of our men were killed."

The Rebels, having now got their Merrimac nearly or quite ready for action, begin to be confident upon the water. The Chaplain writes : —

" Quite a saucy thing was done by a little rebel steamer from Sewall's Point, opposite our camp, on Sunday last. The attempt made was to capture our mail and transport steamer, the Express, which plies daily between the fortress and Newport News. The Express at the time was towing an old schooner, the Sherwood, owned by Assistant-Quarter-master Noyes, and having on board twelve hundred gallons of good pure cold water for the supply of the naval vessels, good water not being easily procured at the fortress. The shells of the rebel steamer all passed over the Express, but it was deemed advisable to cut adrift the schooner and abandon her to the enemy. The contrabands on board the schooner abandoned her, taking the yawl-boat and escaping to the shore, the captain, however, remaining on board, and refusing to leave the schooner. Meanwhile, but very slowly as it appeared to us who were witnessing the matter on the shore, the federal gunboats steamed up and sailed after the rebel adventurer. They were unsuccessful in overtaking her, but poured their shells about her in a fiery storm of thunderbolts. One of our armed ferry-boats pursued the enemy almost to Sewall's Point, running the gantlet between the batteries there and on Craney Island. We temperance men were rather rejoicing to think that the rebels had now a good supply of pure cold water, — an article whose use they appear lately to have abandoned; but I learn to-day that the schooner sunk when near port, having been riddled with our balls. Our gunboats at last ceased the chase, but shelled the rebel camp on Crancy Island, with what success can only be conjectured by us."

And now occurred the greatest naval engagement of the nineteenth century, not only 'in view of the novelty of the combat and the incalculable issue immediately at stake, but because its result went far to settle the question of foreign intervention. Wooden walls would henceforth avail little in maritime warfare, and ships in the heavy iron armor which would be requisite must incur the utmost hazard in a long voyage over a tempest-breeding sea.

Our Chaplain was one of the few eyewitnesses, if not the only one, who has given the full particulars of this event. He thus describes it under date of March 15th, 1862: —'

"The past week has indeed been an exciting one here. The dulness and monotony of camp life have been exchanged for the sounds of the stirring drum, of men marching in battle array to meet any land force which might second the naval armament arrayed against us, and for the flash and roar of the cannon upon our shores. I have been a witness of the entire naval contest; our signal defeat at first, our splendid triumph at the last. Never have I known such alternations of feeling as this last week has brought to me. I have seen the proud American flag struck and humbled, and over it the white signal of surrender to a rebel steamer waving, and my heart sank within me for shame, and then came emotions of stern resentment, and longing to see the affront avenged. I have seen that exultant rebel steamer humbled in her turn before the little Monitor, and the fierce flame-breathing monster towed disabled away to his den, and then came a feeling of exultation, say rather of gratitude to God, whose providence alone sent that deliverance, which no language is adequate to express. Let me now briefly recount events of remarkable interest, avoiding the trite details already before the public, and narrating things as I saw them. The like of this naval engagement, in many respects, the world never saw before; the tremendous interests which hung upon the issue have never been exceeded; and each witness is bound to give his testimony, and give it impartially.

"Never has a brighter day smiled upon Old Virginia than last Saturday. The hours crept lazily along, and sea and shore in this region saw nothing to vary the monotony of the scene. Now and then a soldier might be heard complaining that this detachment of the loyal army was having no part in the glorious victories which everywhere else are crowning American valor with such brilliant success; or a sailor might be noted on shipboard telling how much he hoped the Merrimac would show herself, and how certainly she would be sunk by our war vessels or land guns if she dared make her appearance. At one o'clock in the afternoon the scene changed. Two strangely-clad steamers appeared above Newport News, coming down the river, and a mysterious monster — half ship, half house — came slowly steaming from Norfolk. We did not know, but we all felt, that the latter was the Merrimac. Your correspondent at once went to the large seminary building on the shore, about two miles from the fortress, and so much nearer Newport News, and with an excellent spyglass could see distinctly every movement made. The engagement was a brief one, and as terrible and disastrous as brief. The Merrimac is a slow sailer, but she steamed steadily toward

Newport News, and at once attacked the Cumberland. There can never be a braver defence than the officers and sailors of that frigate made. They fought long after resistance was hopeless; *they never surrendered*, even when the water was filled with drowning men, and the fast disappearing decks were slippery with blood; but all was in vain. With terrible and resistless force the Merrimac steamed at the doomed vessel, and pierced her side with her immense iron beak, at the same time firing her heavy guns directly through her antagonist. The noble Cumberland soon sunk, and her sailors who were yet alive sought safety in the masts yet above water, or by swimming to the shore.

" Meanwhile the Congress had been fired upon by the rebel steamers Yorktown and Jamestown, and also by the tug-boats which accompanied the Merrimac. She had got as near the shore as possible; but when the iron monster turned his attention to her, she was soon obliged to surrender. O how bitterly we all felt the humiliation of seeing the white flag rising to the mast-head above the stars and stripes. I am afraid I felt hardly like a Christian for the moment, if indeed a longing for vengeance upon my country's enemies *be* unchristian. I would have given all I possessed to see that accursed tyrant of the seas, with the rebel pennant defiantly flying, sunk beside her victim, the noble Cumberland. But it was not so to be. We looked for the Minnesota and Roanoke, our helpers in the strife, the first our main dependence, and lo! both were aground and helpless in that fearful hour! It was well, for sure as they had floated, and the Merrimac could have come at them, they, too, must have been sunk or captured. The Merrimac draws more water than either of them. It did seem strange, though, that such a mishap should have chanced to both of these steam frigates, whose pilots ought to have been so familiar with the channel; but the Roanoke for six months has lain in these waters with a broken shaft, which renders her helpless, and the former pilot of the Minnesota had just given way to another and less experienced man. It was all overruled for good.

"The Merrimac now threw her balls thick and fast and heavy upon the camps at Newport News. Strange to say none of these shot or shell did any material damage, though one of them passed directly through General Mansfield's quarters, made wild work with his room, covered the General with splinters of wood, and had it exploded must have killed him. I saw the shell next day, and conversed with the General with reference to it. He has it in his apartment. It weighed forty-two pounds; another by its side, also sent from the Merrimac, weighed ninety-two. The shells were rather badly aimed, and most of them went into the woods, cutting off tops of trees as they fell; but fortunately, nay, providentially, harming no one of the soldiery or the fleeing women and children and contrabands. A little tug had been sent meanwhile from the Merrimac to the Congress to take off the prisoners; but this tug was a mark for the sharpshooters from the shore and from the land batteries, which had been admirably served under General Mansfield's skilful direction, and frightened the Yorktown and Jamestown and the little rebel gunboats from landing their forces. The officers of the Congress and most of the sailors who were not killed, all save twenty-three, escaped to the shore; and the Merrimac, damaged but not disabled by the Cumberland's broadsides, with her commander wounded and several men killed, retired from the conflict, giving a few passing shots at the Minnesota, but reserving her case till the morrow, and slowly steaming up to Norfolk, accompanied by the Jamestown, Yorktown, and the smaller rebel craft.

"That morrow! How anxiously we waited for it! How much we feared its results! How anxious our Saturday eve of preparation! At sundown there was nothing to dispute the empire of the seas with the Merrimac, and had a land attack been made by Magruder then, God only knows what our fate would have been. The St. Lawrence and the Minnesota aground and helpless! the Roanoke with a broken shaft, — these were our defences by sea, — while on land we were doing all possible to resist a night invasion; but who could hope that would have much efficiency! O what a night that was! I never can forget it. There was no fear during its long hours, — danger, I find, does not bring that, — but there was a longing for some interposition of God and waiting upon him, from whom we felt our help must come, in earnest, fervent prayer, while not neglecting all the means of martial defence he had placed in our hands. Fugitives from Newport News kept arriving; ladies and children had walked the long ten miles from Newport News, feeling that their presence only embarrassed their brave husbands. Sailors from the Congress and Cumberland came, one of them with his ship's flag bound about his waist as he swam with it ashore, determined the enemy should never trail it in dishonor as a trophy. Dusky fugitives, the contrabands, came mournfully fleeing from a fate worse than death, — slavery. These entered my cabin hungry and weary, or passed it in long, sad procession. The heavens were aflame with the burning Congress. The hotel was crowded with fugitives, and private hospitality was taxed to the utmost. But there were *no soldiers among the flying host;* all in our camps at Newport News and Camp Hamilton were at the post of duty, undismayed and ready to do all and dare all for their country. The sailors came only to seek another chance at the enemy, since the bold Cumberland had gone down in the deep waters and the Congress had gone upward, as if a chariot of fire, to convey the manly souls whose bodies had perished in that conflict upward to heaven. I had lost several friends there; yet not lost, for they are saved who do their duty to their country and their God, as these had done.

" We did not pray in vain.

'The heavy night hung dark the hills and waters o'er ';

but the night was not half so heavy as our hearts, nor so dark as our prospects. All at once a speck of light gleamed on the distant wave; it moved, it came nearer and nearer, and at ten o'clock at night *the Monitor appeared.* ' When the tale of bricks is doubted, Moses comes.' I never more firmly believed in special providences than at that hour. Even sceptics for the moment were converted, and said, ' God has sent her!' But how insignificant she looked! she was but a speck on the dark blue sea at night, almost a laughable object by day. The enemy call her a ' cheese-box on a raft,' and the comparison is a good one. Could she meet the Merrimac? The morrow must determine, for, under God, the Monitor is our only hope.

" The morrow came, and with it came the inevitable battle between those strange combatants, the Merrimac and the Monitor. What a lovely Sabbath it was; how peaceful and balmy that Southern spring morning! Smiling nature whispered only ' peace,' but fierce treason breathed out threatenings and slaughter, and would have war. Nor would the rebels respect the Sabbath; they know no doctrine but Slavery, no duty but obedience to her bloody behests. War let it be, then, since wicked men so determine, and we have no alternative but shameful surrender of truth and eternal justice. The guilt of violating God's Sabbath be upon the heads of those who will do it, — we may not, indeed cannot, shrink from the terrible ordeal of battle. And soon it comes. At nine o'clock A. M., the Merrimac, attended by her consorts, the war-steamers Jamestown and Yorktown, and a fleet of little tug-boats, crowded with ladies and gentlemen from Norfolk who were desirous of seeing the Minnesota captured, and, perhaps even Fort Monroe taken, certainly all its outlying vessels and the houses in its environs burnt.

"The little Monitor lay concealed in the shadow of the Minnesota. The Merrimac opens the conflict, and her guns shake the sea and air as they breathe out shot and flame. Sewall's Point sends from its mortars shell which burst in the air above the doomed Minnesota. The Minnesota, still aground, replies with a bold but ineffectual broadside. All promises an easy victory to the Merrimac, when lo! the little Monitor steams gently out and offers the monster Merrimac battle. How puny, how contemptible she seemed! nothing but that little round tub appearing above the water, and yet flinging down the gage of defiance to the gigantic Merrimac. It was little David challenging the giant Goliath once again, — the little one the hope of Israel, the giant the pride of the heathen Philistines. Truly our hopes were dim and our hearts almost faint for the moment. The few men on the Monitor are sea and storm worn and weary enough, and their little craft is an experiment, with only two guns with which to answer the Merrimac's many. Who can doubt the issue? who believe the Monitor can fail to be defeated? And if she is, what is to hinder the victorious and unopposed and unopposable Merrimac from opening the blockade of the coast, or shelling Washington, New York, and Boston, after first devastating our camp and destroying its soldiery? That *was the issue;* such might have been the result, smile now who will. Believe me, there were prayers offered, many and fervent, that Sabbath, along the shore and from the fortress walls, as our regiment watched the battle, and sailors must have prayed, too, as never before.

"The Merrimac, after a few minutes of astounded silence, opened the contest. She tried to sink her puny foe at once by a broadside, and be no longer delayed from the Minnesota,

whose capture she had determined upon. After the smoke
of the cannonade had cleared away, we looked fearing, and
the crew of the Merrimac looked hoping, that the Monitor
had sunk to rise no more. But she still lived. There she
was, with the white wreaths of smoke crowning her tower, as
if a coronet of glory. And valiantly she returned the fire,
too, and for five hours such a lively cannonading as was
heard, shaking earth and sea, was never heard before. Literally, I believe that never have ships carrying such heavy
guns met till that Sabbath morning. Every manœuvre was
exhausted by the enemy. The Yorktown approached to
mingle in the fray. One shot was enough to send her quickly
back, a lame duck upon the waters, though she, too, is iron-
clad. The Merrimac tried to run the Monitor down, and
thus sink her; she only got fiercer shots by the opportunity
she thus gave her little antagonist. And so it went on till
the proud Merrimac, disabled, was glad to retire, and, making
signals of distress, was towed away by her sorrowing consorts.
David had conquered Goliath with his smooth stones, or
wrought-iron balls, from his little sling, or shot-tower. Israel
rejoiced in her deliverance, through the power of God, who
had sent that little champion of his cause, in our direst extremity, to the battle. Since then the Merrimac has not
shown herself, and the enemy confess her disabled, and her
commander, Buchanan, ominous name, severely wounded,
four of her crew killed, and seventeen wounded. They admit, too, the valor of our seamen, futile though it was. ‘The
Cumberland's officers and crew,’ says the Norfolk Day-Book,
‘fought worthy of a better cause’; say, rather, worthy of the
best cause in the world, and we who witnessed the fight will
agree with them.

"All that night, as well as the previous and for several
succeeding, our regiments were under arms. I will not detail
the precautions taken to prevent a defeat by land, as, through

the providence of God, an ultimate defeat by sea has been averted. Few of us slept that night, and had we done so most of us would have been awakened at midnight by the fearful cries which came to us from the water, 'Ship ahoy! O God, save us! Fire, fire, fire!' and occasionally a heavy cannon mingling its roar with those fearful cries. I rushed to the shore, with many others, and then a little distance from me beheld the gunboat Whitehall burning, and apparently her crew perishing in the fire or drowning in the waters near. It was terrible, all the more so as we could do nothing to aid, no boat being near our camp. The balls from her shotted guns made even looking on dangerous; one shell struck the United States Hospital at the fort and caused great terror among the inmates, all of whom believed for a while that the Merrimac had come down again and was shelling the fort. Only four of those poor seamen perished in the flames or water, through the mercy of God. The fire came from a shot from the Merrimac, which had the day before passed through the Whitehall and left a little spark smouldering unknown within.

" Amid all these events, disastrous or merciful, our soldiers still live, the fortress yet remains unscathed, and the Minnesota and Roanoke and St. Lawrence, though the first two need repairs, yet fly the old flag at their mainmasts. Above all, the little Monitor floats in triumph, a sentinel on the waters and a strict 'monitor' over the rebels. But for the wounding of her noble commander, Lieutenant Worden, she would have pursued and sunk the Merrimac, and will probably do so if another encounter occurs. She has now another noble commander, Lieutenant T. A. Selfridge of Charlestown, whom I have known from his boyhood, and know to be brave and worthy of the proud Old Bay State. I have visited Newport News, and mourned there the death of the worthy Chaplain Lenhart and the heroic Captain Moore, whom I saw but a few days before, and talked with about his

11   P

intended visit home to Boston. But while I have mourned, I have also rejoiced over our camps, in which none were killed, and our officers and sailors so many of whom were rescued. America will never forget that battle. It will mark an era in the history of the navy. It has taught us a useful lesson, and henceforth we have no more wooden walls as our reliance, but first our God and then plates of steel, and iron-clad frigates and monitors."

Had the Merrimac been victorious, the fortress was ill-prepared for her, and much loss of life and even capture might have ensued. But the Chaplain was unmoved. In a letter to his family he says: " Fear not for me. God cares for me. I never felt less fear than now." Nor did this first fear of battle, which everything indicated would soon be the order of the day upon land, induce him to cast any longing looks homeward. He writes to his wife: " Much as I love you and my children, I am glad I am not with you, nor you with me. My duty is *here;* yours, *there.* In all events, God bless you ! " Referring to the bill which was before Congress for the reduction of the chaplain's pay, he says, " I would not leave, if I had to live on a crust, till the contest is over."

In company with Vice-President Hamlin, the Prince de Joinville, Senators Hale, Sherman, Anthony, and Wilkinson, Hon. Charles R. Train, and many other distinguished officials, he visited the scene of the naval conflict.

" Early on Monday morning we embarked on board the fine steamer King Philip, which had been chartered for the occasion, and had brought the party from Washington. For three days the weather had been very stormy here. Virginia had stood like Niobe, dissolved in tears. Was she weeping over the sins of her rebellious sons? For some cause, certainly, she has been in a melting mood for long and weary months; but no fairer day ever shone than last Monday. Perhaps the hope that these officials, civil, military, and naval, would devise something to crush out the treason which has made Virginia mourn, had something to do with the unwonted smile the face of the country wore that day. Wipe out rebellion from this State, and Virginia will wipe away her tears. At any rate, we saw once again the 'sunny South,' and our faces smiled as well as Nature's at the glad and unwonted spectacle. An excellent band also 'discoursed most eloquent music' on the occasion, from the steamer's deck.

"Our first visit was to Newport News, which we reached after a delightful sail of about an hour. Here the party sorrowfully viewed the charred and blackened hulk of the burnt frigate Congress, and gazed mournfully, but proudly too, on the masts of the sunken Cumberland, — that noble sloop-of-war which never surrendered. By request of Senator Hale, we passed close to and slowly by this sunken vessel, in which are entombed 'the noble men who perished there,' and who had followed that heroic motto of a naval commander, 'Don't give up the ship.' They had died rather than surrender. The band played the 'Star-spangled Banner.' Fitting requiem were those inspiring strains and the eloquent words to which they were adapted. No mournful dirge befits our heroic dead, but rather our country's martial strains with which heart-strings vibrate in unison, as we resolve to emulate those who, on that blood-stained and sinking vessel, even in the death-agony and to the last gasp, 'fought the good fight,' and did conquer, though seemingly vanquished; for

'The saints in all this glorious war
Shall conquer, though they 're slain.'

"As that martial tune was played, some voices joined in singing its words, —

> ' O say, can you see, by the dawn's early light,
>   What so proudly we hailed at the twilight's last gleaming;
> Whose broad stripes and bright stars, through the perilous fight,
>   O'er the ramparts we watched, were so gallantly streaming?
> And the rocket's red glare, the bombs bursting in air,
> Gave proof through' the night that our flag was still there.
> O say, does the star-spangled banner still wave
> O'er the land of the free and the home of the brave? '

"And as we sang or listened, we looked, and lo!. our question was answered: *there* from the topmast of that gallant ship *the star-spangled banner still waved*. The sunshine of that beautiful morning glanced from the pennant of that heroic vessel, still streaming from the masthead as it had done 'through that perilous fight.' General Mansfield has ordered a national flag to be affixed to another of the masts, still to wave in proud defiance to the foe, say, rather, as the most eloquent memorial to mark the grave of those men who had died for that flag and the principles it typifies."

They also visited the Monitor.

"Its iron deck seemed almost sacred as I trod it; for had I not seen that fearful but glorious contest between our little David and the rebel Goliath? and did I not owe perhaps my life to the prowess of the little Monitor? Does not the country owe a debt, also, to that gallant defender, which gold can never pay? We were politely received by Lieutenant Jeffers, her commander, and all parts of the Monitor exhibited, and the tower, or 'cheese-box,' as the rebels called it, was revolved for our inspection. Of course I shall not describe its armament or mechanism. Too freely has that been done by others already. I felt her invincibility, however, as never before, and should now hear that the Merrimac had steamed down for a conflict with almost as much joy as would thrill the hearts of the brave officers and crew of the little Monitor."

He says again in reference to the conflict : —

"No officer was captured of any naval ship or military company on that eventful day. The enemy captured just twenty-three sailors, who went on board one of their tugboats voluntarily, either through mistake or lured by a promise from the perfidious foe that they should be set free on shore at Newport News. These men were carried to Norfolk, one dying on the way. But for the sharpshooters of the Indiana Twentieth from the shore, more prisoners, including officers of the Congress, would have been taken. Nor was a single man killed in camp at Newport News. Two Germans were wounded among the soldiers on shore. Less than two hundred sailors and soldiers in all were killed during the entire naval engagement. The enemy's victory was a bootless one, and I believe will result in good to our cause, by changing our naval tactics, and forcing us to resort to plated steamers and gunboats, instead of wooden walls. Such a floating battery is far better as a means of defence than an entire fleet of wooden ships of war, or half a dozen forts, and much less expensive than are our steam wooden frigates or the maintaining a single fort sixty days."

CHAPTER IV.

THE PENINSULAR CAMPAIGN.

" Glory seemed betrayed."

NEVER did military expedition set out under more favorable auspices than the Peninsular campaign in the spring of 1862. Victory had perched upon the Union banner in a series of momentous battles. Farragut's naval achievement, transcending the rules of military science, as genius and genius only has power to do, had sailed by the embattled forts and seized the Crescent City. This glorious feat wrought up the zeal of the Union forces to a high pitch of enthusiasm, while it dealt to Rebellion a stunning blow, and little was needed to crush it forever.

An immense army started to go up the Peninsula, fired with martial ardor and flushed with hope. The enemy were in no spirit nor force to resist its onward march. But the great expedition paused before Yorktown, and, observing the most cautious rules of military science, advanced upon the place with the progressive parallels of a siege, as if it had the strength of Sebastopol. But the heart of the enemy failed them, and they evacuated. They were slowly and cautiously pursued. They were vanquished in the battle of Williamsburg. But advantage was not taken of victory to strike an effectual blow. Slowly feeling their way, the Union forces advanced. The enemy, meanwhile, by this dilatory progress, gained heart and time and reinforcements. When Yorktown was evacuated, Richmond had been almost destitute. But time had been given to concentrate forces there, and make fortifications. Within a few miles of Richmond the bloody field of Fair Oaks was fought, and the discomfited foe fled to the city. The rebels talked of evacuating the capital, and all expected it to fall; but the Union army did not seize the occasion to attack it. Slowly approaching, the Federals came so near that the clocks of the city could be heard in the Union camp as they struck the hours, and from a high tree, known as the signal-tree, its buildings could be discerned.

But the enemy had been reinforced, not only by men, but by midsummer, which had been permitted to come upon the Union army, breeding pestilence in its marshy camp. This ally, in a heart-sickening, inglorious way, laid more brave Union soldiers under the sod than all the balls and bullets of the Rebellion. The enemy soon made a concentrated attack, leaving Richmond feebly guarded. Now commenced a strategetic movement, as it has been called,* by which the Union army was withdrawn, badly shattered, to the

---

* Chaplain Fuller related, that after the Peninsular retreat he was in conversation with a Frenchman, who spoke very disparagingly of the operations of the Union army in that campaign. To offset it the Chaplain reminded him of Napoleon's retreat from Moscow. "Ah!" cried the Frenchman, "Napoleon never retreated. That was only *one grand retrograde movement!*"

protection of the gunboats. The right wing, as they
retired, fully believed that the other wing was being
hurled upon Richmond; but in this belief they were
destined to cruel disappointment; and they arrived
weary and broken to the river-banks, to learn that
the day was lost, the most reasonable anticipations of
victory rendered vain, and one of the largest armies
known to history, composed of a rank and file of un-
equalled valor and endurance, reduced to a shadow.

This was a disastrous blight upon Union hopes, and
it thrilled painfully through every pulse of the nation.
That most delicate thermometer of public confidence,
finances, sunk immediately. Gold rose to an unprecedented premium, and public securities declined. On
the Saturday when the telegraph announced the sad
finale of the Peninsular campaign, the affrighted silver
dollar and all his progeny of change retreated instantly
to hoarding-places, and the market was left to make
shift, as it might, with postage-stamps and other paper
substitutes.

But we must leave to the deliberate inquest of history the searching out of the causes of this dreadful
national disaster, while we record the Chaplain's notes
by the way.

He writes respecting the encampment before Yorktown: —

"Three times have I visited McClellan's grand and
noble army while it was encamped before Yorktown. The
roads, fearful beyond belief or expression; the uncouth specimens of Southern ' chivalry' and coarse, vehement Secession
women; the rich soil, almost wholly untilled, and evidencing
years of agricultural neglect, — these have been too often

described by correspondents to require any recital on my part. Nor shall I speak of privations and hardships inseparable from the condition of any large army moving rapidly through a hostile country. What do soldiers or visitors to soldiers expect, if not these? I am stopping at the far-famed Nelson house, which Lord Cornwallis occupied while in Yorktown in 1781. It is now occupied as a hospital, and in these rooms, which once were filled with British officers, and but a few days ago with Jefferson Davis, Magruder, and other rebel generals, now our sick officers and soldiers of the loyal army can be found.

"This morning I breakfasted with three rebel officers, captured by us last Sabbath as they inadvertently rode into our lines, believing the Yankees still in front of and not in Yorktown. These officers I found every way gentlemen, and though defiant of the North and a little grandiose in their Southern hopes, our morning breakfast, which was casually made together, passed off very agreeably to me. They declared, in answer to my questions, that they believed a decided stand would be made at Richmond by the rebel army; they thought defeat possible, and that Virginia would be very likely to be evacuated, but that this would by no means end the contest nor injure the South, except with foreign nations, whose assistance they have ceased to hope. The capture of New Orleans they admitted to be a heavy blow to their cause, and they candidly acknowledged that Beauregard, though victorious on the first day's fight at Shiloh, was repulsed on the second day with heavy loss. The blockade they believed a great hardship, and severely felt, but ultimately would do the South good, by making her self-sustaining."

Here he secures some trophies.

"I bring with me many relics, collected at Yorktown. One, a fierce, bloodthirsty-looking pike, used by the rebel

11 *

soldiers. It is fourteen feet in length, adapted to cut or thrust, with a sharp side-knife to cut off an adversary's head or make him captive. I have also a piece of a shell, dug from the old Yorktown intrenchments near the Nelson house, and supposed to have been used in the ancient siege. As we approach the fortress strange sights and sounds salute the eyes and ears. We see the bombs bursting in the air, and hear the big gun Union and our war-ships and gunboats discoursing in thunder tones. We see the fire and thick smoke at Sewall's Point, and as we near the fortress we can distinctly see the rebel Goliath, the Merrimac. The fires from Sewall's Point are growing faint by degrees and beautifully less. It is an animated scene, I assure you, though what it all means we cannot yet make out. We trust it 'means business,' and the business which the country so urgently demands when it asks that the Merrimac and its den, Norfolk, shall alike be taken or destroyed."

His regiment, which had not yet joined the Peninsular army, was employed in the occupation of Norfolk, Portsmouth, and Suffolk. The Chaplain writes, under date of May 12th : —

" This Southern city and its neighbor, Portsmouth, are now centres of interest, and the scenes witnessed on every side are novel and striking. Your correspondent arrived yesterday morning at early dawn, and found the city in full and quiet possession of the national army. The Sixteenth Massachusetts Regiment was the first regiment entering either city; the right wing, with Colonel Wyman at its head, occupying the Gosport Navy-Yard and Portsmouth, of which city Colonel Wyman has been appointed military commandant, the left wing being stationed at the courthouse and jail in Norfolk. Passing up the street, I found the stillness of the Sabbath unbroken, as the soldiers in little squads walked quietly here and there, and the sullen men and women at street corners or behind the blinds of their houses, looked curiously and malignantly at the victors, but were too much cowed down to make any hostile demonstration. Suddenly the stillness was broken by the roar of cannon not far off, and then a few minutes after by an explosion whose concussion shook earth and sea. The Merrimac! was instantly the name on every lip, and a more fearful gloom quickly settled on the brow of every rebel citizen of Norfolk. The fire which the rebels had kindled in the ship had reached first the loaded guns and exploded them, and then the magazine of the world-noted tyrant of Hampton Roads, and she was no more. Soon deserters from her crew arrived, and confirmed the glad intelligence of the destruction of this monster, who had committed suicide in despair of a successful encounter with our champion, the little Monitor. The news was received with very mingled feelings by our troops; they rejoiced that the Merrimac was destroyed; they regretted that she was not captured or vanquished by the Monitor. No other vessel will ever be built on the same model, for she drew too much water, and was too unwieldy for sea or river service, and was at best but a floating battery for harbor defence. Mayor Lamb of Norfolk assured me last evening that she was not injured in her contest with the Monitor, save that her prow, having been bent by the Cumberland's guns, was yet further displaced by a shot from the Monitor, which caused her to leak badly, and necessitated her return to Norfolk.

" Reaching the ferry, I crossed to Portsmouth, finding the Elizabeth River positively yellow with tobacco and covered with a black scum from burning rebel steamers and gunboats, and the ruined navy-yard. These were all fired by the rebels, and were still burning or half concealed by wreaths of dense black smoke. O what a contrast Portsmouth presented to

Norfolk! The burning of the navy-yard, ruining every mechanic in Portsmouth, had filled full the cup of indignation against their traitorous tyrants. Our troops were welcomed as deliverers. Women, and even men, thronged about the advancing column of the Sixteenth Regiment, and insisted on kissing 'the old flag,' weeping tears of joy as they did so. Almost every woman I met, and half the men, bowed and smiled, gladly saying, 'You are welcome.' This was of course not as an individual, for I knew none of the throng, but was a recognition of my connection with the army. The humblest soldier received an equal welcome. Bouquets of flowers were brought us from the blooming gardens, and two citizens earnestly proffered me a breakfast in an eating-house near. Exhausted and hungry from a night's march, diversified only by a ride for a part of the way in a mule-wagon over the worst of roads, I cheerfully accepted the invitation. On entering the house, the good woman who kept it said, 'Well, sir, what will you have? recollect we have to live pretty plainly here.' 'Oh,' was my answer, 'I am used to simple living in the army; give me a bit of beefsteak, and that will do.' 'Steak!' was the exclamation; 'we have none.' 'Very well, some ham and eggs.' 'Eggs! there are none to be had now.' 'Ah! then just some bread and butter, and a cup of tea.' 'Butter and tea!' said my poor hostess; 'sir, the like of us poor folks have n't seen such things for a long time, nor is there a pound of tea to be bought in all Portsmouth.' I rather despaired of any further calling of the bill of fare, and left it entirely to my entertainers, who soon produced some ham, corn bread, rye coffee, and excellent oysters. This I find to have been a luxurious meal amid this starving population. The excitement was intensified when I insisted on paying a quarter of a dollar for my entertainment. 'What, real money!' said the poor woman, and she exhibited it at once

to an admiring crowd, who looked upon it as a memento of
their bygone happy days. I have narrated this incident
accurately, as it shows the almost utter destitution both of
money and provisions on the part of the inhabitants of this
long-oppressed people.

" Leaving the house, my attention was attracted by a
throng swarming to the river. It seemed as if Norfolk and
Portsmouth were shaken to the centre with excitement.
Many whispered hopefully, some mournfully, 'The citizens
are rising against the Unionists.' All such hope or fear was
soon dissipated, for, elbowing my way through the crowd,. I
saw the little Monitor anchored in the stream, and let me
assure you she excited as eager a gaze as could the Merrimac in New York harbor. A great many 'could n't see it.'
' Where ! where is she ? ' they cried, refusing to believe that
the insignificant tub or cheese-box was the dreaded Monitor
who had fought the monster Merrimac five hours, and driven
her back leaking to Norfolk.

" I cannot describe the ruined navy-yard adequately. The
scene is too sorrowful. Fifty large mechanic shops and ware-
houses are smoking ruins; blackened hulks of steamers or
gunboats lie on every side ; huge piles of coal are still burning. The houses of officers alone are saved, and these by
the efforts of citizens, not by the sparing mercy of the rebels.
What folly, as well as sin ! By that conflagration, a fatal
blow is dealt to Virginia, and that by the hands of her professed special friends. This rebellion is making itself infamous, even at the South, by its wanton incendiary fires.
The navy-yard dry-dock yet remains but little injured, only
the front stones being loosened and the gates burned. The
attempt to blow it up proved a failure.

" We are just in time to prevent another crime of slavery.
The Norfolk Day-Book of Saturday, now in'my hands, has
the following advertisement in its columns : —

'SALE OF FREE BLACKS FOR CITY TAXES.

'CITY COLLECTOR'S OFFICE, NORFOLK, May 6, 1862.

' Under the provisions of an ordinance directing the sale of all free blacks who fail to pay their city taxes, I shall, before the door of the City Hall, on Monday, May 12, at 12 o'clock M., SELL the following-named persons for the term specified by said ordinance.'

" Here follow the names of *one hundred and twelve males, and two hundred and four females.* I was at the place at the given time, but found no opportunity to buy a slave, had I desired so atrocious a crime. God be praised, slavery is doomed ! None welcome so loudly, none so gladly, our soldiers as the slaves of these two cities. Whether others be Unionists or not, they surely are.

· " All speak enthusiastically of the noble head of our nation, — the providential man, the Moses of our Israel ! I never witnessed so much enthusiasm about any man as about that plain, homely, gaunt being, who walks unostentatiously among our soldiers, and whom they greet as their truest friend."

The regiment were soon ordered to Suffolk. The Chaplain says, in a letter dated June 9th : —

" We are here, for a time, encamped on the ' Fair Grounds,' less than a half-mile from the centre of the town ambitiously styled Suffolk City. In the whole town, or city if you will, are sixteen hundred inhabitants, two hundred of whom are free negroes. The slaves have mostly disappeared, such Southern riches taking to themselves, not wings, but legs, in times like these, and disappearing rapidly ' between two days.' Many more have been sold into further and more hopeless Southern bondage, to save them from the misfortune their masters assure us freedom is to the black race. The principal street in Suffolk is lined on either side with elm-trees ; the houses are neatly built, and in general in good repair, and, on the whole, the town wears a more trim,

New-England aspect than I have elsewhere seen in Virginia. This was one of the old Whig strongholds in the days gone by; now no place is more bitter in its Secession tone, though growing much more moderate since the occupation of the place by the Sixteenth Massachusetts Regiment, who, by the wise discipline of the officers, and their firm, strict bearing toward the citizens, and by the good order of its private soldiers, have won the involuntary respect of the inhabitants. The absence of any attempt at 'conciliation' on our part, and the unhesitating avowal of our opinions and their reasons, have proved most salutary. A weak policy is always a false one, and amiability is a synonyme for imbecility, and conciliation for cowardice, in the rebel dictionary. The town is on the very borders of the Dismal Swamp, and the location can hardly be a healthy one; but thus far, by strict sanitary regulations and the utter prohibition of the sale of spirituous liquors to the men, the health of the regiment is as good as ever. In the north parish of the town, I am told, two schools exist which are termed *free*. They are supported by a fund accumulated by the earnings of several slaves, who were left by will for that purpose seventy years ago. The slaves are dead now, but the monument of their unrequited toil remains. Of course no colored person is permitted to be educated in these schools. The very children and grandchildren of these swarthy laborers have been and are excluded. Only white children can be benefited by the coined blood and sweat of these sable sons and daughters of Africa. A free institution founded on slavery! Can such an anomaly long exist? Must not either the institution or its foundation perish?"

He thus refers to the Secession females : —

" The women, misnamed ladies, and disgracing womanhood itself, continue to insult our soldiery, relying on the immunity from punishment their sex receives. General Butler's order, rightly interpreted, would do no harm here, and something of the kind is greatly needed.

"I know how difficult it is to deal with such rebels, who forget their sex, and with it decency itself; but if they forget that they ever were ladies, can they complain if occasionally we forget it likewise?"

His regiment is now called to join the Peninsular army. He writes on June 11th: —

"I rejoice that my regiment is not left at ease and in safety as the decisive hour draws nigh. Terrible as is the ordeal of battle, I would not shrink from that fearful sight, nor for whole worlds be absent when word or prayer or feeble act of mine might avail anything to soothe or aid the noble men who fight for all that is dear and holy. I know no holier place, none more solemn, more awful, more glorious, than this battle-field shall be. Let any deem the feeling wrong who will, on that ground I would rather stand than in any pulpit in America, and never can I pray more fervently than on that day that God would bless our dear soldiers and give them success, and scatter before them the enemies of all righteousness, the enemies of man and of God, like chaff before the driving storm. I love peace, love it so much that, were it needful and consonant with my vocation, I would fight for it. 'Blessed are the peacemakers,' and these to-day I believe pre-eminently to be the men who carry a rifle at the shoulder or a sword by the side, and are determined to 'conquer peace,' and to establish it 'by force of arms,' on so firm a foundation that our children and children's children shall never be vexed by war's rude alarms."

Of an historical mansion he says: —

"To-day I have visited the White House here, built on

the foundations of that in which Washington wooed and won Mrs. Custis as his wife, and in which the first years of his married life were passed. Singular to say, the White House is *not white, but brown*. It was recently owned and occupied by Colonel Lee, a son of General Lee of the rebel army, and himself in the same ignoble service. The house is beautifully situated and prettily furnished. An old table and clock which belonged to Washington are still in its rooms, and these are the only relics of the immortal Washington I saw. When our soldiers entered the house, they found the piano open, and a music-book also outspread, as if just used by some fair rebel. On it Mrs. Lee had written, ' Northern soldiers, who profess to venerate the memory of Washington, respect this house, in which he passed the first years of his married life.' They have done so ; the house is uninjured, and carefully guarded, though Mrs. Lee's modest request yesterday, to have the table of Washington and several other things sent to her within the rebel lines, has *not* yet been granted. Opening the music-book I found also the opera *I Puritani*, The Puritans. I wonder how Mrs. Lee and the Colonel like the Puritans of to-day, and whether she rejoices in the triumphs which show the Puritan blood yet runs in their veins, while the descendants of the Cavaliers *run* before Massachusetts Puritans, as their ancestry did before Cromwell's army."

He visited, too, a memorable church.

"We rode through an avenue of trees, which form the entrance to the White House, and soon came to an opening or intervale, which for extent and beauty rivalled a Western prairie. It was enamelled with flowers, and looked as peaceful amid the lofty groves and rugged bluffs, as though it were some happy valley smiling serenely amid frowning cliffs and stately, solemn trees. A half-mile more brought us to a

Q

fountain sheltered by a few stately oaks, beneath which it murmured forth its gentle invitation for the thirsty traveller to stop and drink of its refreshing waters. We were not unmindful of the request, and found the draught a pleasant contrast to the brackish waters common in Virginia. Striking into a bridle-path, we entered a little glen, as charming as I have ever seen, even in the groves of dear old Massachusetts. Passing on as rapidly as my unchristian horse would allow, who resented every application of my spurred heels by kicking viciously, we went through a camp strewn with coats and knapsacks which our soldiers left behind them as they 'went marching on,' and saw anon the quaint old church in which Washington was married. It is beautifully located, amid arching oaks, whose interlaced branches twine appropriate chaplets to his memory. The church is built of bricks imported from England. It is a rude and simple structure, as we judge by the light of to-day, though in its time deemed rather an elegant edifice. None worship there just at present but the twittering swallows, who 'have made there a nest for themselves, even thine altars, O my God.' "

But there were sadder scenes to witness. He writes : —

"I have visited most of the tents wherein lie the sick and wounded, and their inmates bear uniform testimony to the skill and kindness of these noble surgeons who are performing such holy and honorable service at this hour of our country's need. God bless them! I find here also Miss Harriet Fanning Read, the poetess, a native of Boston, who is here nursing and caring for the suffering and the dying. Here too are most excellent and devoted ladies connected with the Sanitary Commission, and our friends at home may be well assured that all possible is done for the sick and wounded of this 'grand army of the Potomac.' "

Martial scenes were now the order of the day. On June 14th he writes : —

" We are encamped on this field, but recently the scene of the most sanguinary encounter which this war has yet witnessed or the country itself ever known. Beneath us and on every side are recent graves, sown thick with men, while the woods all around us are full of the bodies of rebels, as yet unburied, the number of the slain being too great to have yet been entirely disposed of. Arms, accoutrements of every kind, are strewn about, while the two or three houses beneath the ' fair oaks ' which give the true name to this battle-field are completely riddled with balls and shell. The ' seven pines ' are close by, which first gave an erroneous title to the battle-field, which all the resident Virginians call ' Fair Oaks,' which is the designation of the railroad station near.

" This division (Hooker's) is emphatically a fighting division, its general being familiarly termed ' Fighting Joe Hooker,' and is abundantly dreaded by the enemy. I believe the Sixteenth Regiment will not bring upon it any reproach, but will do its entire duty in the approaching conflict. Time will erelong show in reference to this, and may it exhibit an honorable record.

" We are living with republican simplicity here, I assure you. The staff officers have but soldiers' rations, and we all sleep on the ground, and officers and privates share hardships together. But such is a soldier's life, and I hear no murmuring, and have none myself to utter.

" Of course I cannot speak of plans or positions here. Suffice it that we are *close upon Richmond*, and hope soon to enter the rebel capital. How soon or by what movements it would be improper to write.

" All our baggage is left behind, we retaining no more than what can be carried in the coat-pocket or haversack."

On the 17th he writes: —

"We are encamped on the field recently the scene of the most sanguinary strife in the annals of American warfare, for on this spot, when the true narrative of this war is written, it will appear that more lives were lost, more wounds received, than in any other conflict of this struggle, or in any of its predecessors on this continent.

"The terrible evidences of the bloody nature of this fight are all about us. In one grove sixty-seven bodies are buried, and the soil is sown thick with mounds, in which lie heaps of slain.

"Nor do we need to read the record of the past week, written in blood and bones on this plain, though each day has its own dangers and horrors. On Sunday I was three times under fire, — twice in my own regiment and once while on a brief visit to the Twenty-ninth Massachusetts. Early in the morning of that day the shot and shell flew thick and fast over our heads, and we were momentarily expecting a general engagement, and in the evening the same scene was repeated; but prudence was, on both occasions, the best part of rebel valor. At noon of same day, a very fierce attack was made while we were at dinner with the Twenty-ninth, in Meagher's Brigade.

"Add to this a most fearful, raging thunder-storm, in which the artillery of heaven rivalled and drowned at intervals the jarring thunders of our cannon, and you have a day more stirring than could be dreamed of on a peaceful New England Sabbath. On Monday morning, very early, at two and five A. M., we were twice called again into line of battle by similar attacks, but no general engagement ensued, though in these encounters lives and limbs were lost on our side and doubtless on the other. We realize here what war means, and that it implies suffering, wounds, death.

"We make no complaint of privations. They are unavoidable, generally, when large masses of men are moved. And this swampy ground, this cold summer with its incessant rains, the necessity of leaving most of our tents and other comforts behind, render such hardships unavoidable for us. For three nights

'My lodging was on the cold, cold ground,'

with but a solitary blanket for protection. Yesterday we made rude beds of pine-boughs, and are more comfortable in that respect. 'Hard-tack,' or crackers, what the soldiers call 'Hardee tactics,' coffee destitute of any milk or sugar, and 'salt-horse,' as the men term salt beef, were the rations of officers and privates alike, but we are doing better to-day, and shall doubtless be better provided for when our supplies can reach us.

"The rainy days, and strangely cold nights following even the days most glowing and sultry, have tried and must try our constitutions, but sanitary care wards off most of the danger; and all will be well if only we can witness Richmond taken, the rebel army routed, and can hear that Charleston, the head of the snake Secessia, is crushed, and the rebellion dead or dying, and this consummation devoutly to be wished cannot be far off. God speed the day!"

On the 19th he describes an engagement.

"Yesterday witnessed the first bloody skirmish in which the Sixteenth Massachusetts regiment has been engaged. We call the battle a skirmish, — 'Woodland Skirmish,' — it being in advance of the scene of the Fair Oaks battle, or of any place where a fight has yet taken place between us and our foes.

"The camp of this regiment has been some three times exposed to fire, shot and shell reaching us, but producing no casualties; and yesterday a sharp attack upon the left wing

of the army, where we are located in the front rank, called
out this whole brigade under arms. It was deemed best by
General McClellan to order a reconnoissance in force by one
regiment, and ours was selected for the dangerous and important service. At 3½ P. M. the entire regiment was ordered
under arms, and sent forward into the woodlands where it
was supposed the enemy lay, and beyond which his batteries
were known to be. No man shrunk from his duty. Your
correspondent was ill with a sick-headache, but felt it to be
no more than his duty to go forward with his regiment to a
scene which was certainly one of peril, though of honor also.
We marched over the field, where a multitude of graves of
the fallen in the late battle of Fair Oaks met our view; indeed,
we are encamped on that field where Casey's division were
before the last battle. We soon reached the woodlands in
our front, where the regiment deployed as skirmishers. The
woods proved to be full of rebels snugly ensconced in their
rifle-pits, and a large fortification supplied with artillery was
just beyond the woods. The action was soon brought on,
and was short, sharp, and terrible. I can truly say that our
regiment behaved nobly, and I saw no flinching on the part
of any man. The only fault I will find, if any, was that
they were too rash, and pushed forward too determinedly,
considering the tremendous odds both of position and men
against which we were contending. The enemy were certainly in force, five to our one, knew every tree and ravine,
and were protected by rifle-pits. Of course our brave men
fell fast, and soon we bore away, wounded or dying, five brave
soldiers whom I have since buried.

"We drove the enemy back from the woods to their intrenched fortifications, but were unable to hold our ground
or bring off our dead under the murderous fire of their artillery. Double the number of our loss must have fallen killed
and wounded of the rebel forces by the courageous fire of

our men. We took three prisoners. We ascertained, too, the force and position of the enemy, which was the whole intent of the reconnoissance."

On the 21st he speaks of an assault.

" Yesterday afternoon at three o'clock, the battery of the enemy which was unmasked by the Sixteenth Massachusetts Regiment, in their reconnoissance of last Wednesday, opened full fire upon Grover's brigade, then doing guard and picket duty, which here requires an extra brigade for each wing and one for the centre of the army. As the Sixteenth Regiment was then on the advance picket, your correspondent at once proceeded to the field. The 'fair oaks' were struck by many shot and shell, and the enemy's missiles flew pretty lively for about an hour. Several shrapnel shell burst and spilled their contents about our heads in a very disagreeable way. These shells were filled with large bullets, Kentucky rifle-balls, Minie bullets, &c. They fired also some canister shell and a few solid shot. This firing was more severe than any we have yet been exposed to, and the guns were evidently of long range, as some shell passed over our camp as well as the regiment in the field in front. No casualty, however, took place, the shell doing no special damage to us. Artillery firing on men in an open field is really less dangerous, though more noisy, than rifle volleys in wood or field. The Sixteenth certainly gets its share of action and peril now, but the boys are fast becoming accustomed to the smell of powder.

" We hear regularly, morning and evening, the enemy's band playing, and their drum-beat at reveille and tattoo. The object of the assault yesterday was to prevent the further construction of our works and reach our batteries, and if possible destroy our camp. Their effort was in all respects a failure. On the field, attracted by the firing, I met General Kearney, the brave general who lost an arm in the Mexican war, but who rides now into the battle-field with his rein in his mouth and his sword in his remaining hand, an impersonation of military skill and precision, and greatly admired and loved by all the soldiery. He was accompanied by the Count de Paris, who was full of interest in the result of our arms, and seems a truly noble and worthy young man."

On the 22d he writes : —

" Each day brings its own excitement and novel scene ; almost each hour witnesses here in the front line some incursion of the enemy or reconnoissance by ourselves, some wounded, perhaps dying soldier, shot barbarously on picket by the rebels, or some deserter or prisoner brought into our lines and passing through our camp. We occupy the ground on which Casey's division lately were ; a field which, by its graves and yet unburied dead, shows evidences of its sanguinary scenes.

" Every now and then a shrapnel or canister shot or shell reaches the camp, and throws it into a little confusion, though not causing, I believe, so much alarm as rather pleasing excitement.

" Yesterday we had a whirlwind, or wind-spout, which took stray blankets, newspapers, letters, &c. high in air, and passed rapidly through this camp and others, certainly affording us some little variety.

" Yesterday noon an attack was made with artillery upon this division, while the Sixteenth Massachusetts was on the outer picket, causing no small stir, as the shot and shell flew all about us.

" I was under the 'fair oaks,' which gave the name to the recent battle, and where the shell scattered in great profusion. After the attack I gathered one or two handfuls of bullets and Minie balls with which shrapnel shell were filled, and which flew almost like rain about us, yet, strange to say, no one was hurt by any of them."

Another conflict is near. Under date of June 27th he writes: —

" This exciting life, amid the noise of screaming shot and shell, with daily attacks upon our front line, affords incident enough for correspondence, but scarce one quiet moment in which to write. Day before yesterday was one of unusual stir, and marked by a most sanguinary conflict, in which this whole division (Hooker's) was engaged, and in which many a gallant soul breathed its last sigh as it quit its mortal tenement. At an early hour the entire division was notified to be under arms and ready for the field. At seven o'clock the line of march was taken to the woodlands occupied by the enemy, in front of the late Fair Oaks battle-field. The First and Eleventh Massachusetts and Twenty-sixth Pennsylvania were among the earliest to enter the woodlands, where they deployed as skirmishers. The Sixteenth Massachusetts, Eighty-seventh New York, and Twentieth Indiana, and other regiments remained in the outskirts of the woods as support. Action was not long delayed ; soon the forest echoed with sharp volleys of musketry. Each dell and ravine was alive with rebels in ambush. They were courageously driven from these fastnesses, but not without heavy loss on both sides. Just beyond the groves, in a field, the rebels have a battery. Our forces penetrated through the woods to this field, and found themselves under fire from the rifle-pits and battery there. The enemy poured forth in solid column, and with wild hurrahs attacked our soldiery. At this time, many of the First Massachusetts, Second New Hampshire, and Twenty-sixth Pennsylvania were wounded or killed ; but all along the line the enemy were repulsed,

12

and retreated. Wounded rebels, with some prisoners, were now brought in to the spot where your correspondent was standing, and where also the surgeons and some commanding officers were. These rebels seemed defiant, and, though expecting ultimate defeat at Richmond, declared that would not end the war. Their haversacks were pretty well supplied with soft biscuit and bacon for food, but they had no coffee in their canteens, and they said that was 'long since played out in the Confederate army as part of rations.' Their wounded bore their pains less cheerfully and uncomplainingly than our own men, though cared for with equal tenderness. I think my feeling toward the rebellion does not bias my judgment on this point, but the difference was noticeable with all present.

"Toward evening the Sixteenth Massachusetts, Twentieth Indiana, and Eighty-seventh New York were subjected to a fierce attack by the rallying rebels. The first-named regiment had but little share in the earlier portion of the conflict, but at five o'clock were sent forward to support advancing artillery, and the rebels attempting a flank movement, the Sixteenth was encountered by a full brigade of the foe, and endured a cross fire for some little time. This regiment, which distinguished itself in a brilliant skirmish on the 18th instant, fought with much determination now, but was obliged to fall back, owing to the immense superiority of the force arrayed against them. Being reinforced by a portion of Couch's division, it rallied anew under its gallant officers, and thus returned to the charge, the enemy being driven from the field. I sent you yesterday a list of the killed and wounded and missing of this regiment, twenty-nine in number. I did this, not because their conduct in action was more meritorious than other regiments, or their loss greater in a contest where all did well, and many regiments suffered even more than they; but, being with them, I know more accurately the details of their losses.. Twice during the week the Sixteenth Massachusetts Regiment, just arrived on the field, has had a baptism of blood, losing sixty men in casualties on the 18th instant, and twenty-nine on the 25th.* It has proved worthy to stand by the side of other noble regiments from the glorious loyal States. It asks no higher praise or honor.

" The houses and trees beneath which wounds were being dressed by the surgeons presented sad scenes indeed; but many of these were noble and worthy of note. Private William C. Bentley, wounded by the shell of the enemy, both legs broken, and arm and head mangled, yet not immediately killed, displayed great calmness and courage. He declined any stimulating drink or opiate which might dim his consciousness until he had first heard prayer, expressed his religious trust and faith, and sent messages of love and advice to his mother; then he sank into that sleep which knows no earthly waking. Private Francis Sweetser of Company E, Sixteenth Massachusetts, lay wounded through the abdomen, in much pain, but quiet and smiling, as though the hour was full of joy to him. 'Thank God,' he said, ' that I am permitted to die for my country; thank God yet more that I am prepared'; then he modestly added, ' at least I hope I am.' We who knew him, and his humble Christian life in his regiment, have no doubt of the full assurance of his faith, and that all he hoped is now realized in bliss. Of the First Massachusetts there were noble men nobly dying, and of the Twentieth Indiana and other regiments the same could well and truly be said. None can realize the faith and heroism, the high and noble character of our volunteers as a body, who has not witnessed a scene like that.

---

* Afterward, during Pope's retreat, this regiment lost a hundred men in less than fifteen minutes, while charging upon the enemy.

" Our own artillery was not idle, and the havoc among the enemy must have been fearful. Repulsed on every side, they withdrew, and as a result of the battle our pickets were advanced more than a mile nearer Richmond that evening than ever before. The cheering along our lines last night, and the rejoicing bands of music show that the right wing of the army, too, were not idle, while we of the left were exposed in conflict. This advance is very gratifying, and the heavy cannonading of yesterday and to-day proves that the enemy is being driven from his stronghold."

The unlooked-for retreat now commenced. The Chaplain was providentially spared its sufferings. On June 28th he is again at the White House, and writes : —

" Once again I am visiting this now famed and henceforth doubly historic locality. Yesterday morning all was unusually quiet in our camp. It seemed to me an appropriate time to visit White House Landing, and secure some expressage which had been sent me, and forward by Adams's express, which had an office there, some money and other valuables which had been committed to my charge by members of the regiment, for the purpose of safe forwarding. There was then no dream of immediate movement any more than there has been for weeks and even months past, — all was supposed to be triumphant along our entire line. Martindale's brigade was reported to have taken a heavy battery from the enemy, and the evening before our regiment had been summoned from their repose to fall into line to hear two despatches from McClellan as to the success over the enemy at Mechanicsville. An hour before my departure came an order to be ready for a movement at any moment, and as several of us were encumbered with trunks and other comforts of home, deemed superfluous luxuries in camp, it seemed doubly advantageous that I should proceed to White House and see to their safe storage. About the same time sprang up a faintly whispered report of some disaster on our right wing, at a distance from our position; but none seemed to credit it, so opposite was it from what we were expecting. Some panic was said to have existed at White House, from apprehensions of another raid; that, too, was deemed a mere frightful memory of the former disaster in that neighborhood. It did seem best, however, if a movement were soon to be made, to at once disencumber ourselves of all extra baggage and money, and other valuables, and then we should be all ready for action. So at nightfall I started for the White House, sorry to be absent even an hour from camp, but assured of being back again the next morning.

"I found on arriving at White House that all was confusion. The Quartermaster would store no more baggage. Adams's express-office had abruptly departed, and it did seem for a while as if all things under my charge must be abandoned to their fate. I was counselled to take that course, indeed, but refused, and finally succeeded in getting a guard stationed over my baggage, which was left in the open air on the river-bank till morning. Where I was to sleep was a difficult problem. Many tents were struck already, the steamers were crowded, and, homeless and shelterless, I stood on the river's bank at nine o'clock in the evening, hungry, weary, but afraid to sleep on the ground with so many valuables intrusted to my·charge on my person, yet utterly exhausted. At last I did manage to lie down, without mattress or blanket, amid a group of sleepers on the floor of a steamer's cabin, and there slept, and slept soundly too. No New England servant but would 'throw up his commission,' abandon the service very quickly, had he such fare and lodging as is the choicest given to officers or soldiers in the Grand Army. It is well enough, doubtless, that we should

thus learn to prize the comforts of home. Next morning I
succeeded in getting all my stores and valuables into the
hands of a trusty messenger of Adams's express, and getting
my pass, proceeded at an early hour to the railroad station
to take passage for my regiment; but alas for such plans
and my hopes! just as the train was about to leave for its
destination, tidings came that the station above was in the
hands of the rebels, and our communication with the main
army by railroad cut off. Of course there was no way to be
taken but to go down the river in a steamer to Fortress Monroe, and thence up the James River to some point whence the
main army can be reached again. To go forward any other
way would be to advance 'onward to Richmond,' and visit
that city a little prematurely. I prefer to go there with my
own regiment, in due time, rather than under rebel escort
now.

"Then ensued a destruction of all stores and buildings,
which was fearful, yet grand to contemplate. All supplies
were put on board schooners and transport steamers, which
were sent down stream. This was done calmly by the military authorities, but with great energy. A vast deal, however, of public property could not be saved. Soon a large
encampment of tents was in flames. Two long trains of
railroad-cars were burned, with their contents. Every now
and then an explosion took place which filled the air with
fragments and towering columns of smoke and flame. A
huge storehouse of bacon sent volumes of black smoke upward. The stores chiefly abandoned were sutlers' stores,
belonging to a class who excite less sympathy than any other
in the army when they suffer loss. One sutler abandoned a
storehouse containing four thousand dollars worth of goods;
another of one thousand dollars in value. The 'boys' rev-
elled in these, as all things were free that day, and men
procured a good dinner or clothing outfit 'without money

and without price.' As they sorely needed one good meal and to be reclothed, and the sutlers could well afford the supply from their profits, the sight was, upon the whole, a pleasant one. All this time the White House, belonging to the rebel Colonel Lee, stood unharmed. It is a modern structure, and it is a shame that any such house should stand on the site of what once was the home of Washington, to shelter rebels and haters of the country for which he lived and suffered. Few of us grieved when this property of a rebel officer was in flames, also, as by its destruction nothing which Washington ever touched or looked upon was consumed.

" Meanwhile the old scows, filled with bulky stores, were burned, some wagons which could not be removed were burned or rolled over the bank and broken, while old muskets, rebel relics from Fair Oaks, shovels, pickaxes, etc., were committed to the bosom of the Pamunkey, to be concealed there in that muddy stream. Horses careered wildly about, terrified contrabands brought over boats, while the incendiaries, with a good purpose, applied the torch on every side. Surgeons were detailed to destroy such of the hospital stores as could not be removed, which they did effectually. The scene was soon grander, wilder, more brilliant than I have ever witnessed before. The very clouds caught the lurid glow, and reflected in radiant hues the sad, fearful splendor below. Bursting bombs made noise like the shock of thunder-clouds, and scattered fragments about till earth and sky seemed mingled in one awful conflagration. The old theories and pictures of the judgment-day seemed glowingly actualized and painted anew on the twofold canvas of earth and sky. That scene it was a sorrowful but great privilege to witness! Since it must have been done, I am glad to have had such an experience. An artist was sketching it, so that some faint idea will be given of it to the public by a sketch other than this of words. O the desolation, the waste of war! When shall it end, and a righteous peace be declared, without compromise or surrender of justice or the Union?

"This river upon which we are now floating was previously almost a stranger to me, even by its name, so little euphonious. It is the most winding and tortuous stream I ever saw, making such bends as to give the idea, as you see steamers in the distance almost parallel with you, that it is a different stream upon which they must be floating. It plays strange tricks of illusion in that way. It is a singularly broad and beautiful stream, and were it in New England its banks would be lined with smiling villages; now scarce a house is upon its banks, and its shores are either neglected or desolate. In the stream, near where the White House stood yesterday, is an island, where live one hundred and fifty Indians, many of them skilful pilots, and better agriculturists than any white Virginians on the Peninsula. These are the remnant of the once powerful tribe of whom Pocahontas was one. They are passing rapidly away. So is, indeed, everything which once was the glory of fair, but sinful and desolate Virginia."

When the army reached Harrison's Landing, it presented to view many a sad scene. The Chaplain writes : —

. "I have been at this hospital for most of the past week, not as a patient, but caring to the best of my ability for the wounded and suffering sick of my own regiment, and the countless number from the other various regiments of the loyal army, scarce one of which fails to have more or less representatives here. The scenes one is called to witness here are terrible. Ghastly wounds innumerable greet the saddened vision ; men, sick nigh unto death with swamp, pestilential fevers, make their weak moans, asking for pity and for succor; exhausted soldiers, after four days' hard fighting, with scarce any food, plead for a piece of bread, or they must perish with hunger; the dying ask a word of counsel and of prayer, and to transmit some message to wife or child or mother ere the last breath be drawn and the last sigh heave their panting bosoms. The dead, too, lie on the earth beneath the sweet heavens, and their dumb, passionless forms require, as their once spirit-tenants have deserved, that those bodies lately instinct with vigorous life should be decently buried.

"Beautifully situated is this building where we now are. The James River flows silently by, its gleaming waters whitened with countless sails rafting supplies to the hungry army, or its else placid face ruffled by the steamers which come daily to the landing, bringing hospital stores to the wounded and sick, and returning down the stream laden with those whose only hope of recovery or future usefulness lies in the revisiting of their homes and the solace of care and kindness there. Lofty elms line the avenue which leads to this dwelling, and the gigantic cottonwood interlaces its branches with the lordly oak, though causing its vigor to decay, and blighting by its contact. The cottonwood-tree grows almost entirely in the South, and is its representative tree, as the oak is of the North. As these trees intertwine and mingle, yet have distinct organic life and diverse qualities, so has it been with the North and South. Shall it ever be so again, or must the axe be laid at the root of the institution of one of them, and the soil sown afresh with some seed which shall bear a growth homogeneous with, and not destructive to, the other? This is the base of the new line of operations. It is beautiful, and has solid advantages. May its superstructure, the noble army, once of the Potomac, meet with substantial success, and win laurels which shall be beautiful in the eyes of all loyal Americans and of the friends of freedom throughout

12*   R the world. To-day that army is war-worn, and its purposes temporarily baffled; but such men, fighting in such a cause, cannot be permanently defeated; for

> 'Freedom's battle once begun,
> Bequeathed from bleeding sire to son,
> Though baffled oft, is ever won.'

" Lovely as is this situation, it is not more beautiful than the dwelling-house which is in the centre of the town and its skirting woods. It is a fit gem for such an emerald and beautiful setting. The house is of ancient brick, imported from England many years since, whence also came the carved panel-work and cornices in the rooms. President Harrison is reported to have been born in this house, so it has an historic interest already, and will have more in the future. It is elegantly furnished with rosewood and black-walnut furniture. Fine pictures look down upon you from the walls, and the library is filled with costly volumes, many of them books which have crossed the Atlantic ere reaching here. Around the house cluster some twenty or more whitewashed buildings, in which the one hundred and twelve plantation slaves lived, if theirs can be called life, and not existence only. The owner of this house and all its surroundings, the owner, in man's sight, but not God's, of all these human beings, is Powhatan B. Stark, M. D., now a surgeon in the rebel army, and claiming to be a lineal descendant of Pocahontas. He fled precipitately when our transports lined the shores, carrying off to Petersburg all the household jewels and the most valuable slaves also, and ordering the house to be burned by those remaining, an order they did not see fit to obey. He told such slaves as could not be hurried away, that, if they were asked by the Yankees whether they wished to be free, to state that ' they are and always have been as free as they wanted to be '; that order, too, they have failed to obey, but shout hallelujahs over their deliverance from a bondage

which, though not as heavy as usual, was nevertheless griev-
ous, as slavery must ever be to the soul of a man made in
the image of God."

The Chaplain's labors in these fearful scenes were
publicly acknowledged. An army correspondent
says : —

" I know but little of the theological notions of Chaplain
Fuller, but I can tell you that he has got the name, in the
army where he is known, of 'a man going about doing
good.' It matters not how poor or how degraded a man is
who comes in contact with Mr. Fuller, he withdraws from
that contact a better man. 'None know him but to love
him.'"

Another writes : —

" Prominent among those who are active in relieving the
sufferings of the sick and wounded soldiers, I notice the Rev.
Arthur B. Fuller, Chaplain of the Sixteenth Massachusetts
Regiment. Mr. Fuller has been busy at the hospital from
morning till night, administering medicines and words of
comfort to such as were in need."

Shortly before the Sixteenth Regiment unexpectedly
left Fortress Monroe, the Chaplain had obtained a fur-
lough. On his way home the movement reached his
ears, and he immediately retraced his steps, writing
the following letter to his family : —

" I am sorry to disappoint you, by not meeting you this
week; and it is painful to turn back to increased hardship,
when my face was once set homeward. But I learned last
evening, on board the boat, that my regiment had moved forward to occupy Sewall's Point, and thence to Norfolk. I
cannot leave them in their hour of peril, when perhaps my
prayers and counsel may be especially valuable. This is

the first really active service of the *Sixteenth*. Its hardships, its privations, its dangers, I too must share."

When the summons came to join the Peninsular army, he writes to his home : —

" God be praised that we are permitted to do something to serve our country! May He who doeth all things for his glory and man's welfare secure for us a splendid triumph over the forces of rebellion and treason! I pray for my country's redemption, and that even through war may come that freedom for which the bondman sighs, that unity which is the strength of a nation, that righteousness which is her highest glory ! "

From the battle-field he writes home : —

" I am enduring much privation in the way of food, clothing, and exposure. But I do not think it manly to write particulars, as you desire ; indeed, I endeavor not to think about it. Almost every day, and sometimes twice a day, I go out with the regiment in line of battle. I deem this my duty. For nine days I had no change of raiment, not even a clean shirt or handkerchief, and lived on hard crackers and sour coffee. But God blesses my labors, particularly among the sick and wounded, and I am far enough from repining. Of all places in the world, I am glad I am here now. I find no physical fear to be mine. This is a mere matter of organization, not merit. Meet me on earth, if it may be ; in heaven, surely. And know that nothing will make me swerve from my fealty to God, to Christ his Son, to my family, my State, and my COUNTRY." -

But the Chaplain's body was unequal to his spirit, and sank under disease caused by exposure and hardship. His sickness was so severe that the physicians pronounced it incurable in the Virginia climate. He

was urged to seek the recovery of health at home.
Among others, Hon. Frank B. Fay, Mayor of Chelsea, who labored in the army on the errand of mercy
and philanthropy, visited him and urged him to return. His agency had much to do on this occasion
in restoring the Chaplain in life to his family, as it
finally was instrumental in furnishing to them the sad
consolation of weeping over his remains and paying
them the mournful rite of sepulture.

CHAPTER V.

SHADOWS.

"O country, marvel of the earth
    O realm to sudden greatness grown !
The age that gloried in thy birth,
    Shall it behold thee overthrown ?
Shall traitors lay that greatness low ?
No, Land of Hope and Blessing, no !

"And we who wear thy glorious name,
    Shall we, like cravens, stand apart,
When those whom thou hast trusted aim
    The death-blow at thy generous heart ?
Forth goes the battle-cry, and lo !
Hosts rise in harness, shouting, No ! "

BRYANT.

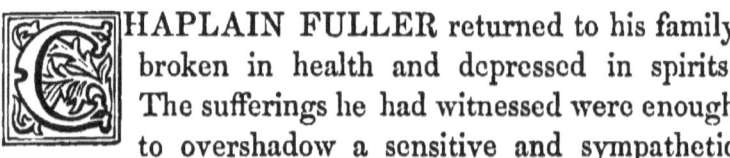HAPLAIN FULLER returned to his family broken in health and depressed in spirits. The sufferings he had witnessed were enough to overshadow a sensitive and sympathetic temperament, such as his ever was. Disease, too, contracted in the malarious swamps of Virginia, had fastened a hold upon him most difficult to be shaken off, and death seemed waiting, at a brief remove, to make the finale of sickness. But it was not these things that clouded the mind of the Chaplain. It was the disappointment worse than death which had snatched victory from the expecting army, deferred the doom of Rebellion, and cast a gloom over the loyal nation.

To share a joy or sorrow with others, we know, intensifies the sentiment, giving it a multiplied force. This almost all have experienced, when the individual heart has shared the sentiment of the circle of family or friendship, or, still more, when it has beat in concordance with the emotion of a popular assembly. But it is impossible adequately to describe, and difficult to realize without actual experience, the power of an emotion in which the hearts of a nation throb in unison. Such was the revulsion of popular feeling when it was at length understood that the enterprise against Richmond had actually been abandoned, and the grand army reduced to a remnant. The blow was broken by veiling the news under the name of " strategetic movement " and " change of base." But the shock vibrated through the loyal nation. Rebellion once more raised its vaunting crest, and loyal resolution was tried by a stern ordeal.

Previous reverses, the " three stinging bees " of Bull Run, Big Bethel, and Ball's Bluff, had only roused and exasperated Union patriotism to fresh enterprise. This new and great disaster stunned the nation for a moment ; it ran so counter to public expectation and to confident hopes held out to the public to the very last, and was so inexplicable, considering the advantages of recent success and of numerical superiority enjoyed by the Federals, at the outset certainly, and up to the last days, if not throughout the tedious protraction of the Union advance. Yet there was little disposition to accuse or recriminate, or even whisper of betrayal. The disappointment was deep and mute ; as nature often seems to be, after some

dread convulsion, or as in the drama of the Apocalypse it is said, after the opening of the seventh seal,
" there was silence in heaven about the space of half
an hour."

The effort of Pope to retrieve the fortunes of the
day with his little army of forty thousand, expecting
aid from the Peninsular army, which a portion failed
to render, was foiled, after the Union army had fought
for many days, with unprecedented bravery and endurance, in a fiery furnace of repeated battles.

But the nation aroused itself to fresh efforts. In
response to the call of government for a new army,
municipalities and individuals poured out money like
water to encourage enlistments, and nobler motives
induced heroes of every condition in life to leave
home pursuits and the bosom of the loved family, to
buckle on the patriot's armor. A host of half a million
came forward as if by enchantment.

During most of the summer, Chaplain Fuller was a
very sick man. For a time the flame of life flickered
so low that it seemed about to expire. He was un-
concerned for himself, though so fully conscious of
his condition that he made some suggestions as to his
funeral. But skilful medical care,* devoted nursing,
and especially the brightened aspect of public determination and renewed confidence, contributed to his
gradual and partial recovery. As soon as his malady
would permit any exertion, he raised his voice in
public to encourage enlistments. But the returning
violence of his disorder compelled him to desist from
such efforts.

* His physician was Dr. Otis E. Hunt, of Weston, Massachusetts.

Now came the rebel invasion of Maryland, finally repulsed, with the aid of the new levies, at the bloody field of Antietam. Soon another campaign was inaugurated against Richmond, and the Chaplain determined to rejoin the army, though his health was by no means restored. He bade a tender farewell to the loved ones at home he was never to see again in the body, and departed in the latter part of October, 1862, to share in the renewed struggle.

Under date of November 4th, he gives an account of his journey, and thus speaks of the Citizens' Volunteer Hospital in Philadelphia : —

"This noble institution is another monument of the untiring zeal and ardent patriotism of the worthy men and devout women in the city of brotherly love. It is under the combined care of the government and citizens. The writer returning, still an invalid, to his regiment, then at Alexandria, found the journey too great for his strength, and was taken again ill in Philadelphia. Finding it impossible to proceed, I was about seeking such ease and care as an inn affords in these bustling days, when it was announced to me that an army hospital just opposite the depot was open night and day, and there could be obtained the medical attendance and the kind care I required. Nor did the statement prove illusory. Though eleven o'clock at night, the hospital was still open, and benevolent physicians and nurses were ready and anxious to be of service to the sick and suffering. I found it even so ; the good Father had put it into the hearts of the citizens of Philadelphia to build this hospital just in the place where it was wanted, that weary and sick officers and soldiers need not have a long and painful ride or march before the kindness of the excellent men and women of the city should be exerted in care of the ill or

wounded. Six weeks ago, not a stick of timber was on
this spot; now a comfortable edifice is here, its arrangements not yet completed, but all deficiencies more than
supplied by the unpaid yet devoted services of the best
physicians and some of the most cultivated gentlemen and
ladies to be met with in any city. Here I found, as daily
visitants, wealthy and refined men and women, who were unwearied in their acts of kindness and attention. God bless
them! I entered there a stranger, yet, leaving at the close
of a few days, felt that I had formed ties of friendship which
time or death can never sunder, and which shall be perpetu-
ated in that land where 'the inhabitant shall not say, I am
sick,' and where no battle shall cause ghastly wounds, or
exposure on the tented field make the frame languid and
weary, but where the tree of life shall cover all with its
outstretched arms and 'its leaves be for the healing of the
nations.'

"The next day was the Sabbath, and I was sufficiently
recovered to visit many sick-beds in that hospital. Here I
found several ill or wounded whose nativity was in loved
New England. I noticed also a fine youth, a Scotch clergyman's son, from Canada. He belonged to the Cameron
(Scotch) Regiment of Highlanders, of whom ninety only
remain, having survived the hardships and wounds of the
battle-field and the stern ordeal of their rough campaign.
All the others have been discharged from the ranks, or
have perished by disease or wounds. Their leader, the
brother of Secretary Cameron, was killed early in the war.
One youth from Vermont was evidently dying. He seemed
glad to have prayer offered, and all our dear New-England
boys welcomed service from one of their own region. Indeed, the religious element was a pleasant feature of this
hospital. Regular services are held each Sabbath, and it
was a request of the soldiers that your correspondent should

hold a short service with them each evening while he
stayed. I never saw any audience of more reverent, eager
listeners than those suffering men. They realize, as few
civilians do, the need of religious support and comfort, and
welcome the humblest effort to afford it. And here let me
say that, contrary to the usual impression, no class of men
are more receptive of religious instruction than those who
compose our loyal army. War develops the worst and the
best traits of character. The Gospel among the soldiers
may meet with bitter opposition from some, with earnest
welcome by others, but, if rightly presented, is heard with
indifference by very few. The next morning our Vermont
soldier died. It was pitiful to hear his cries for mother and
sister then. They were perhaps far off among the green
hills; or did he see them at that home in the heavenly land,
beckoning him on, as he was about to cross the portals of
death? Be this as it may, his last whispered word was
that which I have noted as one of the three which most
often tremble on dying lips, as it is indeed the first which
those lips have uttered, — MOTHER. The other two are
home and *heaven.*

"Resuming my journey when a few days had given sufficient strength, I reached Alexandria, and found the Sixteenth
Massachusetts encamped on the most beautiful spot I have
ever yet seen selected for an encampment. It is the brow
of a high hill, near Fairfax Seminary, about five miles from
Alexandria. By day, the wide prospect of rich autumnal
forest, crowning hill and decking valley, is glorious beyond
adequate description; and on a moonlight night, the soft light
on the landscape, and the gleaming watch-fires from a hundred forts or camps, present a scene surpassing the dreams
of fairy-land. The air here is as pure as the breath of
heaven, and the debilitated and suffering men of Hooker's
old and brave division were fast recovering, when marching

orders came, a day or two since, and they have gone to the battle-field. It was cheering yet sorrowful to take by the hand again the officers of this noble regiment and my brave soldier-boys, if I can longer call 'my boys' those who are now the veterans and tried warriors of many a hard-fought battle. Never did I feel prouder of them; never sadder, than when I saw so many wasted forms or noted how thinned their ranks, or marked the solemn silence as I asked after this man and that whom I had left alive, and now learned, by that silence or a single monosyllable, was — dead. Yet not dead; such heroes must live, on other heights than these, in fields elysian, and be pronounced by the great Captain of our salvation conquerors and more than conquerors through Him that loved them. They have but joined that silent throng who compose the army of the living God, and are ever marching on through Emmanuel's land, and shall one day make heaven echo with their 'Glory hallelujah,' as they chant the praises of Him whom God gave as a 'Leader and Commander to his people.' "

He writes with a more full and free expression of his heart to his family, never expecting it to meet the public eye: " I have reached my regiment safe and sound. How warm the greeting, both upon the part of officers and men! My own family could not be more cordial and more affectionate. It touched my heart. The poor sick men clasped my hands and said, 'Oh, we have missed you so much!' I went from company to company, shaking hands with the officers and men, and came near shedding tears myself, when I found how much they had suffered, and how many were missing, prisoners, wounded, and dead! I feel now that my sickness was providential. I should have died months ago, had I remained in the regiment going through such a terrible campaign.* I was a little sick, and slept in the hospital, last night, but feel quite well this beautiful morning, and shall occupy my own tent. *It was right that I came back.* Sorry as I am to have left you, I should never have been happy, without at least bidding these dear officers and men good-by. Nor should I have known how much they loved me. I never had a parish equally enthusiastic. Many came to the foot of the hill to meet me and carry my valise, and pressed about me with offers of service. The men who were sick at Harrison's Landing declare that they owe their lives to me, and I am praised much beyond my deserts."

The Chaplain found plenty of occupation, and he never confined himself to the limited duties of the regiment, but cheerfully extended his labors to the army division. He writes: " I work very hard among the sick and dying soldiers. We have five large buildings and several tents crowded with more than five hundred sick men, and only two surgeons in attendance, and my services are greatly needed."

His regiment was soon sent forward, but the surgeon pronounced the Chaplain disabled by the state of his health from accompanying them. He writes home to his family: "I shall care for my health and life as much as I can consistently with duty, but I shall cheerfully bear such hardships as are inevitable." Again he says, in the same confidential communication:† "I may rejoin my regiment, who have been

---

* The regiment had a prominent share, not merely in the Peninsular battles, but in the subsequent severe engagements of General Pope.

† It is hoped that the reader will bear in mind throughout these

sent to the front of the line of battle. If I could endure marching and hunger and sleeping on the cold
ground, without even a tent to shelter me, I would go
at once, having no fear of rebel bullets, but I do not
want to throw my life away. There are fifty-two of
the Sixteenth Regiment sick here, and it is plainly
my duty to stay with them, as the sick are my chief
charge."

He soon determines to make another experiment of
camp-life. He writes : —

" Duty calls me to rejoin the brave Sixteenth Regiment at
Manasses, to bear and suffer with them such hardships as
they shall be called upon to endure. Pray Heaven this war
be speedily ended, and all our trials over ; but may it not end
by dishonorable compromise or one backward step by our
good President, or by hoisting the white flag of surrender, or
trailing our starry flag in dishonor before the columns of the
rebels, who bear the black flag of piracy and the stars and
bars of treason. Better war than dishonor. Better still give
up our heart's blood in brave battle, than give up our principles in cowardly compromise. ' *Nothing is ever really settled
that is not settled right.*' May the adjustment of our national
troubles be upon the immutable basis of justice to all men,
freedom to all, and that basis shall be as firm as the rock of
ages, and the peace built upon it shall be enduring as is
eternal righteousness."

A recurrence of his disorder detains him a few
days, during which, however, he visits the sick. He
thus describes the Fairfax Seminary Hospital : —

" This beautiful cluster of buildings is in our imme-
pages that most of the Chaplain's references to himself were made in
the intimacy of confidential correspondence, and without a thonght of
publicity.

diate vicinity. They were previously occupied by an Episcopal Theological School, but several of the professors were
disloyal, and the school is removed or discontinued during
the war. The owners are emphatically loyal men, and the
buildings are rented by the government for our sick and
wounded. Eleven hundred names were on the list as patients
yesterday, many of these from Massachusetts. The little
burial-ground here is sown thick with soldiers' graves. Three
large barracks for the sick have been erected, besides the five
brick buildings. O how wasteful of human life is war, and
how fearful the guilt of the traitors and rebels who have
brought such devastation upon the whole land and filled so
many homes with mourning! I was glad to have looked out
from the cupola of the seminary ere descending into the
chambers of pain. I could not have enjoyed the prospect
above and about me, though glorious in the crimson and
golden splendor of autumn, had I first seen the wounded
in those rooms below. And yet we need often to ascend
some height of vision and look above and far beyond us,
that we may not lose sight of the purposes of Heaven, or of
the brilliant future which it shall give us as the recompense
of all this sickness, pain, and death. Yes, we need to turn
from the bloody and fearful work of war for a time, to hear
no more the stifled groan of anguish, that we may behold the
works of God, and believe from all this evil he will educe
good. God is ever beneficent and kind, and working out his
good purpose, whether the skies are serene and the earth
mantled in autumnal robes of glory, or whether the sky be
overcast and stormy, and the earth covered with its cold
and snowy mantle. He is around and above us, too, in
times of peace and gladness, or now when war makes
gloomy our horizon and fills our hearts with sadness.
Above the clangor of war's clarion, above the roar of the
cannon, more penetrating than the groans of the sick and

wounded and dying of this dreadful hour of strife, let us hear
his voice saying, as our Saviour did on earth, ' Lo, it is I, be
not afraid; peace, be still!' He who makes 'the wrath of the
heathen to praise him,' shall, by even this fearful war, advance
the cause of permanent peace, of true liberty, and a national
prosperity founded on righteousness."

He sees, too, the convalescent and the paroled
camps, which are in the neighborhood. He writes
respecting them : —

" These two camps adjoin one another, and are about two
miles from this place. I visited them yesterday to see such
Massachusetts men as might then be within their limits.
About five thousand soldiers from all the loyal States are
now in the convalescent camp. The men are located each
State by itself. In the Massachusetts portion of the camp I
found all in admirable order, and every tent and street kept
with perfect neatness. All are comfortably cared for; but I
was sorry to see some of our new recruits already in hospital,
and some who should have been rejected at home, and thus
their lives and health saved, and the government not saddled
with the incubus of soldiers unfit to do a day's duty. The
surgeons of our State are as careful as those of any other, but
more care is still needed everywhere.

" A part of this camp is devoted to the reception of recruits
sent hither for all the army, and yet another part to stragglers
from the ranks. This part I did not visit, having no desire
to look men in the face who flee their country's service or
leave the post of duty, without adequate cause, at such a
time as this."

Of the paroled camp at Annapolis he writes : —

" Here are over seven thousand men, who have tasted all
the bitterness of rebel bondage in Richmond and other Confederate prisons. They give a fearful account of their hard-

ships and privations during captivity, and the brutality with which they generally were treated.

"While in the camp, some four hundred and eighty prisoners, just paroled, arrived from Richmond. They were destitute, cold, and hungry. Their overcoats had been taken from them by their rebel captors, and they had suffered much from hunger, but not more, they said, than their jailers themselves; for the rebel army are fearfully destitute of clothing and provisions."

He thus refers to Annapolis : —

"Coming to Annapolis on Saturday, I was struck, even in the twilight, with the forsaken, dull aspect of Maryland's capital. The day revealed its location as exceedingly beautiful, but with none of that thriving, progressive aspect which marks the appearance of every Northern community, where slavery does not curse and destroy with its blight and mildew. The Capitol is, indeed, a finely-proportioned building, erected long since, even before the Revolution; and from its lofty dome, a most glorious landscape lies spread out like a scenic panorama before the vision. Thence you behold the city, with its curious squares, and intersecting streets, and antique buildings, while the river winds its devious way, in beautiful undulations, about and through the city."

A military funeral calls him to the burial-ground. He writes : —

"O, how crowded that burial-ground is with those who, full of hope, and inspired by earnest patriotism, and many of them by devout religious zeal and motive, volunteered for the suppression of this foul and treasonable rebellion which now makes our land desolate ! Shall all these sacrifices be in vain ? Shall these young, precious lives be offered up on our country's altar, and naught be ac-

13   s

complished by it?   Not so! not so! but God shall yet
permit us to dwell in a land purified of the foul stain of
slavery, and the American nation shall become a regenerate
people, loving liberty and working righteousness.   How long,
O Lord! how long ere this shall be?   Tens of thousands of
Christian soldiers on the tented field pray thee to hasten the
dawn of that glad day; while lonely wives and mothers and
children in our homes echo their prayer, and while the
souls of our martyrs in heaven take up the cry of earth,
and mingle its prayers with their praise, as they too say,
'How long ere thou avenge us and our brethren and fellow-
witnesses for Liberty, whose blood calleth from beneath thy
altar?'"

Of the convalescent camp at Alexandria he writes: —

"On Sunday last, in company with several members of the
Sanitary Commission, I visited this large encampment, and
accepted an invitation of its commanding officer to hold religious service there.   As the camp contains some fifteen
thousand men, there was work enough to do without trench-
ing upon the duties of the newly-appointed chaplain of this
camp, who, indeed, welcomed me and shared in the services
of the occasion.   His Honor, Mayor Fay of Chelsea, and his
niece, so kind and attentive to the sick soldiery, were also of
our number, and several members of the Christian Commission were likewise present, and aided in the singing and by
distribution of religious reading.   I think I never was present
on an occasion more interesting.   The singing, in which the
soldiers joined heartily, lent it a charm, and, independent of
the inadequate words spoken, the fact that such a listening
throng of soldiers, all far from home and from so many different States, were assembled, and all eager, all attentive, all
apparently longing for some earnest utterance of needed truth,
might well have touched every heart-string.   Truly it was
good to be there."

The hope of the Chaplain to be able to share the hardships of the campaign with his regiment was disappointed. The diet and exposure at once renewed the violence of his malady, incapacitated him for duty, and sent him to the hospital, to be a hinderance instead of a help. He is reluctantly brought to the conclusion that he must conform to the army surgeon's advice, and relinquish it. He writes home: "You can hardly realize the pain I felt when I found I *could not* share the field campaign without throwing away health and life. I love the regiment, and believe their feeling toward me to be so cordial that I am very reluctant to sever the tie." *

He was consoled, however, by the prospect of serving his country's cause in a new position. He writes to his family: "The President of the United States promises me, through Senator Clark, a commission with full powers as chaplain in a hospital or stationary camp. The Surgeon-General gives the same assurance. But it is necessary that I should resign my present position before assuming the new. I go to the

---

* The following is the surgeon's certificate and order: —

"HOSPITAL OF 16 MASS. VOLS.,
Warrenton Junc., Va., Nov. 16, 1862.

"I do hereby certify that Rev. A. B. Fuller, Chaplain of the 16th Mass. Vols., has been under my care since his return from absence on sick leave, and it is my opinion that his state of health precludes all idea of his remaining in the field. I find that he has Chronic Diarrhœa, and that his disease is aggravated by exposure to cold, injudicious diet, or fatigue.

"It is by my order that the said officer of this regiment remains behind in Alexandria or Washington till such time as competent surgeons pronounce him fit to return to his post.

"C. C. JEWETT,
Surg. 16 Mass. Vols."

camp at Falmouth to-morrow morning, in order to resign. I do this with much regret."

The following is a published account of his leave-
taking with his regiment : —

" On Sunday, Dec. 7, the regiment was drawn up in a
hollow square, at the close of dress-parade, for the purpose
of holding religious services and hearing the farewell address
of their chaplain. The services were deeply interesting.
Rev. Mr. Fuller expressed his great regret in parting with
the regiment, whose officers and soldiers he regarded, after
so many hardships and perils shared together, as his brothers. Nothing but the state of his health, which had suffered greatly from exposure in the field, induced him to
leave them. He should not cease his care for the soldiers,
but according to his ability should continue to minister to
their wants, temporal and spiritual. If the convalescent
camp at Alexandria were made a post-chaplaincy he should
probably be appointed there, and he sought the place because there was most suffering and most opportunity for
usefulness. If it were not, he had nevertheless been assured by the proper authorities of a chaplaincy in a hospital, as soon as he resigned his position in the regiment, and
in either place he would find abundant field for labor and
usefulness. He closed with a fervent prayer for the blessing
of Heaven upon our noble chief magistrate, our country, its
brave, loyal army, and the gallant and heroic regiment with
whom he had seen so much peril and exposure, and whose
members would ever find in their chaplain a friend, wherever
and whenever, in the future, the lines of their lives should
meet."

On the 9th of December he writes his last letter, in
which he says : —

" For nearly a year and a half I have been constantly

with my regiment, except when absent from sickness, and
have learned to regard its noble officers and brave soldiers as
brothers and its camp as a *home*, second only in affection to
my own domestic household. I am here once more, not alas!
long to remain, for exposure to the Virginia summer's heat
and winter's cold, together with privations and hardships
necessarily- incident to campaigns such as ours have been,
these have done their work, and for years I can scarcely
hope to be as well in the future as I have been in the past;
but I have no complaints to make or regrets to express;
what I have seen is worth all it has cost, and I thank God
it has been my high privilege to be with our loyal and heroic
army during its hours of trial and danger. If any regret
were mine, it would be that I am not able to remain with
my regiment longer; but this is, doubtless, in God's providence, all right, and I am grateful that in some hospital or
stationary camp I am still able to labor on for the officers
and soldiers of our army, for whom in hours of sickness, or
when wounded and suffering, none of us can do too much.
Meanwhile I am *here*, *home* again for a little while."

On the 10th of December, his resignation was accepted, and he received an honorable discharge.*

* The following is the order:—
"HEAD-QUARTERS CENTRE GRAND DIVISION.
Camp near Potomac Creek, Va.,
"Special Orders, No. 26.   December 10, 1862.
"The following-named officers, having tendered their resignations, are
honorably discharged from the military service of the United States, on
surgeon's certificate of disability.
"By command of Major-General Hooker,
"Chaplain ARTHUR B. FULLER, 16 Mass. Vols. . . . . .
"JOSEPH DICKENSON, *A. A. Gen'l.*"

CHAPTER VI.

FREDERICKSBURG.

"Nothing in his life
Became him like the leaving it; he died
As one that had been studied in his death."

"I must do something for my country!"

THE Union army had been replenished, the invading rebels driven back, and a new advance was now made upon Richmond. The Peninsula route had proved the most unfavorable that could have been selected, not only by reason of the marshy and unhealthy ground to be traversed, but because it necessitated a division of the Union army. The advance up the Peninsula did not cover Washington, and, unless a force were kept about the city and in the region lying between it and Richmond, a very obvious and effective mode of defence would be left to the enemy, who would have an opportunity to seize upon the Federal capital. If Richmond could thereby be taken, it would be a poor exchange in every point of view; nor could it be supposed that the Federal army would continue .to move against the Rebel stronghold when their own capital was assailed. The Rebels had means of transportation by which they could advance upon Washington almost before the movement was known, and much sooner than the Federal army could be transferred from the Peninsula for its defence. This was proved in the sequel by Jackson's raids against the insufficient armies which were kept as a guard between Washington and Richmond. And the reflecting mind will be satisfied, that it would have been the height of imprudence to add to the great host of the Peninsula the small armies of Banks and McDowell and the few undisciplined forces detained about Washington. The result must have been the ruinous loss of the Federal capital, while it is by no means demonstrable that the further increase of the vast army upon the Peninsula would have changed its fortunes. History will not ascribe the failure of that campaign to lack of numbers or deficiency of courage in the troops, or want of ample munitions of war.

A route was chosen for the new advance upon Richmond, *via* Fredericksburg, which would at least have the advantage of not leaving Washington uncovered. The campaign commenced under critical circumstances. The time of the nine-months volunteers was wearing away, and unless some important blow were struck before their term had expired, the cost of them to the country would be thrown away, nor would they easily be persuaded to enlist again, while it would be still more difficult to obtain fresh recruits.

The cry was, from every part of the loyal country, for an important victory. This would restore public confidence, reduce the premium on gold, and lure forth silver change from its hoarding-places, while it gave to business a fresh impulse.

This, too, would repress the disloyal element in
the Free States, which Federal reverses had emboldened to come forth from its hiding-places and take
advantage of the absence of loyal voters in the volunteer armies, to make itself felt in the elections,
while, though pretending loyalty, it sought popular
pretexts against the government.

To obtain this most needed victory, it was of the
utmost importance to revive the enthusiasm and confidence of the army, which had been somewhat depressed by finding that the unflinching valor and
endurance of the rank and file had not availed to
win decisive success, or even to avoid disastrous
reverses.

Great, therefore, was the anxiety with which the
nation regarded the new campaign. A decisive battle
it was expected, must soon be fought, as it was not
supposed that the Rebels would retire to Richmond
without a sanguinary contest. But should the Union
army prevail in the battle, it was believed that victory would this time be so promptly followed up as
to make sure of the capture of Richmond, and with
this capture the war would be practically ended.

In this state of public expectation, the army of the
Potomac advanced from Aquia Creek till it reached the
Rappahannock. It was determined to cross the river at
the city of Fredericksburg, although this purpose was
disguised by feints at other points. The design was
rendered patent to the enemy by a delay of many
days, caused by the failure to furnish the requisite
pontoon-bridges. Summons to surrender and notice
to remove women and children also preceded the

attack for several days. Meanwhile the active foe had fortified heights at the distance of two or three miles in the rear of Fredericksburg, while they refused to surrender the city, and took measures to obstruct the crossing of the stream.

The 11th day of December, 1862, was the day fixed for the passage of the Rappahannock. The pontoon-bridges had been conveyed to its banks, during the previous night, and one hundred and forty-three pieces of artillery had been so placed as to command the city. During the night rockets had been seen to rise within the lines of the enemy, and at five o'clock in the morning, as the Federals began to construct three pontoon-bridges, two signal-guns were fired by the Rebels.

At six o'clock, when the pontoon-bridges were half completed, a murderous fire from the enemy, under cover of the houses in Fredericksburg, was opened upon our infantry and upon the engineers engaged in constructing the pontoons, and the latter were driven from their work.

Thus the enemy took advantage of General Burnside's forbearance toward the city; and such forbearance ceased to be a virtue. The order was now given for all the guns to be opened upon the city. The cannonade was terrific, and the main body of the enemy's infantry was compelled to retire. Yet, upon a fresh attempt to construct the pontoons, it was found by the enemy's fire that they were still in sufficient force in the city to render the work impracticable. Again our artillery was opened upon the city, firing it in several places. Yet the enemy were not induced to evacu-

13 *

ate. By this time it got to be noon. The Federals
now placed every available battery in position, and, at
a given signal, opened upon the city a terrific cannonade of one hundred and seventy-six guns. The concentrated thunder of this artillery exceeded any previously heard during the war. The shot and shell
went crashing through the houses, firing them in many
places. The smoke of the conflagration and of our
own artillery almost hid the city from view.

It was now three o'clock in the afternoon, and under
the belief that the enemy had been forced to retire, the
work upon the pontoons was resumed. But the fire of
their sharpshooters from cellars, rifle-pits, fences, and
every available shelter, was still so deadly, that the
pontoons could not be laid. A new expedient must
be adopted. The main body of the enemy had unquestionably retired, and though the sharpshooters
were evidently numerous, they were of necessity
somewhat scattered, and might not resist a bayonet-
charge, could it be brought to bear upon them. But
how could the Federals be got over the river? The
boats at hand would not transport much over a hundred, and during their transit they would furnish marks
for more than a hundred rifles. To select a particular
company for so hazardous a service might be invidious,
and should they obey with unwillingness or hesitation,
their example might have a damaging influence. It
was resolved to call for volunteers; for thus not only
would those engaged in the service be best adapted to
it by the possession of superior bravery, but, in case of
a fatal result, should all or the greater number of them
be killed or wounded or taken prisoners, they could not

reproach their commander with requiring of them a desperate service.

The call was made for volunteers. Would it be responded to ? If not, it would scarcely then be practicable to resort to compulsion. The crossing of the river must be abandoned, while at the same time a reproach was put upon the courage of the army, and their failure in the crisis must have a demoralizing influence. Nor was this the only evil to be anticipated. This was the first engagement of the army of the Potomac under the command of Burnside. How many there were at hand to say, " Ah! this proves that he cannot command the enthusiasm of the army! The change of generals has ruined the Federal cause. This results as we expected." How important to prove, in that hour, that the Federal army was composed of patriotic hearts, who understood and prized principles more than men, and were too devoted to their country's cause, too enlarged and intelligent, to identify their cause with any general, even if he enjoyed the popularity, inexplicable on the score of success, which partisan clamor asserted on behalf of a past commander.

Chaplain Fuller was the man to appreciate these considerations, and to feel the momentous issue of that hour through every pulse and fibre of his enthusiastic nature. And he was upon the spot, watching with anxious concern the events of the day. He had, indeed, been discharged from all official obligations to the army; but not from the higher duty which had called him to his army mission. On leaving Washington to resign his chaplaincy, he had said that he should return in a few days, unless he learned there was to be a battle. In that event he should be present at the conflict. To minister to the wounded and dying, on such an occasion, and to inspirit the soldiers by his sympathy and uncompulsory presence amid their dangers, required no army commission. He could do this as one of the self-commissioned, devoted lovers of God and man, who attended, like good angels, upon the army in its contests, receiving their compensation in no earthly coinage.

The view which he took of his duty in the emergency which now presented itself, and the considerations which rapidly passed through his mind and induced him to make one of the volunteers, we are left to infer from knowledge of his character and circumstances; for our inquiries in all quarters have not obtained information of any conversation which he had previous to the act. Indeed, it is scarcely probable that in his decision he made any oral statement of his motives. It was a time for action, and not words. Yet those who knew him, and we trust those who have read these pages, need no verbal exposition from the Chaplain to understand his motives.

Should one in his position respond to this call for volunteers, it would indicate no common devotion. It was a duty which could not be required of him. And for one of his profession to consistently engage in this enterprise would prove his strong conviction that it was a work so holy, so acceptable to God, that even those set apart for sanctuary service might feel called to have a hand in it. His prowess was nothing; yet it was not his unpractised right arm, but his heart, which he devoted to the service, and which would tell on the result, not merely of that special enterprise nor of that battle only, but, by affording a powerful proof of love of country outweighing considerations of safety and life, would have the influence which a living example, and only a living example, can have.

It is easy now to say that it was unnecessary for the Chaplain to volunteer; there would have been enough without him. Such an excuse would have availed every volunteer. The chaplain did not belong to that large class who wait for others, and refrain from self-sacrifice in a good cause, under the pretext that there are enough others to sustain it. The first impulse of such a movement must be improved. Waiting for others quenches its spirit and makes it abortive. His immunity only rendered his volunteering more striking, and more influential in the contagion of example.

The sudden emergency in which the Chaplain decided in a moment how to act, was wholly unexpected by him. He was arrayed in the uniform of a staff officer, which made him a special mark for the sharpshooters. He had been cautioned, early in the day, against exposing himself, and reminded that as he had his discharge on his person, he would not be exchanged if taken prisoner, and if he were killed his family would not be entitled to a pension.* He had also valuables with him. And there was no time to place them in security or to change his costume. That the Chaplain loved home dearly, has fully appeared from evidence furnished in these pages. That, though he was a stranger to fear, he was careful not to throw

* An army officer informs us that he made these suggestions to the Chaplain.

away his life, even in the cause he loved dearest, that
of his country, his correspondence proves. We are
led to the conviction that he deemed the issue of the
hour, and the influence he might have upon it, of more
importance than the life which he staked. He volunteered, musket in hand, and crossed the river in
safety; but fell soon after entering Fredericksburg,
pierced with two bullets, the one entering his chest
through his arm upraised to discharge the musket, the
other piercing his hip. A third bullet struck his breast
laterally, tearing his coat and vest, but inflicting no
wound.

Sergeant Hill of the Sixteenth Massachusetts Regiment informs us that he was the Chaplain's guest at
his last dinner, on the day of his death. "He asked
all," says the Sergeant, "to partake with him, —
teamsters, sergeants, and myself. I told him I feared
he had none too much for himself. 'O yes!' he said,
he had plenty. And, whatever he had, he always
wished to share with those around him."

The following letter from Captain Dunn to the
Chaplain's brother gives an account of the Chaplain's
last moments : —

"In answer to your inquiries, I would say, that, although I
had previously intended, at the suggestion of a mutual friend,
to make the acquaintance of Chaplain Fuller, I saw him for
the first time, in the streets of Fredericksburg, on the 11th
December ultimo, at about half past three P. M., where I
was in command of twenty-five men deployed as skirmishers.
We came over in the boats, and were in advance of the
others who had crossed. Pursuant to orders, we marched up
the street leading from the river, till we came to the third

street traversing it, parallel with the river, and called Carolina Street, I think. We had been here but a few minutes
when Chaplain Fuller accosted me with the usual military
salute. He had a musket in his hand; and he said: 'Captain, I must do something for my country. What shall I
do?' I replied, that there never was a better time than the
present; and he could take his place ȯn my left. I thought
he could render valuable aid, because he was perfectly cool
and collected. Had he appeared at all excited, I should
have rejected his services; for coolness is of the first importance with skirmishers, and one excited man has an unfavorable influence upon the others. I have seldom seen a person
on the field so calm and mild in his demeanor, evidently not
acting from impulse or martial rage.

"His position was directly in front of a grocery store. He
fell in five minutes after he took it, having fired once or
twice. He was killed instantly, and did not move after
he fell. I saw the flash of the rifle which did the deed.

"I think the Chaplain fell from the ball which entered the
hip. He might not have been aware of the wound from the
ball entering his arm, as sometimes soldiers are not conscious of wounds in battle, or he may have been simultane-
ously hit by another rifle. We were in a very exposed position. Shortly before the Chaplain came up, one of General
Burnside's aids accosted me, expressing surprise, and saying,
' What are you doing here, Captain?' I replied that I had
orders. He said that I must retire, if the rebels pressed us
too hard. In about half an hour I had definite orders to
retire, and accordingly fell back, leaving the Chaplain and
another man dead, and also a wounded man, who was unwilling to be moved. It is not usual, under such pressing circumstances, to attempt to remove the dead. In about an
hour afterward, my regiment advanced in line with, the
Twentieth Massachusetts. They occupied the place where

Chaplain Fuller fell; and they suffered very severely, it being much exposed. The Chaplain's body we found had been robbed, and the wounded man bayoneted by the rebel Vandals, while the ground was left to them.

"I think, in addition to Chaplain Fuller's desire to aid at a critical juncture in the affairs of his country, by the influence of his example and his personal assistance, he may have been willing also to show that he had not resigned in the face of the enemy from any desire to shrink from danger.

"I am, sir, yours, &c.,

"MONCENA DUNN,
Capt. 19th Mass. Volunteers."

The Chaplain's body was kindly cared for, as soon as the occupations of the battle permitted, and sent home to his bereaved family. Lieutenant John W. Hudson, of the Thirty-Fifth Massachusetts Regiment, writes that, from some boards obtained by him and Lieutenant Myrick, of Chelsea, a box was somewhat hurriedly made by Charles Campbell, of Wayland, and John Tasker, of Lincoln, while exposed to a desultory shell-fire from hostile guns.

"Into this, towards sunset, we solemnly lifted the Chaplain's body from the rude door on which it lay, having covered it with a white cloth. While this was in progress, Mayor Fay, with a Chelsea lady, who recognized the features of the deceased, came up and offered to pay the expense of transporting the body across the river. Major Willard * went in person to procure the permission of our General for some of our men to pass with this rude coffin across the same bridge over which, two days later, we mournfully saw the mortal remains of the Major himself conveyed in another coffin, which ready hands had quickly improvised.

* In command of the Thirty-fifth Massachusetts Regiment.

"During our work, many from Massachusetts and New Hampshire regiments gathered round, to gaze upon the face of a widely known preacher, an esteemed pastor, a revered and loved friend. Many of them manifested the deepest interest in what we were doing, and lingered about the place till our undertaking was accomplished. Some spoke of the Chaplain as 'their most edifying preacher,' others as 'a most valued adviser,' and others as 'a most faithful friend.' They offered to raise from their ranks the means of transportation."

The same writer, in describing the position where the Chaplain fell, says: —

"There were a hundred hiding-places — in cellars, near windows, and behind the corners of houses, and under the cover of board-fences and trees and outbuildings — from which the deadly rifle might be expected to send its unerring bullet, striking its victim before the sound of the discharge can reach his ears; and no valor of his can save him."

In explanation of the Chaplain's self-sacrifice, he refers to "the need of an example, even to brave men, at such critical moments."

Miss Helen L. Gilson, a niece of Major Fay, was the lady referred to, in the foregoing letter, as accompanying him at Fredericksburg, where both were busied in ministering to the sick and wounded, under the auspices of the Sanitary Commission. She has sketched, in the following terms, some of the last days of Chaplain Fuller: —

"For a long time had I heard of Arthur B. Fuller as a devoted chaplain; and my interest had been awakened to see him; but it was not till a few days before his death that I

T

had the pleasure of an introduction. I then drew from my pocket a well-worn copy of the Army Melodies, of which he was one of the editors, and told him that I had carried it during the Peninsular Campaign, often administering the medicine of music to the sick and wounded; and we were at once well acquainted.

"The next Sabbath, I was one of a party from the Sanitary Commission, who accompanied him to Camp Convalescent. We spent the forenoon in the tents, distributing papers and books. Wherever he went, a crowd of Massachusetts boys gathered; for they all knew and loved him. At two o'clock, the drum sounded, and some five hundred convalescents assembled for religious services. After singing, in which all joined, he addressed them in that simple and earnest way which so wins the attention of the soldiers. Every eye was fastened on him, and each upturned face caught his glow of enthusiasm.

"I wish I could remember all that fell from his lips. I can only quote the following: 'Why, boys,' said he, 'you know what a thrill the cry of "Mail!" sends through the camp; and how eagerly we peruse the dear letters from home. Now the Bible is full of letters from home, breathing a love dearer than that of father, wife, or sister. I have come to read to you a letter from our heavenly home. It speaks the language of more than human affection. Its words are those of encouragement and cheer.'

"The face of the speaker was lighted up with that interest which is more eloquent than speech; and, in spite of the rain and chill atmosphere, not a man moved from his place until the service ended.

"I saw no more of Chaplain Fuller, until we were called to identify his body in Fredericksburg. He lay, surrounded by rebel sharpshooters, who had fallen on the same day with him. Mayor Fay immediately made arrangements to send the body across the river to a place of safety, preparatory to sending it home.

"Chaplain Fuller will long be mourned as one gifted with peculiar power, and singularly adapted to the position which he held in the army. He will ever be remembered as a faithful Chaplain, genial in intercourse, and an earnest man. God alone knows what precious seeds must be sown, that the full harvest may come. 'Except a corn of wheat fall into the ground and die, it abideth alone; but if it die, it bringeth forth much fruit.' More than most of us he believed in sacrifice, — in that consecrated giving, which includes what we *are* as well as what we *have*."

Mayor Fay caused the body to be embalmed in Washington; and it was sent home to the Chaplain's friends. On Thursday morning, just a week after his decease, his lifeless remains were borne back into that home mansion which had been often animated by his living and loving presence.

"But O the heavy change, now thou art gone,
Now thou art gone, and never must return!"

CHAPTER VII.

OBSEQUIES.

"Bring the rathe primrose that forsaken dies,
And every flower that sad embroidery wears:
Bid amarantus all his beauty shed,
And daffodillies fill their cups with tears,
To strew the laureate hearse where Lycid lies."

UBSEQUENT to the private ceremony at the residence of his brother, the public funeral of Chaplain Fuller took place at the First Church on Chauncey Street in Boston on the 24th day of December, 1862.*

"The church was crowded with the friends of the deceased, who wished some opportunity to express their sense of loss, their respect for his memory, and their estimation of his character and services. Governor Andrew and staff, General Andrews and staff, Chief Justice Bigelow, and other prominent public men were present. The escort was performed by the Cadets.

"The coffin was placed in front of the pulpit, and was profusely covered with the most exquisite flowers. One by one the wreaths were placed upon the lid by loving hands, as the

* The funeral was under the general direction of Messrs. William A. Krueger and Thomas S. Williams. The pall-bearers were Messrs. Samuel Smith, C. J. F. Sherman, George P. Richardson, Jr., Henry S. Dalton, Samuel B. Krogman, and O. T. Taylor.

best expression of the cherished memories of the past. The following inscription was upon the plate: —

REV. ARTHUR BUCKMINSTER FULLER,
Chaplain of the 16th Regiment of
Massachusetts Volunteers;
Killed at the Battle of Fredericksburg, Va.,
11th December, 1862,
Aged 40 years.
I must do something for my Country.' "

The following verses were sung from the Army Melodies: —

Sleeping soft, the soldier lies
Calmly, in his bed of blood;
Where, a living sacrifice,
He his body gave to God.

By salvation's Captain led,
In the army of the Lord,
Battle-fields a dying bed
Soft and glorious afford!

There amid the rage of strife,
Clash and roar of conflict grim,
While to God he gives his life,
In the storm, is calm to him.

The first address was from Rev. Rollin H. Neale, who said: —

" My principal difficulty in speaking on this occasion is in controlling my feelings within just bounds. I have seldom heard of a death which so deeply affected me. My first impression was a sense of personal bereavement. I could truly say, 'I am distressed for thee, my brother! Very pleasant hast thou been unto me.' I would not be unmindful of other bereavements which have occurred in our midst.

* Christian Register.

"Putnam and Lowell, Shurtleff and Phillips, Cabot and Willard, and other loved ones, are warm in public sympathy, and the hearts of friends and relatives are freshly bleeding over their graves. But I am sure no one has fallen in this war more tenderly loved, and whose death, in the circle of his acquaintance, has produced a profounder impression than that of the Chaplain of the Sixteenth Regiment. His published letters, so characteristic, frank, and full, have made him widely known. We have followed him from scene to scene, to Alexandria and Fortress Monroe, to the neighborhood of Suffolk and the terrible field of Fair Oaks, to Harrison's Landing, and on board of transports, sometimes sleeping on the vessel's deck and sometimes on the bare ground; but always cheerful, always active, encouraging his 'boys,' as he called them, — ministering to the sick and the wounded, having a good word to say of everybody, and evil of none. We see him ever manly, dignified, uncompromising. He never conceals his sentiments. He condemns rebellion and slavery in the face of their most earnest and bitter advocates, and yet in such a tone of sincerity and kindness as to gain the respect of rebel officers and the confiding love of the poor dying Southern prisoner, whom he soothingly comforted, and at whose cot he knelt in fervent prayer.

"An ingenuous, open-hearted, whole-souled man was our departed friend. There was nothing little, mean, or selfish about him. He was ready to do a kind act or perform any service for a friend without stopping to think what might be the effect upon himself. Some blame him, and perhaps he was imprudent, in the worldly sense of the term, for taking a gun and going into the ranks. But it was just like him. When the battle was raging, and his men, his children, his pastoral charge, were called' to face the danger, it was not in his nature to sit idle in his tent; and if he forgot his headache, and his weakened frame, and as some say his professional character, I should feel rebuked and ashamed, if, as his friend, I attempted to make an apology for him. No, it was an act of generous emotion, of noble heroism, of self-sacrificing patriotism, which will endear him to his associates in the army, and place him high among the martyrs in this struggle. Sure I am that neither the soldiers to whom he ministered as chaplain, nor those churches in New England of which he had been the beloved pastor, will think the less of his religious character now that his blood has been poured out in his country's cause.

" When settled in this city I became acquainted with him. Our friendship was intimate and unreserved. With his earnest, genial, and pre-eminently humane spirit, we forgot our theological differences, and 'wherein we were agreed walked by the same rule and minded the same thing.' Deeply do I sympathize with his relatives, his brothers, his bereaved wife, his orphan children. No public tribute to his memory, no official funeral solemnities, are necessary to exalt him in their estimation. They knew him at home, the sphere he loved the best, amid the thousand sweet and tender charities of life. He loved the circle immediately around him, and cherished an affectionate remembrance of those who had previously been removed by death, — esteemed parents, a lamented brother, an honored sister.

" The quiet rural spot at Mount Auburn which he has described and carefully laid out and adorned for ' our family' now waits to receive all that was mortal of himself. It is hallowed ground, fit emblem of the peaceful rest which his weary spirit has now entered. No more fatiguing marches. Strifes and fears and dying groans shall agitate his soul no more.

'No rude alarms of angry foes,
No cares to break the long repose,
No midnight shade, no clouded sun,
But sacred, high, eternal noon.' "

Rev. E. O. Haven, D. D., was the next speaker. He said :—

" We see before us to-day an extraordinary sight. Ministers of the Gospel of Christ of different denominations pay their tribute of honor and affection to a brother minister who has finished his course, — not as is most common for men of his profession, dying peacefully among his people, breathing upon them a benediction, and bearing testimony to the fidelity of the Saviour in the closing hour of life ; not, as is sometimes the case, expiring suddenly in the midst of official duty, and translated at once from the pulpit to the congregation of the faultless and immortal, — but who died on the field of battle, clad in the soldier's garb, with deadly weapons in his hands, in the forefront of terrible strife.

" Many are shocked at the thought of such a scene. Distant lands will wonder when they hear the report. It will be quoted as an indication of a fearful passion for blood which has usurped the American mind. There are some, even at home, who will timidly inquire, Why is this waste of life ? Why must the ambassador of the Prince of Peace subject himself to the violence of war ? Has there not been a forgetfulness of the proprieties of official dignity ? Has there not been a misapprehension of the duties of a Christian minister ?

" Could he whose mangled body now lies before you, from which the deadly bullet has expelled the noble Christian soul, rise again and speak out as he was wont to do in ringing words, they would not be apologetic, but words of exultation. Were it possible for him to be at once fallen in battle and yet alive with us, I know that he would fill our souls with his own holy enthusiasm. I know that he would make us understand and feel the magnitude of his thought and the love of his heart, when he offered to his country, in what he thought her bitterest trial, the sight of his eye and the strength of his arm, and above all the moral example of his character, won by many years' devotion to the good of his fellow-men. He offered all this to his country, and he did right. It was an overflowing love. He gave away his life for liberty to all men, instead of slavery for negroes, vassalage for the great majority of the whites, and a despotism — greatest curse of all — for a few. He offered his life to inspire the army with noble purpose, and if need be to inspire the nation. He knew that his life might be taken, and is not now surprised; but there comes a voice from his spirit to us saying: Waste not your sympathies in inactive sorrow, but convert the strong tide of your emotion into vigorous thought and powerful action. 'Weep not for me, but weep for yourselves and your children,' or see to it that they are so protected as not to need your tears.

" He was a brave man. He had shown that long before he crossed the perilous bridge and preceded the great army in their passage over the Rappahannock. His bravery was not rash physical courage. His was a cultivated mind and a full heart. Life was to him full of hopes, affections, and ambitions. He had the poet's imagination to paint the future, and the Christian's purpose to produce it. To him life was intensely valuable. The great teacher of modern philosophy has said: 'A little philosophy inclineth man's mind to atheism, but depth in philosophy bringeth men's minds about to religion.' So a little thought makes man a coward, but deeper thought fills him with courage. Our friend was brave because he was a man of thought, of self-control, of obedience to God's law, and of faith. Such a man cannot be timid, for God is in him. He had long ago determined what to live for, — to advocate what he believed to be true, to benefit man, to imitate Christ, to honor God. That I believe he has tried to do. That gave him the courage of an apostle. I am not speaking words of formal eulogy, but what the character of this good man deserves.

14

" He was a philanthropist. His habits of thought, his mode of expression, his life and his religion were pre-eminently practical. He saw the desolations of alcoholic drinks in this and other lands, and devoted his strength at once to promote temperance, and deserves to be ranked among the strongest advocates of total abstinence from intoxicating drinks. He was a friend of popular education, he was a great lover of children, and contributed much influence to make Sunday schools efficient. He advocated every department of practical Christianity. Many of the benevolent associations of this city and State have been cheered in their anniversaries by his ready utterance and eloquent appeals.

" When the nation was suddenly shocked by the eruption of the pent-up volcano of treason and rebellion, when that cruel effort to strike down constitutional liberty, long foreseen by sagacious minds, burst upon the people, then such a sympathetic and patriotic heart as his could not but be thrilled with emotion. His was not a nature to suppress feeling, or to consume it upon himself. He sought opportunity to speak and to act. He was soon in the army as an ambassador of Christ, to bless the soldier and strengthen him for his work. His letters from the camp and field have been read by thousands. He labored faithfully for his country. And when, in the providence of God, a crisis came, — an emergency for which only the noblest souls are fitted, — he sprang to the post of hottest danger. The army saw, the nation sees, all the world shall know, how a Christian like him can give to his country and to right all that he has, even his life. God accepted his offering, as he had that of many martyrs. The family name, highly honored before, has received fresh lustre, and when the historian comes to gather up the jewels that this terrible convulsion has brought to sight, among the names that shall shine with perpetual light shall be that of Arthur B. Fuller."

Next in order was the following tribute from the Rev. E. H. Sears : —

"I have no right to speak of my brother from any such intimate relations as those must have had who met him often in the sphere of his daily duties. I saw him last summer when he came into my neighborhood with his health shattered, his constitution perhaps broken, in the hardships of the Peninsular campaign. Those who saw him then must have known, that with him it meant something to be chaplain of a regiment. There, under the kind ministrations of wife and brother and friends, and breathing the pure country air, he tried to drive out of his system the poison he had breathed into it in the swamps of the Chickahominy. But even when prostrate on his sick-bed, his zeal for the cause to which he had devoted himself burned in him like a flame of fire, and his chief thought was to get back to his regiment, to be with 'his boys,' as he called them, to share their dangers, to minister to their suffering, to nurse the sick and pray with the dying. He returned before half recovered; and when we saw him go away with pale face and faltering steps, we trembled for his life, for we thought he might end it in the hardships of the camp or in the hospital. We did not expect to see him brought home from the carnage of the battle-field. But he took this view of his duties : 'I will not urge others to go,' said he, 'where I am not ready to go myself. I will not preach what I am not willing to practise. I will not ask God's protection of others in dangers which I will not share.' And so on the eve of that most terrible battle of all, when he must have known how fierce the conflict was to be, when he must have known that to thousands before nightfall, 'a heavier sleep was coming fast, than seals the living eye,' he placed himself in the fore part of the danger, and soon fell by two mortal wounds. And I cannot but recognize here the tender adaptations of the Divine mercy as a consolation

to his friends. If he must fall, we could not wish it otherwise. He was spared the long agonics which others have
endured, spared from slow death in the hospital. He passed
with one step through the opening gate, and left the tumult and
the agony behind; one moment in the battle-storm, the next
moment with loved ones gone before in the eternal calm!
The martyr's crown, without the martyr's protracted suffering! He died, in the words of Job, 'when his glory was
fresh with him, and his bow gathered strength in his hand.'

"So, too, in the time of his death, if he was to fall, there
is much consolation. It may be that for all our sins as a
nation — which have been very great — the cause for which
our brother has given his life is to fail. Perhaps it may go
down, for a time at least, in darkness and blood. If so, who
of us would not rather lie as he does in his peaceful coffin?
It is better to die for one's country, than to live on with no
country to die for. If we are to lose all we have held most
sacred and dear, I would say more truthfully a thousand
times than Hector said of the impending ruin of his beloved
Troy,

> ' Let me lie cold before that dreadful day,
> Pressed with a load of monumental clay.'

But if, as we do believe, our country is to rise through this
agony and bloody sweat to a new and a glorified existence,
then, again, how could life be given with such large returns?
The beauty of our Israel slain in its high places for this great
redemption, is raised up and separated to the special sphere
of the Divine mercy.

"There is one lesson which comes to us now, and which
our brother's lips would speak, I doubt not, could they break
their silence in this solemn hour: there are evils more to be
feared than death; and there is something better than life,
and for which life may be joyfully given away. Do not
doubt that the good will be achieved; for God never wastes
the blood of his martyrs."

The closing address was from the Rev. James Freeman Clarke : —

" I first knew Arthur Buckminster Fuller as a little boy. Being a distant relative, I was in the habit of visiting his father's family while a student at Cambridge. They lived at that time in the old Dana House, on the bend of the road from Boston. In the large, old-fashioned parlor, the family sat together in the evening, Mr. Timothy Fuller sitting by one corner of the open fire, with his stand, holding his papers and a lamp, at work preparing for his law duties of the next day, but occasionally taking part in the conversation, usually, as I remember, in moderating what he thought some too enthusiastic statement of his daughter Margaret. She sat talking with her friends as only she could talk, and the younger children studied their lessons or played together ; and among them I well remember the bright eyes and clear, open features of Arthur. Near by sat the mother at her work, serene, gentle, kind, a comfort and joy to all.

" Arthur graduated at Harvard in the class of 1843, which class contained, among other honored names, that of the present President of the College. He graduated from the Cambridge Divinity School in the class of 1847. Among his classmates at the Divinity School, one is a minister of this city, and another is the Colonel of the First Regiment of Carolina Volunteers at Port Royal. Mr. Fuller went to the West, and settled in Northern Illinois as teacher and missionary. I well remember his labor and his zeal in both departments, for I met him on his field of work on the Rock River, and knew how he put his heart into it as into all that he did. And, afterward, when he returned to New England, and was settled over various parishes, I saw him, always characterized by the same activity and devotion. He was an earnest Christian minister, believing in the great doctrine of redeem-

ing love through Christ, and ready to take part with every
Christian brother who was working for the same end. So
it happened, that he often went over the boundary line of
sect, and found himself side by side in brotherly labors in
various religious and philanthropic works with those bearing
other denominational names. They did not like him less for
being a decided Unitarian, finding in him more points in
which they could agree than those in which they were
obliged to differ. And, therefore, we find that they are here
to-day to honor their friend as a brother in many Christian
labors, following, in his own way, the same Master.

" So have the rapid years passed by, until this war broke
out, and Arthur felt it his duty to go as a chaplain. Of his
services there I am not the one to speak, but I know that he
must have been active and kind and useful to the soldiers,
for it was his nature always to be active, kind, and useful.

" Arthur Fuller was, like most of us, a lover of peace, but he
saw, as we have had to see, that sometimes true peace can only
come through war. In this last struggle at Fredericksburg,
he took a soldier's weapon, and went on with the little forlorn
hope who were leading the advance through the streets.
He had not been much in battle before, but more among the
sick in the hospitals. Perhaps he thought it right to show
the soldiers that in an hour of emergency he was ready to
stand by their side. So he went, with a courage and devotion which all must admire, and fell, adding his blood also to
all the precious blood which has been shed as an atonement
for the sins of the nation. May that blood not be shed in
vain. May it be accepted by God as a costly sacrifice, and
may we as a people, when our necessary trials and punish-
ments are sufficiently endured, become that righteous and
happy nation God meant us to be; setting an example to
mankind of a Christian republic in which there is no master
and no slave, no tyrant and no victim, — not a mere rabble

scrambling for gain, but brothers co-operating in building up a grand commonwealth of true liberty, justice, and humanity Let our friends go or stay, let us live or die, —

> ' So we wake to the higher aims
> Of a land that has lost for a little her love of gold,
> And love of a peace that was full of wrongs and shames,
> Horrible, hateful, monstrous, — not to be told,
> And hail once more the banner of battle unrolled!
> Though many an eye shall darken, and many shall weep, —
> Yet many a darkness into light shall leap.'

" Our brother has fallen in the midst of active usefulness, in a life which seemed only half lived. He has gone to join the many dear-beloved friends who have preceded him, — the. upright, industrious father, the saintly, tender mother, the noble child of genius, Margaret, his brother Eugene, his sister Ellen. The few of the family who remain will miss his active, useful friendship and brotherly love. We shall all miss him from among our thinned ranks. But if this teaches us again how ' in the midst of life we are in death,' it teaches us, too, that in the midst of death we are in life. To die thus, full of devotion to a noble cause, is not to die, — it is to live. It is rising into a higher life. It is passing up into the company of the true and noble, of the brave and generous, — it is going to join the heroes and martyrs of all ages, of all lands, who have not counted life dear when given for a good cause. Such devoted offerings by the young and brave, surrendering up their lives, raise us all above the fear of death. What matters it when we die, so that we live nobly? —

> ' They are the dead, the buried,
> They who do still survive,
> In sin and sense interred, —
> The dead! — they are alive!'

" Fathers, mothers, brothers, sisters, friends! You who are in grief to-day, mourning the dear sons, the noble husbands and brothers, who have fallen on all these bloody fields, do

you not also rejoice as you mourn? Do you not also thank
God for the great opportunity he has given you to render up
in his service these precious lambs, these costly offerings?
Ah! I know that you feel thus. I have seen it in your
serene look of inward joy, which tells me you are talking
with your angels. They have not wholly left you. They
go, but they return. To each of these noble brothers of ours
we look and speak from the depths of our truest instincts and
insight.

> ' So we may lift from out the dust
>   A voice as unto him that hears,
>   A cry above the conquered years,
> To one that with us works, and trust.

> ' Known and unknown, human, divine!
>   Sweet human hand, and lips, and eye,
>   Dear heavenly friend that cannot die,
> Mine, mine forever, ever mine!

> ' So all is well, though faith and form
>   Be sundered in the night of fear. —
>   Well roars the storm to those who hear
> A deeper voice across the storm.' "

The addresses were followed by the singing of a
hymn written for the occasion, by Mrs. J. H. Hanaford.

> " Softly sing the requiem holy
>   O'er this still, most precious clay,
> Loving hearts are bending lowly
>   'Neath the chastening rod, to-day.

> " Father! in thy care we leave him
>   Whom our hearts have loved so well.
> Nevermore earth's sin shall grieve him,
>   Now with thee his soul shall dwell.

> " There with loved ones gone before him,
>   He will wait our steps to greet;
> With the sainted one who bore him,
>   Sing the angel-anthem sweet.

"Grieve we not in hopeless sorrow,
O'er our honored hero slain,
Soon shall dawn a brighter morrow,
And we all shall meet again."

"The hearse which bore his remains to their last resting-place in Mount Auburn was draped with the national colors and trimmed with rosettes of black and white, and drawn by four horses wearing heavy black plumes. A large number of mourners followed the remains to the grave, and dropped their tears over the sepulchre of this fallen patriot and philanthropist." *

* Boston Herald.

14 *   U

CHAPTER VIII.

APPRECIATION.

HE‎ libation of the Chaplain's life has been, we trust, accepted, like the sacrifice of Abel, and he has taken his place under the altar with the souls of those slain for the word of God. His devotion touched the hearts of his countrymen; nor was it regarded as out of keeping with the sacred office he had so recently laid temporarily aside, nor as a close unmeet for a life of religious and philanthropic labors. Although it is not a common event for a chaplain to enter the lists of the combatants, yet loyal hearts felt that the exigency of a holy cause rendered the act noble, appropriate, and heroical.

One of the first expressions in reference to it came from the heart of the chief magistrate of Massachusetts, whose patriotic and zealous discharge of his high duties in this our national crisis will win for his name a proud place on the page of history. We insert the letter : —

"COMMONWEALTH OF MASSACHUSETTS.
"EXECUTIVE DEPARTMENT, BOSTON, Dec. 15, 1862.

"RICHARD F. FULLER, ESQ., *Court Street, Boston.*

"My dear Sir: I observe, with grief at the loss sustained by his friends and by the service, but with admiration for his heroic enthusiasm, the death of your brother, the Rev. Arthur B. Fuller, Chaplain of the Sixteenth Massachusetts Regiment, while fighting in the ranks of the Nineteenth Massachusetts as a volunteer, in the battle of Fredericksburg.

"My long and intimate acquaintance with him and all your family render this instance of bravery and of affliction one of unusual interest, as it really is of unusual pathos.

"His conduct was worthy his State and his blood. It will be forever remembered. Nor was it too soon for a good man to die, falling as he did in splendid devotion to a sublime idea of duty, adventuring his life beyond the necessities of his position or the occasion of his office, but not beyond the dictates of an ardent nature, nor, in my judgment, beyond the highest and best idea of the example and decorum of the occasion.

"How many friends at home, how many soldiers in the field, will feel kindled, consoled, and encouraged by this exceptional and more conspicuous act of unselfish and spontaneous patriotism.

"I am faithfully, your friend and servant,

"JOHN A. ANDREW."

Such, too, was the sentiment of the army. We quote from a sermon by Rev. Edward A. Walker, recently chaplain of the 1st Conn. Vol. H. Artillery.

"I have just heard of the death of Chaplain Fuller of the Sixteenth Massachusetts Volunteers, one of the most earnest and faithful officers in the service. I visited him once at Fortress Monroe, and saw the results of his labors in his own regiment, and met him afterward repeatedly in circumstances where his ability and energy were abundantly exhibited. After the battle of Malvern Hill, when our forces removed to Harrison's Landing, and when some five thousand wounded and disabled men were gathered at the old Harrison estate,

Chaplain Fuller rendered himself eminently serviceable, ministering both to the spiritual and physical wants of the sufferers.

"The miserable condition of these men can scarcely be described. After a week of fighting and marching, the heat having been oppressive and the air thick with penetrating dust, they arrived by night in a drenching rain at the Harrison estate. The overseer had been directed, in the event of the coming of the Federal troops, to destroy whatever he could not secrete; but our coming was so sudden as to prevent this. The house was soon filled from cellar to garret by those whose wounds were not so serious as to impede their locomotion. Then those wounded in the legs, or who had suffered much from loss of blood, came feebly up and filled all places about the dwelling that were left, some crawling under the bushes in the garden, others lying by the fences, and others still sinking directly down into the mud, glad of the *sight* of a house and shelter, and of the hope of medical attendance. Within, the floor was so occupied with men, that all passage was for a time impossible. The carpets were covered with mud and stains of blood, while the rich mirrors, furniture, and paintings presented a painful contrast of domestic luxury with all the horrors of war.

"Amid these scenes of suffering, Chaplain Fuller labored with untiring energy, now unobtrusively assisting the surgeons in their more arduous labors, now bringing food and drink to those who were unable to help themselves, now speaking words of comfort and religious consolation to the disheartened, himself at all times cheerful, patient, and helpful.

"With regard to the circumstances of his death, although he was shot with musket in hand while taking part in the attack on Fredericksburg, I cannot believe that he was out of his proper place, or acting otherwise than with a conscientious regard for his duty toward his men. He doubtless felt that his example would inspire them with greater heroism, and therefore willingly sacrificed his life at one of the most critical moments of the war.

"I trust that the record of services so valuable may be preserved. It may well be placed side by side with that of his distinguished sister."

The voice of the press was of a similar tenor. Says one : * —

"He volunteered in the hazardous task of crossing the river, and gave his life as the price of his zeal and patriotism. As chaplain of the Massachusetts Sixteenth, Mr. Fuller has been unwearied in his labors for the material as well as spiritual good of the men, and has exercised over them a remarkable influence. No hardships appalled him, and he always sustained others by his own unflinching courage and his devotion to the great cause he had given himself to serve."

Another,† among its frequent allusions to the subject, says : —

"He was an active, energetic, devoted soldier of the Cross, who did his best to awaken a true religious sentiment in camp, who visited the hospitals, who was an honest almoner of bounties intrusted to him, and who was not only ready to chronicle the heroism of others, but who took his place in the ranks.

"Through his death the Union cause has met with no common loss; for few chaplains in the army have been so active, energetic, and devoted to the interests of their charge, or more fully inspired by a patriotic love of country."

* New York Tribune.　　　　　† The Boston Journal.

Another,* under the head of "The Glorious Death of Chaplain Fuller," says : —

"Ever a lover of liberty and the advocate of freedom to all the human race, of whatever creed or complexion, he has manifested his devotion to his principles by his deeds in the moment of personal peril.

"He fully appreciated the extent and purposes of the rebellion, and the sacrifices needed to put it down, and was willing to labor and suffer with others in the great work.

"His death was feelingly alluded to by the pastors of several of the churches in this vicinity yesterday."

And, in another connection : —

"Rev. Mr. Fuller had his own ideas of the duties of a chaplain in this war. He had previously been a peace man, and he never relinquished his love of peace. But he felt, unless all government is to be at the mercy of traitors, force must be lawful for its defence against the wicked and unprovoked rebellion, — nay, more than lawful, an imperative obligation. It was from this conviction that he accepted the place of chaplain, believing an important part of his duty to be to stimulate the men to a brave and noble bearing as Christian soldiers in the field. He thought a minister should not be like a guide-board, pointing the way it does not go itself. He often said he would not urge the men, or rather 'his boys,' as he styled them, to go where he would not go himself. It was on this principle that he went forward with his regiment, deployed in the van as skirmishers, last summer, before Richmond.

"He was suffering under a violent attack of headache ; but some of the men, as they passed his tent, remarked they wished they had a headache. This determined him to go forward. He was made a mark for the enemy's sharpshooters,

* The Boston Traveller.

and narrowly escaped two bullets which struck trees very near him. This occurrence gave him a strong hold upon the soldiers, who delighted to hear the admonitions of one who did not flinch from the dangers he encouraged them to encounter."

A correspondent in the same paper writes, in reference to the Chaplain : —

" Could hero ever have a nobler sentiment engraven on his tombstone than that which, living, he thus said, and, dying, acted : 'BETTER STILL GIVE UP OUR HEART'S BLOOD IN BRAVE BATTLE THAN GIVE UP OUR PRINCIPLES IN COWARDLY COMPROMISE !'

" Let these heroic words be cut in enduring letters on his monument, — let them be rendered into immortal actions in the lives of his friends."

A Western paper * says, in reference to the Chaplain's funeral : —

" It was attended by a great multitude, among whom were to be found the chief official dignitaries of the State and of the city. And they all honored themselves in thus doing the last offices for the noble dead. For, the devoted servant of his God, he had, as the ardent friend of the soldiers of his regiment, shared their sorrows and sufferings throughout the sad Peninsular campaign ; and in the late passage of the Rappahannock he volunteered to be among the first to enter the boats and receive the fire of the sharpshooters of the enemy. And here it was he fell.

" A man of eloquence, of high culture, of sincere piety, of ardent patriotism, of firm and true courage, he was ever to be found in the place where duty called, no matter what the

* The Northwestern.

personal sacrifice, no matter what the danger. In peace and in war he fought the good fight as a Christian and a hero."

The tone of the religious press was of like import. Says one : * —

" He died a glorious death of devotion to his country, and cheerful self-sacrifice to save its life and liberty. It is not an unfit close to an earnest and warm-hearted Christian ministry.

" From extensive correspondence, I know that Liberal Christianity never had a more valuable Western missionary, and perhaps this is not saying enough, — that, by teaching and preaching through a wide section, he sowed precious seed which cannot perish, doing as much work as any two men, — unquestionably going beyond his physical strength, which was never great, — and leaving through Central Illinois memories which time cannot efface. It was our notorious misappropriation of men which sanctioned the removal of this rarely adapted missionary from those who loved, appreciated, and in some cases idolized him."

And again a correspondent in the same paper writes : —

" I attended, at Chauncy Place Church, the services of music, reading, prayer, and addresses, which united the voices of three denominations of Christian speakers over the lifeless form of our Brother Fuller; not our 'late brother,' for he is more our brother now than ever. All seemed to feel that he had done nobly. I feel that he did wisely, and for him most wisely, in acting promptly, as he did, upon the inspiration of the hour. His case seems to me that of the Magdalen, when she broke the alabaster box of spikenard,

* The Christian Inquirer.

and would have poured out her very life, on the feet of Jesus. Observers, prudent and economical, rebuked her; but the Master, of a diviner wisdom than theirs, said, defending the act, 'Trouble her not; she hath wrought a good' work; she hath done what she could; and wherever the Gospel shall be preached in all the world, there shall this deed of heart-sacrifice go, as a memorial of her.' So will it be in this case. Did the world ever need more than now, — when has our country needed so much as now, — the instant daring of fearless self-surrender?

"It is Ruskin's 'lamp of sacrifice' that Brother Fuller kindled, at such cost to himself, on the south bank of the Rappahannock. Such a soul is a lamp snatched away all too soon for us, and set in the firmament of heaven. We that loved him and valued him even more for his heart than for his head, preferred to keep his beacon-light on our own rocky shores; but God knew better, and took him away.

"I delight, and shall delight, to think of the last day of his earthly life as a splendid exhibition of that impulsive and lofty energy which, put forth for God and liberty and duty, is justly adored by the leading nations of Christendom."

Another says of him: * —

"His love of country required no artificial stimulant, for in his warm heart was the clear flame of patriotism ever burning brightly, communicating its glow and warmth to all with whom he had to do.

"Faithful in the discharge of his duties as a Christian minister at home, he was faithful to his highest conceptions of duty to his regiment. He was a friend to those who looked for friendly counsel, he was a brother to those who needed a brother's sympathy, and in hours of weakness and suffering, the tenderness of his heart, and the self-forgetful-

* The Christian Register.

ness of his spirit, rendered his service to those under his
charge a grateful alleviation of their loneliness and pain. As
a Christian minister, his record is upon the purer tablets
above, and he will live in the memories of those with whom
he has been associated as pastor, preacher, and. friend. His
consecration to a glorious service is now renewed in another
world."

And the same paper thus refers to his funeral : —

"It was a most impressive thought, that he who but a few
months ago had spoken so earnestly in the morning conference meetings of Anniversary week, from the very spot upon
which his body then rested, was lying there silent and cold
in the embrace of death. However moving his appeals had
been when living, there was a greater eloquence in his
marble lips and brow, which told of self-sacrifice, of suffering in the holy cause."

A correspondent in another * writes : —

"Chaplain Fuller spent several days with me at this hospital and the parole camp just before he joined his regiment,
and went into the battle of Fredericksburg, where he fell.
I became very much attached to him, and never have I met
a chaplain in the United States army that in my opinion was
better adapted to the army *work*. His heart and soul were
in it. He spoke plainly, and with great kindness and power
to the soldier. All heard with interest, and many with profit.
Many soldiers at Camp Parole wept like children as he
spoke to them of home and loved ones, and as he pointed
them to Jesus, the soldiers' friend, and instructed them to
copy his noble example, and seek the favor of God. He was
the right man in the right place. He remarked to me on
Sabbath morning, as we were on our way from this city to

* Chaplain Henry C. Henries, in Zion's Herald.

the Parole Camp, 'We all have to turn itinerants in the army, and preach Methodist doctrines.' But he has gone. Side by side he lay with many of the noble and brave on that fatal day. May God bless the dear ones of his household he loved so well."

We quote from still another: * —

" From merely a limited acquaintance with him, we were led to admire his intense patriotism, his self-devotion, and his noble, catholic spirit. The patriot-martyr has fallen. Another precious, cherished life has been laid cheerfully down for the redemption of our country from the barbarism of slavery. Rest, noble hero, with the patriot dead! Green may be the turf above thy mortal form, yet greener and fresher, yea, perennial, shall be thy memory in the hearts of thy surviving friends and thy grateful countrymen!

" While our country shall have a name and place among the nations of the earth, so long will the heroic life and more than heroic death of Arthur B. Fuller be remembered and pointed to as worthy of admiration and imitation."

Nor did his fellow-laborers in the temperance cause forget him. The Massachusetts Temperance Alliance

" *Resolved,* That in the death of the Rev. A. B. Fuller, Chaplain of the Massachusetts Sixteenth Regiment, the Massachusetts State Temperance Alliance has lost a faithful member, who, by his wise counsels and his earnest, able, and eloquent advocacy of the cause of temperance for many years, has contributed greatly to its success, and has won the admiration and shall have the affectionate remembrance of this Alliance."

We must not omit the following testimony of Rev. John Pierpont, written in the Chaplain's lifetime : —

* Herald of Gospel Liberty.

"I know, and for about twenty years have known, Rev. Arthur B. Fuller as a preacher of the glorious Gospel of the blessed God, — a preacher 'sans peur et sans reproche,' — without the fear *of* man or reproach *from* man. Nor, in my humble opinion, is he half so much afraid of the Devil as the Devil is of him."

The Chaplain's widow was not entitled to a pension, as he had been discharged, and had not yet received a new appointment. On her petition to Congress, a special law providing her a pension very promptly passed both Houses without opposition. Hon. Charles Sumner presented the petition in the Senate, remarking, that

"From the 1st day of August, 1861, Arthur B. Fuller had been a duly commissioned chaplain in the Sixteenth Massachusetts Regiment of Volunteers, and had followed its flag faithfully, patriotically, religiously, through all the perils of the Peninsula, and wherever else it had been borne."

The petition having been referred to the Committee on Pensions, they reported,

"That it appears that Arthur B. Fuller was the chaplain of the Sixteenth Regiment of Massachusetts Volunteers; that his health was much impaired by the hardships and exposures of the Peninsular campaign; that after repeated efforts to renew his labors in the camp of his regiment, which were foiled by his sickness returning upon every such attempt, it was finally determined, by the advice of army surgeons, that his malady was such that he could not bear exposure in the field. He was accordingly honorably discharged, on surgeon's certificate of disability, on the 10th day of December, 1862. On the 11th day of December, on the call for volunteers to cross the Rappahannock at the battle of Fredericksburg, he volunteered, and was killed in the service soon after entering Fredericksburg.

" The committee think that, though Chaplain Fuller was technically out of the service of the United States, still he was really in the service of his country and in the line of duty while bravely leading on the soldiers, and dying on the field of battle. They therefore think the petitioner entitled to the relief for which she prays, and accordingly report a bill."

The proceedings of the same Congress in reference to the Conscription bill illustrate the view entertained by the nation of the holy cause of suppressing rebellion and the propriety of clergymen bearing arms in this war. Senator Sumner moved an amendment to the bill, exempting clergymen from military conscription. In support of his amendment he said : —

" In former days bishops have worn coats of mail and led embattled forces; and there are many instances where the chaplain has assumed all the duties of the soldier. At the famous battle of Fontenoy, there was a chaplain in the British army, with a name subsequently historic, who, by his military services, acquired the title of ' the fighting chaplain of Fontenoy.' This was the famous Edinburgh professor, Adam Ferguson, author of the History of Ancient Rome. And only a few days ago, I presented a petition for a pension from the widow of Rev. Arthur B. Fuller, chaplain, who fell fighting at Fredericksburg. But these instances are exceptional. Legislation cannot be founded on exceptions."

" Mr. McDougall. I have as much regard for the ministers of the Gospel as any gentleman on this floor; but I think there is no reason why they should be exempted more than any one of those who profess to believe in the doctrines they teach."

" The men in the days of the Revolution who filled the pulpit not only called the men of the young nation to arms, but they led them to the field; and a man who has faith enough to bear the banner of the Christian faith is fit to be a soldier in any war supported by just principles, any war in the maintenance of a righteous cause. There is not a true believer in the great principles of democracy, as taught by Him who first bore the cross, who is not willing to fight for the maintenance of the great right of a people to maintain themselves in the forms of government. I will ask the Senator from Massachusetts to modify his proposition so as not to include the Methodist clergy, because they are a fighting clergy."

" Mr. FESSENDEN. I have but one word to say. I shall vote against the exemption, for the simple reason that I think it will be an imputation upon the clergymen of my section of the country which they would resent."

The amendment was rejected, and the bill as it passed included the clergy.

CHAPTER IX.

TRIBUTES IN VERSE.

"Begin, then, sisters of the sacred well
That from beneath the seat of Jove doth spring,—
Begin, and somewhat louder sweep the string ! "

FUNERAL OF CHAPLAIN FULLER.

UPON the church altar what form lieth low,
    The flag of his country wrapped round him ?
The seal as of peace sleeps on his broad brow,
    In battle though Azrael found him !
Ah ! this is the chaplain who offered his life,
And, dying for country, won peace in the strife !

The lips of this martyr, now silent and cold,
    Were wont, with their eloquence glowing,
The soldiers to kindle, with loyal hearts bold
    And firm, to the battle-field going :
Where, willing to practise what others he taught,
In van of the peril he fearlessly fought.

Hark ! what martial music is heard in the streets,
    Of mingled gloom, glory, and gladness ?
The throb of the muffled drum mournfully beats !
    The trumpet speaks triumph and sadness, —
A strain swelling proudly in praise of the brave,
But sinking to grief as it leads to the grave !

The train of the mourners thus slowly proceeds,
  By soldiers in sorrow escorted,
With draped carriage drawn by four black-plumèd steeds,
  Its pall with the banner consorted :
And hushed is the crowd where it moves in the street,
Their hearts with the muffled drum seeming to beat!

And now to Mount Auburn they bear the dead brave,
  The soldiers his coffin surrounding,
Who lower their heads as he sinks in the grave, —
  And then, with the volleys resounding,
Is sorrow of martial hearts fitly expressed,
And earth folds the hero to sleep in her breast!

---◆---

REV. ARTHUR B. FULLER.

Servant of God ! thy race is run,
  Life's toils and trials o'er ;
A crown of glory thou hast won
  By Rappahannock's shore.

Thou wast not kissed by fragrant breeze,
  Where Summer reigns the year,
Nor stretched on "flowery beds of ease,"
  When Azrael grim drew near.

'Neath smoke-wreathed sky, in battle-storm,
  While heroes led the van,
With musket clenched and heart all warm,
  He found thee, noble man !

Anon a wingèd death-shot came,
  Unerring, to thy breast ;
It quenched at once the vital flame,
  And brought eternal rest.

It let thy spirit upward soar,
    To join the martyred throng
Who chant, as angels did of yore,
    Sublime, joy-giving song.

Now let the martial pæan swell,
    Loud, sweet, and clear in air!
Toll not a solemn, dirge-like knell, —
    Thy bliss we hope to share;

To tread at last the heavenly strand,
    When *our* course, too, is run;
To stand for aye at Christ's right hand,
    And hear him say, " Well done!"

WILDER.

---◆---

REV. ARTHUR B. FULLER.

" Something for my country!" was thy battle-cry,
    Man's great glory; with Curtius, as with thee.
Nor for "country" only wouldst thou gladly die.
Man's cause was thine, by ready sympathy.
That "something" was thy life, O generous soul!
    Gav'st all! and now to keep thee from the stain
Of blood, angelic music's muffled roll
    Calls Angel Death to count thee with the slain,
To whisper his brief measure in thine ear,
And snatch to heaven their tried and proved compeer.

Christian Register.

---◆---

REV. ARTHUR B. FULLER.

BY CHISLON.

He died, — but to a noble cause
    His precious life was given!
He died, — but he has left behind
    A shining path to Heaven!

Although the tidings of his death
Came like a stunning blow,
So nobly did he fall, we feel
'T is blessèd he should go.

O, none can gain a brighter name,
Or win a deeper love,
Than he who sweetly sings to-day
The songs of heaven above.
We cannot find it in our hearts
To raise a note of woe;
So nobly did he fall, we feel
'T is blessèd thus to go !

NORTON, Mass., Dec. 31, 1862.

REV. ARTHUR B. FULLER.

BY MABELLE.

No dearer the gift, O my Country ! is thine
Than the one which in tears we lay on thy shrine ;
And pray that his life, with its teachings so pure,
May give us the strength which we need to endure.
Since our Father in mercy has set his soul free,
When no more he could do, O my Country ! for thee.

Write his name with living heroes,
Though the noble soul has fled ;
Write it still in golden letters,
Arthur Fuller is not *dead*.

To this work of Christ, his Master,
O how faithful he has been !
As in all his deeds of mercy,
To his suffering fellow-men.

He has watched beside their pillow
    With a father's tender care ;
And no peril, death, nor danger
    Was too hard for him to share.

Cold, white lips have left their blessing
    For the faithful, kindly hand,
Guiding them beside still waters,
    · Leading to the Better Land.

——◆——

NOW AND THEN.

How narrow the terminal bound
    Dividing the now and the then ;
Though scenes it encloses around
    We never may visit again !
It shows, like the cavern of yore,
The footsteps returning no more ! *

These ramparts the moments upraise
    Exclude us forever, alas !
Though soaring love vainly essays
    His wings, o'er the summit to pass.
Nor higher can memory climb
Than serves to look over the time !

Ah ! can it be, brother, that thou,
    Who shared every burden I bore,
Whose life-lamp shone brightly but now,
    Hast passed to eternity's shore,
Where mortal ne'er mixed with the choir,
Save Orpheus, once, with his lyre ?

* " Nulla vestigia retrorsum."

Alas ! that I never shall know
That hand's cordial pressure again,
The living lips' musical flow,
And features all lighted up, then !
That cadence I still seem to hear !
The pleasant laugh rings in my ear !

His body, devoted to Mars,
Was all that rebellion could kill :
His life broke in glorious stars,
That burn in the firmament still !
In Jesus he slept, in the strife,
Where death fitly ended his life !

REV. A. B. FULLER.

BY MRS. J. H. HANAFORD.

Borne o'er death's rolling wave on angel pinions,
Our brother rests
Where blessed Peace rules all the fair dominions,
And War's rude crests,
And martial notes, and hosts arrayed for battle,
Are known no more,
And never swords shall clash, nor death-balls rattle,
Upon that shore.

A hero, in the strife for Freedom dying,
Immortal bays
Shall deck the brow in death's embrace now lying,
And tuneful lays
From hearts sincere his virtues be declaring
Who gave his all, —
Home, health, and life, — obedient on hearing
His country's call.

Yet sad our hearts, who mourn the friend so cherished,
      The noble soul,
Thank God! who lives, while but our hopes have perished,
      And at the goal
Of our short race will bid us welcome gladly,
      And each true heart
Forget the pangs which here it feels so sadly,
      While friends depart.

O Brother! 'neath the shadow we shall wander,
      And think of thee;
Upon thy many virtues sweetly ponder,
      And pray to be
Where thou art resting on the shores immortal, —
      With those so dear
Who earlier entered heaven's gleaming portal,
      And left thee here.

Thou faithful servant of the High and Holy!
      Heaven shall be
Still nearer to the souls that, bending lowly,
      Now mourn for thee,
And with the Everlasting Arm beneath them,
      Float with the tide
Which bears them on where thou erelong shalt greet them,
      The other side.

Hero and Saint! enrolled upon the pages
      Of History,
Telling of deeds sublime to future ages,
      Thy name shall be.
And, better still, the Lamb's resplendent volume
      Thy name shall bear,
Heading, perchance, a long and brilliant column
      Of heroes there.

Farewell for Time! no more we here shall greet thee,
     But, far on high,
Among the angels, we shall surely meet thee,
     No more to die,
And from our lips the chalice, now so bitter,
     Our God will take,
And bid us drink from heaven's fountain sweeter,
     When we awake.

THE END.

Cambridge : Stereotyped and Printed by Welch, Bigelow, & Co.